Praise for
Scrap Everything

"How can you not love a book about smart, savvy women organizing the chaos of their lives into perfect sense? I recommend *Scrap Everything* to anyone who needs a fresh perspective on God's ways."

—LOIS RICHER, author of *Identity: Undercover*

"In this engaging book about relationships, particularly the friendships of women, Leslie Gould takes a different look at the meaning of sacrificial love. *Scrap Everything* is a touching story that not only entertains; it challenges you to think twice about what it means to love your neighbor."

—ANN TATLOCK, Christy Award–winning novelist

"*Scrap Everything* is a captivating tale combining friendship, sacrificial love, and personal growth. The characters are both real and endearing. As a military wife and scrapbooker, I loved reading about people whose experiences and interests parallel my own. I look forward to reading more of Leslie Gould's writing!"

—JANELLE CLARE SCHNEIDER, coauthor of *Homespun Christmas*

SCRAP everything

a novel

LESLIE GOULD

WATERBROOK
PRESS

Scrap Everything
Published by WaterBrook Press
12265 Oracle Boulevard, Suite 200
Colorado Springs, Colorado 80921
A division of Random House Inc.

13-Digit ISBN: 978-0-7394-7685-7

Published in association with the literary agency of Alive Communications Inc., 7680 Goddard Street, Suite 200, Colorado Springs, CO 80920, www.alivecommunications.com.

Printed in the United States of America

Dedicated to Libby Salter,
my dear friend for all these years

You are her daughters if you do what is right
and do not give way to fear.

1 PETER 3:6

*J*ust shoot us." Mark flicked his blond bangs away from his eyes. Elise Shelton aimed her camera at her husband, Ted, and their two sons. The boys groaned in unison as they stood in front of the empty house outside of Fort Carson, Colorado.

"Get it over with," Michael begged.

Elise snapped the shutter. "Just a couple more." She took ten steps to the left to get a better angle of the house.

"You always make us take pictures when we leave a place." Mark crossed his arms.

"I want to remember that we lived here." She couldn't believe the things that she had already forgotten during their years in the army. In another two decades she might totally forget that they'd ever lived in Colorado if it weren't for these photos.

"Why is it always about what you want?"

"What do you mean? All I want are these photos. Everything else I do is for you," Elise said, aware of the hurt in her voice.

Mark scowled. Dark-haired Michael, who was a year younger and a head shorter than Mark, grinned, showing a mouth full of metal. "One more." She held up her index finger. "Mark, keep your eyes open." They were both going into the eighth grade, but no one mistook them for twins. She clicked the camera again.

"These pictures will just end up in boxes like all the rest." Mark headed toward the driveway.

"Every one of those boxes is organized," Elise said, still holding the camera to her eye.

"We know they're organized." Ted kissed her forehead and bounded up the steps to the front door. "Just like everything else in our lives." He turned the doorknob. "It's locked."

"I already checked." Elise followed him with the camera. Thanks to the army, he was nearly as slim as when they married. She raised the viewfinder to his head. His dark hair was beginning to gray at the temples. He turned toward her and grinned, and she snapped the shutter.

Ted pulled his baseball cap from his back pocket. "Onward, ho! Let's move out the wagons."

"Wagon," Mark said. He opened the back door of the Volvo. Ted stopped beside his old red Toyota 4Runner.

Elise never thought to take a photo when they arrived at a new house; too many other things distracted her. In two days they would be in Forest Falls, Oregon, Ted's hometown. It was temporary—one last, ten-month stop so the boys could spend time with their grandfather—then on to Seattle where they would settle for good. It was their plan. Well, her plan anyway.

"Wagon and 4Runner, ho," Ted called out.

"Stop trying to be funny." Mark covered his ears. Michael scooped his football off the lawn as if he were recovering a fumble and scurried around to the passenger side of his dad's vehicle.

"Forest Falls. The best little town in the world." Ted reached out for Elise's hand. "You're going to love living there. You'll never want to leave."

She pulled away.

"I don't want to live in Grandpa's stupid little town any longer than I have to." Mark slammed the car door.

"Mark," Elise chided as she ducked into the car.

"It's true, Mom. You feel the same way."

Elise clenched the steering wheel, and her lower back tightened against the leather seat—the pain as familiar to her as the stress that caused it. She said nothing.

Michael climbed into the front seat of the Toyota. He would chatter for miles and miles, talking Ted's ear off; Mark would sleep until noon, letting Elise enjoy the quiet. Ted turned onto I-25 North, and Elise followed. Pikes Peak towered to her left, and the morning light sifted through the clouds that crowned the mountain. The cool air would soon give way to sweltering heat. They sped through Colorado Springs. Their army days were over. The tension in her back eased. They had made it. Ted had come out alive. The boys were mostly intact.

She was that much closer to finally getting what *she* wanted.

Rebekah Graham twisted her long, auburn hair into a ponytail as she ran down the porch steps of her century-old farmhouse two at a time. "Hey, Pepper," she called out to her twelve-year-old daughter.

"Mom, this old horse is too slow." Pepper sat tall on the palomino. "I want to ride Sky." She blew a wisp of pale blond hair from her face.

"Not yet, sweet pea." Rebekah wedged her hands into the back pockets of her jeans. "You know how Dad feels about you riding that wild thing."

"Dad worries too much." Pepper pulled back on the reins, stopping the old palomino.

"Why don't we ride up into the forest? It's cooler there." Rebekah breathed in the sweet smell of warm alfalfa and manure as she balanced on the middle rung of the corral.

"If I can ride Sky." Pepper grinned. "Just kidding. I'm kind of tired. Maybe later."

"Are you feeling okay?" Rebekah climbed over the fence and landed on both feet in the corral.

Pepper rolled her eyes. "Now you sound like Dad."

Rebekah grabbed the palomino's halter and walked backward, leading the horse around the corral. "Let's see if we can get the old girl moving."

"How about if we scrapbook this afternoon?" Pepper suggested.

"We could do that." Rebekah began to jog.

"Or we could go swimming." Pepper's words bounced out of her mouth.

"Maybe Reid would go with us." Rebekah's thirteen-year-old son definitely wouldn't ride *or* scrapbook.

"He'll want to stay home on the computer." Pepper leaned back in the saddle. "He's so boring."

The three other horses congregated under the shade of the oak tree on the far side of the pasture. Sky, the three-year-old Appaloosa, stamped the ground. Rebekah slowed to a walk and headed toward the gate. The fresh air, the riding, and the chores had made Pepper strong, so strong that Rebekah was ready to consider getting a part-time job or maybe opening a business. She let go of the palomino's halter.

"Let's ride this evening." Pepper pulled the reins to the right.

Rebekah slapped the horse's rump. "Sounds good. We'll take the trail to the falls."

lise fumbled for the switch to turn on the Volvo's high beams, a sure sign that she had become a city girl. She slowed for a turn. An oncoming car startled her, and she flicked the dimmer. For the last month, she had driven to Salem once a week to shop. "What's wrong with the stores in Forest Falls?" Ted had asked each time.

It wasn't just that the shops were small; it was more that the people in them smiled too much. Ted was something of a small-town celebrity, thanks to his dad's bragging, and people expected Elise to be as outgoing as her husband and father-in-law.

Tonight she simply had to get out of the house. The boys came home from football practice poking at each other nonstop, and by the time she finished the dishes, she was desperate to escape. Grocery shopping, even though she needed only a few things, was the best excuse she could muster.

The lights of the car bounced off the evergreen trees. Something moved along the right side of the road. Was it a person? She flicked on the bright lights, and the form disappeared. A split second later a powerful animal leaped in front of her car. She slammed on the brakes, screeching the tires. The creature landed elegantly on the pavement in front of her and then sprang again. Elise pumped the brakes. Shaking, she clenched the steering wheel as the animal—a cat—disappeared into the forest.

A huge cat. A ferocious, graceful, gigantic cat. It had to be a cougar. Elise shivered. She was less than five miles from town, at the most. What kind of town had cougars dashing in front of cars? Another few minutes of running at that speed, and the cougar would be in downtown Forest Falls or at the boys' school. She accelerated the car. There were no cougars in Seattle.

She dimmed her lights and slowed at the city limits. The town was quaint with its old architecture—mostly Victorian and Queen Anne houses—and lovely gardens. The downtown area had brick facade buildings. Ted claimed that tourists actually traveled to Forest Falls on purpose.

She stopped at the four-way in the heart of town. The old hardware store had a new sign: The Scrap Shack. She continued through town, turned left on Cascade Street, crossed over the bridge, and turned into the driveway of their rental. It was a newer home that lacked the charm of the town's original houses, but it didn't matter. She could stand anything for ten months.

Ted met her in the garage. "I was getting worried." He opened the hatch. "I thought you would be home before dark."

"I almost hit a cougar."

"Are you sure?" Ted repacked the groceries in the bags and grabbed all three at once. "There were cougars around here when I was a kid but probably not anymore."

"There's at least one." Elise slammed the hatch.

"Maybe it was a big barn cat." Ted grinned.

Elise smiled at his teasing and took the middle bag from his arms, led the way into the kitchen, and slid the bag onto the counter. "What's this?" She picked up a fluorescent yellow flier.

"The new store in town is having a get-together. I thought you might want to go." Ted pulled out a carton of eggs. "They're broken."

At least the car wasn't broken. Elise read the flier out loud. "Learn to Scrapbook. *Tomorrow!* 10 a.m. *Free!*" She hated exclamation marks and italics.

"Doesn't that sound great? You could make some friends." Ted dumped the eggs into the garbage.

Elise rolled her shoulders. She had met more friends over the last twenty years than she could count. She didn't need any more temporary friends.

"You could do a football scrapbook for the boys." Ted washed egg off the jar of strawberry jam.

"I'd better go check the back of the car." Elise ran a dishcloth under the faucet. She didn't want to find dried egg on the carpet in the morning.

Ted wore a gray army T-shirt and black shorts and jogged in place on the front porch. He quickly opened the screen door for Elise as she grabbed her jacket. "Thanks for being willing to go to the scrapbooking deal," he said. "You'll enjoy it."

He was so eager for her to make friends. "When are you going to get a job?" she teased.

"I have an interview at the Salem Hospital at one." He reached for her hand, a playful gleam in his eyes. "If I get the job, I'll be on call. Will you be able to live without me?"

They started walking to town, hand in hand. "I'll look forward to the few hours by myself!" she told him, but they both knew she didn't mean it. Since their boys had started back to school, the two of them had gone to Portland for a day of bookstore hopping, hiked in the coast range, and cuddled on the couch while reading to each other. They had a list of outings planned—a sort of second honeymoon, thanks to his army retirement checks.

"Maybe you'll meet someone at the scrapbook shop who goes to Dad's church." Ted picked up the pace. He and the boys had gone to church twice in the last month without her. "Or maybe you'll meet one of our neighbors or another mom."

She had avoided neighbors, other moms, and church. It wasn't that she didn't need those things; she did. Just not here, not here in Forest Falls.

It wasn't that she didn't need God; she did. But what was the use of getting involved in one more church for such a short time?

They crossed over the Forest Creek Bridge and into downtown. Ted raised his knees high for a few steps. Elise slowed. If Ted weren't with her, she would walk on by the shop. "We're late," she said. The round clock in the jewelry store window read 10:05.

"Barely. Besides, we're here." Ted stopped. "Didn't some of the army wives in Colorado scrapbook?"

Elise nodded in agreement. One of them talked about it nonstop at the officers' wives' meetings; she had said it was the fastest growing hobby in America. "I don't have time for this, Ted." Elise kicked a pebble, careful not to scuff her black loafer.

Ted nudged her playfully. "I'm only going to work part-time. It's not like you'll have to do everything around the house. You'll have lots of time to spare."

"I'd rather read a book." Elise crossed her arms over her handbag. *Is this how the boys felt on the first day of school, year after year?*

Ted opened the door and kissed her on the lips. "Elise, give the other women a chance to get to know you."

She stepped into the building. Light from two stories of windows bathed the brick interior. "Scrapbooking has a *long* and *vivid* history!" came a voice from above.

Elise climbed the wooden stairs and paused at the top. A woman with long, auburn hair stood with her hands clasped. "Scrapbooking can be traced back to the seventeenth century in Germany." The woman was shapely and tall, probably six feet, or at least close. She wore an orange button-down-the-front shirt over a brown tank top, jeans, and—Elise frowned as she looked down—cowboy boots. "*Both* Thomas Jefferson and Mark Twain were avid scrapbookers!" This perky woman must have made the flier; she spoke in italics and exclamation points too. "Twain—Samuel Clemens—had fifty-seven different scrapbook designs that he sold through Montgomery Ward catalogs."

Thank goodness the rest of the world remembers him for his literature. Elise grimaced. She was doing that negative thing she did when she felt stressed. *It's just a group of women,* she thought. *Small-town women.*

Miss Perky spread her arms wide. "The peak decade for scrapbooking in the past was 1880 to 1890, although during the 1920s, many girls kept journals that included clippings and mementos."

Elise's grandmother had kept a scrapbook filled with graduation, wedding, and birth announcements, all from the *Seattle Times* society page.

"By 1975, with a growing interest in genealogy, scrapbooking came back into vogue." Miss Perky laughed again. "Well, that's my introduction. The rest is history. Today, scrapbooking is a two-and-a-half-billion-dollar-a-year business just in the United States."

Elise shifted from one foot to the other. Where was the coffee?

"This morning we're going to talk about the best books, best paper, and best adhesive materials." The leader stopped speaking when she saw Elise, and her dark eyebrows rose. She smiled broadly. "Oh, *hi!*" she called out to Elise, shading her eyes. "I thought I heard the door, but I couldn't *see* you against the light. Come *in.* You haven't missed a *thing.*"

"I just wanted to look around." Elise stepped forward.

The woman's dark brown eyes danced. "I'm Rebekah! I just opened the shop yesterday." She motioned over the balcony railing. Below, stacks of paper lined one wall, and unopened boxes covered a table.

All the women stared at Elise, smiling. They looked friendly. Too friendly. How could she leave without appearing rude? "I'll just sit and listen."

Rebekah smiled. "Let me know if you want to do the two scrapbook pages after I finish my presentation."

Elise pulled out a cold metal chair. Rebekah broached the subject of creating a theme. "Plan ahead," she said. "I've even been known to dress my kids in outfits that match the paper I have in mind for a certain holiday. Of course, now they're old enough to protest that sort of thing."

The other women nodded and smiled. One woman pointed to the

layout in front of her. Elise craned her neck. Duck paper and stickers sur-rounded a baby wearing a duck sleeper.

Rebekah giggled. "Oh, I'm relieved to know I'm not the only scrap-per mom around. Scrapbooking is like life—sometimes you just have to *make* things happen."

Elise decided she would rather make things *not* happen.

After the presentation, Rebekah beelined to Elise with her hand extended. "Are you new in town?"

"We've been here a month. I'm Elise." She took Rebekah's hand; Miss Perky's fingernails were short and unpolished.

"Where did you move from?"

"Colorado. Before that, Georgia." And before that, Texas, Kentucky, Kansas, Germany, Virginia, Maryland, and Seattle, but Rebekah probably didn't want the whole story.

"Georgia? You don't have an accent."

Elise shook her head. "I was raised in Washington State—in a little town called Cascade Pass. My husband was in the army."

Rebekah put one hand on her hip. "Wait a minute. What's your last name?"

"Shelton."

"John Shelton's daughter-in-law?"

Elise nodded.

"I know John from church. And my son has talked about your boys. They play football, right?"

Elise nodded again. "In fact, I was thinking about making a football scrapbook for them."

Rebekah headed toward the rack. "We have the cutest football stickers."

"Stickers?" Elise followed.

"You don't like stickers?" Rebekah spun the rack around.

Elise quickly shook her head. "These look great." Little stick figures wore helmets and held footballs in various poses. There were baseball, basketball, tennis, volleyball, and soccer stickers too. Elise pulled three sets from the rack.

Rebekah introduced Elise around the room, ending with Sandi Snow, a woman in her fifties with spiked white hair. "John was in the grief group that I led at church," Sandi said. It had been a year and a half since Maude, Elise's mother-in-law, had passed away. Elise turned away from Sandi. Another detriment to living in Forest Falls was that everyone had known her mother-in-law. Maybe they already had an opinion about Elise.

The women visited while they worked, and Elise looked through a rack of paper. Rebekah brought a stack of albums up the stairs. "How long have you been scrapping?"

"Actually, I don't." Elise sat down.

"You do now." Sandi rummaged in a large bag at her feet.

"Oh, I almost forgot to tell everyone." Rebekah dropped the albums onto the table. "A cougar ran through our field late last night. You should have heard it scream; I've never heard anything so hair-raising in my entire life."

Elise's heart raced. She couldn't wait to tell Ted that she was right about the cougar.

"Did you see it?" Sandi asked.

Rebekah shook her head.

"I saw one last night," Elise blurted.

"You're kidding!" Rebekah sat down beside her.

"I was just a few miles from town, and it ran across the road right in front of me."

"Must be the same one." Sandi placed a photo in a small paper cutter and zipped the blade back and forth.

"I hope so," Rebekah interjected. "I'd hate for more than one of those creatures to be around." She spread the albums across the table. "Our neighbors found one of their sheep half-eaten night before last."

"Weren't you going to get a dog?" Sandi asked.

Rebekah leaned back against the cold metal chair. "Patrick says we should. He's afraid the cougar will go after our horses or one of the kids." Rebekah opened a black album and slid it toward Elise.

"Horses?" Elise smiled at Rebekah. "You have horses?" She hoped that she sounded nonchalant.

"Four." Rebekah flipped the pages of the scrapbook. "This would work great for newspaper clippings and photos. What do you think?"

Elise found herself chatting with the other ladies before she remembered that she wasn't supposed to be having fun. *Ted knew I'd do this,* she said to herself, standing to go look at the merchandise.

An hour later Rebekah rang up Elise's book, stack of paper, adhesives, and football stickers. Examples of scrapbook pages hung on the wall behind the counter. A slight girl with light hair and a pixie look was in nearly every photo, along with a tall, dark-haired boy who looked like Rebekah. A man with strawberry blond hair hugged Rebekah in one of the pictures. Twine and thin scraps of leather framed photos of the girl and a horse, buttons and pieces of fabric adorned 4-H pages, and football-like stitching decorated a layout of the boy, outlined with stickers.

Elise pulled out her Gold MasterCard.

"This is just the beginning," Sandi said, leaning over the balcony.

Elise smiled politely, but she knew she would put the entire stack of scrapbooking paraphernalia in the hall closet and forget about it until she packed up the house next spring to move to Seattle. Then she would donate the album and paper to charity.

"I'll give you some advice," Sandi continued. "Be vague with your husband about what you're doing and how much it costs."

"Maybe he'd like to join us since he's retired." Rebekah handed Elise a pen.

"No way!" Sandi called down. "This is our place. In the old days women got together to quilt and gossip. Now we scrapbook."

"Or go horseback riding."

"How do you find time to ride?" Elise asked Rebekah.

"I don't find the time. Not since I decided to open the shop." Rebekah slid Elise's purchases into a bag. "But I need to."

"I used to ride." Elise signed the receipt.

"Come ride with me sometime!"

"Seriously?" Elise dropped the pen into a shack-shaped mug. "When?"

"How about Saturday? I'll close the shop at four."

"Perfect." This wasn't about making a friend—she and Rebekah had nothing in common. It was about riding a horse. Still, Ted would be pleased.

"Great. The next scrapbooking class is one week from today." Rebekah handed Elise her copy of the receipt and the bag. "Bring your photos. We'll learn to crop."

"Crop." Elise repeated the word as if she understood.

"See you Saturday."

Elise tucked the receipt into her purse and headed toward the door.

"Rebekah, what are you getting yourself into? You don't have time—" Sandi's loud whisper followed Elise as she tripped over the threshold onto the sidewalk.

Chapter 2

*R*ebekah leaned against the side of her green Dodge Dakota quad cab and tapped her cowboy boot against the pavement. She had closed the shop fifteen minutes ago. Where was Elise? Perhaps she wouldn't show. Maybe Sandi was right. Maybe Rebekah didn't have time now to get involved with one more person. True, she did need to exercise the horses, but here she was, waiting for Elise and wasting time. Sandi had also pointed out that Elise seemed awfully pretentious. Rebekah agreed. Elise's expression conveyed it all—the same timeless look popular girls wielded in middle school. Still, Rebekah reasoned, the girls she disliked the most from preschool through college had all ended up as her best friends. It seemed, throughout her entire life, that God had connected her with people she never would have chosen. *Why fight it?* she reasoned with herself.

Rebekah opened the door of her truck and climbed in. Elise's fair complexion, blond hair, and small stature made Rebekah think of Pepper. Would her little girl look like Elise when she was grown?

A Volvo station wagon pulled into a parking space across the street. "Am I too late?" Elise called out.

Rebekah opened her window. "I thought maybe you had forgotten."

Elise shook her head.

Rebekah started her truck. "Let's go."

Rebekah waited for Elise to catch up before she turned into the circular drive lined with elm trees. The afternoon sun danced through the grove of spruce trees that surrounded the house. Rebekah led the way up the front steps onto the wraparound porch and through the front door, past the open cherry-wood staircase, and through the living room. Elise commented on the camelback sofa and followed Rebekah through the dining room, around the oak table with mismatched antique chairs. Would Elise realize that she had mismatched the chairs on purpose?

Rebekah swung the kitchen door hard, making it stay open. The kitchen was huge and full of light. The cupboards, all painted white, had been refinished, and a center island and breakfast bar had been added. "My husband, Patrick, and the kids are out in the field repairing the fence." She stopped at the window over the sink. "See? You can barely make them out. They're straight across from the oak tree in the middle of the pasture."

Elise squinted at the three shapes on the edge of the field next to the road.

"You need some boots." Rebekah bumped into a stool at the breakfast bar and headed toward the mud porch. "What size shoe do you wear?"

"Six."

"Figures." Rebekah laughed and looked down at her own feet. "Mine are size ten. Maybe Pepper's will fit you."

"Pepper?"

"My daughter."

The sweet scent of alfalfa swept over Rebekah as her eyes adjusted to the dim light. She loved the barn. Two calico cats scurried behind a bag of feed, a starling flew out the open door, and country music played on the radio. Rebekah snapped it off. "Pepper loves this stuff. She says the horses do too."

She slipped the halter onto the Appaloosa gelding and then slung a saddle and blanket off the saddletree. "This is Sky. He's pretty green and high strung," she said. "Most Appaloosas are, but his dam is a great horse—she's in the next stall—and Sky will be too, soon."

"His dam?"

"His mother. You'll ride her." Rebekah inhaled the rich aroma of the horses as she cinched Sky's saddle. Next she stroked the mare's neck, grabbed another saddle, and propelled it onto the horse.

"Thanks for doing the saddling. My back has been acting up." Elise rolled her shoulders. Rebekah wondered if Elise could saddle a horse regardless. She wasn't much bigger than Pepper.

"Hi!" The barn door slid open. "I saw you guys drive up."

"Hey, Pep." Rebekah stuck her head out of the stall. "This is Elise Shelton."

"Mark and Michael Shelton's mom?" Pepper clapped her hands together. "Tall with long blond hair? Short with curly dark hair and blue eyes?"

Elise nodded and extended her hand. "I'm pleased to meet you. I plan to volunteer at your school library, to keep an eye on my boys."

"All the girls are crazy about Mark."

Elise frowned. "Great."

"Do you like Forest Falls?" Pepper kissed Sky's neck.

"I do. You have a very nice town. Still, it's a bit of an adjustment."

Pepper nodded empathetically. "*I* know. *I* hated it here at first, for the first couple of days anyway."

"When did you move here?" Elise asked.

"Last year." Pepper slipped her ponytail fastener around her wrist and shook out her hair.

Elise turned toward Rebekah. "I thought you grew up here."

Rebekah shrugged. "It feels like it."

"In just one year?"

Rebekah nodded and led the way to the pasture. "I think it's been the hardest on Reid—"

"But he's doing okay now," Pepper interrupted. "He has football and basketball—and the computer. It's suppose to be for both of us, but he never lets me use it." Pepper slapped her hands against her thighs, leaving dusty prints on her jeans. "Where did you two meet?"

"At the shop on Thursday." Rebekah tightened Sky's saddle. "I have a feeling that we're going to end up being great friends." Rebekah cringed at her own words. Her voice had sounded odd—not exactly sarcastic, but not exactly sincere, either. She hoped Elise hadn't noticed.

Elise turned abruptly. "You sound like you've had a vision."

A nervous here-comes-the-truth giggle escaped from Rebekah. "No, it's not that. I just know. I'll tell you later, okay?" She paused, a little embarrassed, and then continued as she swung herself into the saddle. "After we really are friends."

Pepper rolled her eyes. "*Mom.*" The word came out in a moan.

Elise had a confused expression on her face as she grabbed the horn, lifted her left foot into the stirrup, hopped on her right leg, and then hoisted herself into the saddle. She began to laugh.

"What's so funny?" Rebekah asked. Maybe the woman did have a sense of humor.

"Nothing," Elise said. "It's just that this feels good."

"Wait until tomorrow."

Rebekah turned her head as she and Sky led the way up the trail into the forest. Elise adjusted the reins in her hand, threading them over her thumb. "Giddyup." Elise kicked her heels gently against the mare's belly, and the horse jerked ahead. "Whoa!" Elise pulled back on the reins, and the horse halted and then slowly started walking in reverse. "It's been quite a while since I've done this."

"Stop pulling on the reins." Rebekah stopped Sky. "You're telling her to go backward. Just pull once and think *stop.*"

"Think?"

Rebekah nodded. "She can read your mind." Rebekah clicked her tongue, and the horses started forward again. "Riding horses is all about balance," Rebekah called out. "And breathing. Find your balance—plant the pockets of your jeans in the saddle. And breathe from the bottom of your boots. Don't worry. It will all come back to you."

The orange and yellow leaves on the vine maples danced brightly against the rough trunks of the evergreen trees. Huge maidenhair ferns covered the ground. The trail widened, and Rebekah slowed. "You're doing great. You're a natural."

Elise smiled and wrinkled her nose. "How come you don't wear a hat?" she asked.

"I lost it further up the trail. It flew over a cliff on a crazy midnight ride. I haven't had a chance to buy another one." Rebekah glanced upward. "Clouds are rolling in. Are we supposed to get rain?"

"I don't think so."

"Are you a medical person too? Is that how you met your husband?" Rebekah leaned back in the saddle to look at Elise.

Elise shook her head. "I deplore hospitals."

The mare's ears twitched as she lifted her head. "What is it?" Rebekah leaned forward. Sky snorted and stopped abruptly.

The mare pawed at the trail. "What's wrong?" Elise asked.

"I don't know." Rebekah patted the horse. He sidestepped and then reared as a horrible, high-pitched scream tore through the forest.

Rebekah pulled tightly on Sky's reins. "Come on." She and her mount veered off the trail. She flung the rein against Sky's rump and leaned forward, reeling through the cottonwood trees. Rebekah turned her head. Elise was far behind and bouncing like a jack-in-the-box all over the saddle.

The cougar screamed again as Rebekah and Sky splashed through the creek and flew into the field. The screech came from the south, away from the house, down toward the broken fence. Rebekah urged Sky to run faster. The Appaloosa strained. They raced past the oak tree and over the knoll toward the fence line. Terror filled Reid's brown eyes as he stood statue-still with a shovel in his hand.

"Where's Pepper?" Rebekah yelled.

Reid pointed with the blade back toward the tree. The cougar screamed again—this time a hideous shriek. Rebekah shivered. Crouched fifty yards from the tree was the cougar. Pepper stood on the lowest limb and pointed at the cat.

lise dug her heels into the mare, trying to catch up with Rebekah. She didn't want to be left alone in the back pasture with nothing between her and the cat.

"Elise, stop!" Rebekah shouted. She turned toward Reid. "Where's your dad?"

"At the house." The boy's legs shook in his long basketball shorts.

Rebekah raced Sky toward Reid and grabbed the shovel. "Go!" She whipped the horse's backside with the end of the reins and headed toward Pepper.

"Mom!" Pepper's voice came from the tree. Crouching in the grass was the cougar. Elise almost screamed but then saw Rebekah stop Sky halfway between the cat and the tree, lift the shovel, and begin waving it back and forth.

"Mom! Don't let the cougar get Sky!" Pepper yelled.

"Get Reid!" Rebekah shouted to Elise. "Then go to the house for Patrick."

Elise turned her horse. The mare lurched forward, galloping toward the fence as Elise motioned to Reid. He stood, paralyzed.

"Mom!" Pepper shouted again. "Don't let it get the horses."

"Pepper, don't look in his eyes. Hold up your arm. Make yourself look big." Rebekah waved the shovel again.

Pepper held up both hands.

"Hold on. Don't fall out of the tree!"

The cougar crouched lower. Rebekah swung the shovel around her head. Elise tried to grab Reid. A horn honked, and a man jumped out of Rebekah's truck.

Elise turned back toward the cougar—it was gone.

Elise rubbed her hands on her jeans, got out of the car, and walked toward her house. The sunset pulled streaks of pink and orange clouds across the sky. The smell of freshly cut grass mixed with the sweet scent of the roses blooming on both sides of the porch. She kicked off her shoes in the foyer and padded down the hall toward the master bedroom.

"Hey, there," Ted called out from his study. "How was it?"

"Okay." Her voice shook.

Ted stepped into the hall. "Did you have fun?"

Elise nodded and then shook her head. "We saw the cougar."

"The cougar?"

"In the field. It was huge. Even bigger than the other night."

"Elise." Ted wrapped his arms around her.

"It really is a cougar."

Ted nodded.

"It's not a barn cat."

"I believe you."

"Where have you been?" Mark poked his head out of the family room.

"Horseback riding."

"You actually did something fun?" Mark flipped his hair out of his eyes.

"She saw the cougar again." Ted tightened his arms around Elise.

She relaxed against him. "It was right there in the Grahams' field."

"Reid Graham?" Mark snickered. "I definitely don't believe you now."

"The cougar almost got Pepper."

"Pepper?" Mark's voice changed. "Is she okay?"

"Everyone's okay, right?" Ted let go of Elise and stepped back.

"She's fine." Elise rubbed her lower back. "Rebekah called the game department. They'll track the cougar with dogs."

"And kill it?" Mark slapped the top of the doorframe.

"Probably." Ted paused. "Or maybe they'll stun the cougar and relocate it. You can't have an animal that aggressive near people."

Elise rubbed her hands on her jeans again. The heavy feel of dust and the sweaty scent of the horses hung in her nose. "I'm going to take a shower."

"I'm thankful that you're all right." Ted pulled her close again. "That everyone is okay."

She nodded. They'd all been scared, except for Pepper. She'd been worried only about the horses. Come to think of it, Rebekah hadn't been afraid, either—not for herself anyway, only for Pepper.

Elise headed to the bedroom. So much for judging Rebekah by her italics and exclamation marks. The woman was the gutsiest person she had ever met.

"Ted here."

Nineteen years of marriage and Elise still couldn't ignore the middle-of-the-night intrusions. She squinted at the rows of red lights on the night table: 3:47 on a Monday morning. What a way to start the week.

"Surgery." Ted kissed Elise's forehead. "At the Salem Hospital. Car accident."

Fifteen minutes later he bent down to kiss her again, and she decided to get up, lured by the smell of coffee. She poured herself a cup and padded down the hall to the study as Ted slipped out the door.

She had gone to church with Ted and the boys yesterday, hoping to see Rebekah, but none of the Grahams were there. She had seen Sandi from a distance but had quickly turned the other way. She settled into Ted's desk chair and popped open the computer. Ted's home page, the BBC, appeared. His e-mail was minimized at the bottom of the page. He must have checked it before he left and forgotten to close it. Elise clicked the mouse, revealing two messages with usarmy.gov.com addresses. She opened the last one.

> Welcome to the Third Medical Command. Report for duty
> October 8. Please bring your family-readiness paperwork.
> We're on standby to be deployed.

What was Ted not telling her? The e-mail had been sent at 6:30 a.m., September 12. That was today. But it was only 4:15 a.m. Where was the Third located? She Googled the unit. Fort Gillem, Georgia. What was going on?

Elise clicked on the next message.

> Colonel Shelton, I'm looking for an anesthesiologist to
> go to Landstuhl. Interested? It would be a three-month
> deployment. Let me know ASAP.

Elise tried Ted's cell phone; it went right to voice mail. Was he talking to someone else? Or had he turned it off? "Call me," she said. She hoped he would check his messages after surgery. Her hand shook as she hung up the phone. She had waited so long for him to be done with the army. She closed Outlook, and up popped the BBC page with the headline "Two killed in Baghdad suicide bombing."

He'd done his time. Kuwait. Kosovo. Afghanistan. She'd been the supportive army wife, or at least had tried to be. Elise headed back to the kitchen, refilled her coffee cup, and then stared at the picture of Ted and the boys on the refrigerator. She'd taken the photo at Fort Benning when Ted had returned from Afghanistan three years ago. Mark's hair was nearly white from the sun, and he barely came to Ted's shoulder. Michael looked like a little boy. Ted wore his camouflage uniform and beret. He hugged both boys, all three of their bodies entwined, all three of them grinning.

She hated the army.

Ted had told her all he had left was two years in the inactive reserves. He hadn't said anything about being deployed.

She hated Ted.

Not really.

She slumped into a kitchen chair and set her mug down too hard, sloshing her coffee onto the table. She didn't want to be alone in Forest Falls. She wanted to go on day trips with Ted, cuddle on the couch, and plan their future. Ted and the boys were all she had in life. She tried his cell phone a second time, just in case. It went straight to voice mail again. Who else could she call? Her mother and sister lived in Michigan, but they didn't understand anything about the army or Elise's life. Ted had a good job, and he made lots of money. What was Elise complaining about?

Ted was the one person she could count on, or so she thought.

She grabbed a napkin and sopped up the puddle of coffee and then wiped a lonely tear with the sleeve of her robe. She would find a good book to take up the day until Ted came home. A bird chirped a morning song through the window. "God," she whispered, "I thought we'd made it. What's going on?"

Chapter 4

*R*ebekah rolled toward her side of the four-poster bed and opened one eye. Was a light on? "Mom." A deep voice startled her. "Pepper's sick. She's in the bathroom." Reid shook her shoulder. Would she ever get used to his grown-up voice? "Come on, Mom. She's throwing up and crying."

Rebekah swung her legs over the side of the bed, tugging her nightgown down over her thighs, and stumbled into the bathroom. Pepper sat on the floor wearing blue sweatpants and a brown T-shirt with a horse on the front.

"Honey." Rebekah sank down next to Pepper. "What's the matter?"

"I think I have the flu." Pepper tucked a strand of long, fine hair behind her ear.

Rebekah stood and filled a paper cup with water. "Rinse," she said.

"You look white as a sheet." Reid stood in the doorway in his boxers and a T-shirt. "Worse than usual."

Pepper spit the water into the toilet.

"Have you slept tonight?" Rebekah grabbed a ponytail fastener from the glass jelly jar and worked her fingers through Pepper's hair.

"A little."

"Do you hurt?" Rebekah twisted the blond strands into a single braid.

"No."

"Maybe it's appendicitis." Reid crossed his arms. "We just studied that in health."

Rebekah shook her head. "It would hurt if it was her appendix. Thanks for getting me, Reid." Rebekah pulled the bucket from underneath the sink and a stack of towels from the cupboard. "Come on, sweet pea," she said to Pepper. "Let's get back to bed."

She would sleep beside Pepper for the hour that was left until morning. Patrick would never wake up enough to know she was gone. Surprisingly, for all his worrywart ways, he seldom lost any sleep.

How many nights had she spent in Pepper's bedroom over the years? Pneumonia, bronchitis, viruses, the flu—Pepper had caught everything that came around, from the time she came to Rebekah and Patrick as a three-month-old foster baby until she was diagnosed with kidney disease as an eight-year-old.

But then she got better.

Rebekah tucked the covers under Pepper's chin, put the bucket next to the wall, and crawled in beside her daughter. Adopting Pepper had been the first miracle in Rebekah's life. She was sure that God had healed Pepper and given Rebekah a second miracle.

"Thanks, Mom," Pepper whispered. She was silent for a minute. Had she gone to sleep? "Mom?" Pepper wiggled. Of course she hadn't gone to sleep, not without talking first. "I wish we had gotten a picture of the cougar."

"That's a thought." Rebekah wanted to laugh out loud. "Quick! There's a cougar. Grab the camera."

"He was beautiful. Did you see how he stared at me?"

"I think I was too preoccupied with the rest of him to notice."

"His eyes were gorgeous." Pepper stroked Rebekah's face. "He looked like Mark."

"Mark?"

"Elise's son."

Rebekah propped her head on her hand. "How?"

"Mark has blondish hair, like the cougar's, and dark eyes. They look dignified but kind of wild. You know?"

Dignified but wild. Was that what attracted girls these days? Pepper had never liked a boy before. Correction. She probably had liked boys before this; she'd just never mentioned any of them.

"Is Mark nice?"

"He's kind of a loner. His brother, Michael, is nice, though." Pepper yawned. "I like Elise." She yawned again and stretched her arms over her head. "Don't you?"

Did she like Elise? Rebekah wasn't sure. "Hush," she said, evading the question. "Go to sleep."

"I have a call in to the doctor." Rebekah dished up a bowl of oatmeal for Patrick. "It's more than the flu."

"I have a meeting this morning." Patrick picked up the brown sugar bowl.

"I'll let you know when the appointment is." Rebekah dropped the wooden spoon into the pan of cereal.

He carefully poured milk into his bowl. "Do you want me to go?"

"Do you want to?"

"I want to know exactly what the doctor says."

"Then you'd better go." She turned off the burner.

Reid shuffled through the kitchen.

"Good morning, sweetie." Rebekah patted his back. He ignored her.

"What about the shop?" Patrick held his spoon in midair.

"I'll call Sandi."

"Will you pay her?"

"In supplies."

Reid slammed the pantry door. "You didn't buy any more Pop-Tarts."

"They're not good for you." Rebekah held out an empty bowl. "Have oatmeal or raisin bran."

"I'm not hungry."

"You have to eat, and hurry, or you'll miss the bus." She set the bowl on the counter.

Reid slung his backpack over his shoulder. "Where's Pepper?"

"She's still sick."

As Reid headed toward the door, Rebekah eyed the oatmeal. A Pop-Tart did sound good. "Make sure to brush your teeth."

"If the appointment is in the afternoon, then I'll come home after lunch." Patrick rinsed his bowl and placed it in the dishwasher.

"Who will pick me up after practice?" Reid opened the front door.

"We'll be back in time. Don't worry." Rebekah put the milk in the refrigerator. "Did you brush your teeth?"

Reid grunted and slammed the door.

"What did he say?"

Patrick grunted.

"I'll call you." Rebekah blew him a kiss as she headed up the steps to check on Pepper.

Rebekah leafed through the kidney-disease booklet. They'd been waiting in the tiny exam room for over an hour.

"How do you feel?" Patrick asked Pepper for the fourth time in ten minutes.

"Dad." Pepper's feet beat against the metal of the examination table. "Stop asking me that." She swung her minipack off her back and pulled out a package of gum. Next she pulled out her watch. "Three o'clock. I missed art."

Dr. Thomas pushed open the door, shook Patrick's hand, smiled at Rebekah, and patted Pepper on the head. "How's my favorite patient?"

"Fine." Pepper extended the pack of gum. "Want some?"

"Thank you." The doctor took a piece and popped it into his mouth as he sat down on the stool. "Your labs just came in. Your kidneys are not doing so hot. In fact, they've significantly declined since your last checkup."

Rebekah put the booklet back in the rack. "What percentage is she at?"

"Fifteen, but we don't go entirely by the percentage of function. We also consider her symptoms."

Patrick ran his hand through his hair.

"We need to talk about a few things today." The doctor leaned forward. Pepper smacked her gum. "Things like dialysis and an imminent kidney transplant."

"How much time do we have?" Patrick asked.

"There's no way to know. A few months, maybe a year." The doctor paused. "But we have to be ready."

Rebekah reached for Pepper's hand.

"You should be tested as possible donors—the two of you." He looked at Rebekah and then Patrick.

"We have the wrong blood type." Rebekah squeezed Pepper's hand. "Pepper is B, and we're all A." Rebekah had sorted out the blood-type piece of the puzzle when Pepper had been ill four years ago.

"That's right." The doctor paged through the file and then put it on the counter. "Pepper, I'd forgotten that you're adopted. Do you have any contact with your birth family?"

Pepper shook her head.

Rebekah sighed. Did he remember that the birth mother was deceased and that there was no record of the birth father? Rebekah didn't want to explain all of that, not now.

"A bio parent, grandparent, aunt, or uncle might be a possibility." He looked at her. "It would be good to find them—to see who is willing. A related donor is your best bet."

Related. Rebekah squeezed Pepper's hand again. She would do anything for Pepper, give her entire body to her if she could. She had never felt more related to anyone in her whole life.

The doctor continued. "I want you to take a transplant class here and then a dialysis class at the Salem Hospital. We'll hope for a transplant first. We'll have better results if we can avoid dialysis."

"I wanted to clarify one thing." Patrick held up his index finger. "I remember reading that Medicare pays for transplants. Is that still correct?"

"Yes. Tell my receptionist that you need an appointment with Jamie, our transplant coordinator. She will explain everything and walk you through each step. Your insurance and Medicare will cover the transplant. Of course, you'll have other expenses—plus the medicine Pepper will have to take for the rest of her life is very expensive. Your insurance may cover it for only a certain amount of time."

Insurance. When was the deadline for reenrollment? Sometime in September? Rebekah bit her lip. She would look for the paperwork as soon as they got home.

"What can we do in the meantime to help Pepper feel better?" Patrick put his hands on his knees.

"We'll give her antibiotics. She has an infection." The doctor took out his prescription pad. "Pepper, drink ten glasses of water a day, and watch what you eat. No white flour, and limit your sugar. No cola. No baked potatoes. Don't go overboard on protein. Lots of fruits and vegetables and exercise."

"Does riding horses count?"

"Yes." Dr. Thomas stood and patted her head again. "I'm sorry we've come to this so soon, but there's still a lot we can do. Try not to worry."

Rebekah turned off the air conditioning in the pickup as Patrick exited I-5 and headed toward Forest Falls. It was past 5 p.m. Reid would be waiting. Pepper slept in the backseat of the quad cab, a stadium blanket pulled up to her chin.

"We shouldn't have moved to Forest Falls." Patrick slowed for a curve. "Now we'll be going back and forth to Portland, fighting traffic, trying to juggle my job, the horses, Reid's sports, and your shop."

"We'll make it work."

"It was irresponsible of us to move."

"She was better." Rebekah hated the way he analyzed every decision.

"But we knew it wouldn't last." Patrick shook his head.

"I thought it would." The words sounded hollow.

"And I was too influenced by you." He took a deep breath.

"Patrick, we had no reason to believe that she would need a transplant anytime soon. We can't live in fear."

"You're right. But we should have at least lived with some common sense." Patrick accelerated.

"Shh." Rebekah turned her head. Pepper's mouth was slightly open.

"I don't see how we can make it."

"We'll be fine. You heard the doctor. Medicare will kick in." Rebekah paused. "Why do you think they get involved?"

"It's a special program because transplants wouldn't happen otherwise. Insurance companies wouldn't cover them without help, although I think transplants are cheaper than years of dialysis." Patrick passed a semi and then maneuvered back into the right lane.

"How much do you think surgery costs?"

Patrick tapped the steering wheel. "A hundred thousand."

"That much?" No wonder he was worried. "Good grief." What if their insurance or Medicare didn't pay? What if she had missed the deadline?

"Rebekah, we're in over our heads." Patrick turned the truck toward Forest Falls. "Sure, insurance and Medicare will pay the big stuff, but we'll have other expenses. Antirejection meds for the rest of Pepper's life. Loss of income. You won't be able to keep the shop going."

"I can make the shop work."

Patrick tapped the steering wheel again. "We don't have anyone to help."

"Shh. I don't want Pepper to hear this," Rebekah whispered.

He lowered his voice. "We're going to have to sell the farm."

"Patrick, stop."

"And where are we going to find a kidney?"

"I'll call Polly. I still have her phone number."

"No." Patrick's voice rose.

"Why not?"

"It's too much. Her life has been too hard. It's too much to ask."

"The birth aunt, Adrianna, would be in her late twenties by now. Maybe she would be a match. Maybe she has a child."

"Who wouldn't be old enough. You have to be eighteen."

"I think they make exceptions."

"Rebekah, you think everyone makes exceptions." Patrick hit his forehead with the heel of his hand. "Life doesn't work that way."

"You heard the doctor. He said a related donor is best." Her pulse began to race.

"Not in this case. We can't reopen that heartache."

"But it could mean Pepper's life." Rebekah sank against the seat.

"Mom?" Pepper's head popped up behind the seat. "Are we almost home?"

"We're just coming into town, sweet pea." How much had she heard? "We're going to pick up Reid."

"How are you feeling?" Patrick looked into the rearview mirror.

Rebekah was going to scream if he asked Pepper that one more time.

"Sorry." Pepper leaned against the window.

"For what?" Rebekah turned her head.

"For getting sick."

"Pepper, don't talk that way."

Patrick smiled into the mirror. "We'll get through this."

"Look!" Pepper sat up straight. "Ainsley got her new horse!" A red roan grazed in the middle of a field, all alone. Five other horses gathered under a willow tree. The late afternoon light shone golden on the grass.

"The other horses haven't accepted her yet." Pepper craned her neck as the pickup whizzed by.

"She's beautiful." Rebekah's grandfather had a horse the same reddish color when she was a child.

"Ainsley plans to ride her in 4-H. I'm going to instant message her when I get home and tell her I saw the horse already. She'll be so mad!"

"Speaking of 4-H, I think you should take the year off." Patrick slowed for a tractor pulling onto the highway.

"Dad!"

"Don't you think so, Rebekah?"

"The doctor said she should exercise. He said horseback riding was good."

"Riding, not barrel racing."

"Patrick," Rebekah whispered, "the girls barely trot, let alone race."

Patrick followed the tractor at a pace slower than molasses and then turned into the school parking lot. Reid climbed into the pickup. "You're late." Two boys shoved each other in the middle of the parking lot, and then the tall blond kid tripped the smaller, dark-haired boy.

"What are they doing?" Rebekah asked.

"Being boys." Patrick put the pickup in reverse.

The taller boy grabbed the other boy's arm and twisted it. Rebekah opened her window. "Stop that!"

"Mom." Reid slumped in the backseat. "They're brothers, your friend Elise's kids. They act that way all the time." Pepper waved at Michael and Mark, but they weren't looking.

"Sorry, ma'am," the older boy called out. The younger one nodded. A red 4Runner turned into the parking lot, and the two boys ran toward it. A man with a long thin face and short dark hair leaned across the seat to open the passenger door. Rebekah smiled at him. Thank goodness he was out of the army; those boys looked like a handful.

"What's wrong with Pepper?" Reid asked.

"I need a new kidney," she said. "Want to give me one of yours?"

"No."

"Just kidding. You have the wrong blood." Pepper unzipped her backpack and took out her gum. "Want some?"

Reid shook his head. "How do you know I have the wrong blood?"

"Mom and Dad had you tested when I was sick the last time."

Rebekah groaned inwardly. Pepper had misunderstood their conversation with the doctor.

"I don't remember that," Reid commented.

"We didn't have you tested. We already knew that your blood type was A." Rebekah turned the air on again.

"You wanted me to give Pepper one of my kidneys?"

"No, Reid."

"But you would have? If my blood type had been right?"

"No." Patrick pulled out of the parking lot. "You have to be eighteen." He accelerated. "And they don't make exceptions."

"So after I was eighteen, then you would have taken my kidney?" The pitch of Reid's voice rose.

Pepper threw a stick of gum at Reid.

Rebekah ignored them and turned forward, adjusting her seat belt. If she could change one thing in her life, she would make herself Pepper's biological mother. Of course she would keep Pepper exactly the same, except with type A blood. A mother should be able to save her child's life, and she was, without question, Pepper's mother. Rebekah bit her lip. That was exactly what she was going to have to do—save Pepper's life. But how?

Chapter 5

lise absent-mindedly stirred the spaghetti sauce as she read the last page of *To the Lighthouse*. All these years she had wanted to visit the Isle of Skye, where Virginia Woolf had set the novel. She loved Mrs. Ramsay and her flowing thoughts, her domestic life, her interest in her guests and neighbors, and her devotion to art, to her husband, and to her children. She'd lost track of how many times she'd read the novel.

All Elise wanted in life was to have a family and to appreciate art—literature, to be exact. The trip to the lighthouse at the end of the story, without Mrs. Ramsay, was so different from what the family anticipated at the beginning of the novel. Unfortunately, life was like that. Elise sighed. She read the last line: "It was done; it was finished. Yes, she thought, laying down her brush in extreme fatigue, I have had my vision."

Elise closed the book and slipped it back into the bookcase in the living room.

"Hi, Mom." Michael bounced through the back door.

"How was school?" Elise eased the pasta into the boiling water.

"Great. The field trip was to a wetland on the other side of town."

"Hi." Ted closed the back door and kissed Elise on the cheek.

"Where's Mark?" Elise turned the flame down under the sauce.

"Scraping mud off his shoes. He went into the marsh during the field trip." Michael made a two-handed shoving motion. "Reid pushed him in."

"Why?" Her shoulders tightened.

"Because Mark tripped him." Michael swung his leg out, nearly kicking Elise.

"What did the teacher do?" Elise poked a wooden spoon at the pasta, trying to break up the clumps. It was never just that some boy had done something to Mark. There was always a previous scene in the story.

"It was Coach Davis."

"What did Coach Davis do?"

"Nothing."

✄

Elise put the last plate into the dishwasher and wiped the counter.

"Want to go for a walk?" Ted wore his running pants and a sweatshirt. "Mark said he would start on his algebra, and I'll check it when we get back." He pushed up his sleeves.

"I'll put my shoes on." She dried her hands.

"I tried to call you back today, but you didn't answer." Ted led the way out the door and across the street. "Did you read the e-mails?"

Elise nodded. "Can you get out of the inactive reserves?"

"No."

"Ted, we came to Forest Falls so you could spend time with your dad. If we'd known you were going to be deployed again, I could have moved to Seattle." She hurried to keep up with Ted's long stride.

"We came so we *all* could spend time with Dad." They headed down the hill toward downtown.

She didn't answer. The streetlight above them flickered and then came on.

"That bad, huh?" He slowed.

"What?"

"Forest Falls."

"I'm trying." She planned to go back to the Scrap Shack tomorrow.

If she had left the house today, she would have stopped by to find out the latest about the cougar.

"What's your vote in this?" Ted turned onto Main Street. "Do you want me to take my chances with the Third being deployed, or would you rather I go to Germany for three months?"

"Where do you think the Third would be sent?"

"Maybe Afghanistan, probably Iraq."

"Germany or a chance at Iraq." Elise spoke the words slowly. They had lived in Frankfurt for a year and loved it mostly, except for Mark's school experience. He'd been five, and they had started him in German kindergarten. After a month they decided to hold him back a year. "Germany," she answered. It was a no-brainer. "We can visit over Christmas."

"I'll be coming home in January."

"I can't stand another Christmas apart." She'd had three Christmases without him—the first when she was eight months pregnant with Mark, and Ted was in Saudi Arabia before the first Gulf War; the second when the boys were seven and eight, and he was in Kosovo, and she and the boys were in Kansas; and the third when he was in Afghanistan, and she and the boys were in Georgia. Each Christmas had been harder.

"I'll request Landstuhl." He took her hand. "And it's a great idea for you and the boys to come for Christmas."

Three more months of him away, and then what? Would he end up in another reserve unit that would be deployed before his two years were up?

Ted stopped in front of the Scrap Shack. "I used to buy wheels and bolts and drivelines for my go-carts here. It was a hardware store for as long as I can remember."

"I won't have the support that I had when we lived near bases." She kept walking.

"You'll have Dad and his church—and Rebekah and her husband." Ted hurried to catch up with her. "What's Rebekah like?"

"Likable, I guess. All of the women at her shop certainly seemed enamored with her."

The acrid smell of wood smoke filled the evening air. "I want to stop by Dad's place before we head home and tell him what's going on."

John's Chevy pickup was parked in front of his small brick house. A black Jeep pulled away from the curb. Was someone leaving John's house? Elise wondered if he saw many of the friends he and Maude had. Maybe it was a customer stopping by to pick up a cabinet or a table. Years ago he had converted the garage into a carpentry shop. He still took jobs, working nearly full-time. Smoke curled up from the chimney of the brick house as Ted knocked on the back door.

John's Bernese mountain dog, Bear, began to bark. "I'm coming." The back door swung open. "Ted." John opened the door wider. "And Elise. What a surprise."

"Hi, Dad." Ted reached down to pet Bear's thick fur. "We wanted to say hello and talk with you a minute." The dog raised his head. The contrast of the dark around his eyes and the strip of white down the center of his face made him look as if he wore a mask.

"Come in." John hugged his son and then patted Elise on the back. He wore a white, long-sleeved T-shirt, 501 jeans, and fleece-lined slippers.

They walked single file through his galley kitchen. The counters were bare and sparkling clean. He motioned Elise toward Maude's rocking chair. Flames crackled in the fireplace, and Bear settled in front of it.

Ted plopped down on the couch, pulled a pillow out from behind his back, and tossed it to the other end of the couch. "The reserve unit I've been assigned to is on standby to be deployed." Ted folded his hands over his knee.

"To Iraq?" John stood next to Bear.

"Probably." Ted paused. "I've also been offered a position at the Landstuhl army hospital in Germany for three months, which would be much easier."

"Easier isn't always better." John leaned over Bear to throw another log onto the fire. "You don't want to let the unit down." He crossed his arms. Elise sank further into Maude's chair.

"Elise and I have decided on Germany. It's what's best for our family. We haven't told the boys, because I'm waiting for specifics. But it will be hard on them—and on Elise. I moved them here thinking we'd all be together."

"Son, it's only for three months."

Ted nodded. "We could use your help. It would be great if you could hang out with the boys and help Elise if things need to be repaired around the house."

"Whatever I can do."

Elise stopped rocking at the thought of John hanging around the house disciplining the boys and fixing leaky toilets.

"Thanks, Dad." Ted stood.

John knelt next to Bear. "I'm proud of you, Son," he said. "So proud." He turned toward Elise. "Just let me know what you need."

Elise and Ted walked silently past the Scrap Shack and over the bridge. What would they need to do to get Ted ready to go? Switch the insurance back to active duty. Sign another power of attorney. Go over the when-Dad's-away rules with the boys. Buy another laptop so she would have a computer too; the boys had commandeered the old, slow one.

They turned onto their street. "Is that one of our sons? On a skateboard? In the dark?" Ted started to jog. A figure rolled toward them.

"Mom! Dad!" Michael flipped the board into his hands. "Ainsley just IM'd me. She said that Pepper's really sick and needs a kidney transplant."

"Who is Ainsley?" Ted put his hands on Michael's shoulders.

"An eighth grader, but she's a friend of Pepper's."

"Michael, are you sure?" Elise caught up to them.

Ted turned toward her. "Who is Pepper?"

"Rebekah's daughter, the girl the cougar was after." She started walking toward their house.

Michael followed. "They went to Portland today to the doctor."

Rebekah hadn't said anything on Saturday; no one had said a thing about Pepper being sick.

"Why would she need a transplant?" Michael asked.

"Her kidneys must be shutting down, perhaps from disease, or maybe it's genetic," Ted explained.

"But she doesn't look sick, except that she's small." Michael opened the gate.

Elise headed up the porch steps. "Did Reid say anything at practice?"

Michael shook his head. "But both his mom and dad picked him up afterward."

She opened the back door. Michael seemed to know a lot about the Grahams.

"Ainsley said she'd give Pepper one of her kidneys."

"It's not that simple." Ted sat on the window seat and took off his shoes. "You have to go through a series of tests to see if you're compatible. Besides, they don't let minors do that sort of thing."

Mark walked into the kitchen with the phone. "Dad, it's some army guy."

Ted headed down the hall to his study.

"Time for bed." Elise ran her hand through Michael's curls.

"It's only eight thirty," Mark complained as he opened the refrigerator.

"Go read. I'll come tell you good night in a little while." She headed to the utility room to throw in a load of laundry.

Forty-five minutes later Ted opened his study door. "It's all set. I leave in two weeks."

Chapter 6

*C*ome in the house, Reid." Rebekah stood on the porch and leaned over the railing.

"Hook shot from the free throw line." Reid took a step, turned, and arched his arm. Swoosh.

"It's time to go to bed. You've been out here for over an hour."

Reid grabbed the rebound, headed back down the concrete court, and went up for a jump shot. Swoosh. He dribbled near the porch and palmed the ball. "Did you ask me, when you had me tested, if I wanted to give Pepper a kidney?"

"Reid, we never had any tests done on you."

"Would I have had a choice? If I'd been a match?"

"Reid, there's an age limit." Rebekah stepped toward the front door. "No doctor would have taken your kidney."

"That's hard to believe." He bounced the ball from one hand to the other.

"Pardon?"

"It's hard to believe I would have had a choice."

Rebekah walked back to the railing.

"You probably would have taken me to South America or something and had them do it."

"Reid!"

"You love her more. You always have."

What was with him? "Reid, that's not true." Were there tears in his eyes? Rebekah leaned over the railing. "Sweetie, no mother loves one child more than another."

He wiped at his eyes with the back of his hand. "Then you like her more."

Rebekah shook her head. She remembered feeling that way, certain her parents loved her older brother more. "Reid, I love you and I like you—so, so much. Every bit as much as Pepper." She did spend more time with Pepper. Was that what he meant? "Now come on in, sweetie."

He went up for another jump shot. It bounced off the rim.

"Reid, it's nearly ten o'clock. I'm exhausted."

"I'm not," he said, narrowing his eyes, and dribbled the ball, hard, to the other end of the court and up the back steps. She hurried in the front door and met him in the kitchen, intending to hug him, but he rushed by her and up the stairs, taking the ball with him.

"What's wrong with Reid?" Patrick asked, padding into the kitchen wearing black sweatpants and slippers, his hair disheveled.

"He thinks I love Pepper more than him." She sat down and turned off the computer. Pepper had spent most of the evening e-mailing her friends on Rebekah's PC.

Patrick ran his fingers through Rebekah's hair. "Do you?"

"Of course not." Rebekah stood.

"I can see why Reid wonders." Patrick pulled a glass from the cupboard. "I've wondered that myself sometimes." He poured himself a glass of water.

"About Reid?"

"No. About me."

"Patrick." She went and turned off the kitchen light. "I'm too tired for this. Good night."

Rebekah thrust a leg out from under the floral chintz comforter. Moonlight shone through the lace curtain and cast a streak of light on the far wall. Patrick slept on his back with his arms crossed over his chest. A coyote yipped in the night.

Half an hour later she fished under the bed for her slippers and tiptoed into the hall, wearing plaid pajama bottoms and one of Patrick's T-shirts. She poked her head into Pepper's room; her daughter slept with one arm over her head and a half smile on her face, her blond hair fanned across her blue pillow. It was hard to fathom that a disease stalked her body, stalked her life.

Rebekah headed downstairs, making her way through the darkness to the kitchen. She flipped on the light and squinted as she sat down at her computer.

Dr. Thomas had said that a related donor was their best bet. Should she call Pepper's bio grandmother? Or write a letter? She booted up the computer and opened Word. She definitely shouldn't call at 4:30 in the morning. She wrote:

Dear Polly,

I hope this note finds you and your family well.

No. The word *family* brought Mandy, Pepper's birth mom, to mind. How could you be well, ever, if you lost your eighteen-year-old daughter, even if it had been over a decade ago?

Dear Polly,

Sorry it's been a while since I've written.

How long had it been? Rebekah had gone to Mandy's funeral, sent photos on Pepper's birthday for the first five years or so, and then written and sent photos when they had the kidney scare four years ago—not to ask Polly to consider donating but to keep in touch, just in case.

Polly hadn't written back.

Dear Polly,

I'll cut to the chase. Pepper is ill, and we're looking for a
kidney. Would you consider donating yours?

She hit Delete, Delete, Delete until every word was removed from the
screen.

Maybe she should call in the morning, after the kids left for school.
*Polly, this is Rebekah, Pepper's mom—I mean adoptive mom. I was wonder-
ing how you are doing. Are you healthy? Do you have diabetes? High blood
pressure? Any chronic illness? By the way, what is your blood type?* Rebekah
sighed. She could think of no tactful way to do this. She launched the
desk chair backward and bumped into Pepper's boots. The soles were
caked with manure—and in the kitchen. She tossed them onto the mud
porch. Surely Polly, or Pepper's aunt, would agree to be tested. Who
wouldn't be willing to do that for Pepper?

She stood and stretched. She had an hour before everyone needed to
get up.

"Hi, Sky." Rebekah cooed the words as she rubbed the horse's forehead.
He nuzzled his nose against her neck, warming her skin with his soft flesh.
His mother shifted in the next stall.

"Hey, girl," Rebekah called out. "You're next." She brushed Sky's dark
mane and tail and then his inky sides and then over the white spots splattered across his rump. She poured a bucket of oats into his trough and
took off her jean jacket and tossed it over the stall gate.

Sky bumped his head lovingly against Rebekah's arm. "Are you having a good morning?" she asked, rubbing between his ears. He was so

unpredictable. He could be a wild beast one day and a perfect gentleman the next. She couldn't imagine trusting him with Pepper, not yet.

Rebekah poured a bucket of oats into the mare's trough and then began brushing her. "What would you do if something horrible was after Sky?" she asked, working a burr out of the horse's tail. The mare snorted.

The barn door creaked open, and a starling fluttered up to the rafters. "Mom?"

"Back here, honey."

"Will you braid my hair?"

"Just a minute, Pep. Let me finish." Rebekah held her watch toward the light: 6:32. "Feed the other horses their oats." They would have to brush the rest in the evening and hopefully get in a short ride. She raced through her mental to-do list for the day. Check on the back orders at the shop, unpack the inventory that arrived late yesterday, pay the bills, pick up milk and bread on the way home. *Yikes.* She had forgotten to look for the insurance enrollment form. She dropped the brush on the shelf. "Hey, sweet pea, meet me back in the house when you're done. I need to go find something."

Rebekah grabbed her jean jacket and slipped through the barn door. The rising sun glimmered just above the forest, and a flock of birds landed in the plowed field across the road. She sucked in the cool air and hurried up the back steps into the kitchen. The form wasn't on her desk. She turned off the teakettle as she headed into the dining room, snatching a stack of mail off the china cabinet.

"What's up?" Patrick asked as he buttoned his shirt.

Startled, Rebekah jerked up her head. "I need to pay bills today." She thumbed through the stack. Credit card advertisements, a school calendar, the power bill. On the bottom was the insurance form.

"Do you want hot cereal?" he called from the kitchen. "I'm making the instant kind."

"Sure." She unfolded the form and scanned the opening paragraph. *Due date: September 1.* That was three weeks ago.

Chapter 7

*M*om." Michael stood in the bedroom doorway. "We're leaving for school."

"What time is it?" Elise opened her eyes.

"Seven forty-five. We're riding our bikes." Michael paused. "Are you sick?"

"Just tired." She flung the blankets back, climbed out of bed, and slipped into her robe. She hadn't been able to sleep and finally had taken a pill at three thirty. Ted's cell phone had rung an hour later, and he had headed to the Salem Hospital. She stood at the living room window and waved as the boys rode down the street. *Ted. Germany.* They hadn't told Michael. Ted had told Mark last night, but Michael was already asleep. Had Mark said something? Elise poured a cup of coffee and slumped into a chair at the kitchen table.

She swallowed the coffee. Ted always made it too weak. *Ted.* Had he tricked her? Had he known that being deployed again was a possibility but didn't think she would agree to move to Forest Falls if he told her?

She headed to the shower. She was scheduled to volunteer in the school library third period. She would find Michael and tell him then.

Elise scanned the hall. Three girls came toward her, their arms linked. "Hey!" one of them called out to Reid, who stood in front of his locker. "How's your sister? Are you going to give her a kidney?"

Reid poked his head out from behind the door. "Get lost."

Elise smiled. She loved to see other people's kids act out.

"Boy, you're grumpy," the middle girl called out.

"Hi, Reid." Elise took a step toward his locker.

He slammed the door; it bounced back open. He slammed it again.

"Hi," she said again.

He ignored her.

"Hi, Elise!" Pepper hurried toward her. "Don't mind Reid. He's mad at me."

"Why?"

Pepper shrugged. "He's been a creep since last night."

Maybe Mark wasn't that unusual; maybe it was the age. "Pepper, I thought you were sick."

"I'm on antibiotics. I feel better already."

"So it's just an infection?" Elise wanted to laugh. The middle school gossip mill had turned a kidney infection into a transplant.

"Sort of." Pepper flipped both of her braids over her shoulder and waved good-bye as the bell rang.

Elise wove her way down the hall to Michael's math class. He hopped off the back of his chair and onto the seat as Elise entered the classroom.

"What are you doing here?" he whispered.

"I need to talk to you."

"Now?" His head bobbed from side to side.

Elise nodded. "Let's go outside. Tell your teacher you'll be right back."

She sat on the top step; Michael sat three steps lower. Bright yellow maple leaves covered the school lawn.

"Dad had a phone call last night."

Michael shrugged.

"Did Mark say anything?" Elise took her purse from her shoulder and held it in her lap.

"Just that we might move to Seattle after Dad's deployed."

What was Mark up to? "Dad will be gone for only three months."

"Is he going to Iraq?"

"Germany. Mark didn't tell you that?"

"He just said Dad was being deployed—again." Michael cracked his knuckles.

"Have you and Mark told anyone else?"

"No." Michael hesitated. "Well, just a few of my football buddies. They might have told some girls. Rumor is that Dad is going to fight; no one seems to know that he's an anesthesiologist." He grinned and squared his shoulders.

Elise shook her head. The boys had no idea how gossipy small towns could be. "Michael." She leaned forward. "I'm sorry that Mark told you before Dad or I could."

He shrugged. "I should get to class."

"Pepper told me she doesn't need a kidney." Elise spoke the words softly as they headed back into the building.

"No, she does, Mom. The whole school knows." Michael stopped. "Will you be okay while Dad's gone?"

"Sure, honey. We'll all be fine. It's only Germany; it's only for three months."

✂

Elise pushed open the door to the Scrap Shack. "Hi, Rebekah."

"Oh, hi! I was hoping you would stop by." Rebekah put a box of horseshoe charms on the counter. "Sandi told me about your husband."

"How did Sandi know?"

"She's in a Bible study at church with your father-in-law. He asked for prayer for you."

Elise wrinkled her nose.

"How are you doing with all of this?"

"Fine."

"Really? I wouldn't be fine if Patrick was going off for three months." Rebekah slid her hands into the back pockets of her jeans.

"It's just Germany." Elise picked a blond hair off her blazer.

Rebekah nodded. "So this is no big deal to you?"

Elise shrugged. "I'm thinking about taking the boys over at Christmas."

"I've got the perfect embellishments for you." Rebekah hurried over to the travel section and held up a German flag. "You could do a vacation book."

Elise shrugged. She didn't want to hide another scrapbook in the closet. "I'm curious—what happened with the cougar?"

"Oh, that." Rebekah put the flag back on the rack. "The game-department guy didn't find anything. He said to let him know if we see it again."

"Are the horses safe?"

"He said the cougar is probably long gone. They have huge territories, up to ten square miles."

Elise relaxed just a little. "I was going to ask about Pepper too. I heard a rumor, but I saw her at school, and she debunked it. Sorry to hear she has an infection, however."

"She does have an infection, but—"

"She doesn't need a transplant, though, right?"

"No. She does." Rebekah's voice was a near whisper.

"Oh, Rebekah. I'm sorry." Elise stepped backward.

"We've known for a long time, kind of, but I had convinced myself that she was healed. Well, she's not."

"What's the first step?"

"To find a kidney."

"You'll be tested?"

Rebekah shook her head. "There's no point. I have the wrong blood type. I'm going to contact Pepper's birth family."

"Birth family?" Elise asked. "Pepper's adopted?"

Rebekah nodded, a half smile on her face.

"Is Reid adopted?"

Rebekah shook her head. "No."

"So it's an open adoption?" Elise felt confused. She never would have guessed that Pepper was adopted.

"Not really. Her bio mom died when she was a baby. The grandma and an aunt live in Nevada."

"Wow. That's a lot for you to deal with." But at least Rebekah had known for years that Pepper's situation was precarious; it wasn't as though she'd just found out. Elise put her hand against her lower back.

"Parenting two teenagers alone—now that's a lot." Rebekah picked up the horseshoe charms again. "Finding a kidney might be easier."

"Speaking of—" Elise nodded toward the window. Pepper bounced up the sidewalk.

"Mom! Oh, hi, Elise." Pepper hurried into the shop. "I wish I hadn't told Ainsley I was sick. The whole school knows. Now everyone—except for Reid—wants to give me a kidney." Pepper took the charms from Rebekah's hand. "Look at these!"

Elise stood. "I should get going."

"Mom, are we going to ride tomorrow? Before the game?"

Rebekah nodded.

"Can Elise come out and ride with us?"

Elise shook her head. "You'll be too busy."

"I'm closing the shop at four. Why don't you bring the boys out—and your husband? The guys can all eat dinner and then go into town. We'll have plenty of time to ride; the game doesn't start until seven."

"All right." Elise slung her purse to her other shoulder. She didn't want to feel obligated to return a dinner invitation. "Let me bring a pan of enchiladas."

"That would be great." Rebekah took the charms from Pepper. "I'll make a salad and mix up some lemonade."

"See you tomorrow!" Pepper yelled out the door of the Scrap Shack. Elise waved. It had been Pepper who had invited her to ride. Was Rebekah just being polite to have her out again?

Chapter 8

*R*ebekah slapped the hot pads onto her kitchen counter. "Let's get this show on the road so we can go ride." She opened the back door. "Boys, Pepper, time to eat."

Elise pulled the enchiladas from the oven while Ted opened a jar of salsa.

The ball stopped bouncing on the concrete court, followed by a thundering of feet up the steps. Mark shoved Reid through the door. "Watch it," Reid snarled.

"Easy," Elise called out, slipping the oven mitts off her small hands.

"Take your shoes off." Rebekah bristled as she pulled a stack of plates from the cupboard, keeping an eye on the boys.

Reid positioned himself in front of the island.

"Guests first." Mark nudged him aside. Rebekah smiled at Reid and nodded. He crossed his arms. Reid and Michael, with their short dark hair, looked more like brothers than Michael and Mark, although Reid also stood a head taller than Michael.

Pepper opened the back door and slipped off her boots. "Your horses are saddled."

"What about the palomino?" Rebekah stirred the lemonade.

"I don't feel like riding."

"Come here, Pep." Rebekah placed the back of her hand on Pepper's forehead. "No fever."

"I'm just tired." Pepper headed into the dining room.

Rebekah dumped ice into the pitcher. The infection would make her lethargic; it didn't mean anything more than that. "Reid, Dad will be here any minute. He and Ted will take you boys into town. Tell Dad that Pepper can go with him or wait and go with me."

A few minutes later Elise and Rebekah headed out the back door to the horses. Michael and Reid shot hoops, their empty plates stacked in the corner of the court. Mark stood on the corral rail, scratching Sky's forehead.

"Mark likes horses," Reid said in a mocking tone, raising his dark eyebrows as he spun the ball on his finger.

"Stuff it, Reid." Mark climbed a rung higher on the corral.

Rebekah shook her head at Reid.

Michael flashed his metallic grin and then hooted. "Mark's always been crazy about horses."

"Michael, stop." Elise raised her hand against the glaring sun.

"Mark, would you like to ride with us sometime?" Rebekah swung the gate to the corral open. Maybe the kid needed a true friend.

Mark shook his head and jumped down from the rail, drawing away from her.

"My sister used to sleep with her cowboy boots on." Reid swung a hook shot toward the basket. "That's the reason Mom and Dad got this stupid farm, because of stupid Pepper."

"Reid, that's enough." Rebekah grimaced. Reid grabbed the ball and slammed it against the backboard. A flock of geese rose up from the pasture, honking as they formed two lines.

"Good luck at the game." Rebekah swung her leg over Sky. "We'll see you there."

Mark stomped up the back steps to the house.

✂

Rebekah leaned forward as Sky loped up the trail. She held the reins against his dark mane and dug her knees into his side. Every ride was an adventure; it was a thrill to control an animal weighing more than a thousand pounds. She felt ageless as the rhythmic beat of the horse's hoofs drummed along the path, connecting the trees, the animal, and her body. She contained the urge to gallop Sky, to fly through the forest.

She slowed and turned in the saddle. Dusty light drifted through the trees and over the silhouette of Elise bouncing along on the mare.

"Plant your butt, and lean backward." Rebekah stopped Sky. "Lean forward only when you want to go fast or you're coming up a hill."

Elise shifted in the saddle, sitting up straight. "Do the horses remember the cougar?"

"Sure, but as long as they can't smell, hear, or see it, they'll be fine." Rebekah patted Sky's side.

"How long have you been riding?" Elise asked.

"I spent summers on my grandparents' ranch in Montana as a girl." She urged Sky up a rocky spot in the trail. "Were you happy to move to Forest Falls?" she asked as they rode through a dappled patch of shade.

"I'm fine with giving it a try."

"So it's a trial run?" Rebekah kicked Sky gently, urging him over the roots of a western hemlock that had knotted the trail.

"We'll see."

"Don't you like small towns?"

"I grew up in one." Elise sounded a little out of breath.

"I remember." Rebekah smiled. "So, you're just not sure about this small town?"

"I wasn't sure about the one I grew up in, either." Elise laughed. "How old was Pepper when you adopted her?"

"She was a foster baby—our first and last. She came home from the hospital at three months. Then her birth mom died when Pepper was nine months old; we adopted her after that."

"Couldn't you have more babies after Reid?" Elise jiggled the mare's reins and clicked her tongue.

Rebekah shook her head. "I had a hard pregnancy and delivery. I would have tried again, but Patrick freaked out." Her ponytail rose and fell with the horse's motion. "I had been a social worker, so we decided to do foster care. I thought I could navigate the system." She laughed. "We wanted another baby right away but didn't have the money to adopt."

"Why didn't you take more foster kids?"

"Pepper took all my time—doctors' appointments, therapy, keeping her away from other sick kids." Rebekah rode with her left hand on her hip.

"So Pepper was born with kidney problems?"

Rebekah shrugged. "They didn't show up until after she had strep throat for the fourth time, when she was eight. It could have been the infections, or it could have been scarring from when she was in utero."

The trail turned, and they headed for a patch of sunlight. Rebekah tilted her face toward the last of the light filtering through the trees. An orange maple leaf floated toward the trail.

"Do you know the Edna St. Vincent Millay poem 'God's World'?" Elise reached out to the leaf. The breeze lifted it away.

Rebekah shook her head.

"It's about autumn—and beauty." Elise cleared her throat. "O world, I cannot hold thee close enough! Thy winds, thy wide grey skies! Thy mists, that roll and rise! Thy woods, this autumn day, that ache and sag and all but cry with colour." She paused.

"That's beautiful." Rebekah tried not to sound surprised. She didn't know anyone who could recite poetry like that. "I don't know much about literature, but I'm impressed."

"I used to know about literature," Elise said, "years ago."

They rode silently, crunching over dried maple leaves that covered the trail. A bird squawked in the treetops—probably a crow, although Rebekah preferred to think of it as a raven. Sky stepped sideways. "Come on, boy."

The two women rode side by side. Elise held the reins with one hand and tucked a strand of hair behind her ear with the other. "What if Pepper didn't feel up to going with the guys?"

"She'll be okay, but we'll turn around up here." Rebekah stopped at the edge of a meadow. "The grass is covered by wild daisies in late July and early August. Patrick even rode up here with me to pick flowers last month. It was his ride for the year." Fir trees circled the clearing. Rebekah nodded toward the trail. "Sometime we'll have to ride to the falls that are further up the trail."

Elise smiled. "It sounds enchanting."

Rebekah sat back in the saddle. Elise had actually seemed relaxed for half a second.

"So what didn't you like about the small town you grew up in?" Rebekah turned Sky around in the meadow.

Elise concentrated on the mare and frowned.

"Do your parents still live there?" Rebekah prodded.

Elise shook her head. "My dad died in a sawmill accident when I was seventeen. My mom and sister moved to Michigan a year later."

"Why Michigan?"

"A friend told them about a nursing home that was for sale in Lansing. They both worked as nurse's aides, so they bought it with my dad's insurance money. My sister still runs it."

"What about your mom?"

"She watches daytime TV."

Rebekah laughed. "Do you see them often?"

"Every two or three years."

"Not exactly close." Rebekah leaned back.

Elise shook her head.

"I'm sorry about your dad."

"Thanks."

"Were you close to him?"

Elise nodded. She obviously didn't want to talk about her childhood.

They reached a wide spot in the trail. Rebekah decided to try a different topic. "What do you dread the most about Ted being gone?"

"Insomnia."

Rebekah laughed. "I deal with that every once in a while myself." She needed to write the letter to Polly.

"Besides that, everything tends to break or fall apart when Ted is gone." Elise leaned back in the saddle.

"Like?"

"Mark. Michael. Pets, which is why we no longer have cats and dogs. I've buried at least half a dozen over the last fourteen years. Cars. Water heaters. Stoves. Furnaces. Pipes. Bones. Windows. Computers. Couches. Beds."

Rebekah laughed. "I get the picture."

"It isn't pretty."

"No wonder you get insomnia." The trail narrowed, and she pulled Sky ahead of Elise. "What do you do when you can't sleep?" The shadows fell thick and cool. Below, the other horses galloped across the field, cutting through the tall grass.

"Blame Ted." Elise's voice faltered as they headed down the hill. "Or the army."

"Go to the game," Rebekah said. "Please. Cheer for Reid too. I hate to miss seeing him play, but I need to stay home." She sat down beside Pepper on the edge of the four-poster bed.

Elise stood in the doorway of Rebekah's bedroom. Pepper leaned against the headboard, propped up by a stack of pillows. An Oregon Field Guide episode about wild horses played on PBS.

"Can we get one?" Pepper asked.

"One what?" Rebekah put her hand on Pepper's forehead.

"A wild horse."

"No, Pep."

"Elise, you could get one and board it at our place." Pepper scooted up into a sitting position.

"I think you guys have enough going on without adding a wild horse to the mix." Elise waved to Pepper. "Get well. I mean feel better." Elise turned to go. "I'll see you tomorrow, Rebekah, at the shop."

"Thanks." Rebekah stood.

"It's just the infection, Mom, really." Pepper turned on her side. A herd of horses flew through a canyon across the television screen.

Rebekah sat on Patrick's side of the bed with a stack of paperwork and filled out the insurance form. Surely there was a grace period. She would send it in an envelope with Patrick tomorrow. Hopefully he wouldn't look and have another thing to worry about.

"Mom, I really like Elise." The blanket pulled up to Pepper's mouth muffled her voice. "I don't know why you didn't at first." A wild horse ran frantically around a corral.

Rebekah pretended to be engrossed in the form. It wasn't that she hadn't liked Elise—not exactly. No, that wasn't true. She *hadn't* liked her. Now it seemed that Elise was okay, but it wasn't like they were becoming fast friends or anything. How could they when Elise hardly shared anything important?

Rebekah pulled out the pamphlet from the National Kidney Foundation: *25 Facts About Organ Donation and Transplantation.* Rebekah skimmed the information. *A live donor must be 18 years or older.* Patrick was right. *Over 89,000 U.S. patients are currently waiting for an organ transplant; 3,886 kidney patients died in 2004 while waiting....* "Yikes." That was more than ten each day.

"What's the matter?" Pepper propped her head on her elbow.

"Oh, I'm just trying to get through this paperwork." Rebekah shuffled the pamphlet back to the bottom of the pile. "You need to hit the hay, sweet pea. Safe and sound in your own cozy bed."

An hour later Rebekah sat in front of her computer and rewrote the letter to Polly, simply explaining that Pepper needed a kidney transplant and asking Polly if she would consider being tested to see if she was a match. Rebekah wrote that she would call in a week or Polly could feel free to call or e-mail her. Rebekah closed the letter with all of her contact information.

Next she pulled the pamphlet back out from the bottom of the pile of papers. *Recipients with a live donor kidney have a higher survival and success rate than those with a cadaveric donor kidney.* She had never considered a donated kidney not working. She had never thought of Pepper not surviving an operation. She pressed her index finger against her lip. They needed a live donor. And soon.

Patrick's and Reid's voices carried into the house. "He's a jerk. I was wide open over and over." The door opened. "So was Michael. But Mark ran instead."

"And made the touchdowns." Patrick closed the back door.

"Who won?" Rebekah stood and stretched.

"We did." Patrick pulled her close. "How's Pepper?"

"Better."

Reid pushed by. "Want a snack?" she asked.

"No." He dropped his sports bag on the table and stumbled through the dining room, bumping against a chair. He pounded up the stairs.

"Reid!"

"Let him go." Patrick poured himself a glass of lemonade. "He didn't play quarterback; Mark did. Mark knew all day the coach was going to play him but didn't say anything to Reid."

"Poor Reid."

Patrick drained his glass and rinsed it. "Mark hardly passed; he ran nearly every play."

"What did the coach say?" She turned off the computer.

" 'Good job.' We won 32–0. Mark scored all the points except for the two-point conversion." He put his glass in the dishwasher.

"Who had those?"

"Michael."

Poor Reid. She flipped the kitchen light switch. "What do you think of Ted?"

"Nice guy." Patrick goosed her as they started up the stairs. She turned and slapped at him playfully. "A lot nicer than his son. He seemed embarrassed by Mark's behavior. Elise too. They both stopped cheering for Mark by the end of the third quarter."

*E*lise reached into the back of her closet for her suede jacket. She hadn't worn it for a few years. Was it still in style? She tried it on. The reddish brown suede would look perfect on Rebekah.

She sat down on her bed. Had she said too much while riding with Rebekah? Was it corny to quote the poem? She tried to recall the rest of it. "Thou'st made the world too beautiful this year. My soul is all but out of me..." How did it end? She couldn't remember.

Beautiful landscapes, poetry, and good literature all used to do that to her soul—take it out of her. Her first few years with Ted and the births of her boys did too. It didn't seem like much took her soul out anymore. Except horseback riding.

That was why she was going to Midnight Madness at the Scrap Shack. She hoped Rebekah would invite her to ride again.

"I'm not going to the game." Mark wore his red plaid pajama bottoms and white T-shirt; his damp hair hung over his eyebrows. He swung his legs onto the couch, balancing a glass of milk and a handful of vanilla wafers.

Elise picked up the latest issue of *Sports Illustrated For Kids* off the floor.

"You don't want to go to the varsity game?" Michael asked. "Our whole team will be there."

"The whole team hates me."

"You should learn to pass." Michael pulled his sweatshirt over his head.

"We won, you moron." Mark stuffed the cookies into his mouth and grabbed the remote control.

"Come on." Elise folded the blue and white afghan that Maude had crocheted years ago and draped it over the back of Ted's easy chair. "Go to the game, Mark." If he stayed home, should she stay home and miss Midnight Madness at the Scrap Shack?

"Dad, Mark doesn't want to go!" Michael started down the hall.

"That's fine."

Elise followed Michael into the kitchen. "Ted, he has to go. I plan to go to the thing at Rebekah's shop." She had intended to go to the cropping class yesterday morning, but then Ted had made an appointment with a lawyer to get a new power of attorney and to go over their will.

"Go. Mark will be fine."

"See if you can talk him into it." Elise frowned as she put the milk into the refrigerator and the box of vanilla wafers into the cupboard.

Michael held up his hands. "I didn't leave that stuff out."

"I know."

A minute later Ted sauntered back into the kitchen. "He wants to stay home. He'll be fine."

Elise opened the family-room closet door and pulled out several boxes of pictures that she had filed over the years. She didn't have any football photos yet. In fact, she had forgotten to take her camera to Wednesday's game. She would pretend she planned to do a family scrapbook.

Mark flipped the channel from the local news to *King of the Hill*.

"Watch something else." She grabbed a box of photos labeled "Mark/ Baby." She would sort pictures tonight.

Mark changed the channel to *NewsHour with Jim Lehrer*. That would last until she was out the door.

"I'm off." Elise juggled the bag and box. "Call me on my cell if you need anything." She poked her head back into the room. Mark seemed engrossed in a segment about divorce in the military. "The rates throughout the army have more than doubled in the last five years as soldiers are sent on long deployments and couples and families are stressed to the breaking point." Maybe *King of the Hill* would be better. "What do you plan to do all evening?" she asked.

"Hide," he said, slapping a couch pillow over his face.

Elise hurried through the door of the Scrap Shack, clutching her box of photos and her bag. Women milled around on the balcony. A peal of laughter bounced off the rafters followed by a shout. Two cowboy boots flew in the air, followed by two denim-clad legs. Someone was doing a cartwheel. Pepper? No, the legs were too long and the boots too big. Rebekah's head popped up, and her wavy hair bounced around her shoulders as she raised her arms into the air and struck a perfect pose. The women clapped and cheered. Elise edged back toward the door and pushed it open with her hip. She didn't belong here.

Rebekah leaned over the railing. "Elise!" She was a little out of breath. "Come on up!"

Elise raised the box of photos halfheartedly. "I'm late."

"No, you're right on time. We're just getting started."

Elise headed up the stairs and searched the crowd of women. Sandi motioned to Elise. "Over here." She wore an oversized yellow sweater and black hoop earrings, and her short white hair was spiked even taller than it had been the week before.

Elise bumped into a woman with a plate of pizza. "Excuse me." She slid between bodies, turning sideways.

"I'm so happy that you're going to scrapbook." Sandi scooted her album to the side. "I didn't think you would."

Elise smiled.

"You're a little reluctant, right?"

"Just call me the accidental scrapbooker." Elise wiggled out of her jacket.

Sandi chuckled.

"Elise, grab some pizza." Rebekah hurried by with her arms full of reams of paper.

"Rebekah," a woman at the food table shouted, "we're out of napkins."

Sandi stood with one knee on her chair. "Rebekah, I need a pocket for this page—or something. What do you think?"

Rebekah hurried back to their table. "A pink pocket." Rebekah leaned closer. "With a strawberry charm. They're on the rack by the western stuff."

Elise pulled her album out of her plastic bag and muttered. "Midnight Madness. Mania is more like it."

"Isn't it great?" Sandi held up a piece of pink paper. "Rebekah had no idea that so many women would come." Sandi made her way through the crowd to the staircase.

Elise leaned toward Sandi's book. Photos of women eating ice cream covered the layout. They stood around an old-fashioned ice-cream freezer on the porch of an old house. Rebekah's house. And there was a closeup of Rebekah and Sandi laughing, their arms around each other.

"We had a ladies' day." Rebekah pointed a package of napkins at the group photo. "A strawberry ice-cream social."

A minute later Rebekah returned empty-handed. "Are you working on your football album?" She pulled up a chair.

Elise shook her head. "I'm going to start with a family album."

"Mind if I look?" Rebekah pulled a photo of newborn Mark from the box. "Cute." She thumbed through a few more photos. "Where's a family photo?"

Elise shook her head and pulled the box away from Rebekah. "Here's one of Mark and me." She had held the camera out in front of their faces when they got home and had created a slightly out-of-focus image. She had forgotten to ask one of the nurses to take a picture of the two of them before they left the hospital. "Here's one of Ted." Ted wore his fatigues and helmet and stood in front of a tent hospital in the sand, holding Mark's newborn photo from the hospital.

"Elise." Rebekah pressed both photos against her chest. "Ted was gone when Mark was born?"

Elise nodded. "He was in Saudi Arabia, for the first Gulf War." She put her hand out for the photos.

"Did your mom come to help you?"

Elise shook her head.

"Did Ted's parents come to help?"

Elise shook her head again. "They waited until Ted came home." Actually, they waited almost a year.

"That's heartbreaking." Rebekah handed the photos back to Elise.

The shop door buzzed, and Rebekah sprang to her feet. "Hi, sweet pea." She leaned against the rail. "Hi, Ainsley. Come on up."

Sandi dropped a packet of strawberry charms on her layout and then snapped her fingers. "I left my file of borders in my Jeep. I'll be right back."

Pepper handed Rebekah an envelope of photos. "They're of Ainsley's red roan."

Pepper turned to Elise. "Ainsley, this is Mark's mother, Mrs. Shelton." Ainsley blushed.

Rebekah handed each photo to Elise, shot after shot of a horse—by the barn, in the field, under a tree. "What a beautiful horse." Elise smiled at Rebekah. At last, a way to get the conversation focused on horseback riding.

Rebekah laughed, held a photo in midair, and then handed it to Elise. "Look, our charming sons." Mark and Reid scowled at each other, their helmets clenched in their hands.

"Oops." Ainsley reached out her hand for the photos.

Elise placed a navy-blue sheet of paper against the black page of the scrap-book and then arranged three newborn photos of Mark in the middle.

Sandi dropped her keys into her bag and placed a red-checkered strip of paper on the table.

Elise moved the photos into a different configuration. Maybe she should sort the photos first, the whole box. She could keep busy without committing anything to the page.

"A baby-blue border would look striking." Sandi rummaged through her file. "Here." She handed Elise a piece of paper.

"Thanks." Was Sandi warming up to her?

Sandi pulled a page of strawberry stickers from her bag. "Scrapbook-ing is the ultimate in preserving memories—better than photos alone or even video."

"How's that?" Elise rested her chin in her hand.

"See this picture?" It was the group photo of the women with Sandi on the end. "My butt looks really big in it. See this strawberry sticker? Voilà, my big butt is gone." Sandi slapped strawberry stickers around the entire photo.

"You could have just trimmed the photo."

"Cropped," Sandi corrected, then whispered, "The stickers aren't as obvious."

Elise smiled. Revisionist scrapbooking.

A minute later Sandi joined a group of women across the room. Elise sat alone. Rebekah joined the group. All the women laughed at once. Elise sank back in her chair and stared at the lonely baby photos of bald little Mark. A phone began to ring, and a couple of the women in the group ran for their purses. Elise dug in her coat pocket. "It's mine."

"Did Mark go with you?" Ted asked.

"No." Elise almost laughed at the thought of Mark in this crowd of women.

"He's not here. We stopped by Dad's on the way home and just got in. Mark's gone."

"Are his shoes there? His coat?" Elise lowered her voice and turned toward the balcony rail.

"I don't know. How many pairs of shoes does he have? How many coats?"

If she were home, she could tell in ten seconds flat if any shoes, sweatshirts, coats, or jackets were missing. "Is his backpack there? By the door?"

Ted paused. "Yes."

"Have you looked all over the house?"

"Yes."

"Outside?"

"Yes."

Elise thought for half a second. "Did you look on the roof?"

"Yes."

One time, in Georgia, Mark had hidden on the roof. It had taken her ten minutes, the longest ever, to find him. It was after 9/11, and Ted had just arrived in Afghanistan.

"What's wrong?" Rebekah mouthed.

"I'll be right home," Elise said to Ted.

"Everything okay?" Rebekah asked.

"Everything's fine."

"You don't look fine." Rebekah put a hand on Elise's shoulder.

"Mark is missing. I'm sure he's just hiding, but Ted can't find him," Elise whispered.

"Mark must be really stressed about Ted being deployed. You all must be stressed." Rebekah picked up Elise's box of photos and walked her down the stairs. "Let me know when you find him."

Elise nodded. Five minutes later she pulled into the garage. Where would she hide if she were Mark?

Chapter 10

ℛebekah sat at her dining room table with a cup of chamomile tea, too wound up to sleep. Midnight Madness had been an unbelievable success. Thirty-two women, six pizzas, three cartwheels, and scads of sold albums, paper, and embellishments. She hadn't done the paperwork yet, so she didn't know how much money she had made, but it was by far her best day yet.

"Mom." Pepper stood in the archway between the dining room and the living room.

"Sweetie, why aren't you asleep?"

"I had too much fun to sleep."

"Dad isn't going to let you stay out if you don't get right to bed." They'd left the shop in shambles to get Pepper home; Rebekah would have to clean it up before opening in the morning.

Pepper sat beside Rebekah and took a sip of her tea. "What was wrong with Elise?"

Elise. She hadn't called, but surely she had found Mark. "She was needed at home." Rebekah took the mug from Pepper. "You go on to bed. I'll be up in a flash."

Pepper stood. "Mom, what scares you?"

"What do you mean, sweet pea?"

"What freaks you out?"

Rebekah took a sip of tea. "I don't know." She ran her finger over the rim of the cup. "I can't think of anything."

"I'm afraid of raccoons." Pepper yawned.

"Raccoons? Why, sweetie?"

"They're creepy." She yawned again. "Ainsley and I saw one on the way to the shop tonight. It ran across the street, right in front of us." Pepper turned and headed to the stairs.

Rebekah smiled. *Pepper needs a kidney transplant, and she's afraid of raccoons.* Rebekah sat at her desk. She had mailed the letter yesterday, so there was no way Pepper's bio grandma had received it yet. Still, Rebekah checked her e-mails. One from her mother, saying it had been 102 degrees in Phoenix. Three from scrapbook manufacturers. One from Sandi, already thanking her for the Scrap Shack and Midnight Madness: "It's just what the women of Forest Falls need!"

Ten minutes later Rebekah crawled into bed. Patrick slung his arm over her, pinning her to the mattress. She pushed him, and he turned to his side, facing her. "The shop is making money. You don't need to worry," she whispered.

"How's Pepper?" He opened one eye.

"Fine."

"You kept her out too late."

"Shh. Go back to sleep." Rebekah wedged her pillow under her neck. "She's fine."

"Here. You go unlock the door." Rebekah turned off the motor and tossed the keys to Pepper. "I need to make a quick phone call." She called information for Elise's number and then dialed.

A deep voice answered the phone. Was it Ted? When Elise came to the phone, Rebekah asked how things were going with Mark.

"Mark?" Elise sounded puzzled.

Rebekah opened the door of her pickup. "He was missing when you left last night. You said you would let me know when you found him."

"Oh, right. He's fine."

"Where was he?" Rebekah slammed the pickup door.

"I found him right away, in the first place I looked. A cabinet in our garage. He wedged himself into it."

"That's impressive—that you knew where to look." Rebekah pushed open the shop door. "Why was he hiding?"

A high-pitched voice came through the phone. "Mom!" Most likely Michael.

"Just a minute." Elise's voice was muffled. "I have to go, Rebekah. Thanks for calling."

Rebekah struck her boots across the wood floor. Why had she bothered to call?

"Mom." Pepper leaned over the railing. "Bring up more garbage bags; it's a mess up here."

An hour later, as Rebekah flipped the Open sign in the window, Sandi hurried through the door. "What a night." She gave Rebekah a hug. "I haven't had that much fun in years."

Pepper skipped down the stairs.

"Those cartwheels you did. What a hoot." Sandi chuckled.

"Mom."

"Sandi." Rebekah nodded toward Pepper.

"What?" Sandi smiled.

"Mom, you didn't." Pepper stood with her hands on her hips.

"Pepper, you weren't even here. Don't be embarrassed."

"Everyone at school will know. Everyone will talk about it. You promised not to do them anymore." Pepper stomped back up the stairs.

"Uh-oh." Sandi put her hand over her mouth.

"She made me promise not to ever bungee jump again, either, even though I haven't done that since a year before Reid was born."

"How about skydiving?" Sandi took a newspaper out of her bag.

"I've always wanted to do that, but Patrick would have a cow."

"Sounds like Pepper takes after her dad."

"Not really. He worries. She just gets embarrassed. I hate that. It's the hardest thing about having them grow up."

"The hardest?" Sandi spread the *Forest Falls Post* on the counter. "Then thank your lucky stars."

"What's this?" Rebekah turned the paper around. The center page featured a photo of the eighth-grade football team with a closeup of Mark, his arm back, ready to throw the ball. The headline read "New Middle School Quarterback Struts His Stuff."

"It's this morning's paper," Sandi said.

Rebekah read the article. The reporter focused on Mark's talent and Ted being deployed.

Sandi crossed her arms. "Ted hadn't said anything to his dad about a reporter interviewing Mark."

Rebekah raised an eyebrow. "You've already talked to John about this?"

Sandi blushed.

Rebekah shook her head. Elise hadn't said anything, either. Not that she would.

"What was with Elise last night?" Sandi folded the paper. "She was acting weird when she left."

Rebekah shrugged.

"Come on, Rebekah, I know you don't like to gossip, but give me a hint."

"Mark was hiding, and Ted couldn't find him. But Elise found him right away, in the garage." Rebekah bit her lower lip.

"That Mark. There's something wrong with that kid." Sandi rammed the newspaper into her bag. "John thinks Elise has spoiled him."

Rebekah cantered Sky down the dirt road miles from the farm. She wiped her hand across her brow, smearing dust and sweat into a bronze streak across her forehead. Patrick had decided to take a Sunday afternoon nap, and Reid was on the computer. Pepper had stayed in town after church with Ainsley, giving Rebekah the chance to ride long and hard. The road curved, and she dug her heels into the horse, urging him to a gallop. A breeze stirred the willows along the creek. A red-tailed hawk glided toward the forest, and a pair of ducks bobbed in the creek, the male's emerald head bright against the water.

The road wound uphill into the forest. Ahead, the service gate blocked the road. "You have to make things happen," her mother used to say.

"Come on, boy," Rebekah urged. She crouched forward on the horse. He lunged and then ascended, leaving the ground far behind, and soared over the gate.

"Yes!" Rebekah yelled as the gelding landed on his front hoofs and then his back, leaping forward, running faster and faster.

Rebekah turned around at the trailhead, where the logging road ended, and took a breath. The unrelenting drill of a woodpecker reverberated deep in the forest. This southern route to the falls crossed through an old clear-cut and was not as picturesque as the trail from her pasture, but it was great for hard riding. She snapped Sky's rump with the end of the reins. They would jump the gate again. This time even faster.

ed, the boys are ready to leave for school," Elise called down the hall.

Michael and Mark had decided not to ride along to the airport. "We have a game tonight," Michael had said, as if that explained everything.

Elise folded the top of Michael's lunchbag. "Sure you don't want a sandwich?" she asked Mark.

"School lunch is fine."

Michael held his nose.

Mark punched his brother's shoulder. "Let's go."

"You need to tell Dad good-bye." A good-bye to last two and a half months. Elise dropped the lunchbag into Michael's open backpack.

"He's not going anywhere fun without us, is he?" Michael asked. "Like Heidelberg or Switzerland?"

"No, dummy. He's going to sit on that hill in Landstuhl and not even leave the base." Mark spun toward the door. "That's what I would do. I hate Germany."

"Hey," Ted said, catching Mark in midspin.

"So, we're going to move to Seattle when you get back from Germany, right?" Mark butted his head against Ted's chin.

"No."

"I hate this town."

"But, Mark," Michael said in a falsetto, "you're finally learning to play well with others. You passed the ball a record three times at last week's game. All incompletes, but at least you passed."

Mark lunged at Michael; Ted held him back.

"And besides, you're a small-town celebrity, thanks to that article," Michael taunted.

Mark lunged again.

Elise banged the frying pan against the stove. "Come on, Mark, Michael. Tell Dad good-bye. We can talk about the other stuff at Christmas."

"Don't go anywhere until we come over," Michael said. "No castles. No ruins. No skiing. No driving the autobahn."

Ted pulled both boys to him in a big bear hug. He was good at that; affection came more easily to him than it did to her. The bigger the boys grew, the harder it was for her to hug them.

"You be good. Help your mom." Ted kissed each of them on the forehead. "Keep up with your studies."

"I can't breathe," Mark sputtered and then laughed.

Ted squeezed harder. "Play hard at the football game tonight. I'll call as soon as I can." They had splurged and bought Ted a satellite phone, along with a laptop for Elise. Being able to communicate more quickly would be worth it. "I'll be home for most of basketball season." Ted let go of the boys. "I love you guys."

They fell to the floor laughing, a tumble of legs and arms. Mark's size overpowered Michael, and Michael's dark curls contrasted with Mark's straight blond hair.

"Bye, Dad." Michael jumped up and hugged Ted one more time. "I love you."

"We're going to be late," Mark muttered as he headed toward the door.

"They're so different," remarked Ted. He stood beside Elise at the window as the boys pedaled their bikes down the driveway.

"Yes. They show things differently." She hoped it was that. Mark seemed so cold, so heartless at times. The boys turned the corner.

"I'm going to finish loading the software on your computer, then we need to leave." Ted reached for her hand as he walked by. "Patrick said to call him if you have any problems with it. Call Dad for everything else."

Elise crossed her arms. "Like if some psycho comes around after reading in the paper that you've been deployed?"

"It was harmless, Elise. Really."

The active army had reinforced, over and over, to be discreet about deployments: Don't put yellow ribbons in front of your house; don't speak with the media; do everything possible to protect your family. Ted had given the reporter permission to interview Mark without asking Elise. He didn't even think about whether he needed to consult her, he'd said. He thought the article would be a boost to Mark—that was all. She preferred to go out of her way to play it safe, not to take risks. Ted didn't understand how responsible she felt for the safety of their family when he was gone.

She sat down at the table and opened the box of photos from Midnight Madness. She was tired, bone weary. The familiar feeling that they had taken a wrong turn, that they had misread the map, was afflicting her again. It was the same feeling she'd had during the first Gulf War and, to a lesser degree, during Kosovo.

She hadn't felt that way during Ted's Afghanistan tour; she'd felt no warning, no buildup, no question that Ted should go and care for the soldiers after the 9/11 terrorist attacks. She had felt God's hand on her family. She had felt strong. She had slept. Elise had considered it a blessing that her family could make a contribution. So many had suffered, and Ted, who had been at a meeting in the Pentagon just a few weeks before the attacks, had been spared.

Elise pulled half of the photos from the box. Why did she feel as if they had taken a wrong turn this time? He was only going to Germany. Was it because they were in Forest Falls? Would she be at peace if they were in Seattle?

She thumbed through the photos. Mark in his bathtub, Mark in his stroller, Mark in his swing—the miracle swing. Other babies had fathers, grandparents, aunts and uncles and cousins. Mark had *the* swing. That was all the help she had.

She thumbed through the photos, putting them in order. Ted, wearing his uniform, holding Mark on the tarmac at Andrews Air Force Base, the chartered 747 behind him. She hadn't slept at all the night before and hadn't taken anything to help her sleep. She hadn't wanted to be groggy for Ted's homecoming; instead she was exhausted. She hadn't truly believed that Ted had come home alive until she felt his hands on her face and his lips on her mouth, until he took his startled-eyed son in his arms. That night Ted got up with Mark. The baby howled, terrified by the stranger who had invaded his world. Maude and John flew out the next Christmas, two weeks before Mark's first birthday. It was the first time they had seen their grandson. By then Elise was six months pregnant with Michael.

Elise shuffled through the photos. Ted, his parents, and Mark wore parkas, gloves, and hats in front of the White House; Maude had worried about the cold and had squeezed Mark's cheeks every few minutes to see if he was warm. Elise posed below the Lincoln Memorial, holding Mark on her hip against her bulging belly.

"I looked happy," she said quietly. They had been crazy to have two babies fifteen months apart. It had brought out the worst in Elise. Mark suffered the most.

Elise stood and poured coffee into her Starbucks travel mug.

"Are you ready?" Ted wore khakis and a blue polo. Years ago the army had stopped having soldiers travel in their uniforms, stopped sending them off as sitting ducks. Still, she always expected him to wear his uniform when deployed. He carried his laptop case in one hand, a garment bag and a mid-size suitcase in the other.

Elise reached for her travel mug. "Ready."

✄

Ted drove the Volvo north on I-5. Farms and nurseries flew by, Mount Jefferson reigned in the distant autumn haze, and the outline of Mount Hood was visible further north. Two horses stood under an oak tree. "What do you think Pepper's chances are of finding a kidney?" Elise asked.

"It's a bit scary. So many people need transplants."

They rode silently. A grove of fir trees flew by; a narrow bridge over Forest Creek slowed them down briefly. Ted drummed his fingers on the steering wheel. He tried to contain himself, she knew. She thought of the soldiers in the Shakespearean tragedies who had been giddy to go off to war. At all these call-ups, all these times, Ted had been giddy to go, giddy to do his duty—giddy to leave her and the boys.

She wasn't being fair. Ted had never been eager to leave them. The time away was hard on him too; he missed so much of the boys' growing up. He cried the first time he held Mark, cried on the tarmac with all his army buddies swarming around him, because he knew that the five months he'd missed of Mark's little life were gone forever.

When Ted got the call about Afghanistan, Mark asked Elise, "Why is Dad so happy?"

Elise took a sip of coffee. He was only going to Germany this time, and the boys would hardly change. As they crossed the Boone Bridge, spanning the Willamette River, the traffic slowed.

Ted reached for her hand. "Will you go back to Rebekah's shop?"

Elise shrugged.

"Rebekah seems like a good woman; she'll be a friend."

"It's only for a few months, Ted. I'll be fine." She hoped she would be fine.

"Don't try to be too self-sufficient." Ted squeezed her hand. "God wants us to rely on others."

It was a conversation they'd had over and over. Elise knew it was up to her to take care of the boys. Ted seemed to think other people would help her, but over the years, no one had. Not her mother. Not his parents. She had to be independent. It would be harder on her to hope that others might help her and then be disappointed when they didn't.

Ted turned onto I-205. Twenty minutes later he took the exit to the airport. "I'll stop at the departures area; there's no use in you going inside." He pulled along the curb in front of the Delta counter. They both climbed out and met at the back of the Volvo. Ted hugged her, holding her close. "I'm sorry. I know this isn't easy for you."

"We'll be fine." Elise tucked her head under his chin. "We'll see you in just over two months. That's nothing." She relaxed.

"Move your car!" the security guard yelled, waving for her to leave.

"I'll call when I get there." He kissed her mouth. "Thanks, Elise, for keeping everything together the way you do. I know this isn't what you expected."

Elise cried on the way home, cried as she drove over the bridge, past the river and the stand of fir trees, past the two horses huddled under the oak, past the farms and nurseries. She cried because Ted was supposed to be retired. She cried because she didn't walk into the airport and wave until he disappeared, as she always had before. She cried because she couldn't feel her soul. No, that wasn't true. But it didn't feel like the same soul. It felt like an old, worn-out soul.

She turned off I-5 onto the winding road toward Forest Falls. She didn't want to be a single parent again. During the golden years when the boys were eight and nine, even nine and ten, being a mother felt easy. Now it felt as if they were toddlers again. Giant, unpredictable, independent toddlers. Make that toddler. Singular. Mark in the garage, wedged into the cupboard. Mark at Rebekah's, shoving Reid through the door. Mark on the field, running recklessly with the football.

Elise turned on the windshield wipers against the light rain. It was the first rain since they had moved to Forest Falls, and she hoped it would end by the time the football game started. The CBS News jingle chimed on the radio. The music still made her stomach lurch. On the first day of the first Gulf War, she had been driving home from Mark's pediatrician appointment when the jingle had announced that the bombing had started.

A doe and fawn bounced through the field to her left, and Elise gripped the steering wheel. She turned her windshield wipers to high against the sudden torrent of rain. *Germany is the epilogue,* Elise told herself. *Nothing ever happens in an epilogue. The happy reunion at Christmas will conclude our army story. What does Rebekah always say—"You have to make things happen"?* Elise laughed. She would make this story end even if it meant putting a picture of Landstuhl on the last page of a scrapbook entitled *Our Life in the Army.*

She had the urge to drive through town and east to Rebekah's, to saddle the mare and ride all the way to the falls, even in the rain. She felt hollow. She would go home, fix dinner, and get the boys to the football game. She accelerated. She would do basically the same thing day after day, relentlessly, with little adult contact and little support, until Christmas break. She hoped she could sleep tonight.

The deer jumped the fence. Where was the fawn? Elise pumped the brakes. The car fishtailed on the wet pavement and then veered to the right. The air bag exploded in her face as the car slammed to a stop with a sickening clunk.

ebekah leaned against the shop counter with the phone to her ear, winding the cord around her fingers. She had been on hold twenty minutes. Twice before, earlier in the day, she had hung up when customers came into the store. Neither had purchased a single item. How could a woman shop in a scrapbooking store and not buy anything?

Rain began to pelt the window. Passersby hurried for cover.

"Thank you for holding," a female voice said.

Rebekah explained the problem. Their insurance hadn't paid for the visit to Dr. Thomas.

"There's an issue with your paperwork." The voice continued, "We haven't received the reenrollment form. It was due September 1."

"I sent it in."

"Before the deadline?"

Rebekah paused. "Close to the deadline. We've had your insurance for the last fourteen years."

"No, you're new with us."

"No, my husband has worked for U-Tech for fourteen years." Rebekah leaned against the counter.

"He started a new position at a new site last year."

"So?" Rebekah turned toward her scrapbook layouts behind the register.

"We start a new account when an employee is transferred."

Rebekah took a deep breath. "That's ridiculous."

The woman ignored her. "Let's see. Your daughter has a preexisting condition."

"It's not preexisting. She's been enrolled with you for eleven years." The pitch of Rebekah's voice rose.

"But she's twelve."

"We adopted her when she was one. She didn't have the condition when we adopted her." *At least, we don't think she did.*

"I see."

What? What do you see? "Perhaps I should speak with your supervisor."

"My supervisor is out today. I'll look into this and call you back tomorrow."

Rebekah dropped the phone into the cradle and ran her index finger over the scar on her lip. When she was nine, her brother had pushed her, hard and on purpose, over the handlebars of her bike onto the pavement. As their mother drove her to the doctor, her brother told a detailed story about Rebekah swerving for a cat and bouncing over the curb and somersaulting onto the street. Rebekah sat in the backseat holding a dishtowel to her bloody face and shook her head while her mother soaked up every nuance of her brother's fabricated tale.

Her family was like that—they were gifted at telling lies. Patrick was forever telling her to stop exaggerating. That's what she had done on the phone about missing the deadline. Exaggerated.

Rebekah picked up the duster and ran it over the rack of glossy cardstock. She needed customers. Sandi hadn't stopped by all day, for the first time since Rebekah had opened the Scrap Shack. She dropped the duster onto the counter and pulled the latest issue of *Simple Scrapbooks* from the rack and skimmed through the magazine. A military layout caught her eye. The headline "Thanks for Serving" with flag stickers, dog-tag cutouts, and photos of a soldier and his family taken on an army base filled the spread. She would make a card for Elise, a thank-you for their sacrifices. She had the exact same stickers in stock.

The door buzzed. A customer. Sandi hurried through the door, closing her umbrella. "What's with the rain? It's coming down in sheets."

"And driving all my business away."

"I was on my way to the post office and thought I'd stop in to say hello." Sandi leaned her umbrella against the counter. "What are you working on?"

"A patriotic card for Elise." Rebekah folded a piece of cardstock.

"How is Elise doing?"

"I don't know. I haven't talked to her." Rebekah positioned the flag sticker.

Sandi shook her head. "She's an odd one. I guess we'll see her at the game." Sandi turned the card around. "Hopefully Mark will pass tonight, but I'm not going to hold my breath."

It couldn't be easy being Mark right now. It wasn't easy being Reid now, either—or Pepper, for that matter. Michael was the only one of the four who seemed settled.

Sandi picked up her umbrella. "I'm off. See you soon."

Rebekah held up her glue stick in farewell.

Rebekah tucked Elise's card into the pocket of her jean jacket and swung her truck into the school parking lot. She dashed across the wet pavement to the field, clutching her jacket and stadium blanket.

"Up here!" Sandi wore a bright red quilted coat and waved both hands. Patrick and John sat on either side of her.

"Where's Elise?" Rebekah asked John as she spread a blanket on the damp bench. The rain had stopped, and the evening had turned clear.

He shook his head. "I haven't talked with her all day, but Ted called to say his plane was delayed."

Rebekah sat next to Patrick and held a second blanket on her lap. The boys ran a lap around the field.

"Mark and Michael were late for warmups." Patrick nodded toward the field. Mark was the last player in the line of runners. He skipped from foot to foot for the final fifty yards.

Santiam, the visiting team, kicked off. Reid caught the ball and ran it to the forty-yard line. The center snapped the ball, and Mark snatched it into his arms and sidestepped for a few yards. Michael fell into the Santiam line, but Reid rushed forward, wide open. Mark didn't hesitate. He dashed between two defensive players and broke into a sprint, the ball tucked against his side as if it were as precious as a newborn baby. Ten, twenty, thirty yards. The defenders fell back. Forty. Touchdown. John sprang to his feet. "That's my grandson!"

"Brilliant." Patrick clasped his hands together.

"Way to go, Forest Falls!" Rebekah stood and clapped. "Too bad Elise missed it." She searched the stands and sidelines. Mark took off his helmet and faced the stands. John waved.

Mark ran in the two-point conversion. Just two minutes into the game it was 8–0. Michael yelled something as the boys reached the sidelines, and Reid bumped into Mark. Ten minutes later the coach put Reid in as quarterback and Mark in as the wide receiver, along with Michael.

"I hope he's not rusty." Patrick stood.

"He'll be fine." Rebekah clapped her hands together.

"There's Elise!" Sandi stood beside Patrick. "You missed Mark's touchdown. And the two-point conversion."

Elise waved and climbed the stands to sit next to Rebekah.

"Everything okay?" Rebekah asked, handing Elise the card.

"Kind of." Elise looked at the envelope. "Thanks." She slipped it into the pocket of her suede jacket.

Reid threw an incomplete pass to Michael.

"What happened?" Rebekah spread the blanket over her lap and onto Elise's.

"I slammed into a boulder on the way home from Portland. On the shoulder. It messed up the Volvo's undercarriage."

"*What* happened?" John leaned across Sandi.

"I had a little accident. The car's in the shop."

Reid completed a pass to Michael, but Santiam's defenders tackled him immediately.

"What made you hit the rock?" John asked.

Elise sighed. "A deer ran out in front of me, and I slammed on the brakes and then spun around. The road was slick from the rain and the oil on the pavement; at least that's what the tow-truck driver said."

Reid passed again. Another incomplete.

"Was anything chasing the deer?" Rebekah asked.

"I don't think so. She had a fawn with her at first, but then it was gone." Elise paused. "I was frightened that I'd killed the fawn. I was so relieved to get out and see that I'd hit a big rock."

John whistled loudly. "How bad is the car?"

"They'll give me an estimate tomorrow."

"Why didn't you call me?" John asked.

"I have Triple A."

Reid passed again. Michael caught the ball and ran—ten yards, twenty yards, thirty yards. Touchdown. The crowd exploded. Rebekah and Elise jumped to their feet.

"Boy, those Shelton brothers sure can play ball!" the announcer shouted.

"That's my other grandson!" John called out.

"Both of your boys are fast." Rebekah held the blanket with her elbows as she clapped. Mark shuffled off the field and turned, legs apart and arms crossed, toward the game.

Pepper and Ainsley ran up the bleachers at halftime. "Mom, look at Ainsley's cowboy boots."

Ainsley held up a suede boot that sagged around her leg. "They're slouch boots."

"They don't look very practical for riding," Rebekah said.

"They're fashion boots, Mom." Pepper giggled. "She got them at Target."

"They're made for strutting," Ainsley added.

Strutting. Sandi flashed Rebekah a smile as Elise pulled a pair of gloves from her pocket.

"Can I get a pair?' Pepper asked.

"Of course not." Patrick stood and rolled his shoulders. "We can't afford any extras right now."

"How about some popcorn then?" Pepper flashed her dad a dazzling smile. She wore her hair in a casual bun that came off looking like an updo, with wispy blond tendrils floating around her face.

Rebekah searched her pocket and pulled out a ten. "Get me some too."

"Is popcorn good for her?" Patrick asked.

"It's not exactly good, but it's not going to make her kidneys shut down, at least not tonight."

Pepper snatched the money, clamped her hands over her ears, and bounced down the stairs.

"Bring back the change," Patrick called out.

Ainsley strutted after Pepper, carefully holding her camera.

Rebekah leaned against Patrick at the beginning of the fourth quarter. The score was sixteen to seven. The coach put Mark back in to play receiver. Reid sidestepped behind the line. Mark jumped up and down, wide open.

"Reid, pass the ball," Rebekah shouted. Patrick elbowed her.

Reid passed to Michael. Incomplete. Reid attempted three more passes to Michael but didn't pass to Mark the entire quarter. With one minute left in the game, Rebekah stood; Elise folded the blanket.

Reid went back for a pass. Michael ran wide and waved his arms. Mark sped toward the goal line. Reid hesitated and then passed to Michael. Complete. Michael ran for the touchdown: 24–7. Rebekah scowled. Reid had blatantly favored Michael. At least Mark hadn't favored anyone; he simply hadn't passed. Poor Mark.

Coach Davis jogged onto the field and chatted with the referee as the boys headed to the bench. Mark yelled at Reid. Michael yanked his helmet off and shouted at Mark.

Elise stood. "This isn't good."

Mark grabbed Michael by the arm. A camera flashed. Reid moved in slow motion, trying to get between the brothers, but tripped and fell to the ground.

Patrick stepped forward. Rebekah grabbed his arm, but he pulled away and ran down the bleachers. Mark propelled Michael toward the bench. Michael shoved his brother, said something, and then smiled, showing his silver streak of braces.

Rebekah reached for Elise's hand as Mark walloped his brother in the mouth.

The camera flashed again.

Chapter 13

"No!" Elise gasped. Rebekah squeezed her hand, but Elise pulled away, trying to see better. Mark hit Michael again, and Michael fell to the ground. John jumped to his feet and thundered down the bleachers after Patrick. Elise hurried down the steps, mortified, as Coach Davis ran from the field, pushed through the sea of players, and knelt beside Michael.

John ran onto the field and grabbed Mark's arm, but Mark jerked away. Patrick, looking befuddled, pulled Reid up off the ground.

Blood poured from Michael's face. Mark stood with his helmet in one hand and his other hand behind his back. Fans left the stands, shaking their heads. John knelt in front of Michael, next to the coach.

"Get me a towel," Coach Davis yelled. The manager tossed one, and it landed on Michael's head. Mark took another step backward. Elise ran down the last few steps and crossed the track to the field.

"Your nose isn't broken. I think you took most of it in the mouth." Coach Davis pulled down on Michael's lower lip. "Which is a bummer considering the braces." He turned toward Mark. "Show me your hand."

Mark obeyed. "Your brother's braces didn't do your hand any favors, either. Get me the first-aid kit," Coach Davis called to the manager.

Elise had no idea what to do—yell at Mark or comfort Michael. John held the towel against Michael's face.

She stood outside the circle as Coach Davis finished taping butterfly bandages to Mark's hand. "Son, this is tough," he said. "You have more raw talent than I've seen in years, but I can't allow this. You're off the team."

John stood. Reid smiled. Elise took a step away from the crowd as Mark brushed his blond hair away from his eyes. He drilled the coach with hateful eyes and swung his helmet back and forth. He turned and walked away.

✂

Elise started the engine of the Toyota; other parents stood outside the locker room waiting for their kids, chatting together. Were they talking about her? What was taking the boys so long? She pulled out the envelope from Rebekah and opened the card. *Call me anytime. I want to help.* Reid pushed the door open, and Patrick put his arm around his son's shoulder as they walked around the side of the gym.

The door swung open again, and Michael hurried to the 4Runner.

"Where's Mark?"

Michael turned to the backseat and then shrugged. "I thought he was out here."

Elise shook her head.

"He never came into the locker room, Mom."

Elise pressed her fingers against her temples. "He must have gone straight home."

Mark's jersey was wadded in the middle of the garage. She pulled in over it. His cleats were in the kitchen, and his pants were on the staircase. She surveyed his room. His running shoes and black hoodie were gone. She hurried back down the stairs to the garage, followed by Michael. Mark had dumped his helmet in the corner, where his bike belonged.

Dear Lord, what do I do now? Elise knelt on the concrete and pulled his jersey from beneath the 4Runner.

"Boy is he in trouble." Michael whistled and headed back into the house.

Elise pulled her keys from her pocket. Maybe Michael could spend the night at Rebekah's so Elise could search for Mark. Her other choice was to call John. She hurried into the kitchen and picked up the phone. "Rebekah, it's Elise."

"What's wrong?" Rebekah sounded tired.

"It's Mark. I can't find him. I'm sure he's just hiding again, but his bike is gone."

"Did you call the police?"

"I'm going to in just a minute. I was wondering if Michael could spend the night at your house so I can look for Mark."

"Sure. Bring him out. I'll go with you to look for Mark."

"No, that's okay."

"Elise, don't be ridiculous. Of course I'll go with you."

"Did you call John?" Rebekah asked as she climbed behind the wheel of her truck. She had insisted on driving.

Elise shook her head. "I think he's fed up with Mark after tonight."

"What about Ted?"

"I left a message on his cell."

Elise liked to tell Ted everything. She had heard of an army wife who didn't tell her husband she was diagnosed with breast cancer until he came home from Iraq. *How brave,* Elise had first thought. Now she realized how bizarre that was. How had the husband felt when he got home?

Rebekah slowed as they passed the school. "Would he go back to the football field?"

"I don't think so." Elise squinted into the dark night.

Rebekah stopped at the city park, and the two women shone their flashlights along the creek bank, through the playground, and into the covered picnic area. Elise bent down and looked under the tables, waving the flashlight back and forth.

Her cell rang. She fumbled the phone from her pocket, sure it was Mark. It was the officer on patrol asking if she had found her son.

"We can go ahead and file a missing child report. I can meet you at your house or the station."

Rebekah dropped Elise off at the police station. "Drive north," Elise suggested. "Maybe he decided to head to Seattle." Elise climbed out of the rig. "Thank you, Rebekah."

Rebekah nodded, her ponytail swinging back and forth. "I'll come back in half an hour."

Elise pulled the 4Runner into the garage. Mark's bike was still missing. Pain pulsed through her lower back. They had searched every alley and roof in town and twenty miles to the north. Elise put her flashlight and purse on the kitchen counter. Rebekah said not to worry about Michael, that she would put him on the bus with her kids.

Elise hunted through the house again: in her bedroom, behind the couch in the family room, in the hall closet, in Mark's room, in Michael's room. She walked into the backyard and blew her breath into the cold night. Was Mark warm? Was he safe? She stepped backward to the fence and scanned the roofline. No Mark. Before she had kids, she imagined that being a mom would come naturally to her. But now she wasn't so sure. Had she been too permissive with Mark? too strict? too demanding? not demanding enough?

Rebekah had assured her that she'd never heard of a child being abducted in Forest Falls. Mark would be fine. It was just a matter of his coming home or their finding him. Numbly, she reached into her coat pocket for her phone and called Ted again. No answer. Was he still in the air? Had his flight been further delayed?

She tried one more time.

"Hello."

"Ted!"

The phone cut out, then came back. "I'm in Frankfurt—" It cut out again.

He had arrived. She paced up and down the patio and then punched the speed dial a third time.

"Hello."

"Mark is missing."

"Pardon?"

"Mark." She tilted her head back to look at the stars.

"He's hiding?"

"I don't know. He's been gone since last night."

"Elise—" The phone cut out again.

She rubbed her hand over her face and shuffled back into the empty house to start the coffee. She would wait ten more minutes; hopefully Ted would be out of the airport by then. She sat at the kitchen table, her arms wrapped around her coat, around her body, shivering, aching for her husband. Had she ever felt so alone?

A head passed the kitchen window, and footsteps fell on the porch. She rushed to the door. It was John.

"Ted called. He told me to get over here—although he didn't say it that nicely."

What did Ted expect his dad to do? Save the day?

Elise's cell rang. "Dad's on his way." Ted sounded out of breath.

"He's here."

The landline rang. John stood in the middle of the room, his hands in the pockets of his leather jacket. "Here." Elise tossed him her cell. "Talk to Ted."

She grabbed the phone off the coffee table, expecting the police.

It was Rebekah, sounding too chipper. "Hey, I decided to do the chores when I got home, so I came out to the barn."

John held up the cell and shrugged.

Rebekah continued. "I heard something stir in Sky's stall. I thought maybe the calico had her kittens. But—"

"Mark! He's at your place?" She had been over that road four times tonight. Why hadn't she seen him?

John crossed his arms.

"Yep. He's still sprawled out in Sky's stall. The horse is standing over him."

"I'll be right there." She would get Mark, bring him home, and send him to bed, and then she would cry. He was safe. And then when he woke up, she would... She wasn't sure what she would do, not yet.

"Elise." Rebekah's voice grew fainter. "There's a problem. He doesn't want to go home."

Elise turned away from John. "What do you mean?"

"He wants to stay here."

Elise put her hand on her hip. What did it matter what Mark wanted?

"You know, I used to work with troubled teens. Sometimes they need a breather. He could stay here for the day and cool off, maybe ride the horses. Sandi is going to work at the shop today while I catch up on things around here."

"Thanks, but he needs to come home." Elise hurried into the kitchen and grabbed her purse and keys. "I'm on my way, Rebekah. Thanks so much for your help."

"I'll go with you." John picked up his keys.

"No. It's fine. You go home and go back to bed." She would call the police officer on her way to Rebekah's.

"Bed? It's 5:00 a.m."

"I can handle this. I'll deal with him after he's gotten some sleep."

"That boy needs a strong hand."

"I agree with you." Elise dangled her keys.

"Then let's go."

John would scold Mark the whole way and then tell him to shower and get ready for school, maybe throw in a hundred push-ups for good measure. Mark would be embarrassed and sneak into bed and feign sleep. And then what? John would pull him out of bed? Yank him onto the floor? Drag him down the stairs?

"Elise." John started after her and then stopped in the doorway between the kitchen and the garage.

She slammed the door to the 4Runner and turned the key. Nothing. She checked the headlight knob. It was on; she hadn't heard the warning chime, and the truck was too old to have an automatic shutoff switch.

"Elise, I'll drive you." John crossed his arms. "What other choice do you have?"

Chapter 14

*R*ebekah swung a bale from the stack. The dim lights of the barn and clean smell of the cedar shavings soothed her exhaustion. She cut the wire and carried a bundle of hay between her gloved hands and tossed it into Sky's stall. Golden straw landed on Mark's black sweatshirt.

"Mark, wake up." She stood on the bottom rail. "Your mom is on her way."

He bolted to his feet, flinging his arm against Sky's rump. The horse sidestepped away from the wild-eyed boy. Rebekah didn't envy Elise one bit when it came to raising this kid.

He sank to his knees, and Sky sniffed his head.

"Do you like my barn?" Rebekah stepped down and crossed her arms. Mark shrugged his shoulders.

"Do you mind the smell of horse manure?" She wiped her boot on the rail.

"You're weird."

"I know." Rebekah smiled. Her grandfather had asked her the same question all those years ago, but he hadn't use the word *manure*.

Mark shrugged. "It smells okay. I don't know. It doesn't really smell."

"Reid thinks it stinks."

"So does Michael."

"Pepper thinks it smells good."

Mark nodded.

"My grandpa said that you can tell a horseperson by how they answer that question."

"Can I go back to sleep?" Mark slumped in the hay.

"As long as you wake up when your mom gets here. She's taking you home."

"I don't want to go home." Mark put his head in his hands.

"I know." Rebekah leaned over the rail. "But your mom is worried sick. She's been out looking for you all night. So have the police."

Mark shrugged.

"Didn't you know she would be scared to death?"

Moon shapes sagged under Mark's watery brown eyes.

"Where's your bike?"

"Behind the barn." He flipped his hair over his eyes.

Rebekah leaned against the rail. "Would you like to ride one of the horses sometime?"

Mark groaned. "My mom's going to kill me."

"She hasn't killed you yet, so she probably won't today."

Mark leaned back against a bale of hay and pulled his hood over his head.

✂

Rebekah poured oats into the mare's trough. "What would you do, girl?" she whispered. "What would you do if Sky were such a handful?" Rebekah had seen so many well-meaning parents rush and take charge of their kids when what they really needed to do was listen. You had to have a relationship with the kid; that was the most important thing.

The mare snorted.

"Is that right, girl?" Rebekah rubbed between the horse's ears. "Do you think that controlling a kid is like controlling a horse?" You had to gain the horse's trust; that was most important.

A car door slammed. Then another.

"Mark? Rebekah?" Elise pushed open the door. John stood behind her. Mark hid his head in his arms.

Rebekah stepped out into the middle of the barn, surprised to see John. "Hi! Hey, John."

John stood in the middle of the barn with his arms crossed. "Mark—," he began.

Elise interrupted by putting a hand on John's arm. "Rebekah," she said quietly, still holding John's arm, "where's Mark's bike?"

"Out behind the barn."

Elise turned to John. "Could you go get it?"

John looked a little longer at Mark and then headed toward the back door of the barn. Rebekah had to admit she was impressed by Elise's quiet strength.

"Come on, Mark." Elise leaned against the railing. Sky turned and brushed his nose against Elise's arm.

"I don't want to go home."

Rebekah swallowed hard.

"Grandpa's going to kill me." Mark put his head in his hands.

"Well, not this morning anyway. He promised to wait until after you get some more sleep." Elise's elbows must have been digging into the top rail of the stall, but she didn't move away from her son.

Mark stood and rubbed Sky's neck. "Did you call Dad?"

Elise nodded.

"Is Michael okay?" Mark stood and walked toward his mother.

Elise nodded a third time. She reached out and stroked Mark's hair. Amazingly, he didn't pull away.

"I didn't mean to hit him."

"How could you not have meant to hit him?" Elise asked quietly. "You punched him in the mouth."

"How's your hand?" Rebekah butted in.

Elise looked at her with steady eyes. Rebekah stepped back. Clearly

Elise had things under control. Should she leave? Go help John with the bike?

Mark shrugged, pressing the gauze against his sweatshirt, his eyes focused past his mother and on Rebekah. "You know how Michael and Reid are always bugging me about not passing. I get so nervous during a game. All I can think to do is run."

Rebekah nodded. It was his way of saying he was sorry—to both of them.

"Come on, Mark." Elise opened the stall gate. "Let's go home."

Rebekah sat at her computer with their bank account open. She had finished the chores and let the horses into the pasture.

Patrick's slippers slapped against the dining room floor and into the kitchen. "Good morning." He tied his burgundy robe as he headed toward the coffee maker. "What are you working on?"

"Bills." Rebekah yawned.

Patrick shook his head. "Did Elise find Mark?"

"He was hiding. He's okay."

"Where was he?"

"In our barn."

Patrick stood with the pot of water in midair. "Why was he in our barn?"

"He felt safe there, and he likes the smell."

Patrick shook his head. "Right."

Rebekah logged out of the account. She would work on bills when she wasn't so tired. "Remember, I'm taking Pepper to her 4:30 doctor's appointment today. And then the transplant class is tomorrow." Rebekah yawned again.

"I have a late meeting today." Patrick measured out the coffee.

"I'll ask Elise if Reid can go to their house after practice."

"Do you think he's safe there? With Mark?"

"Patrick, don't be ridiculous." Rebekah pushed back her desk chair.

"That kid's a loose cannon." Patrick flipped the switch on the coffee maker.

"I think he's just having a hard time, with Ted leaving and everything. Besides, Sky likes him." She stood. "Patrick, show the kid some grace." She stretched as she pushed her computer chair closer to the desk with her knee. "By the way, we both need to go to the transplant class."

"I'll take tomorrow off."

"Mom!" Pepper pounded down the stairs.

Rebekah hurried toward the dining room. "What is it?"

"There are raccoons in the tree outside my window! Make them leave." Pepper's shiny hair flew around her face.

"Good grief." Patrick stood in the kitchen doorway.

Rebekah headed up the stairs.

"What's with her?" Reid stood against the hallway wall. "I thought we were having an earthquake."

Rebekah banged on Pepper's window. Three raccoons, a mother and two smaller ones, ran along the branch of the big leaf maple.

"Mom, look!" Pepper screamed as she pointed down the road, through the yellow and orange leaves of the tree. Sky was trotting up the road. A logging truck was barreling down the hill toward him.

lise eased onto a dining room chair, careful to sit straight, and pulled the box of photos toward her. Reid and Michael would be here in half an hour. She was thankful that Rebekah had asked if Reid could hang out at their house. She had been afraid the Grahams might want to keep their kids away from Mark. What punishment should Mark have? Community service for involving the police? Being grounded for a month? No television, computer, or video games for two months?

"Elise?" John knocked on the front door as he swung it open.

She hurried toward the entryway. Mark's breakfast dishes were still in the sink, and the drapes were still closed. She caught her image in the dining room mirror. No makeup, pale skin, and drip-dried hair.

"I came to jump Ted's rig." John held his hand out. "I need your key."

"I can call Triple A." She had meant to call hours ago.

"Let me do it."

She opened the foyer table drawer. "I'll help you push it out of the garage." She kicked off a slipper.

"I have a charge box."

"Oh."

"How's Mark?" John asked.

"He's asleep."

"What is his punishment going to be?"

"I'm going to talk to Ted about it when he calls."

John headed to his truck. Sandi sat on the passenger side. Elise shut the front door and then chided herself. She didn't need to be obviously rude. She kicked off her slippers, stepped into her gardening clogs, and headed outside.

Sandi opened her window. "Hi."

Elise waved. "How are you?"

"Fine. Sounds like you've had some excitement."

Elise smiled. Did the whole town know? "It all worked out okay," she said.

"I helped at the Scrap Shack this morning so Rebekah could get some things done at home. She had to close the shop early this afternoon to take Pepper to Portland."

The whole town did know. Elise crossed her arms and then, aware of how defensive she looked, uncrossed them. "Poor Rebekah."

"She was just relieved that Mark is okay." Sandi fidgeted with her tennis-ball-sized hoop earring. "You must be about ready to wring his neck."

Elise nodded. "He was very sorry."

"Did he say why he did it?"

"No." Elise kicked at a pebble in the driveway.

"He told Rebekah that he was headed to the mountains."

Elise rubbed her lower back and grunted some noncommittal response. She wasn't about to discuss this with a gossip. But it did make her wonder. She had loved *My Side of the Mountain* as a child. The thought of gaining independence and making it on her own had been so appealing—when she was ten. Of course, as a parent she saw the story a little differently. Had Mark read the book? She didn't think so. Had he planned to hang out in the forest for a couple of months? He'd dropped out of Cub Scouts as a nine-year-old.

"John and I went to our Bible study at church after I was done at the Scrap Shack." Sandi leaned forward. "We prayed for you—for Ted too—but especially you."

"Thanks." Elise ran her hand through her limp hair. "So, Sandi, what do you do? Are you retired?"

"I work part-time as a hospice nurse."

"And that's how you know John? From when Maude died?"

Sandi shook her head. "I was acquainted with John and Maude through church, and then John took my grief class."

Elise forced a smile. What if John married her? How horrible for Ted. How horrid for all of them. That's all they needed—a stepmother, stepmother-in-law, and stepgrandmother. Sandi was so different from Maude. "It's chilly." Elise rubbed her arms. "Would you like to come in for some tea?"

Sandi shook her head. "John will be done in a minute. Will I see you on Friday night for Midnight Madness?"

"Hopefully." Elise said good-bye and then turned toward the house, relieved to be going in alone.

"All done." John wheeled the charge box out of the garage as Elise reached the front door. "Let the car run for fifteen minutes or so, or go for a drive."

"Thanks." Elise stepped back onto the sidewalk.

"Mom, phone." Mark wore his pajama bottoms and dirty black sweatshirt and stood next to the 4Runner.

"Just who I was looking for." John motioned for Elise to go first into the garage.

She took the phone. "Hello?"

Mark started into the house, and John followed him.

Elise hurried after them into the kitchen.

"Hi." It was Ted. "How are things?"

"Fine. Your dad came over to jump the 4Runner." Elise headed to the hall. Had Mark gone into Ted's study? Had John followed him?

"How's Mark?" Ted sounded tired.

"Fine." Elise started down the hall.

"I know things are hard for him, but he needs to suffer the consequences for this."

"I know. I was thinking community service."

"That's a good idea. Ask Dad. He might know of an older person in the church who needs yard work done or something."

"I'll ask around." Elise heard voices upstairs. Had John followed Mark up to his room? She heard steps on the landing and hurried to the kitchen, not wanting John to find her lurking. "Ted, I'll call you back in a few minutes. Your dad is just leaving."

"That kid," John said as he headed to the garage. "He's the most obstinate person I know." Elise followed him and waved to Sandi. John shook his head as he backed out of the driveway.

Elise sat back down at the dining room table and picked up a photo of Mark dancing in the middle of their condo in Virginia with a string of beads around his neck. She stood in the background, nine months pregnant. On the back she had written: "Waiting for Michael."

Elise carried the photo up the stairs. Mark had been happy. He'd never been easy, but he had been happy. When had he grown so miserable?

She knocked on his door. No answer. She pushed it open. He stood at his window.

"I found this picture," she said, stepping over his dirty jeans and a pile of smelly socks.

He shrugged, the black hood of his sweatshirt covering his head.

"Look."

He turned and took the photo. "Is it Michael?"

"No, it's you."

"I look really stupid with those beads around my neck."

Elise shook her head. "No. You look really cute and, well, happy."

He handed the picture back.

"Mark, honey, I love you." Elise reached out and patted his arm. He pulled away. She wished that she could cradle him like a baby again. She wished that she could hug him, a good solid hug, not a half hug or a pat.

"There's a squirrel in the tree," Mark said. "He jumps from that limb to the roof and then back again." He pushed his window open wide and stuck his head outside. "It's about a four-foot jump. That's pretty far for a squirrel, don't you think?"

Elise had no idea what was a long way for a squirrel to jump. "I talked to Dad about your consequence."

Mark closed the window and slouched on his bed, his nostrils flared.

"We decided on community service. We can ask Grandpa—or the pastor—for the name of someone at church who needs yard work or house projects done, someone who is sick."

"The Grahams need help." Mark sat up a little straighter. "Pepper's sick, and Rebekah can't keep up with the horses. She told me that this morning. That's why she was out in the barn so early."

Elise massaged her lower back with one hand. Helping the Grahams wouldn't be her first choice for Mark. She still felt unsettled about his not wanting to come home. "We'll talk about it later."

"Mom, we're here!" Michael's voice carried up the stairs. She hadn't started dinner. She would call for a pizza—maybe two pizzas since Reid was here too. She headed back downstairs with the photo.

"Do you plan to come to Midnight Madness on Friday?" Rebekah stood in the entryway while Pepper helped Reid find his backpack, sports bag, and shoes.

"I'm not sure." Elise wadded a greasy napkin in her hand.

"Is it Mark? You don't want to leave him alone?"

"Yes."

"Ask John."

Elise wanted to laugh. "I don't know if that would be a good idea."

"Mark could go to the game with Patrick. Give him some options.

Ask if he wants to stay home. If he runs, you know you really have a problem. If he doesn't, maybe last night was a fluke."

"But what if he does?"

"Then you have a problem." Rebekah smiled.

"I'll let you know what I decide to do."

"Mom." Mark stood behind Elise, a piece of pizza in his hand. "Did you ask Rebekah about the community service?"

Elise clutched the napkin. "No."

"Community service?" Rebekah turned from Elise to Mark.

"My punishment." Mark spoke as he chewed. "We wondered if I could help take care of your horses."

Elise grimaced. Mark assumed she was in favor of his helping with the horses. It *would* be easier than arranging a project to help someone they didn't know. She forced a smile.

"That would probably work. I'll talk to Patrick." Rebekah shoved her hands into her back pockets. "Did Reid tell you about our scare this morning?"

Elise wasn't sure if she was talking to her or Mark. They both shook their heads.

"Sky got out of the pasture where the fence needs to be repaired and decided to go for a run down the highway."

Elise's hand flew to her face.

"Is he all right?" Mark asked.

Rebekah clasped her hands together. "A logging truck was coming down off the mountain. Pepper and I were in her bedroom and went tearing out the door, yelling and waving. Pepper was in her pajamas and barefoot." Rebekah continued. "I was in my socks—"

"Mom!" Pepper called from the dining room. "I wanted to tell the story."

"What happened?" Mark asked.

"Sky ran into the field across the road at the last minute." Pepper stopped beside Mark in the entryway. "And we got him back in the pasture and patched the fence."

"Thank goodness." Elise turned to Mark. "Go check on Reid, okay?" She patted his shoulder. "Tell him I put his shoes by the back door."

Pepper followed Mark.

"It looks like he's taking responsibility," Rebekah whispered.

"How's Pepper?"

"Okay."

"Any word on a donor?"

Rebekah shook her head. "She won't get on the list until Friday. She has B blood, the least common, so I'm not as hopeful about the list, unless a universal donor is a match."

Elise's stomach lurched.

"That's why I'm counting on someone in her birth family to donate a kidney. It would be best."

Michael thundered down the stairs, followed by Reid and then Pepper.

"Thanks for having him." Rebekah reached for the sports bag. "I owe you a favor."

"Hardly. Thanks again for everything you did last night." Elise closed the door behind them. Thank goodness Michael hadn't heard the conversation about blood types. She didn't need him asking any questions.

Chapter 16

E lise babies him. That's why she stayed home tonight." Sandi poured Dr Pepper into her red plastic cup.

The Scrap Shack door buzzed.

"Hi, Mom!" Pepper and Ainsley thundered up the stairs.

"Pepper, how was your transplant class this morning?" Sandi raised her cup.

"Fine."

"Did you get on the list?"

"We did," Rebekah answered. "We have a plan. We're on a list, but at the same time we're going to look for a live donor."

"Where?" Sandi took a drink of pop.

"Don't worry." Rebekah laughed. "I won't be taking tissue samples from you."

"I would get tested—seriously," Sandi said. "But I wouldn't qualify, because I have high blood pressure."

"Thanks." Rebekah stood. "Honestly, though, things will work out." Going to the meeting and putting Pepper's name on the list felt like a big step.

"Where do you plan to find a kidney?" Sandi asked.

Pepper grabbed Ainsley's arm and headed to the sticker rack.

Rebekah lowered her voice. "I sent a letter to Pepper's birth grandmother."

"Oh, that sounds complicated." Sandi pulled a folder of paper from her bag. "So the list you put Pepper on last night is a cadaver list?"

Rebekah nodded.

"What kind of list?" Ainsley spun around.

"Cadaver," Rebekah answered.

"Like, dead?" Ainsley slapped her palm over her mouth as she turned toward Pepper. "You're going to get a dead person's kidney?" she asked between her fingers.

"Ainsley." Rebekah placed her hands on her hips. "We all do what we have to. Whoever gives—" She stopped. Elise stood at the top of the stairs. Rebekah turned back to Ainsley. "Whoever gives Pepper a kidney will be giving her a wonderful gift. If it's from a cadaver, we will be forever grateful to the family. We will pray for them and thank God for them. But we will never be repulsed by their gift."

"Okay." Ainsley stepped backward, her hand still over her mouth.

"Mom." Pepper's face was red.

Ainsley looked as if she was going to cry. Rebekah put her arms around both girls. "I'm sorry. I'm tired. But I don't want to hear negative stuff about kidney transplants. We have to be positive."

The girls ducked away from Rebekah and went downstairs.

Elise pulled out a chair across the table from Sandi. "What happened?"

"Tell you later." Sandi smiled. "But let me warn you. Don't mess with Rebekah or her baby."

"I heard that." Rebekah crossed her arms.

"Come sit down." Sandi pulled out the chair next to her. "You're exhausted, Rebekah. You've got to slow down."

"And control my mouth."

Sandi shook her head. "No, that was fine. Sit."

"Elise, how's Mark?" Rebekah pulled out a chair.

"Okay. He stayed home. He was watching an old Pink Panther movie, so I decided to come, just for a while."

"How's Ted doing?" Sandi asked.

"Fine. Our conversations keep getting cut off. I think our satellite is on the wrong side of the moon or something. He's already started working, so he feels good about that."

"Mom," Pepper called up the stairs, "where are the horseshoe charms?"

"Excuse me." Rebekah started down the stairs.

An hour later Elise slipped on her coat to leave. "When can Mark help with the horses?"

Rebekah leaned against the table. Patrick had reluctantly agreed. "How about Sunday, after church?"

Elise hesitated. "That should work."

Rebekah tidied the calligraphy pens in the center of the table. "Why don't you come out too, stick around? We can all ride. Mark too. I would love to see him on a horse."

"I'll ask him." Elise paused. "Thanks, Rebekah, for everything."

Rebekah leaned against the balcony as Elise walked out of the shop. She looked so small, so lonely, so afraid.

"I think it's time to liven things up." Sandi stood and clapped her hands. "How about some cartwheels?"

"Mom." Pepper slapped her hand against the table.

Rebekah held her hands over her head.

"Mom!"

"Just kidding, sweet pea. I wouldn't do that to you." Rebekah poured herself a cup of Dr Pepper and winked at Sandi. "It's up to you, girl."

Sandi collapsed on her chair, laughing.

Rebekah crossed the lawn and met Elise and her boys by their car, in front of the corral. "How's your hand?" she asked Mark.

He grunted.

"Aren't you going to ask about the inside of my mouth?" Michael asked.

"Sorry, but I'm not worried about it getting infected with barn bacteria." Rebekah tousled his curly hair. "Reid's waiting for you."

"Have fun with the horses." Michael bolted toward the house. "Rodeo Queen." Reid started down the back steps, dribbling his basketball.

"Come on, Mark." Elise nudged him toward the barn.

"Are you all right with Michael hanging out with Reid unsupervised?" Rebekah asked. "Patrick had to go into the office."

Elise hesitated.

"They can reach Patrick on his cell. No problem."

"Okay."

Was Elise uptight about the boys staying alone? They were almost fourteen. Rebekah pushed the barn door open.

"Over here." Pepper led the saddled gelding out of his stall. "We thought that we would ride first and then muck out the barn. It looks like it might rain."

"Can I ride Sky?" Mark asked.

"Nope. Only Mom rides Sky. You get the quarter horse. He's safe for beginners."

Rebekah opened the Appaloosa's stall door and handed Mark the reins. "Lead him out to the corral. Maybe you can ride him in a few months."

"Did you know that horses have seventy senses?" Pepper sat on the palomino while Mark hoisted himself up on the quarter horse.

"That's ridiculous." Mark wiggled his Adidas into the stirrups. "There are only five senses."

"But theirs are so fine tuned that they have subsets of each sense."

"Sight, hearing, smell, taste, and touch. How can there be subsets? Are they aliens?"

Elise swung her leg over the mare. Rebekah smiled as she mounted Sky. Elise seemed more relaxed every time she rode.

"Kind of." Pepper led the way. "For example, horses never get lost. They have an amazing homing sense."

"Homing sense. Would that be under smell or sight?"

Pepper rolled her eyes. "Another example is that their ears move around, and they can absorb more sound than we can."

"That's still hearing."

Pepper shook her head. "I read it in a book. They have seventy senses."

"Are you sure you didn't read it on the Web? Maybe some kook's blog?"

Pepper touched her chin with her index finger. "Maybe I did." She laughed.

"Let's ride to the falls today." Rebekah slowed Sky until they were in the back. Mark rode like a pro; he would do fine on a long ride.

A half hour later they passed through the meadow and then up a rocky incline. "This is where I lost my hat on my midnight ride." Rebekah nodded over the ledge.

Elise leaned to the side and then quickly away from the deep canyon. "Whose land is this?"

"The Forest Service's."

A few minutes later they passed into another grassy area. "We call this the upper meadow. Want to rest?" Rebekah asked.

Pepper and Mark dismounted. Elise's legs shook a little as she climbed down. The horses began to graze.

"Did you know that grass-fed horses eat eleven to thirteen hours a day?" Pepper plopped down in the middle of the clearing.

"How boring." Mark tossed a dirt clod at Pepper's feet.

"Mark." Elise wiped her hands on her jeans.

"We saw a cougar a couple of weeks ago." Pepper tossed the dirt clod back at Mark.

"I know." Mark tossed another dirt clod over her head. "My mom's seen it twice."

Rebekah smiled. They were talking as if she and Elise weren't along. "Maybe it's in the forest right now." Mark tiptoed around, taking exaggerated steps.

"Nah. The horses would let us know. It's one of their senses."

"The cougar sense? Is that sense number sixty-one?" Mark shook his head.

Pepper nodded. "They stayed huddled for two days after we saw the cougar, or else they wanted to be in the barn. I watched them from my window. But on the third day, Sky went to sleep in the field, and then I knew the cougar was gone."

"Maybe it will come back." Mark sat down.

"Maybe." Pepper pulled a piece of grass through her teeth. "I'd like to see it again. Do you know how rare it is to see a cougar? I feel chosen." She grinned. "But if it comes back, it might get shot. I don't want that to happen."

Rebekah adjusted the cinch strap on Sky's belly.

"They like horse meat," Pepper added matter-of-factly.

"Their first choice is deer, though," Rebekah said, sitting across from Pepper and Mark, "and there are lots of them around here. A deer a week and then supplemental meals, such as raccoons." Rebekah made a scary face at Pepper.

Pepper wrinkled her nose.

"And girls." Mark jumped to his feet.

Elise threw a dirt clod at him.

They rode along the creek. The sound of rushing water grew louder. "It's right after this bend," Rebekah called back. A fallen, rotting tree blocked the trail, and one by one the horses jumped over it. The mare nicked her hoof against the trunk, stumbled, and then caught herself. "It's okay, girl." Elise bent forward and patted the horse's neck.

The trail curved, and Elise gasped. Rebekah leaned back in her saddle and smiled. A sea of water tumbled over a high cliff, crashing off a granite wall and then splitting into two separate falls before it plummeted into a pool that fed the creek. Giant rhododendrons and sword ferns grew along the banks of the pool, and towering old-growth fir nearly obliterated the sky. Boulders and fallen logs lined the creek, and moss covered the rocks. Mist flew into their faces.

Mark stopped the quarter horse.

"Amazing, isn't it?" Rebekah smiled.

Elise and Mark nodded. "It's enchanting." Elise breathed deeply.

"What's the matter, Pepper? Are you speechless?" Mark asked.

She giggled. "I've been here before."

Mark turned the quarter horse onto the trail that led under the falls. Pepper followed.

"I came here once at night, in the summer—the night I lost my hat," Rebekah said. "Don't tell Patrick."

"By yourself?" Elise looked stricken.

"There was a full moon."

"What was it like?"

"Light reflected off the pool. The water glistened, and the trees were silhouetted against the starry sky." Rebekah took out her digital camera and shot a photo of Pepper and Mark under the falls, then she pointed it at Elise. "Smile." Elise grimaced, but the mare held her head high.

Rebekah clucked her tongue and directed Sky to follow Pepper and Mark, who rode ahead, laughing. Mark plucked a pine cone from a low branch and tossed it at Pepper. She caught it and threw it back. Rebekah took a photo of their backs and the rumps of the two horses.

✄

"Brush the horses down." Rebekah hung Sky's bridle on the peg. "Then we'll all muck out the barn."

"I'll brush Sky." Pepper leaned against the saddletree. Mark flashed her a dirty look.

"I'm going to make some lemonade for everyone." Rebekah pushed open the barn door and squinted at the sunlight. Michael and Reid were shooting free throws. Patrick stopped his car across the road at the mailbox. It was Sunday; there wasn't any mail. He pulled a handful of envelopes out. Rebekah sighed; she'd forgotten to get it yesterday. She waited as he steered his Honda under the elms. Patrick unfolded his long legs from the car and waved a piece of paper at her. He wore gray slacks and a white dress shirt. "It's from our insurance company. They denied payment."

"It's just a snafu. We were late with our reenrollment, but it's no biggie. They just reenrolled us for what we had last year."

"It's more than that, Rebekah. It says denied. D-E-N-I-E-D."

Chapter 17

*E*lise stood in the center of Mark's room, resisting the urge to pick up the damp towels, dirty socks, and wrinkled jeans that covered his floor. "Mark, you need to get up now." His alarm had gone off thirty minutes earlier. "Michael is ready to leave. You're going to be late."

Mark's yellow walls, walls he deemed too happy and wanted painted, were bathed in sunlight. Elise closed the window. Had he been out on the roof last night? A robin landed on the ledge and pecked at the wood. She took a closer look. Breadcrumbs. Had Mark been feeding the birds? Or maybe the squirrels.

He poked his head out from the covers. "My hand really hurts. I did too much yesterday. I think it's infected." He flung his hand over the side of the bed.

She examined his wound. It looked exactly the way it had the day before. "Your hand is fine. Take a couple of Tylenol. Hurry or you'll be late."

"He's stubborn, Mom." Michael swallowed the last of his orange juice. "You need to be stricter with him."

Elise refilled her coffee cup. This was why she wanted Ted out of the army. The boys needed him more and more the older they got; she needed him more and more the older they got.

"You're going to miss playing rugby in PE," Michael yelled up the stairs.

"What?" Elise stood in the hallway, her robe cinched around her waist.

Michael held his finger to his mouth. "Not really, Mom. I just thought it might get his attention."

"I'm not going," Mark yelled back.

"I'm out of here." Michael grabbed his lunchbag off the counter and hurried to the garage.

Elise climbed the stairs again. "Come on, Mark. I'll drive you."

"I said I'm not going."

Elise sat on the edge of the bed.

"I hate that school." He pulled the covers over his head again. "The only reason I said I liked it before was because of football. But the only reason I said I wanted to play football was to make Dad happy."

"Mark, you have to go to school. It's the law."

"How about if I go work at Rebekah's barn today? That's all I really want to do. I don't need school for that."

"If your hand hurts too badly to go to school, then you definitely can't work with the horses. You'll have to wait a few days." She resisted the urge to slam his door as she headed down the stairs.

Elise pulled the shoebox of photos from the closet and sat at the table. Had Mark reached the age where she couldn't make him obey? couldn't make him go to school? Having him home made her uneasy. She slipped the photos of Mark into an envelope. Next was a newborn photo of Michael with his full head of wild hair. He'd weighed nine pounds at birth, three pounds more than Mark had, and he'd slept through the night after the first month. Ted thought newborns were the easiest thing in the world.

Maude and John had flown out in June when Michael was six weeks old. Maude pointed out, every chance she got, that Michael was an easier baby because Elise was more relaxed. She said it over and over. Was that why she could nurse Michael but Mark had stopped at three months? Was that why Mark clung to her, climbing on top of Michael when she fed the baby? Why Mark cried at loud noises? Why he had to have an old ratty flannel spit rag wrapped around his hand and wedged against his cheek in order to fall asleep? She hadn't felt very relaxed with Michael, but she guessed she was, at least compared to when Mark was a newborn.

Michael was constantly being held in his photos—by Ted, by her, by friends who worked with Ted at Walter Reed Army Medical Center, by the older ladies at the church they attended, and by his grandparents. Mark had adored his brother—loved him too much. If Elise left them alone for a second, Mark would try to carry Michael, squeeze him, or cover his face with kisses. Blond, big-eyed Mark with his chubby hands and thunder thighs was constantly mauling Michael.

Maybe it shouldn't have been a surprise that the unruly toddler had turned into the stubborn teen upstairs. She wished she could pull the darling little boy from the photo; he would let her hug him. She sorted through a group of photos of the boys wearing red cowboy hats with strings under their chins. In the last one, Mark was buck naked except for the hat and a pair of black boots. Maude and John had brought the boots—one of the few gifts from them that weren't handmade. She moved the photo to the bottom of the box.

Where were those boots? She hoped she had stashed them away as a memento. If Mark continued to ride, maybe she would buy him a new pair. He had done a good job brushing the horses and mucking out the barn yesterday.

She sorted the photos again, stacking all the ones of just Mark. She would find more of his photos and make him his very own album, as a surprise. Women at the shop spoke of the deeper connections they had with their children by creating books for them. Some of them even claimed that scrapbooking had brought healing to their relationships. She would work on a family album later.

An hour later Mark, wrapped in a blanket, stumbled down the stairs and collapsed on the family-room couch.

"I'm going downtown for a few minutes." Elise buttoned her jacket. "I'll be right back."

Mark grunted.

"Rebekah?" Elise climbed the stairs to the shop balcony. "Where are you?" Rebekah usually rushed to the door the minute she heard the buzzer.

"Down here."

Elise hurried down the stairs.

Rebekah stood in the doorway to the storeroom with her cell phone to her ear. "I'll be right out."

Elise spun the rack of western stickers.

"What kind of mistake?" Rebekah's voice carried from behind the door. "But we don't have secondary insurance. I already told you I faxed that form this morning." There was a pause, and the storeroom door opened again. "And it shouldn't be reenrollment. I was told that since you didn't receive the form in time you rolled over our choices from last year." Another pause. "Of course." Rebekah's eyes were tired. "I'm on hold," she said to Elise. "What do you need?"

"Another scrapbook. One for just Mark."

Rebekah nodded. "Oh, just a second—" She leaned against the counter. "Oh, good. I knew it couldn't be the enrollment. So it's been a big mistake?" Rebekah's face fell; she headed back to the storeroom.

Elise pretended to be engrossed in the spiral scrapbooks.

After a minute Rebekah's voice rose again. "It isn't a preexisting condition. We adopted her eleven years ago." Another pause. "My husband has worked for U-Tech for fourteen years." A longer pause. "A different plan? You're kidding!" Rebekah shoved the storeroom door open.

Elise stepped to the backside of the display.

Rebekah stood at the counter and scribbled on a notepad. "Dialysis isn't good for children. Their kidneys play an important part in brain development and growth and red blood cells." Another pause. "She'll definitely need a new kidney before then." Rebekah's face reddened as she spoke.

Elise peeked around the scrapbooks.

Rebekah clenched the pen. "She's not going on dialysis." Rebekah held the phone tightly against her ear. "I need to speak with your supervisor." Another pause. "Fine, I'll call back in the morning."

Elise examined a few more albums. "Everything okay?" she asked, holding a midnight blue album in her hand.

"It will be. The insurance company is claiming that Pepper's kidney disease is a preexisting condition and that we have a waiting period of two years—so we have fourteen months left to go."

Elise shook her head.

"However, they will cover dialysis. Does that make any sense?"

"Ridiculous." Elise placed the album on the counter. "What are you going to do?"

"Contest it. What else can I do? And find Pepper a kidney." Rebekah picked up the album. "This is perfect for Mark. How is he?"

Elise shrugged. Mark's problems seemed minuscule compared to what Rebekah was going through. "He didn't go to school again today."

"Send him back to the barn. The work and fresh air will do him good." She rang up the amount on the cash register. "Seriously, if he doesn't go to school tomorrow, take him to the barn. You two can ride."

Elise pulled out her MasterCard. "Thanks, but he says his hand is too sore to go to school. I told him that it's too sore to go to the barn then too."

Elise snipped the dead yellow roses into the bucket. Her hand slipped, and a thorn stabbed through her glove. Mark and his bike were gone, again, but it was the middle of the day. Maybe he'd just gone for a bike ride. She was too embarrassed to call anyone anyway. She would wait until Michael got home, maybe until dark.

"Mom?"

"Where did you go?" Relieved, Elise jabbed the clippers toward Mark.

"Football practice, just to watch." Mark took the bucket from her.

"Why didn't you leave a note?"

"I did. By the pictures on the table."

"I didn't see it." She stooped to pull a weed that grew in the crack of the sidewalk. It had grown chilly, and dark clouds were gathering on the horizon.

"Coach Davis asked me if I wanted to play in the last two games of the season."

"And miss only one game for hitting your brother?'

Mark nodded.

"That doesn't seem like much of a consequence." Elise headed toward the side of the garage.

"But you're making me do community service," Mark said, following with the bucket.

"That's not for hitting your brother; that's for running away." Was one afternoon at Rebekah's enough?

Mark was silent.

"Did Coach Davis bring it up with you?"

"Yes." Mark dumped the bucket of wilted roses into the yard debris bin. "Michael feels all right about it."

"What made the coach change his mind?"

Mark shrugged.

Elise thought it had been a fair consequence. She rubbed her forehead with the tips of her glove. *If he gets back on the team, will he think it's okay to be violent? To react in anger and attack others? If I don't let him play football, will he refuse to go to school?*

"If you play football, you'll have to give up things at home, like the computer and TV."

Mark nodded. Was that a hint of a smile?

"Let me think about it some more and talk to Dad. And talk to your coach." This was when she really missed Ted. She hated talking to coaches, the kings of boy world. She didn't even know the language. She had as good as decided, and Mark knew it.

An afternoon of work at Rebekah's was probably enough. In fact, having him go out there more would only make things harder—for her. What if he didn't want to come home again?

Elise took the bucket and walked to the front of the house to prune the rest of the roses. The shears slipped in her hand and fell to the lawn. She bent to pick them up and then straightened slowly. Why did it bother her that Mark enjoyed being at Rebekah's? Elise positioned the shears again. Was it that Rebekah knew how much he wanted to be there? Was she afraid that Rebekah thought she was a bad mother? Did she care more about what Rebekah thought than what was best for her son?

ebekah thumbed through the shop's mail: a catalog from Inky Fingers Stamping, a flier from Scrapbooking Disney Style, and the letter that she had sent to Polly. *NOT AT THIS ADDRESS* was written in block letters in the corner of the envelope.

She sank onto a metal chair and put her head in her hands. Now what? Why hadn't Polly let her know that she had moved? Rebekah sat up straight. *Yikes.* She hadn't let Polly know they had moved, either. She dialed information and asked for Sparks, Nevada. No Polly Gaines listed. She tried Adrianna Gaines. No listing. Adrianna might have married. How would she track Polly down?

She needed to pick up Pepper in fifteen minutes to go to Portland for a doctor's appointment. Sandi was coming by to watch the shop. She pulled out her address book from her purse and then tried the phone number she had written down. Maybe Polly had kept the number. The phone rang ten times. Rebekah tried again. "Hello?" a scratchy voice asked. A child cried in the background.

"Is Polly available?" Rebekah doodled Pepper's name on the pad of paper.

There was a rustling, and the woman coughed. "I think she's at work." The phone went dead.

Rebekah dialed again. "Is this Adrianna?" She thought of the girl at her older sister's graveyard service all those years ago.

"This is Rebekah—"

"Listen, I work nights. Could you call back later?" The phone went dead again.

Rebekah circled the number in her address book. At least Polly was still alive. Sandi waved through the window. The door chimed. "Cool paper." Sandi held up a sheet with a white and brown cow design and then a sheet with a leathery look from the western section, which was positioned just inside the door. "I can just imagine what Pepper has planned."

"Speaking of, I promised we would stop by Old Navy on the way home."

"Take your time. I brought my scrapbook to work on, and John is going to bring me lunch." Sandi held up a handful of puffy stickers in sun, star, and moon shapes. "You're going to have to hide these from Pepper."

"I know." Rebekah tucked the returned letter into her purse.

"Do you have any homework to do, sweet pea?" Rebekah leaned her head against the clinic wall and closed her eyes.

"I need to finish my Spanish, *madre*." Pepper kicked the exam table and unzipped her backpack. "Will Jamie meet with us all the time, or will other nurses too?"

"Jamie is the transplant coordinator. She'll guide us through the whole process." Rebekah opened her eyes.

"It seems like a good job." Pepper kicked the table again.

It did seem like a good job—except for those people who died waiting for a transplant.

Jamie smiled as she came through the doorway. "Ooh! Cute outfit, Pepper!"

Pepper grinned. She wore a blue shrug over a long-sleeved, brown T-shirt.

"I like those colors together." Jamie sat on the swivel stool.

"Me too. All my stuff this year is blue and brown—clothes, note-books, scrapbooking stuff." Pepper sat tall.

"Cool." Jamie opened the file. "Dr. Thomas will see you in a few min-utes, but first I wanted to check on how things are going. I know that you're on the cadaver list. Rebekah, you mentioned looking for a live donor."

Rebekah nodded.

"Where are you with that?"

"Still making phone calls." Rebekah avoided Pepper's gaze.

Jamie made a note. "So, at this point, the list is our best bet?"

Rebekah nodded. *Maybe*. She didn't want to talk about it in front of Pepper. She didn't want to talk about the insurance company mix-up either. She needed to call Jamie and speak to her privately about both.

"Mom, can we go by Nordstrom too?" Pepper flipped down the visor of the truck, opened the mirror, and examined her mascara.

"No, we're only going to Old Navy, and stop looking at yourself. You look beautiful." Rebekah pulled into the mall parking garage.

"But there's a Nordstrom here at the other end of the mall."

"I know Nordstrom is here." She'd shopped there before she had kids. "I can barely afford Old Navy; I don't have the time or the money for Nordstrom." Rebekah parked the truck.

Pepper flipped the visor back into position and opened the door. "Who do you have to call?"

"Call?" Rebekah grabbed her purse.

"About a kidney."

It sounded so absurd. As if she was going to call Dial-A-Kidney or something. Should she tell Pepper? No. "Oh, I've just been talking to the insurance people about stuff."

Pepper led the way across the parking lot to the sidewalk. "Hey, I found a kidney on eBay last night."

"It's illegal to buy human organs—not to mention sell them." Rebekah had already checked. "How much was it?" She opened the door to the mall.

"Two and a half million dollars."

"Yikes."

"Mom?"

"What, sweet pea?" Rebekah led the way into Old Navy, scanning the store for blue and brown tops. At least Pepper's fashion obsessions narrowed her choices.

"Do you think my birth mom would have been willing to give me a kidney if she had lived?"

"You bet." Rebekah put her arm around Pepper. *Willing yes, capable no.* At least Mandy had Pepper before she contracted hepatitis and who knew what else.

"How did the appointment go?" Sandi slipped her scrapbook into her bag.

"Fine." Rebekah flipped her hair over her shoulder.

"Really?"

Rebekah sighed. "The appointment was fine. Everything else is falling apart. I can't get hold of Pepper's birth grandmother, and our insurance company is driving me crazy."

"Rebekah, I've never seen you stressed."

"I'm not stressed." Rebekah sank into a chair.

Sandi laughed. "You are. I know these things."

"You know what would be fun? A retreat. A scrapbooking retreat." Rebekah put her hands between her knees.

"When?"

"As soon as possible."

Sandi stood. "I can call the church about the lodge. It's only fifteen miles from here." She pulled her cell from the side pocket of her purse.

"In the mountains?"

Sandi nodded as she dialed. "It would be perfect. I've done retreats there before. I'll see if it's available this weekend."

Rebekah clapped her hands together. "It doesn't matter if it's a small group."

"What about Midnight Madness? And Saturday?"

"We'll have Midnight Madness at the lodge, and I'll just close the shop on Saturday—put a sign in the window. Anyone who really wants to scrapbook over the weekend will be with us, and I'll take merchandise to sell."

Sandi held up her hand and began talking on the phone. She nodded to Rebekah. "Great! I'll pick up the key on Friday morning." She turned to Rebekah. "We're all set."

lise kicked the tire of the 4Runner. It was flat. The Volvo was back in the shop for a rattle that had showed up the day after the repair work was completed. The mechanic assured her it needed only an adjustment and she would have it back by Monday afternoon. She pulled her phone from her purse on the passenger seat. No service. Rolling farmland surrounded her. A tractor inched along a half-plowed field on a distant hill. She leaned against the 4Runner and exhaled into the cold air. Too bad Ted wasn't standing here with her; he would be thrilled with the country setting. His experience growing up in a small town had been so different from hers.

She just wanted to get the grocery shopping done and then get home to do chores. Shopping in Forest Falls had become even more of a problem since the article in the paper that had mentioned Ted being deployed. Not only did strangers smile at her in the grocery store, but now they approached her to offer their support. Two women from church had stopped by last week—one with a loganberry pie and the other with snickerdoodles. Both had stayed for nearly an hour.

The boys were still asleep when she left. Michael would get up soon and watch cartoons all morning. Who knew when Mark might pull himself out of bed—probably not until she got home.

She zipped her jacket and pulled the 4Runner's manual out of the jockey box. Where would the spare be? In the back? Or under the rig? She lifted the hatch and tugged on the carpet. There it was. At least she wouldn't have to get under the truck to pull it out. Elise unscrewed the bolts and yanked on the tire.

She slumped against the bumper. The spare was flat too.

A horn honked, and a white pickup pulled off the road. It was John.

"What's the matter?" He slammed his door and walked toward her. He wore a short-sleeved white T-shirt and Levi's.

Wasn't he cold? Elise stood up straight. "Flat tire—and a flat spare."

"That's not like Ted to leave a spare unfixed. It must have gone flat on its own." John took the tire and threw it into the back of his truck. Elise headed to the passenger side of John's truck.

"Not so fast." John pulled a box of tools from the bed of his truck. "I'll get the tire off too; we need to get them both repaired."

Ten minutes later they were on the road to Salem, listening to country music. John turned the volume down.

"Where were you headed?"

"Grocery shopping."

"They have stores in Forest Falls."

Elise changed the subject. "Where are you off to so early on a Saturday morning?"

"To measure a kitchen in Salem for cabinets. It's going to be my fall project."

A line of quail scooted across the road and then floundered into flight at the last moment. John neither slowed nor swerved.

"How about if we drop the tires off and then I'll drop you off at the grocery store." John took a hairpin curve with ease, crossing one hand over the other. "There's one close to the house where my appointment is."

Elise held a latte with one hand and the handle of the shopping cart with the other as she waited for John outside the store. He pulled to the curb.

"Want a coffee?" she asked, placing hers in the cup holder.

"A plain, black coffee would be great. None of that foamy stuff." He jumped out of his truck and began loading her groceries, placing them inside the large plastic tote in the back of his truck.

Five minutes later John pulled onto the freeway toward Forest Falls and took a drink of his coffee. He swallowed quickly and said, "Ted called last night."

Elise nodded. John didn't have e-mail. That was one of the reasons they had purchased a satellite phone.

"He said that you and the boys are going to Germany for Christmas." John kept his eyes on the road. "I haven't talked with Ted about this. I wanted to run it by you first."

Elise's lower back tightened.

"Please be honest."

She put her coffee in the cup holder.

"What would you think if I went too?"

Elise forced a smile. What was the chance that he would really go? "I think that would be great." Her back began to hurt.

"Think about it. Talk to Ted and the boys."

Elise leaned against the seat and closed her eyes. She had never been alone with John, without Ted or Maude. She had no idea how to tell him she wanted the trip to Germany to be a family vacation, just her and the boys and Ted. Besides, would they need to book another room if John joined them? She couldn't imagine him bunking with the boys.

"Here we are." Fifteen minutes later John had the tire back on, the spare secured in the back, and the groceries transferred to the 4Runner.

Elise waved as she turned the key. She turned it again. Nothing. She opened her door as John started to pull away. He stopped and jumped out of his truck.

"The battery's dead."

"Did you leave the lights on again?"

"I don't think so." She checked. "Yes." Her hand flew to her face.

"I'll come back with the charge box." He eyed the narrow shoulder. "It's too dangerous to pull my truck up here. Let's get the groceries back in my rig."

"No, it's okay. Just call Triple A for me when you get into town." Elise hopped back in the 4Runner. "You've done enough already."

"Elise, don't be ridiculous. Help me with the groceries." John opened the back of the 4Runner. "You might need a new battery."

Elise nodded. "I'll take it in on Monday, after I get the Volvo back."

Michael greeted her at the kitchen door. "Mom, can we go play football with Reid and his dad?"

"Go grab a bag of groceries."

Michael stuck his head out the door. "How come Grandpa is here?"

"The 4Runner broke down."

"You have the worst luck with cars." Mark yawned and pulled on the drawstring of his pajama bottoms.

"Go help." Elise nudged him as she pulled chocolate-chip-cookie-dough ice cream from the bag.

"So can we go?" Michael hurried back into the kitchen.

"Go where?" John put two bags on the counter.

"To play football with the Grahams." Michael pulled a loaf of bread from a bag.

"We have to go back out and jump Dad's truck. I'm tired now, but by then I'll be exhausted."

"Please," Michael begged like a four-year-old.

"How about if I take them, Elise?" John stood in the kitchen doorway, a bag in each arm. "You and I can go get the 4Runner, and then I'll pick them up and meet Patrick. I'll stop and get them some lunch"—he looked at his watch—"a late lunch on the way to the field."

"Are you sure? I've taken up most of your day already."

John slapped Michael on the back. "I'd love to do it."

"Thanks." Michael hugged his grandfather.

"You'd better get dressed." John pointed at Mark.

"And call Reid. And put the groceries away." Elise closed the freezer. She would have some peace and quiet this afternoon or maybe time for something she wanted to do. "I wonder if Rebekah plans to ride this afternoon," she said out loud. "It looked like the shop was closed when we drove by. Maybe she took the day off to work on the farm."

"I don't think so." John dangled his keys. "She's at that scrapbooking retreat."

"Retreat?" Elise turned toward him. "What retreat?"

"Oh, a bunch of the ladies got together at the lodge to scrapbook or whatever it is that they do," John said casually.

"Well, I guess horseback riding is out." For once Elise was glad that John was so oblivious to her feelings. She couldn't hide the hurt in her voice.

Elise rummaged through the box of photos, too tired to read or do housework. Too hurt, really. Try as she might, she couldn't shake the rejection she felt every time she thought of the Forest Falls women at a retreat she wasn't invited to. She had wasted her day without the boys, and they would be home soon. John had called to say he and Patrick were taking the boys out for burgers. That was two hours ago.

The front door swung open. "I still can't believe that pass, Mark!" Michael flung his sweatshirt onto a dining room chair. "You should have seen it, Mom. I went up for the pass, and the ball just dropped into my arms. They didn't stand a chance against the Shelton boys!"

Mark and Michael high-fived each other.

Elise stood. "Did you guys have fun?"

"We had a great time." John slapped Mark on the back.

Mark nodded.

"And the boys were no trouble at all." John smiled broadly. "No back talk, no fighting, and no sulking."

"Thanks." Elise crossed her arms. "Boys, what do you tell your grandfather?"

"Thank you," they chirped in unison.

"You're welcome. I hope we can do it again sometime." John started to walk out the door and then turned back toward Elise. "See you at church tomorrow."

She nodded. Maybe. Why should she go to church and try to get to know people better when the women she did know hadn't invited her on their retreat? She turned toward the boys. "It's after nine. Both of you need to go to bed."

"I want to e-mail Dad first. Tell him about the pass I caught." Michael headed to the family room.

"You mean the pass that I threw." Mark ran after him.

"Why can't you do that in a game?" Michael grinned.

"Whatever. I get the computer first." Mark slammed his hand down on his brother's head, and they both fell to the floor of the hallway in a heap and began to wrestle.

Elise stepped over them, thinking of the scene in *A River Runs Through It* when the mother pushes her way between the two fighting brothers. "You can e-mail tomorrow." Elise's boys were already too big for her to break them up, even when it was a friendly wrestling match. "Get ready for bed."

Mark jumped to his feet. "Mom, I'm not going out for basketball."

"Why?"

Mark shrugged and headed to the kitchen.

Was it his grades? Or Ted's being gone? She had better check in with Mark's teachers soon. She stepped into the study and opened Outlook. One e-mail from Ted.

Sorry I couldn't call tonight. I got delayed at work. Lots of
surgeries. Have you bought tickets for December? Make
sure to get travel insurance with them. Love, Ted

She e-mailed back.

I did buy the tickets. I'll e-mail the info tomorrow.

Of course she had purchased travel insurance. But she didn't want to
think about travel insurance; she wanted to think about sleigh rides, nut-
crackers, and castles covered with snow. She added:

The boys will e-mail tomorrow. Right now they're wrestling
in the hallway. Are you missing home?

And then:

P. S. What did you say to your dad about us going to
Germany?

She was too hurt to tell him about not being invited to the scrapbooking retreat. So much for Ted's optimism about the women of Forest
Falls.

"You idiot. You almost tore my ear off." Michael came running
toward the study. Mark's laugh followed.

Elise stepped into the hall. "Michael, go to bed." He dashed up the
stairs.

Mark sat down in the middle of the hall.

"I just got an e-mail from Dad. He's looking forward to us coming to
Germany for Christmas." She wanted to give Michael a minute to get
ready for bed before another ruckus ensued. "Brush your teeth," she yelled
up the stairs.

"I hate flying," Mark said and started up the stairs.

Elise walked to the table and cleared the photos. She needed to do laundry, unload the dishwasher, and decide about going to church. She longed for some time of worship, but she knew now for sure that she was not accepted in Forest Falls. She hated to give up the horses, but she would not interact with Rebekah again. She counted the months on her hand. Eight. Eight more months until they moved to Seattle and left Forest Falls for good.

Chapter 20

*R*ebekah unpacked a box of paper, the phone tucked under her ear. Pepper sat on the balcony watching *Arthur* on the little television her grandmother had given her last year for Christmas; she had begged to bring it to the shop. D.W.'s whiny voice was getting on Rebekah's nerves, but she was happy that Pepper still watched her childhood shows. She was at that wondrous age between girlhood and womanhood.

Rebekah dialed the number. The phone rang seven times. She would let it ring twice more.

"Hello."

"Hi, Elise. Rebekah here."

"Hi."

"Want to ride up to Portland with us? I need to take Pepper to a doctor's appointment."

"I don't think so."

"Please? Sandi told me that both of your cars broke down again."

Elise didn't answer.

"Look, Elise. I feel really bad about the scrapbooking retreat. Sandi thought I had told you, and I thought Sandi had. We both just assumed you didn't want to—or couldn't—go. You know, that you didn't have anyone to watch the boys."

"Oh."

Oh. Lovely. She was ticked, and Rebekah didn't blame her. It was a low blow. She and Sandi hadn't figured out the mix-up until Sunday morning.

"We would really like to have you come along."

"To go to the doctor's appointment?"

"We're going to stop by the Western Store. I know you need boots for when you ride with us." Rebekah stifled a yawn. The retreat had been a lot more work than she'd expected.

"When do you need to leave?" Elise sounded resentful.

"Fifteen minutes."

"I could use some boots."

Rebekah smiled.

Elise walked toward the pickup, her suede jacket in one hand and her purse in the other. "Hi." Her voice had a scratchy, sleep-deprived sound, and her hair was damp. "Hi, Pepper," Elise said as she climbed into the front seat.

"How are you?" Rebekah asked.

"Tired, that's all."

"How come?"

Elise shrugged. "I stay up too late when Ted is gone. It's hard to get to sleep." Elise seemed to be interested in the willow trees along the creek as they crossed the city limits.

An hour later at the clinic, Rebekah pulled out Pepper's insurance card for the receptionist. The woman read from the computer screen. "Payment denied." She paused. "For the last five appointments."

"I know." Rebekah shivered.

"Ask Jamie to help you. We have to appeal this sort of thing every now and then."

Rebekah sat down across from Pepper and Elise.

"What's in your bag?" Elise nodded toward Pepper's small Nike backpack.

"Gum. Trident bubblegum."

"What else?"

"Blue and brown paint chips. I want to paint my room. And *Arthur* trading cards."

"Arthur? The aardvark?"

Pepper nodded. "Mark and Michael probably used to watch it."

"Yes, they did, and I read plenty of *Arthur* books to them over the years."

"I still like the show. And the Web site." Pepper opened her backpack. "Oh, I also have some polka-dot fabric—blue and brown. I'm going to make a cushion for my chair, the one I painted last week. And I have some horse stickers and some free song stickers for my iPod."

"You have an iPod?"

"No. Not yet." Pepper nudged her mom.

Rebekah shook her head.

"Mom, can we go by the scrapbooking store on the way home? The big one?"

"No. We're going by the Western Store. Besides, we have our own store now." Rebekah flipped the pages of the magazine.

"But the one close to Lloyd Center has so much cool stuff. Lloyd Center! Can we go there too?"

Rebekah pretended to read the magazine. "We went there just a few days ago."

"It's been way over a week—just so you know."

"Pepper Graham." The nurse stood at the door to the waiting room. Rebekah and Pepper stood.

"Oh, I also have my urine sample in my bag," Pepper said, turning toward Elise. "Want some gum?"

✂

The Western Store took up an entire block. Rebekah breathed in deeply. Leather, feed, and fertilizer. She quickly found the halter and bandage she needed for Sky.

"I need new boots, Mom. My feet grew." Pepper turned down the boot aisle.

"I can't afford new boots right now."

"Aren't these cute?" Pepper held up a short, blue and green, gator-print boot with a square toe. "It's a Fatboy. They're really trendy right now."

"Pepper, I can't afford trendy."

"Those *are* cute." Elise picked up a brown Fatboy boot. "What size do you wear?"

"Six and a half."

"I thought your feet grew." Rebekah concentrated on not rolling her eyes.

"They did, Mom. I used to be a size six. My boots are too tight. I'm not kidding."

Elise turned the boot over and checked the bottom.

Rebekah wandered off and sat down in a leather chair, the bandages in one hand and the halter in the other, her purse over her shoulder. She leaned her head back and closed her eyes.

"You asleep?"

"Almost." Rebekah sat up straight. "Did you find some boots?"

Elise nodded.

"Fatboys?"

"They're cute." Elise sat down next to Rebekah.

"What's Pepper doing?"

"Deciding."

"I'm not buying her new boots." Rebekah sat up straight.

"She knows. I am."

"Elise, I can't let you do that."

"Sure you can. I don't have a daughter to buy things for. Let me buy for Pepper." Elise's eyes brightened.

"I'll trade you boots for scrapbooking stuff."

"That means I'd have to get serious about scrapbooking."

"You'll scrapbook." Rebekah flinched, thinking about the retreat.

"We'll see." Elise hugged the box. "Let me buy the boots. You let me ride your horses."

Pepper stood in front of the mirror, admiring a pair of red boots. Rebekah shrugged. "Okay. Thanks."

"What did the doctor say?" Elise slipped out of her jacket.

"The same. Transplant within the next six months if at all possible. Her kidney function is just below fifteen percent. The coordinator is going to call our insurance about the preexisting-condition fiasco."

"Any word about the list?"

"The doctor doesn't deal with that. Kids have priority on the list, because of everything the kidney affects—growth, all of that. But still, it's a long list."

"What's the hardest part for you?"

Rebekah paused. Was Elise really interested? "The hardest part is not being able to give Pepper one of my kidneys. I should be able to. I love her more than anyone in the world loves her. Don't you think I should be able to?" Rebekah slumped in the chair.

"I'm sorry." Elise squeezed Rebekah's hand.

Surprised by Elise's warmth, Rebekah continued, "Wouldn't you want to be able to do that for your kids?"

"I've never even thought about it," Elise answered. Her face contorted just a little.

"Be thankful that you haven't had to. It's horrid."

Pepper paraded in front of them, wearing a pair of blue boots. "Those are really cute." Elise stood and headed to the hat aisle. Rebekah followed her.

"How about this?" Elise tried on a green straw cowboy hat.

Rebekah picked up an orange one. "I've wanted to take Sky to the coast and ride on the beach. Want to go next Saturday if Sandi will watch the store for me?"

"Maybe, if John will watch my boys." Elise paused and looked at herself in the mirror. "How would we get the horses to the beach?" She took the hat off her head and then took the orange one from Rebekah.

"The trailer."

"That old rickety thing behind your barn?" Elise plucked a blue hat off the shelf.

"It works fine."

"Have you pulled it before?"

"Yes." Rebekah stood on her tiptoes. Where was Pepper?

"When?"

"Every week to 4-H through the spring and summer."

"How many times to the beach?" Elise headed toward the boot department.

"None." Rebekah ran her hand through her hair. "What are you doing with all those hats?"

"Buying them. For you, Pepper, and me."

"Elise."

"Hush."

✂

"Is it safe for Pepper to eat ice cream?" Elise whispered as they stood in line at Baskin-Robbins.

"As long as she doesn't eat a whole gallon," Rebekah whispered back.

Pepper sucked on a pink spoon from her sample of Very Berry Strawberry. She tilted her head. "Mom, they're playing country."

Rebekah listened. Sure enough, even in Portland.

"I love this song." Pepper held the spoon in her hand. *"But she's somebody's hero,"* she sang along. *"A hero to her baby with a skinned-up knee."*

"I especially like the line at the end of this song about Momma being in a nursing home and being fed with a spoon." Rebekah winked at Elise.

"The keeper of the Cheerios." Pepper sang through the whole song. "It's by Jamie O'Neal. She's singing about you guys."

Elise shook her head. "I don't think I'm anyone's hero." They inched forward in the line.

"You are." Pepper blew a bubble. "I hope I'll be a mom someday. If I can't have kids, I'm going to adopt."

"You'll make a great mother," Rebekah said as she approached the counter. Boy, they had a long way to go before thinking about grandbabies.

"Who all went on the retreat?" Elise asked after she ordered her frozen mocha.

Rebekah tried to sound nonchalant. "Sandi, Pepper and Ainsley, and a few other women." Rebekah paid the cashier.

"How many altogether?" Elise's voice sounded scratchy again.

"Twenty." Pepper reached out her hand for her cookies-and-cream ice-cream cone. "Isn't that cool?"

Rebekah elbowed Pepper.

"What, Mom?" Pepper grabbed a stack of napkins.

"Wow. What a great turnout." Elise's voice fell flat.

Rebekah handed Elise her mocha. Why did life never seem to progress past junior high?

Chapter 21

Elise scooted onto the seat and slammed the door of Rebekah's pickup.

"Look at my little sweetie," Rebekah said with a smile. Pepper stood next to the barn with her arms crossed and a fierce scowl on her face. "I told her we're going to check things out—to see if it's safe for me to take her next time."

"She's going to make you pay for this one."

Rebekah nodded, her two braids bobbing back and forth. "Never underestimate the power of a pout. I can just imagine what she's going to talk Patrick into today—probably shopping." Rebekah swung the pickup and horse trailer onto the highway and accelerated. "How are the horses doing?"

Elise turned her head. The trailer window was filthy, but she could make out Sky jerking his head up and down. "Sky doesn't look too happy. I can't see the mare."

Rebekah wore her orange hat. "How are things with Ted?"

"Pretty routine. Lots of surgeries. He's found a church. It's cold and wet in Germany too. He said the 4Runner's spare shouldn't have gone flat; he checked it when we left Colorado. And he doesn't know why his army checks haven't been coming through."

"You're kidding. The army doesn't pay?"

"Eventually they pay."

"Yikes. What have you been living on?"

"Savings."

"Must be nice," Rebekah muttered as she slowed for a curve.

Elise leaned back against the headrest.

"Do you remember our conversation about small towns way back when? What business did everyone know of yours in Cascade Pass?" Rebekah pulled to the right to allow a car to pass as the pickup strained up a hill.

"The usual stuff."

"Like who had dinner at whose house?"

Elise laughed. "We didn't really have dinner at anyone's house."

"How come?" Rebekah tipped her hat back.

"We kept to ourselves."

"And did what?"

"Everyday stuff. Homework. Housework." She paused. "We spent one week every summer in Seattle at my grandmother's house. We would all go to the market and wharf. Dad would take me to the art museum and the library. Twice we went to the Space Needle. Every year my mother would cry the whole way home."

"Were you close to your father?"

Elise nodded.

"You were in high school when he died?"

"Senior year." Elise yawned and then sat up straight. "Look, a deer." She pointed to the right of the road. "I hope there isn't a cougar behind it."

Rebekah laughed. "If there was, Pepper would be even more bummed that she didn't get to come along."

Elise turned the subject to the kids and school. She had decided to ride to make Rebekah feel better about not inviting her to the retreat. No, that wasn't true. She decided to ride because she wanted to ride. It was that simple. She wanted to ride, not talk about the past.

✄

A gust of wind whipped Elise's green cowboy hat from her head as Rebekah led Sky backward down the rickety ramp from the trailer and onto the asphalt. Sky reared. Rebekah pulled firmly on the reins as Elise chased her hat across the parking lot. Elise clamped it back on her head and pulled the tie to the front.

Rebekah laughed. "Here, hold on to Sky."

Sky turned his head and pawed the ground. Elise clasped the reins tightly. What if he got away from her? The mare backed out of the trailer in one swift motion. Rebekah and Elise saddled the horses and then led them down the trail toward the beach.

Elise's hat blew off again. She dismounted and chased it into the surf, snatching it from the foamy waves. Rebekah rode toward the mare, grabbed her reins, and handed them back to Elise. "Push the dealy all the way up to your chin," Rebekah said, "like mine."

Elise did and then unzipped her parka and breathed in the salty air. It was windy but warm.

"We must be getting a balmy breeze from Hawaii." Rebekah handed Elise her reins and wiggled out of her fleece. Sky held his ears back.

What did the horses think of the beach, the crashing waves, and the smell of the ocean? They trotted along the edge of the water. Elise rolled her shoulders. Breathe and balance.

"How did you and Ted meet?" Rebekah rode closest to the waves.

"I worked in a bookstore in Seattle, and Ted came in looking for a specific poem."

"Was he taking a poetry class?"

"A community class at the church on his block. He was expanding his horizons." Elise squinted under the brim of her hat as she talked. She hadn't thought to bring her sunglasses.

"So then what?"

"I finally found the poem. He didn't know the author. Just the title: 'When You Are Old.' "

"Sounds cheery."

"It's really beautiful but sad. It's by William Butler Yeats, about growing old and love fleeing and pacing upon the mountains overhead."

"Sounds depressing."

"Exactly." The horses splashed through a creek that cut through the sand, and Sky bounded ahead.

Elise ached for Ted. The first week he was gone was tolerable; one less person to interact with meant a little bit more time to herself. She would stay up and read or watch a movie she wouldn't watch otherwise. But after the first week, loneliness would seep into her bones, into her heart. As the weeks marched on, the loneliness turned into an ache. It wasn't that love had fled. It wasn't pacing the mountains overhead. It was suspended by a turning satellite, an unpredictable army, and miles of uncertainty.

"Be careful who you make sacrifices for in this life," her mother had once told her. "You can't help who you fall in love with," her father had said not long before he died. Those were the only two pieces of advice her parents had given her.

Sky's dark form lunged up the bank of a wider creek that flowed into the ocean. The muscles of his thighs rippled as he moved. The mare stumbled. Elise held on tightly.

"What happened after you found the poem? Did he ask you out?" Rebekah tipped her orange hat back on her head.

Elise nodded, her cheeks flushed from the sun and wind. "We sat on the wood floor of the bookstore and read the poem, and we both felt, I don't know, a little haunted. He said, 'That's awful. I hope that never happens.' For a moment I thought he was married." What she didn't say was that she had already checked out his ring finger and had determined there wasn't even a tan line. "But he wasn't. He asked me if I wanted to have tea the next day."

"Tea?"

"We took the ferry to Victoria and had high tea at the Empress Hotel."

"You're kidding!"

Elise shook her head and smiled.

"Boy, Ted doesn't waste time, does he?" Rebekah adjusted her cowboy hat. "Did he tell you right away that he was a medical resident?"

"No. He didn't tell me for a month. That's when I figured out that he was eight years older than me. He kept that a secret too. He didn't tell me at first that he owed the army six years, either."

"But you married him anyway."

"The army wasn't that big of a deal in the mideighties. Absolutely nothing was going on. The cold war was ending. The Berlin wall came down soon after that. He would serve his six years, and we would move back to Seattle, where he would go into private practice. No big deal. Then that tyrant I'd never heard of invaded that little country I'd never heard of, and my whole life changed."

"Saddam Hussein? Kuwait?"

Elise nodded as the mare picked her way over a rocky spot on the beach.

"Why did Ted stay in after his six years were up?"

"He loved the first Gulf War. Crazy, huh? I was home barely surviving while he was deciding that he had never done anything so meaningful in his life as taking care of wounded soldiers." Elise was ready to change the subject. She concentrated on holding the reins and then kicked at the stirrup strap with her foot to straighten it. "How did you and Patrick meet?"

"Portland State University. I was the bigmouth in our biology class. He was the cute geeky kid who blushed at everything I said. I couldn't get enough of him."

On the way back, as they headed north, the wind grew stronger. Elise pulled her hat tighter against her head. They rode along the water's edge, hoping for some protection from the stinging sand.

Rebekah tightened the string against her neck. "I was wondering about your mom. Did the townspeople help her after your father died? Were they good to her?"

Elise shook her head. "My mom was never really accepted. My dad was well liked, but my mom was aloof, never really made friends." She was saying too much; still she continued. "When I was in junior high, she had an affair with a man in town. Everyone knew except me. Finally two girls at school cornered me during PE and questioned me about my mom and this man. I denied it. 'No, it's true,' they said. 'Everybody knows.' They were right. Everyone did know."

"Yikes. I'm sorry." Rebekah leaned toward Elise.

"It was really awful."

"And then what happened?"

"The man and his family moved to Everett. He had a son my age that all of my classmates really liked. And that was it, sort of. But then people really had a reason not to like my mom."

"What about your dad?"

Elise paused and then shook her head. "I don't know. It wasn't really anything I could talk to him about. I do remember him crying in church one Sunday around that time. But that was all. It made me feel awful, but I was too afraid to ask him about it."

"He stuck with your mom?"

Elise nodded. "They didn't talk much. She was disappointed in him, that he didn't make more money, that he hadn't become a manager. He was a small man who did really hard labor. A high-school dropout who went straight to the mill. He loved to read, but he had no education."

"Wow. Is that why you don't want to stay in Forest Falls? The small-town stuff?"

"No." Elise didn't want to offend Rebekah. "I like Seattle, that's all."

"How did your parents meet?" Rebekah asked.

"Dad worked in a mill outside of Seattle for a year, and my mom's cousin worked at the same place."

"What did your mom's family think when she married and moved to Cascade Pass?"

"I'm not sure. She always made it sound like her family was rich; she would talk about the dances she went to, the dresses she wore, and all that. But I think they were just middle class. Her mother's family had money before the stock market crashed—they owned a mill. They used to be part of the society scene, but that money was long gone before my mother was born."

"But she missed the city life?"

Elise nodded.

"Kind of like you."

"Kind of."

The reflections of the horses shimmered in the shallow water. A purple and red kite soared overhead. "Look, a sand dollar." Rebekah jumped off Sky. "It's perfect." She climbed back on.

"What about your parents?" Elise asked.

"They live in Arizona, thank goodness. Not that I don't love them, but there's always a lot of drama and hurt feelings when they're around, and then they want to control everything—at least my mother does. I haven't told them how serious things are with Pepper, because she would rush up here and try to take charge, I think."

"Do they like to play the part of the hero?"

Rebekah laughed. "Of course. Don't we all? But they're not heroes."

"More like comic relief?"

"You've got it. They're forever trying to sneak things by each other. My mom and her purse collection. How many purses does one woman need? My dad and his golf clubs. He's in search of the perfect putter."

The horses continued at a fast walk.

"I think you're a hero." Elise loosened her grip on the reins. Her face reddened; she was definitely saying too much.

"What do you mean?" Rebekah led the way back to the water's edge.

"You rescue everyone."

"Please." Rebekah shook her head.

"Look at your determination about Pepper. And don't forget the cougar. You should have seen yourself rushing toward it, totally unafraid."

"No. I was afraid."

"It didn't show."

"Does my fear about Pepper show?" Rebekah turned her head toward Elise.

"Are you afraid?"

Rebekah slowed Sky to a walk. The tide was coming in and swirling around the horses' ankles. "When she was sick before, I was never afraid. A while back Pepper asked me what I'm afraid of, because she's afraid of raccoons. I told her nothing, but I lied. I'm afraid that she'll die. I'm not always afraid of that, but at times I wake up in the middle of the night and feel like I've been punched in the heart."

Sky stopped to sniff a pile of kelp.

"I have to be optimistic." Rebekah sat tall. "I have to go to Nevada to find Pepper's birth family."

"Will you just show up?"

"I guess so. If they won't answer the phone, I can't very well tell them I'm coming." Rebekah pulled on Sky's reins.

A sea gull flew low in front of the Appaloosa. He spooked and jerked his head back. Surely someone in Pepper's birth family would donate a kidney. Or would they? Talking about the past was better than talking about this. Thank goodness Rebekah hadn't brought up blood types again.

Chapter 22

*R*ebekah held up a piece of silklike Asian paper for her customer. "That's perfect," the woman said. She fanned out the stickers of paper lanterns in her hand. "I heard at a crop party the other night that you have a great travel section here."

"Where are you from?" Rebekah asked.

"Portland."

Rebekah clapped her hands together; she couldn't wait to tell Patrick. A few minutes later Sandi and John hurried into the shop, rosy faced and bundled in their jackets. Sandi pulled her tie-dyed fleece cap from her head. "We were out walking. Isn't it a gorgeous day?"

Rebekah smiled. It was actually overcast and threatening to rain.

Her cell phone rang. "Excuse me." It was probably Pepper wanting to go to Ainsley's after school.

It was the kidney transplant coordinator. "I have the paperwork for your insurance appeal. I just need you to sign the forms," Jamie explained.

"I'll come up tomorrow." She walked toward the storeroom.

"I can fax it."

"No, I'll be up in the morning. I don't want any problems with lost faxes or any of that." She told Jamie good-bye and hung up the phone. Sandi laughed at something John had said. Rebekah smiled. What was going on between those two?

"Last game of the season is tomorrow night. Is Reid ready?" John asked.

"I'm sure he is." Rebekah ran her hand through her hair. "Speaking of tomorrow, Sandi, I hate to ask—"

"I can watch the shop in the morning, but I work in the afternoon."

"Perfect." Rebekah's face showed her relief. What would she do without Sandi? "I should be back by noon. I just have to sign some insurance papers at the hospital." Rebekah paused.

"What is it?"

"I may have to go to Nevada sometime and look up Pepper's bio family. I haven't told Patrick yet—"

"Rebekah, just let me know, and I'll work my schedule around it." Sandi put her hands on her hips. "I'll watch the shop whenever I can. Just get the insurance stuff figured out, and then find our girl a kidney, okay?"

"Ready?" John buttoned his jacket.

Sandi waved to Rebekah. "I have my key. I'll see you by noon."

"Thanks," Rebekah said. "Hey, one more thing."

Sandi started to laugh.

Rebekah continued. "I was wondering. Would you two want to come to our house for Thanksgiving?"

"Sure." Sandi smiled at John.

He hesitated. "It's Elise and the boys. I'm not sure what their plans are."

"I'll ask them to come too." Rebekah slipped her cell phone into her jean jacket.

"That's not what I meant." John put his hand on Sandi's shoulder. "I feel like I should be with them, at their house or mine."

Rebekah nodded. "Or mine. It'll be fun."

"Hey, Elise." Rebekah jumped from her truck, carrying her stadium blanket, and hurried across the parking lot of North Fork Middle School. "Listen, I was talking to Sandi and John yesterday about Thanksgiving. I'd like to have all of you—Sandi and John and you and the boys—come to my house. Would it work for you?"

Elise swung her arm into her coat. "I hadn't even thought about Thanksgiving."

"It's only a couple of weeks away."

Elise pulled on her hat. "I think that would work. John will be there?"

Rebekah nodded.

"With Sandi?"

"Yep. Isn't it wild? What's going on with those two?"

Elise shook her head. "I have no idea."

Rebekah and Elise stopped at the fence to watch their sons.

"Hey, Reid." Mark drilled the ball across the field. Reid caught it and shouted, "Why can't you pass like that in a game?"

"Those boys." Rebekah pulled her gloves from her pockets. "Come on, let's go warm up our seats."

"I forgot my blanket. I'll be right there." Elise headed back to her car.

Patrick sat on the top row of the bleachers. "What are you doing way up here?" Rebekah asked.

"Taking in the view." Patrick put one arm around Rebekah. "How was your trip to Portland?"

"Fine. I think I could drive it with my eyes closed."

"Well, don't."

"Run another lap," Coach Davis yelled. The boys jogged around the track in slow motion as if they might fall forward and land on their face masks at any moment.

"Where's Pepper?"

"With Ainsley."

Elise started up the bleachers, followed by Sandi and John. Rebekah nudged Patrick. "Look at those two."

He shaded his eyes. "It's not our business." He squeezed Rebekah's gloved hand.

"They're coming for Thanksgiving."

"They are?" Patrick let go of her hand.

"So are Elise and the boys."

John stepped forward to shake Patrick's hand. The center snapped the ball; Mark caught it and ran.

Rebekah followed the boys to the bus after the game, a 14–0 victory for Forest Falls, and searched for Reid.

"Coach Davis let Mark back on the team only because he feels sorry for him. Because his dad is in Iraq," one of the defenders said.

"Germany. His dad is in Germany." Reid stood on the first step of the bus.

"I thought Mark said Iraq," the other boy said.

Reid shook his head.

"I wish they'd never moved to Forest Falls," another boy said. "Oh, well. At least basketball will be better. Mark's grades are too bad to go out."

Were Mark and Michael in the group? Rebekah craned her neck. No, they stood with Elise by her Volvo.

"Reid," Rebekah called out, "do you want to ride with me?"

He shook his head. "I'm taking the bus."

"Dad's picking Pepper up at Ainsley's, but I'll meet you at school."

Rebekah stopped by Elise's car. "Good game, you guys."

"Thanks," Michael said.

Mark nodded.

Rebekah headed to her truck. If Mark's grades were too bad to go out for basketball, would Elise allow him to help more with the horses?

Rebekah slammed the oven door with a twist of her hip. She'd made bacon and eggs for breakfast.

"How many people did you invite for Thanksgiving?" Patrick tied his tie.

"Just Sandi and John and Elise and her boys." She pulled the sash on her robe.

"Mark?"

"He's been fine."

"You're going to pull off Thanksgiving, get the insurance figured out, and find a kidney? All in the next two weeks?"

"Patrick, I have a plan. I promise."

"She needs a kidney soon. I called Dr. Thomas yesterday."

"Why did you call the doctor?" Rebekah stirred the orange juice.

"Because you don't give me straight answers."

"I do give you straight answers."

"No, you don't. You keep telling me everything will work out."

"It will. Patrick, I promise you. It will." She pulled the clip out of her hair and let it fall around her shoulders. Patrick didn't seem to notice.

"The doctor said her protein levels are high. That if she doesn't have a kidney in the next few months, she may have to start dialysis. If she starts dialysis, chances are higher she'll reject a donor kidney. Plus it could affect her brain development and everything else."

"I told you that." Rebekah twisted her hair and wound it back on her head.

"No, you didn't."

"I told someone that." Who had she told? She specifically remembered telling someone. Had she told Elise and forgotten to tell Patrick?

"I think I should start going to the appointments with you."

"And miss work? What good would that do?" Rebekah poured four glasses of juice.

"Mom!" Pepper slid into the kitchen, socks on her feet, blue boots in her hand. "Do you think these boots will look good with my outfit?" She wore a short, flouncy, brown skirt and a long-sleeved, blue T-shirt with a brown camisole underneath it that showed around the neckline.

"I don't like that outfit," Patrick said, crossing his arms.

"Why?"

"The boots will look great, sweet pea." Rebekah turned off the burner.

"When did she get the boots? I thought you were going to stop spending money." Patrick caught Rebekah's eyes.

"I didn't buy the boots." Rebekah pulled the tray of bacon out from under the broiler. "Elise did."

"You shouldn't have let her."

"She said that since she rides our horses, she wanted to get the boots for Pepper. She got a pair for herself too." She wouldn't mention the hats.

"Dad, why don't you like my outfit?"

"You look too old." Patrick grabbed a piece of bacon.

What was up with him? Rebekah shoved her hands into the pockets of her robe. "It's a cute outfit. Tell Reid it's time for breakfast."

Pepper slid back through the dining room, swinging her boots back and forth.

"You're too soft on her. You let her wear whatever she wants. She manages to get someone to buy whatever she wants." Patrick tightened his tie.

"No, that's not true. She wants an iPod."

Patrick shook his head. "Rebekah, she needs a kidney, not trendy clothes and an iPod."

"I'm not buying her an iPod. Believe me. And I'll find her a kidney." Rebekah headed to the kitchen door. "I'm going to get dressed."

"How?" Patrick called after her. "How are you going to find a kidney?"

lise walked around the school cafeteria tables, her boots clicking on the brown linoleum. Lunch duty was not her favorite volunteer position; she would rather be in the library. But she had told the secretary she would fill in wherever she was needed.

Michael and Reid waved, just a little. She smiled. The rain pelted the windows. Mark walked into the cafeteria alone without acknowledging her.

"Hi, Elise." Pepper pranced through the doorway in her boots. She held her right foot out. Elise held her foot up too.

"You have matching boots!" Ainsley squealed. "I want a pair."

"We could each trade a boot and do that blue and brown look." Pepper grinned at Elise.

Elise glanced down at her boots and then at the rose-colored sweater set Ted had given her for Christmas last year. Did they go with the boots? Not really, but at least Pepper approved.

"I have pictures from the last game and some more of my horse." Ainsley dug in her backpack and handed Elise an envelope.

More photos of the horse, then pictures from the game. Mark throwing a pass. Reid on the sidelines. Elise's hand froze around a photo of Mark's fist smashed against Michael's face on that awful, horrible night. Then a photo of Michael bleeding and one of Coach Davis bandaging Mark's hand. "Look at these," she finally said.

"Oh, those." Ainsley's expression grew sheepish. "Do you want the doubles?"

"No." Elise started to hand them back, then hesitated. "Yes." She took the three photos and headed over to the closet where her purse was stashed. She couldn't criticize Sandi for revisionist scrapbooking and then turn down an offer for photos of one of the worst moments of her life.

Three boys in the back corner of the cafeteria raised their voices. Elise headed over. They quieted when she grew closer. Mark, Ainsley, and Pepper cut in front of Reid and Michael in the lunch line. The kids came through with trays of chicken strips and fries, and the boys had milk on their trays. Michael hadn't wanted a sack lunch that morning. The smell of the fried food turned Elise's stomach. She wiped down tables, interrupted the beginning of a food fight, and tried not to stare at Mark and Michael. Mark's eyes darted around the cafeteria as he talked with Ainsley and Pepper, Michael tried too hard to be part of the conversation, and Reid migrated over to a group of basketball players. Michael followed after a few minutes.

"Mrs. Shelton." The boys' English teacher, Mr. Jenkins, came toward her with his tray. "I need to talk with you. Could you come by after school?"

"Can you tell me a little now?" Her anxiety rose. She didn't want to wonder, to worry all day.

"Michael is doing fine." He clutched his tray. He was maybe twenty-five, and this was his first teaching job. "Mark hasn't turned in an assignment in two weeks."

"Really? He's been doing his assignments. I sit with him every evening when he does his homework." She thought Mark was pretending he didn't care his grades were too low to play basketball. Maybe he really didn't care.

"I haven't seen a thing."

Mark laughed at something Ainsley said, and Pepper looked embarrassed. Even when he laughed, Mark had a faraway look in his eyes.

"Is it too late for him to turn the assignments in?" Elise asked.

"I gave him until yesterday."

"So it's too late?"

"I'm afraid so." Mr. Jenkins met her gaze.

"I wish you had told me—e-mailed me, given me a call."

"Mark should have told you."

Elise nodded. Yes, in an ideal world, Mark should have told her. "His father is in Germany with the army right now." Mr. Jenkins shifted his feet. He probably thought she was making excuses for Mark; he was probably right. She sighed. "I'll talk with him."

"Hey, Pepper." Michael headed back over to Mark's table. "What's your blood type?"

Elise wiped another table.

"Why?"

"Mark wants to give you a kidney." Michael laughed.

"No, I don't." Mark stood on his chair.

"Sit down." Elise called out.

Mark scowled.

"You have to be eighteen to donate a kidney," Pepper said, pulling the sleeves of her sweater over her hands.

"Pepper doesn't want Mark's kidney anyway." Ainsley stood. "Come on, Pepper."

"What's your blood type?" Michael sat down beside Pepper.

"Michael wants to give you his." Mark stood. "Don't you, Mikey?"

Pepper patted Michael's back. "You're sweet."

"So, what is it?" Michael shot Mark a mean look.

"B something."

Michael turned toward Elise. "Mom, what's mine?"

"AB positive, I think." Elise wandered over to where her purse was and checked her cell phone, hoping Michael wouldn't ask about her blood type.

"I'll e-mail Dad tonight. He'll remember." Michael hurried after Reid. "See you after practice, Mom!"

Mark grunted as he walked by.

Elise turned the chicken soup to simmer and stepped to the kitchen window. Dusk cast a golden glow over the backyard. This was her witching hour; when the boys were small, it was the time of day when they fell apart, when fathers with normal jobs were coming home to save the day. But Elise had been on her own to play another game of Stratego with them or to turn on the television so she could make dinner.

Mark stood in the doorway.

"Where are you going?"

"For a walk." He wore his black sweatshirt.

"Where to?"

"Just around."

"I need to talk with you first." She covered the soup. "Mr. Jenkins said you haven't turned in an assignment for the last two weeks."

"He's a creep." Mark slouched against the counter.

"Mark, the issue is your assignments."

"He sits at his desk and surfs the Web while we read."

"That's not the issue, either."

"How can I respect a teacher who does that?"

"Why don't you turn in your assignments after you do them?"

Mark shrugged. "I hate English."

"That's not the point, either." Elise poured herself a glass of water.

Mark opened the cupboard and pulled a handful of animal cookies out of the bag.

"It's too close to dinnertime."

"Nag, nag, nag."

"What will it take for you to turn in your assignments?" Elise leaned against the counter.

"Tell Mr. Jenkins to stop surfing the Web. Shouldn't he be grading papers or something?" Mark said with a full mouth.

"Shouldn't you be turning in papers for him to grade?"

"He doesn't grade anything anyway. If he likes you, he gives you an A. If he hates you, you get a D. Or an F."

"Michael turns in his work."

"He likes Michael. Everyone likes Michael. And Michael gets A's." Mark stuffed another cookie in his mouth and grabbed three more. "Bye." He spit crumbs with the word.

"We're eating in thirty minutes. As soon as Michael gets home from basketball practice."

Mark slammed the back door.

Elise yanked the lid off the pot and grabbed the salt and frantically shook it into the soup. *That kid.* She headed down the hall to the study. Three new e-mails. The first from Mark's science teacher.

> Mark hasn't turned in an assignment all week. He's been staring out the window. I sent him to the office today.

Great.

The second e-mail was from Ted:

> Michael, so good to get your e-mail. Didn't realize you had a Hotmail account you could use at school. Decided to send this home so Mom could be in on the conversation.
>
> You are AB, so you can't give to Pepper. Mom actually has B blood, and so does Mark. The Rh factor, the positive or negative, doesn't matter when it comes to donating a kidney. Mom would have to be tested extensively, because having the same blood doesn't necessarily mean a match. It is very complicated. Mark is too young to donate a kidney.
>
> Mom said that all of you are going to Patrick and Rebekah's for Thanksgiving and that Grandpa will be there

too. That's great. I'm happy that our family is becoming
friends with the Grahams.

How is basketball going? I miss you. Please give Mom
a hug. Tell her I'll call later.

Love, Dad

Elise hit Delete. Thank goodness Ted had sent it to her account and
not Michael's. All she needed was for Michael to obsess about her donating a kidney to Pepper. What was Ted thinking? She had two kids, a house,
and cars to manage. Were her kidneys even fit to donate after all the
painkillers she had taken through the years? Did the drugs damage her kidneys? Did the drugs she took while she was pregnant damage Mark? Were
his problems her fault?

She logged off the computer. At least this deployment was better than
usual. She had been sleeping for the most part. She stayed up too late, but
she hadn't had the perpetual insomnia and sleep deprivation that had sent
her to the edge before. And her back hadn't seized up like so many times
in the past.

Now if only Mark would pull his act together.

Elise spread the next several photos from the box on the table. John hadn't
said anything more about going to Germany with them at Christmas, and
she had avoided bringing it up. She didn't want to tell Ted that she would
rather his dad not go.

"Neuschwanstein Castle," Michael said, leaning against the table.

"Do you remember?" He'd only been four.

He nodded and pulled out a chair.

"And this is Hohenschwangau Castle." Elise pointed to the next
photo.

"I remember that too."

Mark walked through the room and held his nose. "Not Germany."

Michael crossed his arms. "I still don't get it, Mark. Why did you hate it so much?"

"Get lost." Mark punched Michael in the arm and sauntered out of the room.

"Mark!" Elise jumped to her feet.

"Don't worry about it, Mom. It didn't hurt."

Elise sat back down. She was too tired to go after him. "It's time to get ready for bed. I'll be up to check on you in a few minutes."

"I have a question first." Michael scooted his chair back. "What's going on between Grandpa and that lady with the white spiky hair?"

"Sandi?"

Michael nodded. "They were sitting together at the game, and Pepper said that all of us are going to her house for Thanksgiving—Sandi too."

"I don't think anything is going on. I think they're just friends."

Michael shook his head. "I think something is going on." He headed up the stairs.

Elise straightened her back as she flipped through photos of the boys posing in front of a set of armor; the boys wearing lederhosen, ready for a Volksmarch; and all four of them standing in front of the Rhine River on a fall day, the leaves of the trees along a stone wall bright orange and scarlet.

They had invited Maude and John to visit them in Germany. Ted had even offered to pay for the tickets, but they had declined. Why hadn't they come then instead of John wanting to go now? Maybe it was Maude who hadn't wanted to travel. She had been well then, or so they thought. She had heart problems at the end, unusual for a woman in her early sixties. She'd always been a little uptight; perhaps flying scared her.

Now John felt he could go. Still, she wanted it to be a family vacation. Maybe they could go back to Europe with John in a year or so. He could meet them in Seattle, and they could all fly together.

They would spend Thanksgiving with John at Rebekah's this year. Wasn't that enough?

Elise put the photos back in the box. She would e-mail Ted about his dad wanting to go with them, but she would wait to say anything about Sandi. Hopefully that would blow over. She logged on to her computer and opened Outlook; she had an e-mail from Ted.

> I talked with Dad this evening. He's decided not to come
> to Germany at Christmas.

Could John read her mind? Or had he decided he would rather spend Christmas with Sandi?

Chapter 24

*R*ebekah spun around in her kitchen, the skirt of her dress twirling around her legs. She loved Thanksgiving. She bumped into Patrick, who stood at the island arranging raw vegetables.

"Sorry, honey."

Patrick frowned.

"Please don't be grumpy."

"I'm not."

How could anyone be grumpy when the robust smell of the turkey roasting permeated the house, accented by the sweet smell of the candied yam casserole as it warmed on the stovetop? "You are. What's bugging you?"

"Let's see. Pepper needs a kidney, you have a new business, and there's a cougar stalking our farm."

"What are you talking about?" Rebekah took his hand. "We haven't seen the cougar for weeks and weeks. It's long gone."

Patrick pulled his hand away. "We're in a bad spot. You've totally minimized all of this."

"No." She pulled the meat thermometer from the drawer. "I haven't."

He crossed his arms. "It feels like everything is falling apart."

"Come on, Patrick." Rebekah stabbed the turkey's thigh with the thermometer. "God has given us each other, a wonderful family, this farm. You have a good job."

"We're here!" Sandi opened the back door and hurried in, followed by John.

"Hi there." Rebekah hugged them both. "Happy Thanksgiving!"

"You look so pretty." Sandi set her pie container down on the kitchen table. Rebekah looked down at her brown and burgundy paisley dress, mostly covered by a frilly apron Pepper had given her for Christmas last year. Sandi wore big hoop earrings and a sweater with a red and orange turkey that looked like a second-grade art project.

"Patrick." John shook the younger man's hand. "How are you?"

"Fine." Patrick dipped a carrot stick in ranch dressing. "Have a carrot."

A dog barked. "Did you bring Bear?" Rebekah asked.

John nodded. "He likes being out in the country. I didn't take him hunting this year. I thought a day on your farm would make him happy."

"We're happy to have a dog around. I keep meaning to get one."

Patrick shook his head.

"Patrick, every farm needs a dog. You said so yourself, for protection."

"I know, but that was before life got so complicated. Who has time to train a dog now?" Patrick dipped another carrot.

Rebekah nudged Patrick with her hip. "Why don't you go get Reid and pass a ball around?" That would be good for Mark and Michael when they arrived. They could all play football until the turkey was done.

"It's raining." Patrick sounded like Eeyore.

"Hardly."

"What's with hubby?" Sandi asked as Patrick yelled up the stairs for Reid.

"He's worrying. Again."

Reid thundered down the stairs, and John headed to the front door. Sandi took the lid off the pie container.

"Is that Dutch apple?" Rebekah asked.

Sandi nodded.

"My favorite."

"I know."

Bear barked. "Have you told Patrick about going to Nevada?" Sandi pushed up the sleeves on her sweater.

"Shh." Rebekah opened the oven door again. "I can take only so much of his doom and gloom." That wasn't the entire reason she hadn't told him. She didn't want to hear his reasons for her not going. How else was she going to find a kidney?

"Rebekah, don't get your—" Sandi began.

"Sorry we're late." Elise came through the back door, carrying a big crystal bowl. Mark followed her.

"Not a fan of football in the rain?" Sandi asked Mark.

Mark grunted and headed toward the dining room.

"Hi, Mark." Pepper's voice was followed by the clatter of a plate. "Want to help set the table?"

"Is it getting pretty wet out there? Should I call the guys in?" Rebekah called after Mark as the door swung shut.

"They're fine under the trees. Mark is just ignoring his grandfather, that's all." Elise set the bowl on the counter and brushed a strand of wet hair from her face.

"What happened?" Rebekah shut the oven door.

"John came by yesterday with a load of wood for our fireplace and asked Mark to get off the couch and help unload the truck." Elise crossed her arms. "Mark told his grandpa to shut up."

"Yikes."

"Yikes is right." Elise peeled off her wool coat and hung it by the door above the pile of boots. She wore a powder-blue angora sweater set and tan linen pants. "Mark wouldn't budge."

"Elise, how awful." Rebekah put her arm around her friend.

Sandi sighed. "Good thing that John decided not to go to Germany with you at Christmastime."

"John, will you pray?" Rebekah clasped her hands together.

"Dear God, we thank you for your blessings on this Thanksgiving. Thank you for family who are friends and friends who are family. Bless

this time we have together, and please protect Ted while he serves you overseas. Amen."

Rebekah took a serving of potatoes and passed them on to Elise. "It
must be so hard to be away from Ted on holidays."

"This will be the last. We'll be with him for Christmas." Elise looked
suddenly uncomfortable.

"Because we're going to Germany!" Michael added.

"Sounds like the trip of a lifetime," John said, spooning cranberry
sauce next to his turkey. "That will be great for all of you."

"You should come, Grandpa." Michael scooped mashed potatoes
onto his plate.

Mark coughed.

John shook his head. "Thanks, Michael. I don't think that would be
best right now."

Mark snickered. Elise concentrated on ladling gravy onto her potatoes.

"How come we never get to go anywhere?" Reid asked.

"Because your sister needs a kidney transplant." Patrick repositioned
his water glass.

"Honestly, Patrick." Rebekah passed the candied carrots on to Sandi.

"We never went anywhere before she needed a kidney transplant,
either." Reid's silver knife clattered on the antique china plate.

"We went to Arizona last Thanksgiving." Pepper raked her fork
through her potatoes.

"That doesn't count. It was just to see Grandma and Grandpa."

John cleared his throat.

"Oh, sorry, Mr. Shelton. I didn't mean anything by that." Reid
blushed.

"Yes, he did." Mark snickered again.

"Knock it off, Mark." Michael reached around Pepper and thrust the
basket of rolls into Mark's chest.

"Rebekah, is your china a family heirloom?" Elise asked. "It's beautiful."

"It came from my grandparents' ranch."

"That was back when farms made money." Patrick speared a sweet pickle.

"It was a ranch, not a farm." Rebekah grimaced and then clapped her hands together. "Do over. Let's go around the table and say what we're thankful for. I'll start." She sat up straight, Reid rolled his eyes, and Pepper heaped gravy on her potatoes.

"I'm thankful for the scrapbooking store and the new friends it has brought our way."

Sandi sat tall. "I'm thankful to be here. It's been a long time since I've been part of a family, let alone two."

John smiled across the table. Sandi blushed just a little.

"Your turn, Mark." Rebekah nodded at the boy.

His head bobbed. "What are we doing?"

"Saying what we're thankful for, you idiot." Reid shook his finger at Mark.

"Reid, stop it." Rebekah scowled over the centerpiece of minipumpkins and gourds.

"I'm not thankful for anything." Mark grinned.

"Come on," Pepper said. "You have to be thankful for something."

Mark tilted his head. "I'm thankful that we're moving to Seattle next year, away from Forest Falls." He shoveled a forkful of mashed potatoes into his mouth, smearing gravy across his upper lip.

"I'm thankful you'll be in Seattle next year too." Reid put his elbow on the table.

"Reid." Rebekah moved the centerpiece so she could see him better. "That's enough."

Bear began to bark. Pepper jumped, scraping her chair against the floor, and rushed to the window. "He's running across the field."

"Maybe he sees a deer." John craned his neck.

"Pepper, come sit down." Patrick waved his fork around as he talked. "I would like to have one civilized meal this year."

"Bear is going toward the forest. He just jumped the fence!"

"Come on, Pep. Back to the table." Rebekah cut her turkey.

Pepper sat down. "What happens if Bear finds the cougar?"

John swallowed and then said, "He'll tree it. A decade ago people could hunt cougars using dogs. Now it's illegal."

"Will he hurt Bear?" Reid asked.

"No." John passed the broccoli salad to Michael. "The cougar will just stay in a tree until Bear goes away."

"What if Bear doesn't come back?" Michael asked.

"He'll come back. He'll be fine." John smiled at his grandson.

"But Bear won't hurt the cougar?" Pepper asked.

John put down his knife and fork. "What's the big attraction to the cougar?"

"He's gorgeous. Big eyes. That fawn-colored fur. And he's so fast."

So much for the I'm-thankful game. "I wish we had a dog like Bear," Rebekah said.

"How about if I loan him to you?" John put his fork down. "As long as Bear likes it here, and until the cougar issue is resolved."

"He kind of looks like a raccoon, like he's wearing a mask, even though he's a dog," Pepper commented.

Rebekah shook her head at Pepper. "Well, he's nothing like a raccoon. He's not going to climb the tree outside your window." Rebekah turned to John. "I can't let you loan him to us. Bear will miss you."

"I'll come visit him. I'd feel a lot better, especially with Elise and the kids riding." John smiled. "Besides, he makes Sandi sneeze."

Rebekah put the last of the china away and collapsed in her desk chair. Maybe Pepper's grandmother had e-mailed. She turned on the computer and then noticed the light blinking on the answering machine. They'd missed a call. She pushed the button.

"Wednesday, 3:45 p.m." Yesterday afternoon. No one had checked the messages last evening. "Hey, Rebekah, it's Jamie. I just got off the phone with your insurance company. The appeal worked. Pepper has been fully reinstated. Happy Thanksgiving."

Rebekah clapped her hands together. "Patrick!" She ran into the dining room and then up the stairs. "Patrick." He sat at the computer next to Reid. "Jamie figured out the insurance."

"That's great! What did she do?"

"I don't know. She left a message yesterday afternoon, but we missed it." Rebekah massaged Patrick's shoulders.

Reid shook his head.

"Hey." Rebekah flapped her apron string at Reid. "This is a big deal. We have a lot to be thankful for."

"All you think or talk about is Pepper and her kidney. I'm sick of it."

"Reid." Patrick put his arm around his son. "We're concerned about Pepper, but that doesn't mean we're any less concerned about you."

Reid shrugged Patrick's arm away. "No, Dad, that's not true. Well, maybe it is for you, but not for Mom. She's totally obsessed with Pepper."

"No, I'm not." Rebekah untied her apron.

Reid nodded, his head bobbing up and down. "When was the last time you did anything for me? Bought anything for me? Made anything for me?"

"I do things for you all the time." Rebekah crossed her arms.

"Like what?"

"I grocery shop, cook, do laundry. Wait, you're almost fourteen. You should be doing your own laundry."

Reid turned back toward his computer.

Patrick squinted his eyes and barely shook his head at Rebekah as he mouthed, *Let it go.*

Rebekah turned and headed down the stairs. She was ready for Reid to grow up. To think that she used to work with troubled teens, that she actually had the audacity to believe she knew what she was doing.

Chapter 25

*J*t was too late in the evening for caffeine, but Elise poured herself a cup of Rebekah's free coffee anyway, hoping to wash away her day-after-Thanksgiving lethargy. Only a handful of women had shown up for Midnight Madness. Pepper was having an overnighter at Ainsley's house, and many of the women were out of town for the holiday or had guests. She picked up a copy of the *Memory Makers* magazine that Rebekah had dropped on the table.

"I'm thinking about buying Adobe Photoshop." Sandi punched a hole in a tag and ran a piece of yellow yarn through it.

"Why?" Rebekah asked.

"No mess. You download everything and print the page. Voilà. You're done." Sandi pulled more yarn from her new tote.

"But there's no texture." Rebekah started for the stairs.

"And no mess, no storing all this stuff." Sandi pulled a letter *S* from a page of stickers and rubbed it onto the tag.

"Where are those photos from?" Elise put down the magazine and nodded at Sandi's page.

"My farm." Sandi rubbed a *U* on the tag.

"Your farm?"

"I sold it five years ago."

"Why?" Elise leaned against the table.

"I couldn't keep it after my husband died." Sandi positioned an *N*.

Elise put her hand on her chin. "I'm so sorry. How did he die?" She had known Sandi for almost three months. How had she missed that she was a widow? She had assumed Sandi had been single all her life.

"He had a massive stroke; he was only sixty-seven." Sandi rubbed an *F* on the tag. "I switched to hospice nursing after that."

"Do you have any kids?" Maybe there were other things about Sandi's life that Elise had missed.

Sandi shook her head. "We were older when we married. I was in my midforties, and he was in his late fifties. He'd been married before but didn't have any kids."

"Sandi." Rebekah hurried up the stairs with a box. "Just keep your stuff here if you don't want it cluttering up your house. That goes for all of you. I should get lockers installed."

"No." Sandi rubbed another letter on the tag. "You should just carry Photoshop."

Rebekah pulled up a chair next to Sandi and slid the box of animal cutouts onto the table. "Oh, your sunflowers. I remember you talking about them. You miss those, don't you?"

Sandi nodded and placed an *L* on her tag. "Rebekah, you should plant sunflowers at your place, along the fence line."

Rebekah turned the album around for a closer look at the layout of sunflower photos. "Would the horses eat them?"

Sandi smiled. "I have no idea. You could always find out." She repositioned the album in front of her and affixed the tag with the word *Sunflowers*.

Elise scanned the room. Maybe there were things about the other women that she had missed too.

"Are you getting ideas for Mark's book?" Rebekah asked, nodding toward the magazine.

"Not really. I like to read the stories on the layouts, but sometimes the words are too small to read." She turned the magazine around. "Like this layout. Here's a preemie baby with a whole bunch of tubes and a story with lots of tiny, tiny words."

"It's called journaling." Rebekah opened the box. "Pepper is going to love these cutouts."

"I have a magnifying glass." Sandi dug in her bag.

"Oh, good." Elise pulled the magazine closer.

"What do you hear from Ted?" Rebekah asked

"Don't ask." Elise held the magnifying glass over the layout.

"Why?"

"He spent last weekend touring castles on the Rhine." Rebekah laughed.

"Must be tough, huh?" Elise put down the magnifying glass.

"Come on, Elise. It is tough." Sandi took out the next page of her album. "I hear about the emergency surgeries, burn victims, amputees. All sorts of hard stuff."

Elise bristled.

"I wonder if they still do scrapbooking in Germany," Rebekah mused. Was she changing the subject on purpose? "After all, that's where it started."

"They didn't nine years ago. That's one of the things I liked about it." Elise cringed at the sarcasm in her voice. "Sorry." Elise looked through the magnifying glass again. "I still can't see the words; they're just too tiny."

Sandi took the glass.

Elise flipped to the next page in the magazine. "Look, a layout of a little boy throwing a tantrum. I love it. Reality scrapbooking."

"Let me see." Rebekah leaned over.

Elise read the headline. "*You're cute even when you're angry.* Forget what I said. There's nothing real about this." She spread out the magazine so everyone could see.

Sandi leaned over the table. "Love the metal frames around the photos. Is that a Photoshop layout?"

Rebekah shook her head.

"It has to be. That mom couldn't have time for all of this." Sandi spread her arms wide. "Not with all those tantrums."

"But, Sandi, you can't even figure out how to download your photos." Rebekah went back to sorting the cutouts. "How are you going to run Photoshop?"

Sandi blew Rebekah a kiss.

"It's that whole revisionist scrapbooking mentality." Elise flipped the page.

"Speaking of…" Sandi stood. "You should see the photos that Ainsley had at the retreat."

Rebekah held up a raccoon cutout. "I can't wait until Pepper sees these. She hates raccoons."

"What are the pictures of?" Elise closed the magazine.

"Sandi." Rebekah warned, scooping the cutouts into her hand.

But Sandi looked directly at Elise and said, "Mark hitting Michael." She poured herself a Dr Pepper.

"I've already seen them." Elise stood. "In fact, I have the doubles." Elise glanced at her watch but couldn't focus. Why had Sandi brought up those photos? "I told the boys I would be home at a reasonable time." She grabbed the magazine and her coat, headed for the stairs, and then stopped. "Rebekah, I need to buy the magazine. I almost stole it."

"I'm coming." Rebekah dumped the animal cutouts into a box and followed her downstairs.

Rebekah scanned the bar code. "I don't know what's with Sandi," she whispered.

"Don't worry about it." Elise pulled out a ten-dollar bill.

"I have a favor to ask." Rebekah gave Elise her change.

Elise nodded.

"Patrick's going out of town on business tomorrow morning. He has meetings in Chicago on Sunday and Monday." Rebekah slipped the magazine into a bag. "Would you want to go with me and take the kids to Portland on Sunday after church? They could ice-skate while we shop."

Elise wanted to laugh. Some favor. "Sounds like fun. I'll talk to the boys."

"I haven't started my Christmas shopping this year." Rebekah handed Elise her change. "Yours is all done, right?"

"Mostly. But I'm not doing much for the boys since we'll be in Germany."

Rebekah started to say something and then stopped.

Elise waited.

"I'll see you Sunday then, if not before." Rebekah walked Elise to the door and then hurried toward the stairs, back to the other women.

"Come on, Mark. Get up. We're going to be late for church." Elise stood in the doorway of Mark's room. Icy rain pelted his window.

Michael thundered up the stairs. "Mom, the phone is for you."

"Mark, get up."

"I don't feel well." He sounded pathetic.

"Get up."

"Mom, the phone." Michael waved it in front of her face.

Elise jerked Mark's pillow from under his head, took it with her, and then grabbed the phone, expecting Ted. It was Rebekah.

"Hey, I have a favor to ask. Can you drop me off at the airport after we go ice-skating?"

"What's going on?"

"I have a ticket to Reno, to see Pepper's birth grandma. Don't tell my kids. They think I'm flying to Phoenix to see my parents."

Elise ducked into the bathroom. "What time does your flight leave?"

"Six."

"I guess we can all go in my Volvo." Michael and Reid could fit in the jump seat—barely. "When do you come back?"

"Tomorrow evening. Sandi said she would pick me up—and watch the shop during the day. But do you think you could spend tonight out at my place? That way you guys could feed the horses when you get back. And you could get all the kids off to school."

"Sure." Elise opened the shades in Mark's room.

"Thanks. See you in a few minutes at church."

Elise started down the stairs. "We're running late. If we're not there, I'll swing by your place to pick you up."

"Mom, I want to go to church." Michael was dressed and ready to go.

"Rebekah, if Michael's there, give him a ride to your house, okay?"

Mark sped around the rink, his arms flying back and forth.

"He's good." Rebekah snapped her digital camera.

Elise nodded. "He skated in Colorado, played hockey some."

"I bet he loved it."

"No, he wasn't crazy about it." That's the way Mark was with sports—good without trying, but not passionate.

Reid skated by and made a face at Rebekah. She laughed. "We used to skate when we lived here. Reid didn't really like it then, either."

Michael zipped by, chasing Mark, and Pepper followed.

Elise held a pretzel in both hands, waiting for it to cool. "When did you decide to go to Nevada?"

"I got the ticket on Wednesday."

"Before Thanksgiving?"

Rebekah nodded.

Elise shook her head. "Why did you wait until today to tell me you were going?"

Rebekah shrugged. "I wasn't sure until today that I was actually going through with it."

"Have you been there before?"

"I went for Mandy's funeral—Pepper's birth mom." Rebekah held her digital camera away from her body, tracking the kids in the screen. "She overdosed when she was eighteen. Pepper was nine months. I didn't take her with me." Rebekah zoomed in on the kids. "I was afraid that Polly, Mandy's mother, might change her mind, that she might want to adopt Pepper."

"Did Mandy's mom know who you were then?"

"Yep." Rebekah snapped a picture of Pepper waving her arms from side to side, speeding after the boys.

"So you talked with her? All of that?"

Rebekah nodded.

"What is she like?"

"She was overwhelmed back then. They'd had Mandy in treatment. Then she ran away and ended up in Portland. Polly came to Portland once and took Mandy home. She ran away again and got pregnant with Pepper. Polly and her husband separated, and finally Polly felt like she needed to put her energy into her youngest daughter."

Rebekah waved as Reid came around again. "Are we about ready to leave?" he asked.

"Five more minutes." Rebekah took another picture. "I'm taking Pepper's scrapbook. I think when Polly sees what a great kid Pepper is, she'll help me. How could she not?"

"I hope she will." Elise took a deep breath. "What does Patrick say?"

"He doesn't know. Don't say anything, okay? If he calls."

"What am I supposed to say?" Elise took a bite of the pretzel.

"That I'm out. He'll probably call my cell anyway." Rebekah dropped her camera into her purse. "Time to go." The kids zipped by again, Michael on Mark's heels, Pepper close behind.

Mark laughed as he spun in a circle toward the middle. "Catch me," he taunted and sped off to the bench.

Rain hammered the roof of the Volvo and fell in sheets over the windshield. "We're spending the night at Reid and Pepper's." Elise's muscles tightened all the way down her back. "I told you that this morning."

"No, you didn't."

"I did. That's why I told you to throw pajamas, clothes for tomorrow, and your toothbrush into your backpack." A semi sped by.

"No, you told me to bring my backpack."

Elise arched her back, trying to ease her anxiety.

Mark crossed his arms. "I don't want to stay out there."

"Hush."

Michael, Pepper, and Reid slept in the backseat.

Elise's cell rang. She scooted her purse toward Mark. "Answer it. I can't talk right now. It's raining too hard."

It was Ted. Mark gave him one- or two-word answers. "Fine. I-5. Portland. Mom's driving." Mark turned toward her. "Dad wants to know if Michael got the e-mail he sent, the one on blood types. No one ever e-mailed him back."

Elise glanced in the rearview mirror. It was too dark to see Michael. Was he really asleep? "I don't know," she lied.

Mark kept talking to Ted. "Dad says he'll send it again, so Michael can read it."

Mark talked to Ted a little longer and then hung up. "He said he'll call you back." Mark paused. "Maybe you should get tested to see if you could donate a kidney to Pepper, since Rebekah can't."

"Is that what Dad said?"

Mark shook his head.

The rain slowed, and Elise turned the windshield wipers down. "Did you finish your homework?" She pulled into the middle lane to pass a truck.

"You're changing the subject."

"Mark." She sat up straight and caught Pepper's reflection in the rearview mirror. "Your father's gone. I can't donate a kidney." She had thought it through, even more today after being around Rebekah and Pepper. She was sympathetic, very sympathetic, but Ted was in Germany. She couldn't risk herself for someone else's child; she needed to take care of her own two kids.

"I was right." Mark drilled her with his eyes. "You do think only about yourself."

Chapter 26

*R*ebekah stood at the window of her room in the Fairfield Inn. Ten rings. Maybe seven thirty was too early to call. She had awakened at five and gone swimming at six. The sooner she could speak with Polly the better.

"Hello."

"Polly, it's Rebekah. Pepper's mom—adoptive mom. Please don't hang up." Silence. But no dial tone. That was good. "I'm in town. In Sparks. I'd like to see you, just to chat. Just to get some information."

More silence.

"I can come out to your house or meet you at a coffee shop, wherever you like, whatever time you like. I just have to make my five o'clock flight." Was she there? "Polly?"

"If I meet with you, will you leave me alone?"

"Yes."

"You can come here. Make it nine thirty. I have to be at work by eleven."

Rebekah collapsed onto the bed. "Thank you, God," she whispered.

Her cell began to ring. *Patrick.* She slid the phone under the pillow. She would call him after she talked with Polly.

Rebekah sidestepped a pink and purple bike with training wheels sprawled across the sidewalk as she hurried to Polly's front door. It was the same split-level that Rebekah had visited over a decade ago. She knocked firmly. No answer. She knocked again.

"Coming."

A gray and tired Polly opened the door. Her hair was cut short, and wrinkles lined her eyes and mouth. She wore a blue tunic and pants, and she was smaller than Rebekah remembered, not much bigger than Pepper.

"Hello, Rebekah."

"Polly." Rebekah hugged her. Polly stiffened and patted Rebekah's shoulder.

"Mom, can you pick up Cadee after school?" A woman stood in the hall. She had blond hair, but much darker than Pepper's fairylike hair. She wore a short skirt and combat boots.

"Adrianna, this is Rebekah. Mandy's little girl's mom. Do you remember her from the funeral?"

Adrianna shook her head.

"Hi." Rebekah smiled. Adrianna was twelve or thirteen at the funeral, Pepper's age.

"Nice to see you." Adrianna crossed her arms. "What's this about?"

"Rebekah just wanted to stop by."

"Do you want me to stay, Mom?"

"No, Adrianna. Get ready for work."

"So can you pick up Cadee?"

"Sure."

Adrianna waved her hand and headed back down the hall.

"She works in a restaurant—sometimes during the day, sometimes at night." Polly fussed with a faded pink doily hanging on the back of a torn recliner.

"May I sit?" Rebekah waited until Polly sat on the couch and then planted herself a half foot away and opened the scrapbook.

"Mandy had a fish named Pepper—a bug-eyed, black goldfish."

Rebekah attempted a smile. Thank goodness Reid wasn't along; Pepper would never hear the end of being named after a fish.

"Mandy was little then, seven or eight."

"You must miss her."

"I don't miss the bad times." Polly shook her head.

"Do Adrianna and Cadee live with you?"

Polly nodded. Rebekah moved closer with the scrapbook. "Here's Pepper on her favorite horse, an Appaloosa named Sky. She only rides him in the corral, but she rides the other horses all around our farm."

"She looks happy."

"She is."

Polly pointed to Reid. "Your son has grown up."

"They both have. Here's Pepper with Bear. He's a dog that has been staying on our farm. Long story. Anyway, I took this picture on Thanksgiving." And put it in the scrapbook last night. "She loves animals."

"So did Mandy."

"And here she is on her first day of school this year."

"She looks like Mandy."

Rebekah nodded. "I think so too."

"Like a little pixie." Polly shifted her weight. "I don't have much time. I have to get to work. I go in at mealtimes, at the nursing home."

"Oh."

"I hurt my shoulder. I'm on partial disability."

"I'm sorry." Rebekah turned toward Polly. "Did you get my letter?"

Polly blushed.

Rebekah slipped out of her blue blazer. "Pepper is sick; I came to ask for your help." Rebekah closed the scrapbook.

"The kidney problem?"

Rebekah nodded. "As I said in the letter, she needs to have a transplant soon."

"She's on a list, right?"

"Yes, but the list takes a long time. We're looking for a related donor who has a compatible blood type. Then that person would need to be tested to see if the tissue matched."

"I'm not strong."

"What about Adrianna?"

"She's not like Mandy was, but she couldn't handle something like that. She's not exactly stable."

"The procedure is much easier than it used to be, and the recovery is minimal."

Polly shook her head. "Something will come up for Pepper. I'm sorry; I can't help you."

Rebekah slumped back against the couch.

"You need to go."

Rebekah gripped the scrapbook. "May I send you photos of Pepper from time to time? Could we stay in touch?"

Polly clasped her hands together. "Please don't tell her that I said no. I don't want her to be disappointed in me, not any more than she already is."

Rebekah reached for Polly's hand. "She's not disappointed in you, honestly." *She has a good life*, she wanted to say, *except for needing a kidney.*

Polly pulled her hand away and stood. "Good-bye now."

Rebekah clutched the scrapbook. "Polly, I'm sorry."

"What for?" Polly swung open the door.

"For asking." *For your life. That Mandy died. That you'll never know what a wonderful person Pepper is.*

"Go on now."

Rebekah sat in her rental car. Polly backed a Ford Escort out of her bare garage and waved, just a tiny toss of her hand, as she drove by. Adrianna stared straight ahead.

Polly hadn't cried at Mandy's graveside service. Adrianna was there, and a group of her friends, huddled together for warmth against the December wind. The minister was the funeral home chaplain, and there were no neighbors, no friends from Polly's work, no grandparents, no father. Polly had told Rebekah matter-of-factly that Mandy's dad had taken a job on an oil rig in the Gulf and said he couldn't make it. Rebekah missed Mandy then—missed her commentary about her family, about her mom's despair, her father's anger. Mandy had kept a few of her visitations with Pepper, but most of the time she just didn't show. A few times she'd said she wanted to be a good mom to Pepper, but she never followed through with appointments or classes.

I need to get home. Rebekah felt a sense of urgency. Maybe she could get an earlier flight. She would drive straight to the airport. She would rather wait in Portland until Sandi could pick her up than spend another minute so far from home.

Rebekah closed her eyes as the plane took off. She hated the feeling of being pinned to the chair, totally out of control. Ten people died each day because they needed a kidney transplant. A tear slid from her eye. She swept it away. *God,* Rebekah prayed, *don't make me face life without Pepper.* She opened her eyes and turned her head toward the tiny patch of window she could see past the young man sitting next to her. Clouds rolled in over the bare, brown hills that fell away as the plane ascended. Another tear pooled. She searched her pockets for a tissue and then her purse. The tear escaped. She wiped her face with the sleeve of her jacket.

A flight attendant hurried by and then returned a minute later with a packet of tissues. She patted Rebekah's arm. "Let me know if you need anything else."

"Thanks," Rebekah whispered. How could Polly be so heartless? Rebekah blew her nose. Why had she put so much trust in Polly? The plane hit turbulence, and the fasten-your-seat-belt light came on. The sky darkened with rain clouds. Lightning flashed. More tears raced down Rebekah's face. Her twentysomething seatmate pressed his nose against the window.

"We're having a little turbulence." The pilot's voice came across the loudspeaker, deep and reassuring. "We'll be out of the storm in a few minutes."

Another bolt of lightning flashed, this time closer.

Rebekah wadded the tissue in her hand.

Pepper was in the middle of a storm, but she didn't act like it. She never seemed to worry about when she would have the transplant—or if. She accepted that she would. Why didn't she worry?

Because she trusts. That quiet voice.

Rebekah sank against the chair and gripped the armrest.

Trust me.

God, I do trust. I'm just trying to do everything I can to figure this out. No, she didn't trust—not as she used to, not as she had when Pepper was a baby and when Pepper was ill four years ago. What had changed?

Rebekah, give up control.

She leaned against the headrest as the plane flew out of the storm, escaping the ominous clouds. Lightning flashed miles away. Rebekah closed her eyes. Maybe she didn't know how to trust anymore; she was so used to making things happen, to taking charge.

How could she change?

lise wiped peanut-butter cookie batter off Rebekah's kitchen counter. The entire kitchen sparkled, and soon it would smell of freshly baked cookies. She had also caught up the laundry, vacuumed, and changed the sheets on all the beds. She couldn't donate a kidney, but she could at least make things a little easier for Rebekah. She thought about riding the mare during the afternoon, maybe even Sky, but the rain never let up, and she knew the trail would be slick.

She stirred a pot of stew. The bus would drop off the kids in just a few minutes. Her purse, slung over the back of a dining room chair, began to ring. Elise grabbed her phone. It was Ted. She wandered into the living room as they talked. "Rebekah should be home in a few hours, then the boys and I will go home." Ted brought up blood types. Elise stood at the bottom of the stairs. At least she didn't have to worry about any of the kids hearing her talk.

"You should get tested, Elise."

"Ted, that would be ludicrous."

"Why?"

"I'm a single mom, remember?" She walked to the front window. The school bus stopped down the road.

"Everyone would help you."

"Who would help me?"

"Dad, the women from the shop…" Ted hesitated. "People from church."

"Rebekah asked Pepper's birth family if one of them could donate a kidney."

"And?"

Elise watched Pepper swing her backpack at Mark. Reid ran ahead. Michael walked backward. Was he yelling something at Mark?

"I'll let you know what Rebekah found out." Elise headed back into the kitchen. "She was pretty sure they would agree to be tested."

They talked about Ted's weekend trip to the castles. "Don't tell Michael," Ted joked.

The kids clambered up the back steps and through the door. "Dibs on the computer," Pepper yelled.

Reid pushed ahead and tore through the kitchen with Mark and Michael behind him.

"The kids are home." Elise held the phone tightly against her ear. "Call back soon, okay?"

Mark sat down at Rebekah's desk and turned on her computer.

"Help me with the horses, Mark." Elise slipped a tray of biscuits into the oven and set the timer.

Pepper jumped down from her stool at the breakfast bar and grabbed her raincoat off the hook. "Mom's computer is really slow, but Dad took his laptop, so this is your only choice since Reid won't let you use his. His is slow too; he wants a new one for Christmas."

"Come on. We need to get the horses fed." Elise pulled the hood of her parka onto her head.

"Why can't Reid and Michael do it?"

"Because I asked you, Mark." She slipped on work gloves. "You had an hour after school to relax. Now it's time to work."

"Mom, that's not fair." Mark turned toward her.

"Come on, Mark. I need your help." Elise opened the back door. A gust of wind yanked it from her hand. She knew once Mark got to the barn, he would be happy to help.

Pepper zipped her jacket, and Mark followed her out the door. "Get a coat," Elise commanded.

"I'm fine."

Bear poked his head out of his doghouse, which John had hauled out to the farm, and then followed the trio to the barn, sniffing their hands as they walked. Elise struggled against the wind and pushed open the barn door. "Okay, Pepper, tell us what we need to do."

"Feed and water the horses, put out more hay, and scoop the poop."

"Mark, you water. Pepper, you feed them. I'll start scooping. Whoever is done first can put down the cedar shavings."

Elise put her hand out to Sky. Why was she always surprised when a horse responded so positively? He brushed his head up against Elise's face and then nuzzled her neck. "Are you happy to see me?" Elise rubbed his forehead.

"Do you think the cougar is out tonight?" Mark asked Pepper.

"Not in the rain." Pepper poured oats into the bucket.

"What do you think, Sky? Is the cougar going to come out of the forest?" Mark stood on the railing of Sky's stall.

"Don't scare the horses, Mark," Pepper commanded

"He doesn't know what I'm saying."

"Sure he does." Pepper spread oats in the palomino's feeding trough.

"You're full of it."

"Mark." Elise headed to the back door with the shovel. "Stop it." She didn't need sibling squabbling between children who weren't even siblings. "Mark, help me with the door. Please."

He swung it open, and she backed out into the storm, flinging the poop from the shovel onto the pile, the wind whipping off her hood.

"Use the wheelbarrow." Pepper nodded toward the green wheelbarrow in an unused stall.

"Good idea." Elise placed the shovel in it.

"Yeah, good idea, Mom." Mark grinned and rubbed his arms with his hands.

Elise struggled to get the wheelbarrow inside the stall.

"We leave it outside the stall," Pepper said. "It makes it easier."

"I see." Elise shoved the wheelbarrow; the gate swung against it. She lost her balance, and the wheelbarrow shot through the gate and toppled over.

Mark began to laugh.

"I'm going to pull the biscuits out of the oven." Elise headed to the barn door. She had forgotten to ask Michael to listen for the timer.

Bear barked furiously and paced along the pasture. Elise turned toward the forest as Bear vaulted over the fence, his massive body lunging into the night. "Bear!" she yelled, cupping her hands around her mouth, trying to shout above the wind that howled through the spruce trees near the house. He tore through the field. Along the edge of the willows near the creek was another animal. Was it a deer? No. It was too low to the ground.

A horrible scream brought Pepper dashing out of the barn. "Where's the cougar?"

Another wail filled the air—worse than a woman's screech, worse than a baby in the night or a fight between two tomcats.

"Bear is chasing it into the forest." Elise pressed her body against the fence.

"I can't see either one of them." Pepper jumped on the railing.

"It's getting too dark. They're too far." Elise pushed her hood from her head, but she couldn't hear the cougar or Bear. The rain beat against her face.

"Bear!" Pepper shouted. "Come back!"

✄

Elise sat at the head of the oak table. Pepper sat sideways in her chair, her feet pointed toward the kitchen.

"What are these?" Michael asked.

"Hockey pucks." Mark slid a biscuit across the table.

"The stew is very good." Reid slurped a spoonful as he talked.

"Thank you." Elise put her spoon next to her plate. "Pepper, you should eat."

Pepper drummed her fingers along the oak table. "When is Bear going to come home?"

"I didn't think you liked that dog." Reid sawed away at a biscuit.

"I never said that." Pepper went to the back door and opened it, called Bear's name, and then closed the door. "How far would he go?"

"Maybe he went home to Grandpa." Mark pushed his plate toward the middle of the table.

Elise shook her head at him.

"Was that a bark?" Pepper opened the door again.

"You're imagining things," Mark yelled after her.

"He's back!" Pepper rushed outside in her socks.

Elise hurried after her, into the night. Bear crawled under the fence, his coat soaked and matted. Pepper knelt beside him and rubbed him with her hands. The storm had calmed.

"You're going to get wet." Mark stood on the deck.

Pepper took Bear's head in her hands. "He has a scratch on his nose." She turned to Elise. "Do you think the cougar did it?"

"He wouldn't have a face left if the cougar did it." Mark turned and went back in the house.

"It was probably blackberry bushes." Elise knelt down by the dog. The scratch started near his eye and ended on his nose. Should she call John?

"Mom, phone." Michael ran down the steps.

Elise took it, expecting Rebekah.

"Hi."

It wasn't Rebekah; it was Patrick.

"Reid said Rebekah is in Phoenix." Patrick's voice was agitated.

"Uh-huh." Elise ducked into the kitchen, hoping Pepper would stay outside with Bear.

"I called her parents. Her mom tried to cover, but I know Rebekah isn't there. Where is she?"

"I think she's on her way home."

"Elise," Patrick's voice cracked, "where did she go?"

Elise swung open the kitchen door. The boys apparently had gone upstairs.

"Elise?"

"Nevada."

Patrick was quiet for a long moment. "Thanks. I'll keep trying to reach her on her cell."

hanks, Sandi." Rebekah grabbed her overnight bag from the back of Sandi's Jeep. Bear ran to meet her, his tail wagging. "Thanks for watching the shop too."

"My pleasure."

"Do you want to come in?"

Sandi shook her head. "I'm going to stop by John's. He has dinner ready."

Rebekah leaned against the seat. "You just said there's nothing going on with you two."

Sandi shrugged. "There isn't."

Rebekah shook her head and smiled. "Right. Well, hopefully, I'll see you tomorrow." She slammed the door and turned toward the house. Bear stayed between her and the fence. "What is it, boy?"

The back door flew open. "Mom, we saw the cougar!" Pepper ran out on the deck in her socks. "Bear chased it for a really long time."

Rebekah cringed. "I didn't think it would come back."

Elise stood at the door. "How was your trip?"

"Fine." Rebekah followed Pepper through the door, dropped her bag, and then whispered to Elise, "I'll tell you later."

"What did Grandma and Grandpa send me?"

"Send you?"

"Me and Reid. They always send us stuff."

"Not this time, sweet pea." Rebekah hadn't thought to buy them gifts at the airport.

Pepper's face fell.

"Pepper, please take off your socks." Elise stood at the sink and scrubbed a pot. "You're tracking all over the floor."

"Oops," she said, peeling her socks from her feet. "It's the second pair I've gotten wet tonight."

Rebekah patted Pepper on the head. "The kitchen looks great."

"Elise did a ton of work." Pepper wadded her socks in her hand.

"You shouldn't have." Rebekah hung her coat on the rack.

"I didn't do that much."

"How close was the cougar?" Rebekah put her purse on her desk.

"In the field. Bear chased it back into the forest," Elise answered.

Reid sauntered into the kitchen. "Hi, Mom."

Rebekah hugged him, pulled him close. "Take my bag upstairs, would you?"

"Pepper, please go tell Mark and Michael to come down." Elise dried the pot. "Patrick called," she said to Rebekah.

"Figures." Rebekah slipped out of her blazer.

"Reid told him you were at your parents'." Elise dried her hands. "Patrick said he had tried your cell."

"He did. About a million times."

"He also tried your parents. I ended up telling him you were in Nevada; I couldn't lie." Elise hung the towel on the refrigerator handle.

Rebekah pulled a chair out and sat down at the kitchen table. "I've made a mess of things."

"Patrick will understand once you explain."

"No, he was right. I shouldn't have gone. It was too much to ask of Polly. Life is too hard for her. I was only thinking about my own desperation."

"And Pepper's needs."

Rebekah rested her chin on her hand.

"When does Patrick come home?" Elise asked.

"Tomorrow." Rebekah bit the scar on her lip. "Unless he takes a late flight tonight. Elise—" Rebekah wanted to ask her about trust. Did she trust God to take care of Ted? to take care of her and the boys?

Pepper pranced back into the room. "Mom, I have a doctor's appointment on Wednesday."

"Really?"

"They left a message. It's at 2:15."

Rebekah checked the calendar. "Reid has a basketball game that afternoon."

"He can come to our house before the game," Elise said.

"I wonder if I can get Sandi to watch the shop again. I hate to keep asking her."

"I don't think she minds. If she does, John could watch the boys, and I can watch the shop."

"Thanks." Rebekah put her arm around Elise. "Thanks for everything."

Elise hugged her back, a dainty hug, but still, it was something.

Rebekah headed up the stairs with a stack of clean towels that Elise had left in the dryer. All of the laundry was caught up for a few minutes, thanks to Elise, until the kids took their dirty clothes off. Rebekah couldn't remember the last time she didn't have piles of laundry to wash. Reid sat at his computer on the landing, and Pepper stood over him, both of her hands glued to the back of the chair.

"It's my turn," Pepper wailed.

"Use Mom's computer."

"It's too slow."

"It's as fast as this one." Reid slammed his back against Pepper's hands and clicked onto his e-mail.

"I want to check my mail." Pepper yanked her hands out from behind her brother's back and planted them on her hips.

"Pepper, go downstairs." Rebekah crammed the stack of towels into the hall closet.

"He always gets his way." Pepper yanked on the back of Reid's chair.

"I wish we'd never adopted you." Reid stood and pulled the chair back toward the computer.

"Stop." Rebekah stepped between her children. Why would Reid say that? "Pepper, go downstairs. Reid, you have five minutes." Rebekah crossed her arms, opened her mouth again, and then closed it.

"You know what's ironic?" Reid hunkered over the keyboard. "That Dad is a computer geek, and we have the slowest computers in the entire state."

"Be thankful you have a computer." Rebekah headed down the stairs.

Reid pushed back from the computer and stood over the railing. "Mom?"

"What, Reid?"

"Thanks for sticking up for me in front of Pepper."

"Reid, that's not what I did." She climbed to the top stair. "And you shouldn't have made that comment about wishing we hadn't adopted Pepper. That's hurtful."

"You know what else is ironic?" Reid hunkered back down in his chair.

"What?"

"That Pepper thinks you favor me when she's so obviously your favorite."

"Reid, that's not true."

"Mom!" Pepper called from the kitchen. "Your computer just froze."

"It's time for bed anyway. Pepper, you can use this computer tomorrow," she yelled, her voice growing shrill. She was too tired to deal with them for another second. She turned back to Reid. "I do not favor Pepper."

"Do you remember when I wore my socks outside and you made me buy my own?"

She did. They were living in Portland, and he would run outside and shoot baskets in his stocking feet. "And?"

"Pepper wears her socks outside all the time, and you don't even tell her not to."

✂

An hour later, after Rebekah had checked the horses and fed Bear, she pulled back the comforter. Clean sheets. Rebekah's eyes filled with tears; Elise had done too much. Just as she settled her head on her pillow, Bear began to bark, and a car turned into the driveway. A door slammed.

Rebekah hopped out of bed and stood at the window. Patrick grabbed his laptop and bag out of the trunk and tipped his head back, scanning the house. Did he see her? Could she fake being asleep? She climbed back into bed.

He would double-check that both doors were locked, drink a glass of water, and make sure the dryer was off before coming to bed. Five minutes later she heard his footsteps on the stairway and then across the landing. "Rebekah, I know you're awake." He turned on the lamp. "All you had to do was answer your phone."

She turned toward him. "I know. I should have."

"I was frantic." He sat down on the bed.

"I'm sorry."

"You can't imagine the things that ran through my head."

Actually, she could.

He stood and hung up his jacket. "I thought we had decided we wouldn't ask Polly about donating a kidney."

"You decided that." She sat cross-legged on the bed. "But I shouldn't have asked Polly."

Patrick's hand froze on the top button of his shirt.

"You were right." She knew he liked to hear those words, but she didn't often say them. "I need to trust God for a kidney. I'm just not sure that I can."

Patrick sat down on the bed. "Maybe it would be easier for you to trust if I stopped worrying so much."

Rebekah nodded.

"I'm sorry." He put his arm around her.

She shook her head and began to cry.

Patrick handed her a tissue and took her in his arms. "It will be all right."

"I know."

"Why are you crying?"

Rebekah shook her head. She leaned against his shoulder, soaking his shirt. Fear. That's why she was crying. She was so afraid.

The smells of the shop comforted Rebekah—the Murphy Oil Soap she used on the old oak floors, the hint of coffee, and the crisp scent of paper. She flipped the sign from Closed to Open. Sandi had moved the patriotic section to the front. It looked good.

Rebekah turned on the computer to make fliers for the Thursday morning class and Midnight Madness. What should she teach on Thursday? Creating timeless albums? Was it possible? Pepper's first album was full of gingham-patterned paper that Rebekah now despised, but maybe in another decade she would find it endearing.

Elise hurried by the window and through the door of the shop. "I had a few errands to run and thought I would stop by. How are you doing?"

"Fine."

"Fine?"

"Not so fine." Rebekah opened Word to make the flier. "I'm in a funk."

Elise unwound her green scarf from around her neck.

"Listen to what the transplant coordinator told me this morning." Rebekah stepped away from the computer. "We were chatting on the phone about the list and surgery. She said that kidney transplants are considered elective."

"What?" Elise held her scarf in midair. "That's ridiculous."

Rebekah continued, "You have to have a liver, pancreas, heart, and lungs to live, but you can survive on dialysis. So technically almost any surgery can bump a kidney transplant."

"Except nose jobs, right?"

Rebekah nodded. "And liposuction."

Elise unzipped her jacket.

"Oh, well, surgery is a ways off." Rebekah shrugged. "Now we'll wait and see what happens with the list and work toward dialysis, just in case."

"Have you talked to Patrick?"

"I apologized. He came home late last night." Rebekah leaned against the counter. "What are you up to today? Besides errands."

"I'm going to volunteer in the library this afternoon—after I run into Salem to get money pouches for the boys to carry their passports."

Rebekah picked up a box of Disney products off the floor. Maybe she could host a card-making class that would appeal to Pepper and her friends. "Check on Pepper after lunch, would you? We had a rough morning."

Elise nodded and flung her scarf back around her neck.

Rebekah's cell rang. "Mom, I'm not feeling so hot." Pepper's voice fell flat.

"What's the matter?"

"I can't concentrate, and I feel kind of sick. And itchy."

"I'm on my way." Rebekah stuffed the phone into her pocket.

"Is Pepper sick? I can watch the shop while you go get her." Elise pulled her scarf off again.

"But you need to get to Salem."

"No. I can go tonight."

"I'll bring her here and see how bad she is." Rebekah grabbed her purse and hurried out the door.

A few minutes later she stood in the middle of the school hall during passing period. Reid and Michael jostled each other.

"Hey, Reid," she called.

He turned.

"Pepper's sick."

He shrugged.

"I came to get her."

"She's faking. She probably just wants to go shopping." He hurried ahead, slapping Michael on the back.

Rebekah had volunteered in the school last year, but that felt like ages ago. She felt lost as she hurried into the office. "Hi, sweet pea. Do you feel like you can go back to the shop with me?"

Pepper nodded.

"How much water have you had today?"

Pepper gathered her coat and backpack. "None."

"Did you drink much last night?"

"Not really."

"What did you have for breakfast?" Rebekah led the way through the crowded hall.

"A donut."

Rebekah stopped. "Where did you get a donut?"

"From Ainsley."

"Pepper, you can't eat that stuff. I thought you made yourself whole-wheat toast."

"I didn't have time to eat it." Pepper wiggled into her silver ski coat as they headed out the front door of the school. "This morning was crazy."

It had been. It had taken Rebekah a few extra minutes to pull herself out of bed and to wake the kids since they didn't get up when their alarms buzzed. Then the drain on the trough had plugged, and water had spilled over into the field. Bear had rolled in the mud and then splattered Pepper while she let the horses out, so she had to change—all before the bus arrived.

"Let's get you something to eat and plenty of water. You're probably just dehydrated and overloaded with sugar." Rebekah kicked through a pile of wet maple leaves in the parking lot and reached behind the driver's seat of the truck for a bottle of water. She tossed it to Pepper. "I have oatmeal at the shop and some apples."

Rebekah pulled onto Main Street. "Look, they're putting up the Christmas decorations," Pepper said, pointing ahead. "Who's at the shop, Mom?"

"Elise."

"That was nice of her."

Elise was turning out to be a dependable friend after all. Rebekah smiled as she parked under a garland of greenery and white lights wound around the pole outside the shop.

Pepper turned around in her seat. "Dad just pulled up behind us."

Rebekah climbed out of the truck. "How come you're not at work?"

"I decided to take comp time." Patrick pulled his jacket from the car. "What's wrong with Pepper?"

"She's not feeling well."

"I had a donut for breakfast." Pepper grabbed her backpack from the truck and headed into the store.

"Why did she have a donut?"

Rebekah opened her mouth and then closed it. "Never mind."

"When is her next appointment?" Patrick's pitch rose.

"Tomorrow." Rebekah hit the automatic lock on her key.

Patrick opened the door to the shop. "I'll take her."

"You said you would stop worrying." Rebekah lowered her voice. Pepper ran up the stairs.

"I'm not worrying."

Would it make it harder for Patrick if he took Pepper? Would he start obsessing about what percentage she was at? where she was on the list? her diet and exercise? Rebekah turned toward her husband. "They'll check her kidney function. We'll know how much closer she is to dialysis. They'll probably want to go ahead and put a shunt in her arm, just so she's ready."

"They'll do the shunt tomorrow?"

"No. They'll schedule that for later."

"I'll take her home now." Patrick started toward the stairs. "Come on, Pepper."

"Make sure she gets some good food."

Patrick nodded. "How soon will she have to start dialysis?"

Rebekah shrugged. "Ask tomorrow."

urn up the heat." Elise closed the garage door and headed for the kitchen. "And turn on the lights." She hated a cold, dark house. She and Mark had picked Michael up after basketball practice and headed to Salem for dinner and the money pouches.

Michael rushed through the house, turning on lights as he went. Mark headed down the hall.

"Don't get on the computer." Elise put her purse on the dining room table.

"I haven't had a chance to check my e-mail all day. The Internet was down during study hall."

"Check it tomorrow. It's too late tonight."

"It will only take a minute."

"Mark, don't get on the computer."

He stood in the study doorway, his hand raised against the doorframe, his bangs hanging in his eyes.

"Mom, I have a book report due tomorrow." Michael sat at the dining room table and dug into his backpack.

"Why didn't you start it earlier?"

"I did. I finished it Saturday."

Elise turned toward the hallway. "Does that mean Mark has a book report due too?"

Michael nodded.

"Mark," Elise yelled, "did you finish your book report?"

"Almost."

"Come show me."

"Just a minute."

Michael pulled everything from his backpack and then put books, notebooks, folders, pens, and pencils back in one at a time. "The thing I don't like about going to a small school is having the same classes as Mark." He zipped the pocket and stood.

"Why?"

"None of the teachers like him. It's embarrassing." He slung his backpack over his shoulder.

Elise headed to the family room. "I told you not to check your e-mail."

Mark quickly minimized the screen. "I'm not. I'm working on my report."

Twenty minutes later Elise checked the family room again. No Mark. She climbed the stairs. His door was closed. She opened it. His room was dark, and he was asleep or at least pretending to be.

Elise left the school library at 3:10, as the last bell rang, and searched for Mark in the hall. She couldn't find him. Michael hurried toward the gym for practice, and she followed him, but he scooted into the locker room. She headed back to Mr. Jenkins's room and found him sitting at his computer. She cleared her throat.

"Mrs. Shelton." He stood.

"I wanted to check on Mark's book report. Did he turn it in?"

Mr. Jenkins shuffled through a stack of papers on his desk. "Here's Michael's. No, I don't see Mark's."

"May he turn it in tomorrow?"

"Has he completed it?"

Elise nodded. "He was working on it last night."

"If it's done, I'll accept it tomorrow."

Elise hurried to the Volvo and scanned up and down the streets as she drove home. Gray clouds billowed on the horizon against the tree-covered hills. She had given the boys a ride this morning, and Mark had told her his book report was done, but she hadn't had time to check it.

Where was Mark now?

She parked the car in front of the house and pulled the mail from the box. Three bills and a postcard from Ted from Heidelberg.

She sat at the dining room table, eyed the box of photos, and sighed.

"Hi." Mark came through the front door. "What's up?"

"Nothing." Elise turned her head. "Why didn't you turn in your book report?"

"I did."

"Mark, I checked with Mr. Jenkins. You didn't."

"He must have lost it already."

"Mark, show me your report."

He grabbed a handful of cookies and turned to go upstairs. "I told you I turned it in."

Elise followed him, swinging her arms back and forth as she climbed the stairs, and knocked on his door. No answer. She opened it. He stood with his window open. "Mark, reprint your report and turn it in tomorrow."

He dropped a handful of cookie crumbs onto the ledge. "I don't think I saved it."

"Then rewrite it and turn it in tomorrow."

"Could you please leave? That song sparrow in the birch tree wants some crumbs, and you're scaring him."

Elise hurried out of the pharmacy with a bottle of Dramamine for the plane ride and pulled the hood of her parka over the top of her head.

Mark often got nauseated when they traveled. She would give him a dose when they left Portland on their direct flight to Frankfurt. She hoped he would sleep for a good chunk of the way.

Her anger at Mark had driven her out of the house and on a walk downtown. The last light of the day began to fade.

It had been raining for the last week. The pungent smell of wood smoke mixed with the scent of the damp air and earth. She marched along in front of the Scrap Shack. Pepper waved frantically and ran to the door. "Hi!"

Elise slipped through the door and flipped her hood off.

"Elise." Rebekah stood. Sandi sat at a table, pulling merchandise from boxes.

Elise picked up a package with a little gadget inside. "Fastenater," she read. "What is that?"

"It's like a stapler." Pepper held up a light blue metal object. "But the staples are decorative, kind of like brads."

"How is everyone?" Elise unwound her scarf.

"Fine." Pepper held out her arm. "I got this new dealy at the doctor."

Elise took Pepper's hand. She couldn't see anything. "Where is it?"

Pepper took Elise's hand and positioned it just down from the crook of her elbow. "Here."

The blood in Pepper's arm rushed back and forth. Elise cringed. "What is it?" It felt like a little alien had possessed Pepper.

Rebekah laughed. "They attached a vein and an artery yesterday. It will make the vein strong enough for dialysis."

"Dialysis? Has it come to that?" Elise felt Pepper's arm again, felt the B blood rushing through the artery to the vein. She stepped backward.

"We're getting close." Rebekah opened another box.

Elise felt a little queasy. What would Rebekah think of her if she knew she might be a possible match but was unwilling to be tested?

"One more week until you fly out, right?" Sandi asked Elise.

Elise nodded, unable to speak.

"John said that Ted is worried about his old unit. The one in Iraq."

"Really?" Elise found her voice. Ted hadn't said a word.

"Seems an anesthesiologist has been sick, and the other ones are exhausted." Sandi ran a price sticker over another package.

What was Sandi getting at?

"Those tent hospitals really sound like something." Sandi slapped another sticker on a package.

"They're state-of-the-art." Elise picked up a Fastenater package. She would start on Mark's book when they got home from Germany. "The operating rooms are totally sealed, air-conditioned, and fully equipped. Just like a regular operating studio."

"Does Ted want to go to Iraq?" Sandi asked.

"Sandi." Rebekah tossed a Fastenater package at her. "Don't talk that way. Elise and the boys are going to Germany for Christmas. She doesn't want to think about Iraq."

Sandi shrugged her shoulders. "John thinks Ted wants to go."

Elise sighed. It wasn't Sandi; it was John. He should stay out of it. "I'm sure there's a part of Ted that wants to go, but he promised years ago that he wouldn't volunteer without me being one hundred percent in favor." Elise dropped the package on the table. "Orders are one thing; volunteering is another." Her cell phone rang. "It's Ted. Bye, you guys. See you soon."

"Sandi…" Rebekah's voice faded as Elise headed out the door.

"Hi, Ted. You saved me from Sandi telling me your dad's opinion."

"About?"

"Never mind." She walked quickly. "How are you?"

They chitchatted for a few minutes. Was he going to bring up her blood type again? He hadn't re-sent the e-mail to Michael.

"Do you remember Robert Steward? He was in my unit in Afghanistan." Ted's voice grew serious.

She did. A short, stocky man with four daughters.

"He's been in Iraq, in Balad, with my old unit. He's sick. They're flying him to Landstuhl today, then most likely on to Brooke Medical for more tests."

"That's who Sandi was talking about. Ted, it's really awkward when you tell your dad stuff before you tell me."

"I'm sorry."

"What's wrong with Robert?" She ducked under the awning along the beauty shop.

"They don't know. He's been sick with intestinal problems for a couple of weeks; it could be a parasite."

She hurried across the street. Robert's wife, Bea, was a strong, no-nonsense person. She also had lived in Georgia while Robert and Ted were in Afghanistan together. Her two older girls had gone to the same school as Mark and Michael. "Where's Bea now?"

"Illinois, in her hometown. I think she'll meet Robert at Brooke." Ted paused. "They're looking for someone to take his place."

"Ted." She started up the hill, toward the bridge.

"I just wanted you to know."

"Why?"

"Colonel Shelton to OR." A woman's garbled voice could be heard in the background.

"I'm being paged."

"Don't vol—"

"I love you."

He was gone.

epper!" Rebekah stood at the bottom of the staircase. "We're leaving."

"I just need to get my paint chips, to show Ainsley."

"We have to leave now!" Rebekah crossed her arms. Pepper had already missed the bus.

Reid stood in the dining room. "I have a test first period."

"I know." Rebekah threw him the keys. "Go start the truck. We'll be right out."

"This is what I mean, Mom. You spoil her."

"And scrape the windshield." It had frosted overnight but promised to be a clear, sunny day. Rebekah started up the stairs. "Pepper—"

"Mom, Ainsley is leaving for California tomorrow. I have to show her what color I've decided to paint my room."

Rebekah stopped in Pepper's doorway. "I'm going out to the truck right now. If you're not in it by the time I drive away, you'll stay home today or find another way to school."

"Fine. I'll call Dad." Pepper opened her desk drawer.

"No, you won't call Dad. He misses enough work as it is." Rebekah turned on her heel and grabbed her coat.

Pepper ran out of the house as Rebekah put the truck in reverse, her coat and backpack in one hand, her shoes in the other. She dove into the backseat, laughing. "It's a good thing the ground is frozen. Otherwise my socks would be covered with mud."

Rebekah turned onto the highway. "It's a good thing you get your allowance tomorrow, because you're buying three new pairs of socks."

"Mom," Pepper pouted in the backseat, "that's not fair."

Reid smiled. Rebekah turned on the radio.

Rebekah hurried down the back steps and climbed the fence into the pasture. She walked quickly, clapping her hands against the frosty afternoon, and then began to run along the fence line. The shop had been busy with husbands and kids coming in to shop for Christmas. She had sold twelve gift certificates, lots of tools, and several albums. The ladies had stayed away, though, doing shopping of their own.

The late-afternoon light faded as the sun set behind the hills. Another few days and it would be the winter solstice. The cold air bit at her lungs, and Rebekah slowed to a jog. She had a destination: Sky had a favorite pole that he kept leaning against, which needed to be reset. She was going to flag it and hopefully fix it after church in the morning. Mostly, she just needed some fresh air and time alone before tackling the house. Her parents were coming for Christmas.

She had hoped that this would be a happy Christmas, that a kidney would be lined up for Pepper, that their worries would be over. Mandy had died just before the first Christmas Pepper was with them. It had been bittersweet. Rebekah had grieved for Mandy's lost life, for Pepper's loss, and for Polly's. But hope had grown in Rebekah that Pepper could be legally theirs. She and Patrick had prayed every day together. They had set aside a weekend and fasted, begging God for his direction, for what was best for Pepper. Rebekah knew God was in control, that it was up to him.

Even four years ago when Pepper was so sick, she had relied on God.

What had changed? Patrick had always been a worrier, but it had grown worse since they had moved from Portland to the farm, and opening the shop had added to his worries. But it wasn't his fault she had stopped trusting.

Low clouds settled over the forest, and the fog rolled slowly down the hill toward the pasture. Were they irresponsible to have moved? Had she taken too big a risk in opening the shop? Was that why she was having a hard time trusting God? She frowned. She had been feeling as if her decisions, her desires, had made things worse and that it was up to her to make things right.

God, she prayed, *please teach me to trust you again.*

Don't be afraid.

Rebekah slowed to a walk, out of breath. Fear. She was so afraid, afraid of losing Pepper, afraid of losing everything. She stopped at the post and grasped the top with her gloved hands. She shook it, hard. It definitely needed to be reset. Sky whinnied, far away. The other horses had already gone to the barn. She knelt and ran her hand along the dirt around the pole. Perhaps a mole had dug close by. A tuft of fur fell from the wire. She picked it up. Golden fur. She stood. Maybe it was from a coyote, maybe not.

Sky whinnied again, this time closer. She whistled. The last of the light faded as the horse ran toward her through the fog. "Come on, boy." She grabbed his mane and swung onto his back. "Let's go home."

Rebekah sat next to Patrick on the hard wooden pew. Candles lit the sanctuary, and greenery filled every windowsill. One week until Christmas Day. The choir filed off the stage as Elise squeezed in next to Rebekah. Michael and Mark shoved each other into the row behind, next to Pepper and Reid. Mark wore sports pants and a sweatshirt, and his hair stuck out in twenty directions.

The winter sun shone through the stained-glass window of the nativity scene to Rebekah's right, making the blues, reds, and purples of the window vibrate in the intense light. Pastor Jim stood on the platform, leaning his tall, lanky body forward slightly. He stroked his goatee and then began speaking about Mary and Jesus. It wasn't the typical baby-in-the-manager sermon. He read from John 2, about the wedding in Cana. "Do whatever he tells you," Mary told the servants before Jesus turned the water into wine.

"Why did Mary have such confidence in Jesus?" Pastor Jim asked as he sat down on a white stool. "Because she knew he was kind and compassionate and could be trusted with both the big and small things in life."

Kind and compassionate. Rebekah's eyes filled with tears. He felt compassion toward Pepper. He could be trusted. He could turn their water into wine.

Patrick nudged her. Was he getting the same thing out of the sermon? He nudged her again and pointed at her purse. It was vibrating. She dug out her cell. It was an incoming call from the hospital. She tripped over Elise's small feet as she struggled out of the row and dashed up the side aisle. Pepper's and Reid's faces floated by. She reached the double doors and hit Talk. *Dear God, sweet Jesus, could it be?*

"We have a kidney," Jamie's voice sang. "It looks like a match. We need you up here ASAP."

Thank you, God. Rebekah tried her hardest to walk down the aisle. Was she running? God had taught her to trust again and had provided a kidney, all in one moment.

"Mary knew Jesus was her Savior. Not only was she willing to tell the servants to trust him, but she was willing to trust him too." Pastor Jim paused.

First she tapped Pepper, then Elise and Patrick, motioning to each to follow her.

"Christ's kindness continues to all of us today, every day." The pastor smiled. Rebekah smiled back. She was sorry to disrupt his sermon, but she knew he would understand. Patrick shook his head. "Come on!" she mouthed, grabbed her Bible, and led the parade out the door to the steps of the church.

"We have a kidney!" She hugged Pepper, then Patrick, and then Elise. "We need to go now."

Pepper beamed and slipped her arms into her coat.

"Now?" Patrick's arms dangled at his side.

"Now." Rebekah turned to Elise. "Can you take Reid and feed the horses tonight and in the morning? And Bear? My parents are coming Wednesday, but I'll ask them to come tomorrow, because I know you fly out on Tuesday. I'll call Sandi too. And Reid. Tell him I'll call as soon as you guys get out of church."

Elise nodded. "Just let me know what else you need." She wiped away a tear. Rebekah hugged her, and then Elise hugged Pepper. "I'll be praying for you, sweet pea."

Elise had called Pepper by her pet name. Gratitude washed over Rebekah. "Thank you, Elise. Isn't it incredible? My phone rang just as the pastor spoke about Christ's compassion and kindness."

Elise nodded. "Mary, his mother, trusted him."

"And I will trust him too."

Sandi threw open the door. "What's up? I was in the balcony and saw all of you leaving."

"There's a kidney for Pepper!" exclaimed Rebekah as she reached over to hug Sandi.

"I'm going to get the truck," Patrick said. He took Rebekah's Bible and ran down the stairs, two at time.

Sandi broke away from Rebekah and hugged Pepper.

"You know what this means?" Pepper asked.

What is she thinking? Is she afraid? Rebekah stepped toward her daughter.

"Someone died."

"Oh, sweet pea, you're right." Rebekah's heart sank as she wrapped her arms around Pepper. "Let's pray for the family—pray that they will feel Christ's compassion and kindness, that they will trust him." Rebekah reached for Pepper's hand and for Elise's; they reached for Sandi's hands. "Dear Lord," Rebekah prayed, "thank you for teaching me to trust again." Then she prayed for the family of the donor and for a successful surgery for Pepper.

Chapter 31

*A*s Rebekah said, "Amen," Elise hugged Pepper again—relieved for Pepper, relieved for herself. Would she ever tell Rebekah she had type B blood? Probably not. Elise turned toward her friend. "We can stay at your place tonight if that helps."

"Really? I know you're busy. I didn't want to ask."

"It would work great; I'm almost packed."

Rebekah laughed. "You would be."

Sandi slipped back into the church, but Elise stood on the steps of the church as Patrick pulled Rebekah's truck onto the street, hugging her arms around her body until they drove away. She turned and headed through the carved double doors of the church.

"May you be blessed this Christmas by Christ's kindness and compassion." Pastor Jim smiled. A young woman walked slowly down the aisle with a candle to mark the fourth Sunday of Advent. The congregation stood. Elise slipped into the pew. It was going to be a wonderful Christmas, maybe the best ever. Pepper would have a new kidney, she and the boys would be in Germany, and Ted would be home for good in just three weeks.

Forest Falls wasn't all bad. She still wanted to move, but visiting would be easier now. She could stop by the shop, maybe ride with Rebekah. They would keep in touch; she was sure. Maybe the Grahams would come to Seattle to visit.

As the congregation sang "Joy to the World," she turned her head and caught a glimpse of Sandi and John in the balcony. When they came back to visit, would Sandi and John be married? Maybe this Christmas wasn't going to be absolutely perfect; she still felt guilty about not wanting John to go to Germany with them.

Pastor Jim stood with his hand over his brow and scanned the congregation. "Can anyone tell me why the Grahams left early?"

"There's a kidney waiting for Pepper!" Sandi called out from the balcony. The congregation began to clap. Elise sat down.

Pastor Jim held up his hands. "Let's pray."

Elise packed the last of her rolled clothes into her suitcase. In three weeks, Ted could deal with Mark's schoolwork. They could go to Seattle and look at houses, check out schools, and decide what part of town they would live in.

She headed down the hall to fold the load of clothes in the dryer. The basketball bounced against the garage. "Mark?" She poked her head into the family room. "I thought you were out playing basketball."

"I got bored."

"You need to pack pajamas and a change of clothes to go to Rebekah's."

He shook his head. "I'll do it later." The zooming sound of the computer game buzzed in her head.

"We need to leave in a few minutes."

"Leave?"

"To go to Rebekah's."

"We're spending the night? Again?"

He hadn't registered a word she'd said. "Turn off the computer." Her frustration rose. She took a deep breath. Pepper was getting a kidney. She could deal with Mark. He hated to travel, hated Germany. He was probably just feeling anxious, and she needed to show him compassion. "On second thought, play one more game, okay, Mark? Then you can get packed."

He turned his head. "What's with you?"

She smiled.

He fixed his eyes back on the computer game. "I don't want to feed the horses."

"You enjoyed it before."

"No, I only pretended to."

"Mark," Elise scolded, "your father and I didn't raise you to act like this. Pepper is getting a kidney, and we need to help them."

"Get Reid and Michael to help. They never do anything with the horses."

"They don't like to ride."

"Who says that I do?" Mark's plane went down, and crash noises exploded out of the speaker as he threw his hands up in the air.

"That isn't the point. Anyway, you can't stay here by yourself."

Mark started another game.

"One more game." She held up her index finger.

"Right." Mark leaned to the left, pulling on the joystick.

Bear barked as Elise pulled into Rebekah's driveway, under the bare elms. The horses trotted toward the fence, their heads held high. Elise grabbed her overnight bag as the boys piled out of the car. "Mark and Michael, grab your backpacks." The wind whistled through the tops of the spruce trees.

Elise rubbed Bear's head and started toward the horses, her bag slung over her shoulder. "Hi, there." She rubbed Sky's neck. He tipped his head to the side. "Did you know Pepper is getting a kidney today? I bet she already told you, huh? I bet she gave you a long good-bye."

Rebekah had said that Pepper would have to stay in Portland for a

month in case she had an emergency, first in the hospital and then with
their old neighbors. Rebekah and Patrick would take turns staying with
her. Sandi had promised to run the store on her days off; Rebekah
expected to juggle the other days; Elise had offered to help once she was
back from Germany.

Elise scratched Sky between his ears, and Reid pulled the spare key
from a fake rock under the deck and unlocked the door.

"I'll need help with the horses in about an hour." Elise dropped her
overnight bag in the kitchen. "Hey, Mark." She turned toward the desk.
"Let me on Rebekah's computer—"

"I'm just checking my e-mail."

Who did he expect to send him a message? "Let me know when
you're done. I forgot to check mine before we left."

Elise started on the breakfast dishes in Rebekah's sink. It must be un-
settling to get a call and have to rush like that, just grab a few things and
then be gone. Did Pepper have any idea what she would be going through
in the next month? Surgery. Steroids. Antirejection medication. Poor thing.
What an ordeal.

"You have one message from Dad." Mark stood.

"Mark, why are you reading my e-mail?" Elise turned toward him,
alarmed.

"I'm not reading your e-mail. I just pulled up your account."

Elise hesitated. "Okay, thanks." She dried her hands and sat down at
the computer.

> I have something I need to talk with you about. I'll call at
> 6 p.m. your time.

Her heart raced. What was he up to? She had only one guess. Iraq.
No, he couldn't go to Iraq. He couldn't be gone any longer than the three
months she'd been counting off, day by day, hour by hour.

Chapter 32

epper sat on the preop bed with her backpack spread over the white cotton blanket. She sorted out her *Arthur* trading cards, paint chips, and fabric swatches. "Do you like this fabric with this paint?" she asked Patrick.

"It's fine." He turned to Rebekah. "What's taking so long?"

Rebekah shrugged. Who knew? Maybe it always took this long.

The sixteen-year-old boy in the room next door was wheeled out and through the double doors. "I talked with his mom." Rebekah sat on the end of the bed. "He's having a shunt in his brain repaired."

Patrick ignored her. "Are you sure everything was a match?"

"You heard Jamie. She said the tissue samples looked great." Rebekah would spend the night in the hospital with Pepper, and Patrick would stay with their old neighbors. She wasn't sure what to do about Christmas. Maybe Patrick and Reid could have Christmas morning with her parents on the farm and then they could all come up to Portland.

Pepper yawned and stretched her arms over her head, pulling the hospital gown nearly off her shoulder.

"I wish I had an iPod." Pepper put her cards and paint and fabric samples back in her bag.

Patrick shook his head.

Pepper pulled out knitting needles and yarn.

"When did you learn to crochet?" he asked.

"It's knitting, Dad. No one crochets anymore. Ainsley taught me." She slowly moved the yarn around the needles.

"Did you bring a book?" Rebekah asked.

Pepper opened the bag, peered in, and then dropped the bag on the bed. "Nope." She yawned again.

"Do you want to take a little nap? It will make the time go faster." Rebekah fingered the yarn.

Pepper shook her head. "I'm hungry."

"I know."

"Why did they want us up here so soon?" Patrick asked.

"Mom, why don't you and Dad get something to eat?" Pepper stretched again and dropped her knitting into her backpack. "I think I'll try to sleep."

"Why don't you go to the cafeteria? I'll stay with Pepper," Patrick said as he sat on the edge of the bed.

"Why don't you both go?" Pepper yawned again. "The nurse can page you when it's time."

"No, I'm not going anywhere." Rebekah sat on the other side of the bed.

"Mom, Dad, please. I'm fine."

They sat in a booth in the sleek, nearly empty cafeteria. Patrick played with his paper cup. "Something's wrong."

"Patrick, nothing's wrong. Hospitals are like this, remember?" Rebekah took a bite of vegetable soup. "You should eat something."

He shook his head. "Are you sure Elise is okay staying at our house?"

"She wouldn't have offered if she wasn't. Honestly. That's one thing about Elise; she's not impulsive about offering to help."

"She's been a good friend to us, hasn't she?" Patrick took a sip of coffee.

Rebekah nodded. Elise had. What would their family have done without Elise and Sandi during the last few months?

"Now Ted will be home soon," Patrick said. "After things are settled with Pepper, maybe I can get to know him."

It would be good for Patrick to have a friend in Forest Falls. He hadn't really connected with any of the other dads. He and John got along well, but they didn't have much in common. Rebekah finished her soup and crinkled the cracker wrapper into the bowl.

Patrick drummed his fingers on the table. "I'm going nuts," he said. She put her hand over his.

"I can't stand this any longer," he said. "Maybe we should pray again." Rebekah smiled and bowed her head.

"Rebekah and Patrick Graham to preop." The voice over the PA system startled her.

"Amen," Patrick said as he leaped to his feet.

The nurse met them beside Pepper's bed, where Pepper lay fast asleep. "Dr. Thomas is on his way," the nurse informed them.

"Dr. Thomas?" Patrick rubbed his forehead. "Shouldn't he be scrubbing for surgery?"

Rebekah shrugged and sat back down on the edge of the bed. Pepper stirred and flung her arms over her head.

Patrick paced along the curtain. Rebekah stood. Patrick sat in the chair and stretched out his legs, sinking low.

Dr. Thomas pushed through the curtain and stepped into the room. Both Rebekah and Patrick jumped to their feet.

"I have bad news," Dr. Thomas told them without preamble.

"Oh no." Rebekah reached for her daughter's hand. "Should I wake Pepper?"

Dr. Thomas nodded as Patrick slumped back into the chair.

"Sweetie, Dr. Thomas is here." Rebekah shook Pepper gently. "You need to wake up."

"Am I done?" She rolled toward Rebekah and opened one eye. "Is the surgery over?"

"No, sweet pea." She guided a strand of blond hair from Pepper's face. "You haven't been in surgery. Dr. Thomas has something to tell us."

"Are you awake, Pepper?" The doctor moved closer to the bed.

Pepper sat up and nodded.

"I go over each kidney meticulously before doing a transplant. I'm so sorry to tell you that the artery on this kidney isn't long enough to attach. It's not the right kidney for you."

lise's cell began to ring. She spread the *Country Living* magazine facedown on Rebekah's camelback sofa and wiggled the phone out of her pocket. Ted was early.

She told him that Pepper was getting a kidney, that it had all worked out, that they hadn't needed her after all.

"That's great." Ted's voice sounded tired and far away.

She asked what he needed to talk to her about.

"Elise, this is going to be hard, but I need to go to Iraq."

"What? You said you would never volunteer." She stood.

"If I don't volunteer now, I'll get orders within the year. It would be better for me to go and be with a unit I know, with people I trust."

Elise planted her hand on her lower back.

"It will be less disruptive for you and the boys if I go now than if I come home and we have to go through all of this again."

How could he be so sure? "Would you go while we're still in Germany?" she asked, imagining another fear-filled good-bye.

He didn't answer.

"Ted?"

"Elise, I need to leave tomorrow."

She sank back onto the couch. "No."

"Elise, I'm sorry."

"Ted, I can't do another Christmas without you." She pulled a cushion to her chest. "And you told me you would never volunteer. The boys need you. I need you. Think about us."

"I have—nonstop—but I need to do this. It would help so much if I had your support."

She couldn't give him her support. Why hadn't he discussed this with her? "You said that you wouldn't volunteer." Her voice was whiny, desperate. Could the boys hear her? She headed to the front door and out onto the porch.

"I've thought and thought about this. I think it's best for all of us if I get it over with. It will only be a short time."

"How long?" She leaned against the railing.

"Two months max."

Christmas in Forest Falls without Ted. What a nightmare.

"You and the boys could still come to Germany."

"No." She wasn't going to deal with Mark by herself in a foreign country.

"Elise, I'm sorry."

Fog rolled over the field across the road. A single finch fluttered in the bare maple tree. The spruce trees around the house bowed in the wind.

"Elise, I love you."

She pulled her sweater tight with one hand. What was she afraid of? That Ted would never come back? That he would leave, die, like her father? Is that what she had been afraid of all these years? That he would choose to go? Her father hadn't chosen to go, but he had given up something—the hope that things would ever get better before he died.

"Elise, are you there?"

"Ted, call me later. I can't talk right now." She hit End and wrapped both arms around her middle and leaned against the railing.

Michael pushed open the front door. "Mom, what's wrong?"

Reid towered behind him. "Is Pepper all right?"

"Pepper's fine." Elise dug a tissue from her pocket. "Everybody's fine. Just give me a minute, okay?"

Elise started her cleaning rampage in Rebekah and Patrick's room; she stripped the bed, vacuumed, and dusted. Nothing was nicer than coming home to a clean bedroom. She scrubbed the upstairs bathroom and headed to the stairs with her arms full of dirty sheets and towels.

"Mom." Michael stood. "What's going on?"

Mark flipped his bangs from his eyes.

"Let me start this load of wash, and then I'll tell you." She carefully made her way down the stairs.

At least Pepper was getting a kidney. Elise sighed. Was she angry with Ted? Yes. Was she angry with God? How could she be angry with God when he had just provided a kidney for Pepper?

She wedged the sheets into the front-load washer, measured out the soap, and spun the dial. She felt forgotten by God.

Be strong, she coached herself as she headed back up the stairs. "Mark, Michael," she said as she reached the landing, "Dad is going to Iraq."

"After we get back from Germany?" Michael turned from the game he and Reid were playing.

Elise shook her head. "No, tomorrow. We're not going to Germany."

Michael jumped from his chair. "Mom, how can he do this to us?"

"Dad's going to Iraq?" Mark asked quietly.

Elise nodded. "He feels—"

"Can't we go to Germany anyway?" Michael dropped the joystick.

Mark stumbled over his chair and fled down the stairs. Elise followed. The back door slammed. She stopped in the living room, in front of the picture window. Mark ran to the fence. Sky trotted toward him, and Bear brushed against his leg. Mark buried his face in Sky's mane. Tears welled in Elise's eyes and cascaded down her face.

A barn swallow flew above Elise's head as she ducked into Sky's stall, fighting back more tears. All three of the boys agreed to help with the chores without protest. Elise and Mark spread the cedar shavings. She inhaled the sweet smell of alfalfa mixed with cedar. Michael doled out the oats, and Reid pushed the wheelbarrow out the back door.

Bear began to bark as a vehicle pulled into the driveway. Maybe Rebekah's parents had taken a much earlier flight. Elise pushed the big door open far enough to slip through. It was Rebekah's truck. Patrick climbed out and then Pepper.

"What happened?" Elise's heart sank.

"The kidney wasn't right." Patrick rubbed the back of his neck.

Elise's hand flew to her mouth. "Oh no." She hadn't imagined that the transplant wouldn't work out.

"We have to wait for another one." Pepper slipped her backpack over her shoulder.

"I'm so sorry." Elise hugged Pepper. Rebekah came around the back of the truck, and Elise hugged her too.

Rebekah swiped the pads of her fingers under her eyes. "Unbelievable, huh?"

Reid and Michael came around the side of the barn.

"Son." Patrick started toward them. "The artery on the kidney was too short, so the transplant didn't happen."

Reid stood still, his long arms dangling at his side, his eyes big.

"It's okay." Pepper craned her neck to look behind Michael. "Where's Mark?"

"In the barn." Elise ran her hand through her hair. Were her eyes still red?

"Is everything okay?" Rebekah asked.

"Ted's going to Iraq."

"Oh, Elise." Rebekah put her arm around her friend. "He'll go after you come home from Germany, right?"

"No." Elise tried to smile. "He leaves tomorrow."

Chapter 34

*R*ebekah sat at the breakfast bar with yesterday's paper spread out in front of her. She had convinced Elise and the boys to spend the night; she hadn't wanted them to go home alone with such bad news. Now she wasn't sure she should have asked them to stay.

"Why did you agree to move here?" Mark slammed the cupboard door, a box of Cheerios tucked under his arm. "Why didn't we move to Seattle?"

"I'm sorry you're unhappy here." Elise leaned against the counter. She looked uncomfortable.

"You should have stood up to Dad. He's gone, and we hardly ever see Grandpa."

Rebekah stood. Mark was blaming Elise; poor Elise. "Mark," Rebekah interjected, "I was surprised to see you up so early this morning." He'd been at Reid's computer when she pulled herself out of bed.

"I never went to sleep." Mark poured cereal into the bowl.

"Mark." Elise sat down slowly. "You may not stay up all night, at our house or anyone else's house."

That explained his foul mood. Rebekah poured herself a cup of coffee. "Do you want a cup?" she asked Elise.

Elise nodded. "Please."

"Are you okay?" Rebekah handed her the cup.

"My back is out."

"Do you want some ibuprofen?"

Elise shook her head. "No thanks. I already took some."

"So what are we doing for Christmas?" Mark asked with his mouth full.

"We're going to Grandpa's."

"Great. With his girlfriend?"

"Her name is Sandi, and I'm not sure she's his girlfriend."

"Come on, Mom. What planet do you live on?"

Rebekah smiled and sat back down at the breakfast bar. She started to suggest that they join them for Christmas but caught herself.

Mark took another bite. "We should move to Seattle while Dad is gone. That would serve him right."

Rebekah raised her eyebrows. Boy, Mark was on a rampage.

Michael pushed open the kitchen door. "I still don't get why we can't go to Germany. It's not like we have anything better to do." His eyes were red and puffy.

Elise stood and put her arm around Michael.

"It's not fair," Michael whispered.

"I know." Elise pulled him close. "I'm as disappointed as you are."

He pulled away. "You're lying. We would be going if you were as disappointed as I am."

Elise rubbed her lower back. "I'm going to get a shower, and then we need to head home."

Michael slumped on a stool.

After Elise was out of earshot, Rebekah asked, "What did you guys get your mom for Christmas?" Rebekah wrapped her hands around her coffee mug.

Michael looked at Mark. Mark shrugged.

"We were going to get her something in Germany." Michael poked Mark's arm.

"Why don't you come by the shop this afternoon or later this week? I'll give you some ideas."

Michael nodded.

Mark shoveled another spoonful of cereal into his mouth. "This is going to be the worst Christmas ever."

Rebekah stood, yawned, and headed upstairs. She couldn't solve Mark's problems; he was going to have to figure out how to handle his angst on his own.

Rebekah stood in the middle of the balcony, taking in the shop as if she had never seen it before.

"Your shop is charming, just charming." Her mother turned around, her gold snowflake earrings bumping against her neck. She wore a navy-blue sweat suit and a gold visor over her blondish hair and clutched a gold purse. "I love the light from the windows. But you could use some new furniture."

"Grandma." Pepper plopped down on the secondhand couch. "Here's my latest scrapbook."

The door buzzed, and Rebekah headed down the stairs. The furniture was fine. The couch was a little worn, the metal chairs had dings, and some of the tables were chipped, but everything was functional.

Mark and Michael stood just inside the door. "Hi." Mark crossed his arms over his black sweatshirt.

"Hey, guys."

"We came to get something for Mom." Michael pulled his University of Oregon cap from his head.

"Do you want to get a gift certificate? Or a tool?" Rebekah asked.

"A tool?" Mark flipped his bangs from his eyes.

"For scrapbooking." Had he expected power drills and screwdrivers?

"We each have twenty bucks," they said in unison.

The boys decided to pool their money and buy a gift certificate for their mom. They finished the transaction, and then Michael stepped forward and craned his neck. "What's up there?"

"A work area. Pepper's up there with my mom." Rebekah headed for the stairs. "Come on up. You can meet her."

Mark and Michael zipped past Rebekah and raced up the staircase.

"Mom, these are my friend Elise's sons, Mark and Michael."

"Ma'am." Mark stepped forward and extended his hand. Michael copied his brother.

Rebekah smiled at their good manners. "This is my mother, Darla." The boys stood side by side.

"So nice to meet you." Darla closed Pepper's scrapbook.

Pepper stood. "Mark rides with us sometimes."

"Once." Mark flipped his bangs again. "I rode once."

"Whatever." Pepper rolled her eyes.

"What do you hear from your dad?" Rebekah took the scrapbook from her mom.

"He arrived." Michael shrugged his shoulders. "He's fine."

"He just IM'd me last night." Mark crossed his arms. "He said he would e-mail tonight."

The door buzzed again, and Rebekah hurried downstairs to wait on a customer. Another last-minute gift certificate. She expected the boys to follow her, but they stayed. Pepper's giggle floated down. Mark was probably teasing her. That was good; maybe he'd lightened up since Monday morning.

"So it's your father who just got sent to Iraq." Rebekah's mother's voice always carried. "Pepper was telling me about you."

Another giggle.

Rebekah started back up the stairs.

"We talk quite a bit. He has a satellite phone, and we e-mail all the time." Michael sat down on the couch next to Rebekah's mother.

"Now what does your father do?"

"He's an anesthesiologist." Mark spun the rack of sports stickers around.

"Oh, a doctor."

Rebekah knew her mother would be impressed.

"Too bad he's not home. Maybe he could find Pepper a kidney." Darla twirled her snowflake earring.

"Mom." Rebekah's boots clicked on the last stair. "Doctors don't find kidneys." Especially not army anesthesiologists.

"Actually, he did find Pepper a kidney." Mark stepped away from the rack.

"Yeah, right." Pepper sat back down by her grandmother.

Mark flicked his head. "At least he found someone with the same blood type."

"Who?"

Mark turned toward Rebekah and said, "My mom."

lise finished up her shopping—trying to compensate for the last-minute change in plans—and decided to swing by the Scrap Shack. It was only a couple of minutes until closing time.

"Mom!" Michael said as she walked in the door. He glanced back at Rebekah and shoved something into his pocket.

"Hi, guys. What are you doing here?" Elise wore wool pants, black granny boots, and a wool coat.

"We just stopped by." Mark pulled his hood onto his head.

"To see Pepper," Rebekah said. She was smiling, but Elise could see that something was bothering her.

Pepper stood at the railing but walked away when Elise looked up.

"I hope they weren't too much trouble," Elise said.

"Not at all." Rebekah smiled stiffly and then said, with obvious reluctance, "Oh, and they met my mom. She's upstairs. Would you like to meet her?"

"Sure. Mark and Michael, wait if you want a ride." Elise followed Rebekah up the stairs slowly. Her back was hurting more than ever.

Mark grunted and stayed by the door. Michael followed Rebekah and Elise up the stairs. Rebekah made the introductions.

"So," Darla said to Elise with a vinegar smile, "you're the one with B blood."

"Mom!" Rebekah said. "It's none of our business—"

"I'm not saying it is," Darla said. "I was just making sure that Mark had the story straight…"

Elise didn't hear anything else. She mumbled an apology, then rushed down the stairs and out the door. The boys followed her to the car.

Elise pulled the Volvo onto the street. She wanted to hide. She wanted to go far, far away. She would talk with Mark about blabbing her blood type to Rebekah later, after she calmed down.

"Mom." Mark slumped in the front seat. "I was IM'ing Ainsley, and she said that Sandi told Pepper that Dad *volunteered* to go to Iraq."

Elise gripped the steering wheel. "It's complicated."

"Why didn't you tell us?" Mark asked.

"I was going to. He figured if he didn't go to Iraq now, he would get orders in a year or so. This way he could go with his old unit, and then his service would be over."

"You always said he wouldn't volunteer."

She rolled through the four-way stop. "That was our agreement." The only way Mark could have found out about her blood type was if Ted had told him. "How did you know about my blood type?"

Mark shrugged.

"Mark, my blood type is none of your business."

"It's the same as my blood type, so I think it is my business."

Elise slowed. "Did Dad tell you that?"

"No."

"Then how did you find out?"

"I have my ways." Mark crossed his arms.

"E-mail." Michael slumped against the backseat.

"Pardon?"

"He checks your e-mails."

"How?"

"He looks at the preview pane without actually opening the message."

She pulled over to the side of the street. "Mark, you have no right to read my e-mail." What else had she and Ted e-mailed back and forth? "And I couldn't give Pepper a kidney even if I was a match."

"Why not?"

"I've told you, and now it's even worse. Dad is in Iraq. You and Michael, if you haven't noticed, still need a parent around."

"That's lame." Mark scowled.

"And I've had some medical problems—my back injuries."

Mark nodded toward the white pharmacy sack between the seats. "Here we go again."

"Mark." She missed the turn toward their house and turned right to go around the block. Now she would need a password on her e-mail account. She would have to have Ted tell her how to do that—or ask Michael. "The bottom line is, you may not go on my e-mail account; it's private." She stopped at the four-way stop.

"It's private," Mark mocked and opened the car door. "I'm walking." He slammed the door and shoved his hands in his sweatshirt pockets.

Michael scooted toward his door.

"Michael."

"I'll just keep him company." He opened the door and then paused. "Mom, Rebekah said she would never expect you to donate a kidney. She wasn't upset that you hadn't said anything about your blood type."

Elise gripped the steering wheel.

"Really, Mom. Don't be mad." He closed his door and ran after Mark.

Elise took a pain pill, changed into a pair of sweatpants, and sat down on her bed, her eyes falling on the family picture on the dresser, taken just last year in Colorado as they snowshoed near Winter Park. Ted stood with his arms around the boys; Mark's face was tanned from snowboarding, and Michael grinned like a goofball. Elise stood a step away—she had just handed the camera to a stranger and asked him to snap the photo. The

Rockies towered behind them, sunshine glinting off the snowy peaks. She turned the photo facedown. She would take a nap and forget about Ted being in Iraq. She would forget about Pepper and the B blood that coursed through both of their bodies. She would forget about Michael's disappointment and Mark's anger.

"Mom." Michael pushed open her door. "I really want to go to Reid's. He said I could spend the night. His mom and dad say it's fine."

"No. Tomorrow is Christmas Eve. They deserve some family time." She pulled back her covers. "I'm going to read for a while."

"There's nothing to do." Michael yanked the door shut.

She opened *Their Eyes Were Watching God.* Janie and Tea Cake had just survived the hurricane. Did she want to keep reading? Her vision blurred. She had to read through the hard part about Tea Cake to get to the end, to find Janie transformed and independent, changed by love.

Mark stood over her. The room was dark, and her hand still clutched the book. "I was IM'ing Pepper. She said that they're going to ride tomorrow and invited us to come out because Rebekah is closing the shop at noon."

"No." Elise's voice sounded far, far away. "I'm sorry. It's too close to Christmas." She rolled away from him. "And stop IM'ing."

Ted's time in Germany was supposed to be an epilogue to their army story. She hadn't bargained for a whole new chapter. She hadn't bargained for Iraq. She pulled the blanket over her head.

Sometime later Mark dropped a bag on the bed beside her. "Rebekah brought this by. It's fudge. She asked if we were coming out tomorrow."

Elise shook her head.

The next time she opened her eyes it was pitch dark. "Dad's on the phone." Michael dropped the receiver beside her head.

The red dots on the clock came into focus: 10:15 p.m. "Hello?"

"Michael said your back is out. Are you doing okay?"

"I'm fine." Did she sound as groggy as she felt? "Are you okay?"

"Safe and sound."

She exhaled and sat up against the headboard. Had she taken one or two pain pills? It felt like three. "Ted." She felt loopy. "You know when I was pregnant with Mark and you were gone and my back still hurt from the car accident the year before?" She paused. "Do you think the pills hurt him?"

"How many pills?"

"Just one at a time. A few times."

"Hurt him? How?"

"You know—how he doesn't like school, how he gets so angry."

"Elise, the pills probably didn't hurt him."

"I shouldn't have taken the pills." She wanted to go back to sleep.

"Other things have made him angry, and lots of kids don't like school." Ted paused. "Michael told me what happened at Rebekah's shop."

"Ted, I'm not donating a kidney; Rebekah doesn't even want me to. I have our boys to take care of, remember?" Elise scooted back down on the bed.

"The pills might have hurt your liver but not your kidneys."

"Ted, stop. You're not here. You don't get a say in this."

Silence.

"I'll try to call on Christmas Day," he finally said. His voice sounded hurt.

"Talk to you then." When she woke again, it was 6 a.m. She patted Ted's side of the bed before she remembered—it was Christmas Eve. Ted was in Iraq.

✄

"I'm going to take a shower." Elise shuffled down the hall to her room.

"May I go to Reid's?" Michael asked, following her.

Elise bent over, slightly. "His grandparents are there."

"So?"

"They need family time." Elise sat on her bed.

"He said it's fine." Michael pushed her door open.

"I'm sorry; not today."

Michael slammed the door. Elise stood and opened it to find Mark smirking down the hall, pointing at Michael. The cords in Elise's neck tightened to match the muscles in her back. Why hadn't she insisted last summer that they move to Seattle?

She stood in front of her dresser and searched the mirror. Her hazel eyes were too big against her pale face, tiny wrinkles gathered around her downturned mouth, and her hair was dull.

"Merry Christmas," she muttered out loud. John had graciously invited them to spend Christmas with him as soon as he found out Ted was going to Iraq. Elise sat on her bed again. She hoped John could contain his pride. She shook her head. He had to be worried, just as she was.

And Sandi would be there. Had they planned a private Christmas? Just the two of them? She hadn't been willing to share Christmas with John, but he had been quick to include them.

Chapter 36

*R*ebekah scooped an armful of gold wrapping paper off the living room floor and shoveled it into the fireplace. Her mother picked a theme every year; this time it was gold snowflakes. The fire curled the edges of the paper and quickly consumed the wrappings.

"We shouldn't burn that." Patrick wadded more paper into a pile. "I heard on the radio that it can start a roof fire. I'll get a bag."

Pepper tore paper from a small box. "Oh, Grandma!" She pulled out an iPod. "It's just what I wanted."

Rebekah shook her head. She had told her mother not to. Reid read a gold snowflake tag, smiled at his grandmother and then his grandfather, and shredded the paper off a Dell computer box. "A new PC. My own PC." He smirked at Pepper. "Dad, it has a DVD burner."

"Really?" Patrick smashed wrapping paper into the bag.

"Thanks, Grandma and Grandpa!" Reid wadded the paper into a ball.

Rebekah's father stood.

"Bill, what do you need?" Patrick asked.

"More coffee."

"I'll get it for you." Rebekah headed into the kitchen with her father's mug; he followed.

His dark hair had grayed, but his step was still spry and long. "All these gizmos." He winked at Rebekah. "I have no idea what they even are. Your mother seems to know, but I'm out of touch. It makes me miss the ranch, the simpler days. If I was lucky, I might get a new hat. That was a big Christmas."

"That putter you got looks pretty nice." Rebekah poured the coffee.

"It is. I picked it out myself." Her father winked again. "You know, honey, I'd do anything to give you what you need for Christmas, what you really want."

Rebekah nodded.

"A kidney for Pepper. That's what would really make this a happy day." Her dad drew her close and pulled her head against his shoulder.

Rebekah plunged the meat thermometer into the prime rib. It was their customary mouth-watering Christmas dinner, a tradition held over from holidays on the ranch. Her eyes and nose smarted from the heat of the oven and the richness of the beef. Another fifteen minutes and it would be done. Rebekah pulled out the crystal from the top shelf of the antique hutch.

Her mother took each goblet and set it on the breakfast bar. "I noticed it was a lean Christmas for you and Patrick. You didn't get the kids much, and you didn't get each other anything."

"We're trying to be frugal, planning ahead for Pepper's transplant." Rebekah climbed down from the stepstool.

"But you have insurance, right?"

Rebekah nodded. "And Medicare. They have a special program for transplants. But I won't be able to work, and I should pay Sandi while she fills in for me—and whoever else I need to hire. Plus we'll have copays on all of Pepper's antirejection medication."

"A few copays can't be too much."

"It adds up. She'll have to take over thirty medications."

"Good grief." Darla swung a towel over her shoulder. "I wish I could help, but we've had some unexpected expenses ourselves."

"It's fine, Mom. We can handle this. We just need to be careful." Her father had sold his parents' ranch in Montana several years ago and used the money to buy a home on a golf course outside Phoenix. Surely the ranch money wasn't all gone.

"Too bad the transplant didn't work out." Darla filled the sink with water. "I never got the scoop on your trip to Nevada. Is Pepper's family a possibility?"

Rebekah bumped against the stepstool. "Pepper's family?"

"You asked them for help, right? When you went to Nevada? Patrick called back and said that's where you were. I didn't ask you about it over the phone. I thought you might be embarrassed that I knew."

When they first took Pepper as a foster child, Rebekah's mother would ask how "that drug baby" was doing. Then after they adopted Pepper, she would ask how the foster baby was. "Pepper," Rebekah would say over and over. "Her name is Pepper. She is not a drug baby or a foster baby. She is our daughter."

For the first several years, Darla bought Reid nicer presents than Pepper. Finally Rebekah pointed it out. "Oh," her mother had said, "I had no idea."

No idea. Rebekah was sure her mother had no idea now, either.

"Pepper's family?" Rebekah couldn't help but play dumb.

"Rebekah." Darla squeezed soap into the water. "You know what I mean. Her real family."

"Her biological family? Her birth family? Is that what you mean?"

"Of course it is. I just can't keep track of the right terms. What did her real grandma say?"

"Mother, you are her real grandma."

"I know." Darla tossed the dishcloth into the water. "Rebekah, stop tormenting me."

"Neither her birth grandmother nor her birth aunt is in any shape to donate a kidney."

"How about to help financially?"

"Mom." Rebekah pulled the china from the bottom shelf of the hutch. "I would never ask them to help. Besides, they're as poor as church mice."

"I didn't know. Don't get in a snit. It's just that you've done so much for Pepper."

"Mother, stop."

Darla put the goblets in the rack, and Rebekah began to dry them.

"Mom!" Pepper skipped into the kitchen followed by Reid, trying to imitate her. "This iPod holds a thousand songs."

"What a waste of money." Reid poked Pepper in the side. "You're just going to load it with country."

"Pepper, do you like country-western?" Darla dried her hands on the end of Rebekah's dishtowel.

"I love it!"

"Me too!" Darla walked toward the table with two goblets. "But I never liked horses the way you do, much to your grandpa's disappointment. Have I told you how we met?"

Pepper shook her head and smiled at Rebekah.

"We missed you at Thanksgiving," Darla said as she dropped her napkin in her lap.

"We had friends over," Reid replied. "Their dad is in Iraq."

"He wasn't there at Thanksgiving, though; he was in Germany." Pepper took half a whole-wheat roll.

"I met his wife. Right? And his boys." Darla smiled.

"You did?" Reid speared the largest slab of prime rib on the platter.

"They were at the shop on Friday." Rebekah sighed.

"They were?" Reid giggled. He avoided the Scrap Shack at all costs.

"It's a shame Elise won't give Pepper a kidney." Darla smiled at Rebekah.

"Mom, don't start this again."

"What are you talking about?" Patrick held the butter knife in midair.

"It was embarrassing," Pepper said. "Mark told us Elise has B blood, and then Elise felt really bad."

"Has she considered getting tested?" Patrick passed the butter on to Reid.

"No. She's a single mom right now with a husband in Iraq, and she has a bad back or something like that." Rebekah skewered a slice of meat. Why did Elise have to have B blood? It only complicated things.

"One of their boys is a bit of a challenge," Patrick said to Darla, as if that explained everything.

"I thought they might come today." Reid passed the spinach salad with the cranberries on to his grandfather.

"They're having Christmas with Sandi and John," Rebekah explained. What she didn't say was that Elise had been ignoring her attempts to reconnect, which probably wasn't such a bad thing, considering her mixed-up emotions.

Pepper took the salad. "We're glad you're here now, Grandma and Grandpa, even if we didn't see you in November. And at least Mom saw you after Thanksgiving."

Rebekah's dad opened his mouth, Darla elbowed him, and Patrick rolled his eyes.

"What?" Pepper asked.

"No, you're right." Rebekah passed the rolls to her mother. "At least Grandma and Grandpa are here now."

After Christmas dinner, Pepper attempted to download songs onto her iPod, and Reid set up his computer. Patrick floated between the landing and the kitchen while Rebekah loaded the dishwasher. Her parents dozed on either side of the sofa.

Rebekah picked up the phone.

"Who are you calling?" Patrick asked.

"I've been thinking about Elise and what a hard Christmas this must be for her."

Patrick walked over to Rebekah and wrapped her in an embrace.

"I'm just calling—"

"I know what you're doing. Call her. She's with Sandi and John, right?"

Rebekah dialed John's number. Sandi explained that Elise's back was hurting and that she had gone home about an hour ago with the boys.

"She must be stressed," Rebekah replied.

"She seemed really uptight," Sandi said.

"I'll call her at home." Rebekah dialed Elise's number, and Michael answered. A few moments later she had a groggy Elise on the line. "Merry Christmas."

"Hi, may I call you back?"

"Are you doing all right?"

"My back hurts."

"Can I do anything to help? Have the boys over? Bring you some soup?"

"Thanks. But we're fine. I'll be better tomorrow." The line went dead without a good-bye.

lise opened one eye. Was it over? She looked at the clock: 3:52 a.m. *Thank you, God, for December 26.* She padded down to the bathroom and then out to the living room. White lights twinkled on the artificial tree.

"Mom." Mark sat in Ted's chair.

"What are you doing, honey?"

"I couldn't sleep."

"It's the middle of the night!" She sat down on the couch.

"I know."

"Is Michael in bed?"

"Since midnight or so." Mark flung his leg over the arm of the chair.

"What's the matter?"

Mark shrugged. "This was the worst Christmas ever."

Elise slipped a pillow behind her back.

"Dad called."

"Why didn't you wake me?"

"We tried." Mark stood. "I asked him why he volunteered."

"What did he say?"

"Same thing you did, but it made more sense when he said it."

Elise rubbed her fingertips under her eyes.

"Did you know that the Garden of Eden was near Iraq?" Mark asked.

"It's possible."

"Isn't that ironic?"

Elise nodded. Was it ironic?

"Here Dad is near where humanity began…" His voice trailed off.

"And?" Elise yawned. What was Mark talking about?

"And look how horrible things have gotten."

Elise tipped her head back. Desert Storm. Kosovo. 9/11. Afghanistan. Iraq. Mark's life had been shaped by war; it had crashed, over and over, straight through his childhood. She never would have chosen this for him.

"I think Dad really wanted to go." Mark slumped back down in the chair.

Elise did too. "How does that make you feel?"

"I hate that question. It's so fabricated."

Elise paused. "How did Dad sound?"

"You know Dad. He was his usual optimistic self."

Elise pulled the red and green afghan off the couch and covered herself with it. Maude had crocheted it ten years ago. She put it out only at Christmastime.

"I understand why Dad volunteered."

"Why?"

"Loyalty. He wants to help."

Elise stayed silent. Loyalty or pride? Someone else could have gone.

"He said volunteering doesn't mean he's not loyal to us."

"What do you think?"

"I think you're mad at him. I think you blame him for this, and I think you take your back pills to escape, to hide."

Elise wrapped the afghan tight and stood. She wanted to go back to bed.

"Don't blame him, Mom. It doesn't help. It's like he's gone and you're not here either."

✄

Elise was sitting at the table, numbly staring at the newspaper, when her cell phone rang. She pulled it out of her robe pocket.

"Merry Christmas."

She imagined him standing in front of the field hospital, sand blowing around his face, his beret pulled down on his forehead. Or would he wear a helmet? She sighed. "That was yesterday."

"Merry day after Christmas. How was it?"

"Fine," she said, annoyed with his cheery voice. "Where are you?"

"In my barracks. Do you feel better?"

"A little."

"Mom!" Michael hurried into the breakfast nook. "Can I go to Reid's?" His curls were mashed on one side of his head.

"It's Dad." She put her hand over the receiver. "Wait a minute."

The doorbell rang. "Michael, get the door."

"Is everything okay?" Ted asked.

"Fine. How are you? How was Christmas in Iraq?"

"I miss you guys."

Elise was silent.

"Are you punishing me?"

"Mom, Rebekah is here."

Elise changed the subject. "Mark said that he asked you about volunteering."

"Mom! Rebekah is here."

She nodded at Michael.

Ted sighed. "I'll e-mail you. E-mail me back, okay? Have Mark show you how to use instant messaging. If I'm on, we can talk back and forth."

"Does that work?"

"I instant messaged with Mark for a while last night. It's not the same as talking on the phone but better than e-mail."

"I'll try it."

"Elise, I love you."

"I love you too." She did, really she did.

"Mom." Michael's face contorted.

"I'll come back later." Rebekah stood in the dining room.

"I'm off the phone." Elise wiped her hands on her robe.

"I was worried about you." Rebekah stepped forward. "Are you coming to the shop today?"

"I'm not sure."

"Do the boys want to hang out at the house? Patrick and my parents are there. Mark can ride with Pepper. Reid got a new computer that he would love to show Michael."

"Please, Mom." Michael tugged on the sleeve of her robe.

Elise shook her head.

"Mom," Michael groaned and disappeared into the family room.

"What's wrong?" Rebekah shoved her hands into her brown corduroy coat.

"My back hurts."

"Patrick could come get them." Rebekah smiled.

Elise shook her head. "Thanks, though. I appreciate it."

Rebekah crossed her arms. "Okay. Hey, new topic. I felt horrible about Mark bringing up your blood type."

Elise shrugged. How much should she try to explain? "Mark went through my deleted e-mails, trying to find something from Ted about volunteering, and he came across one about blood types."

"So you e-mailed Ted about your blood type?"

"No. Michael had. Before he knew he had to be eighteen, he was hoping he could donate a kidney to Pepper."

"That's sweet." Rebekah averted her eyes. "Come by the shop. Sandi will be there. I'm having an after-Christmas sale."

Elise tried to smile. "I'll see." She knew she wouldn't. What did Rebekah think of her? What would the other women think? "Well, thanks for coming by. Tell everyone hello if I don't make it to the shop." She immediately regretted saying that. She didn't want anyone to mention her name.

Rebekah opened the door and then turned. "Please, Elise, let me know what I can do to help."

Elise nodded, the cords in her neck taut. "Thanks." This would be a lot easier if Rebekah weren't being so nice.

"Let's go to Seattle," Elise said at dinnertime. She always sat at the head of the table with the boys on either side when Ted was gone.

"For good?" Mark slurped his minestrone soup.

"No. To visit."

"I have basketball practice." Michael pushed his bowl toward the center of the table.

"You do?"

"Wednesday and Friday."

That pretty much took up the entire week. "Can you miss?"

"I don't want to miss." Michael stood. "Besides, wouldn't driving that far be bad for your back?" He picked up his dishes and headed for the kitchen.

Elise ignored the fact that he hadn't asked to be excused.

Mark grabbed another piece of bread. "Maybe he could stay at Reid's."

Elise shook her head. "He's right. That's too far for me to drive." She didn't want Michael to stay at Rebekah's. They all needed a break from each other. Besides, she didn't want to owe Rebekah any favors.

She stood and shuffled to the kitchen. Maybe she couldn't go to Seattle, but she needed to get out of Forest Falls sometime soon. She had a bad case of cabin fever. "Michael," she called down the hall, "it's your turn to do the dishes."

He didn't answer.

"Michael."

He stormed out of the family room to the middle of the hall, waving his hands. "That's what I hate about living here."

"What?" Elise crossed her arms. "Doing the dishes?"

"Everything. The chores. Not being able to go anywhere."

"What do you mean? Mark and I want to go to Seattle. You're the one with basketball practice."

"All I want to do is go out to Reid's."

Elise leaned against the wall. "Michael, they have company. We can't go barging in."

"No. It has nothing to do with them having company. It only has to do with you." Michael slammed the family-room door.

Elise headed up the hall and back to the kitchen, avoiding Mark's smirk.

ye!" Rebekah called after Reid and Pepper as they jumped out of the pickup and headed for the school. It was the first day back after Christmas break, and they had missed the bus. This time it was Reid's fault.

Reid jogged into the school, meeting Michael at the door.

"Pepper!" a group of girls yelled. Ainsley ran ahead and hugged her, and the other girls gathered around. Pepper opened her backpack and pulled out a pack of gum. She wore a long brown sweater over her jeans and, of course, the boots that Elise had bought her. Her hair was in a high ponytail.

God, I'm still trying to trust you, honestly, Rebekah prayed. *I just don't know what you're doing.* Kids take priority. Jamie had told her that again, just last week. When Rebekah asked how long it would take for another compatible kidney, Jamie said she didn't have an answer. "It could be tomorrow—or next year."

God, we don't have until next year.

Rebekah pulled out of the parking lot and onto Main Street. A light rain began to fall. By the time she reached the shop, it had turned into a downpour. She sat in the truck with the windshield wipers on high. *Trust me.* That little voice. *Don't be afraid. Trust me.* She turned off the motor and dashed into the shop.

Rebekah sat on the gymnasium bench, her corduroy coat wrapped around her. Sandi waved from the breezeway door and hurried over to the bleachers. John followed.

"Is Patrick coming?" Sandi asked.

Rebekah nodded. "He's running late."

"Where's Pepper?"

"She went to Ainsley's after school, but they should be here by now."

John sat down on the other side of Sandi.

Rebekah reached behind Sandi and patted his back. "Hi, John. How are you?"

"Just fine." He took off his wool cap and placed it on the bleacher. "How's that dog of mine doing?"

"Great. Things have been pretty quiet now that the cougar knows we have a security guard." Having Bear meant there was one less thing to worry about. Not even Patrick had mentioned the cougar for a few weeks, although she hadn't told him about the tuft of fur she'd found. "What do you hear from Ted?"

"Nothing but good things. They're doing lots of surgeries. During his off-hours he plays with the Iraqi children, mostly soccer. He misses his boys."

"There's Elise." Sandi pointed toward the door.

Elise stood with her camera, watching the boys warm up. Reid passed the ball to Michael, who made a perfect lay-up. A slight smile passed across Elise's face as her camera flashed.

The buzzer sounded, and the boys huddled with the coach. The cheerleaders started chanting. Elise sat on the first bench on the other side, her camera in her lap. Rebekah relaxed.

"Any word about the transplant list?" Sandi asked.

Rebekah shook her head.

Sandi leaned closer to Rebekah. "I heard that Elise has B blood."

"Who told you that?"

"John."

"Who told him?"

"Michael."

Rebekah shook her head. Where was Pepper? It wasn't like her to be so late. She dialed Ainsley's home number. No answer. Could she trust Ainsley? Maybe they'd eaten a dozen donuts after school. Where were they? Was Pepper safe?

Reid tipped the ball to Michael, and Michael went up for a jump shot. Swoosh. The score was 28–23. Forest Falls was ahead. The halftime buzzer sounded. Rebekah stood. "I'm going over to Ainsley's to see where those girls are."

"Do you want me to go with you?" Sandi grabbed her coat.

"No, I'll be right back."

"Hi, Elise," Rebekah called out as she walked by. "Michael's doing great!"

Elise smiled. "So is Reid."

Rebekah cringed at their shallow exchange as she opened the gym door and stepped into the torrential rain. She drove slowly away from the school toward Ainsley's house. What if Pepper was out in this cold? Why hadn't they called for a ride? Surely they wouldn't have walked. It was over two miles, and the first mile was along the highway. Pepper had told her that Ainsley's brother would give them a ride. He was, what, a junior? Maybe a senior? The shop had been full of customers when Pepper had called. What had Rebekah been thinking?

Nothing was going right.

Rebekah slowed, but Pepper was nowhere in sight. What if Pepper intended to meet her at the shop? She headed toward the highway. The windshield wipers squeaked at a rapid pace, frantically swiping the sheets of water away. She took a deep breath. She was annoyed, really annoyed with Pepper. And who else? Elise. With the whole kidney thing, with having to feel careful around Elise now.

And she was annoyed with God. She couldn't help herself. *Why can't I give Pepper a kidney?* It was as if God had forgotten them. Rebekah clutched the steering wheel. She was starting to sound like Patrick, like a broken record. God must be getting tired of her whining. It had been easy to trust when Jamie said there was a kidney, but look at her now.

The windshield wipers squished out their squeaky rhythm. *Trust me. Trust me. Trust me.*

"Stop it!" she shouted out loud as she pulled into Ainsley's driveway and snapped off the wipers. The house was dark, and there wasn't a car in sight.

Chapter 39

*R*eid tipped the ball to Michael, and Michael ran for a fast break and another perfect lay-up as Elise snapped the shutter. She smiled, pleased she had caught the action.

"That's my grandson!" John boomed, jumping to his feet.

Partway through the second half, Sandi and John walked around the court and sat on either side of Elise.

"We've missed you at the shop." Sandi folded her quilted jacket over her lap.

"I've been busy."

"Ted called this morning." John leaned forward, his hands clasped. "He had tried to get you, but your cell phone was off."

"He didn't leave a message."

"He said they got shot at last night."

"John." Sandi nudged him. "Maybe Ted didn't want Elise to know that."

Elise winced. What else did John know that she didn't? "Is everyone okay?" Elise gripped her camera.

"Just fine."

"How did Ted sound?" Elise's voice shook just a little.

"Great. Fit and raring to go. He did three surgeries last night." John wrapped his hands around his knee.

Elise rolled her shoulders. "I'm dying of thirst. I'm going to get a drink." She tucked the camera into the pocket of her suede jacket and hurried out to the breezeway. She saw Pepper leaning against the cinder-block wall while Ainsley flirted with a group of older boys.

"Hi, Elise." Pepper walked toward her. Her down jacket was soaked, and her hair hung in wet strands.

"Sweetie," Elise put out her hand, "you're all wet."

Pepper nodded.

"And you look exhausted." Elise quickly took off her coat. "Here, wear my jacket."

"Thanks." Pepper slipped out of hers and dropped it by the wall.

"I'm getting something to drink. Do you want something?"

Pepper nodded, pulling Elise's coat around her.

"And how about some popcorn?" Elise took her wallet from her purse.

"Please." Pepper shivered. "I went to Ainsley's after school, but we didn't have any dinner. Her mom had to take a neighbor to Salem. Then her brother gave us a ride, but he dropped us off downtown, and we walked here."

"I think your mom went looking for you." Elise paid the cashier.

"Uh-oh."

"Here, use my cell. Give her a call."

Pepper dialed the number just as Rebekah hurried through the door, her cell phone in her hand.

Pepper held up Elise's phone. "That's me calling you."

"Where have you been?" Rebekah's cowboy boots echoed through the breezeway. Ainsley and the older boys stopped talking.

"Mom." Pepper slipped out of Elise's coat.

"Pepper." Rebekah shoved her cell back into her pocket. "I looked everywhere."

Pepper tossed the coat to Elise as she hurried toward her mother. "Shh. You sound like Dad."

"I don't care who I sound like, young—"

Elise ducked back into the gym.

Elise waited in the Volvo for Michael. Why hadn't she brought a book? The rain pelted the roof of the car and cascaded down the windshield. She had forgotten how much it rained in the Northwest—day after day, week after week, month after month.

Her cell phone rang. *Ted.* She hoped he wouldn't bring up the kidney stuff. The last two times he had called he had urged her to be tested; she didn't want to dread his calls.

"How are you?" he asked. They talked about the surgeries and about the mortars that had fallen on base. "It was nothing." They covered the basketball game, the boys, the weather, and how Mark was doing in school.

"I need to keep checking in with his teachers," Elise said.

"What if you don't? What if you leave it up to Mark?"

"What do you mean?"

"Well, maybe the less responsibility you take, the more he will."

"What if he flunks?"

"Better for him to fail now than next year."

"What if he ends up taking this year over?"

"It will be his choice."

Easier said than done. She shook her head in the darkness.

Ted changed the subject. "It sounds like Dad spends a lot of time with this Sandi."

"Oh, I don't know," Elise said.

"He sounds happier. The happiest he's been since Mom died," he added.

"Does it bother you?" She slouched against the seat.

"No. Maybe a little. Mostly, though, I think it's a good thing, a really good thing for him." The rain let up just a little. Michael followed Reid out of the locker room. Elise turned her head. Rebekah's truck was parked on the far side of the parking lot with the engine running. Pepper was probably in the backseat, wrapped in a blanket.

"Here comes Michael. I'll let you talk to him while I drive home." She turned on her lights. "I love you."

Elise locked the back door behind her and turned toward the kitchen table. Mark held the phone between his head and chin. "Uh-huh." A half-filled bowl of Frosted Flakes sat on the table in front of him. He ran a spoon through the milk and cereal. "That will work."

Had Ted called Mark as soon as he hung up from talking to Michael?

"I'll see you tomorrow. Bye."

It couldn't be Ted.

"Hi." Mark smiled. He seemed in a good mood. "How was the game?"

"Good. They won."

"How did you do, Mikey?" Mark shoved the spoon into his mouth.

"Fifteen points, seven assists."

"Cool." Mark took another bite, spitting a drop of milk onto his chin.

"Who was on the phone?" Elise picked up the box of cereal. She stopped. Mark should put it away. Never mind. It was faster if she did it.

"Patrick. He wants me to help with the horses. He said that he would pay me to muck out the barn and exercise Sky in the corral and maybe ride the other ones." He stood.

"Don't forget your bowl and the milk." Elise was surprised that Patrick would ask. Even though he had complained beforehand, Mark had enjoyed the couple of times they had cared for the horses. She was pleased that Patrick felt Mark was capable, although Rebekah had probably suggested it.

Mark grabbed the bowl.

"The dishes in the dishwasher are dirty."

He put the bowl in the sink.

"Mark?"

"Huh?"

"Your bowl. And the milk."

"Right." He turned back to the table.

Maybe helping with the horses would take Mark's mind off Ted. "When does he want you to start?" Elise asked. She wasn't opposed to him helping Rebekah, not like she had been in the fall.

"Tomorrow, after school. I can ride my bike. He said he would give me a ride home."

Elise turned back from the refrigerator. "That road is pretty narrow. I'll drive you."

"I'll be fine."

"You'll have to be careful."

"Mom, I know."

"What do you want to do for your birthday?" Elise asked. Another week and he would be fifteen.

"Go to Seattle."

"For a trip?"

"Duh, Mom. But moving would be better." Mark headed down the hall; the milk was still on the table. They had visited Seattle the year before, a family trip after moving to Colorado. They had stayed at the Edgewater Hotel, gone to the market, and taken the ferry to Victoria and then over to Vancouver for a couple of days. It had been a wonderful vacation.

"Mikey, now you're a hotshot basketball player, huh?" Mark's voice was too loud.

Elise hoped they didn't get started. She couldn't handle a wrestling match tonight. Why hadn't Mark gone out for wrestling? It would make all of their lives easier. But he'd be off the wrestling team with his poor grades.

"Mark," she called out. "Put the milk away. Put your bowl in the dishwasher. Get ready for tomorrow."

"Hotshot." Mark's voice was louder. "Golden boy—except for your dark hair. Wait, I was supposed to be the golden boy."

Elise couldn't make out Michael's response.

"Double hotshot." A door slammed.

"Mark!" Elise started down the hall to the family room. Mark had Michael pinned to the floor. "Get up."

"We're fine. Aren't we, Mikey?"

"I want to take a shower and get to bed." Michael moaned.

"No. Don't you have homework to do? An A paper to write? Another science fair to win?" Mark flipped his hair out of his eyes with the toss of his head.

"Mark, get off him."

Mark stood and slapped both hands on his jeans and then jumped as if he were shooting a basketball. "Hotshot," he sneered and ambled out the room. The stairs creaked as he headed up to his bedroom. Never mind the milk and bowl.

"He's stressed about school," Elise said.

Michael headed to the downstairs bathroom. "You make excuses for him. I'm sick of it. And I'm sick of living here."

Elise pursed her lips. Maybe Michael *would* want to move to Seattle.

"I want to go live at Reid's house."

Chapter 40

A shovel scraped against the concrete floor as Rebekah squeezed through the barn door. The sweet warmth of the horses greeted her. Sky's stall was clean, with fresh hay spread across the floor.

"Mark, how are you doing?"

He poked his head out of the stall and smiled. He wore a black stocking cap. "I'm good."

"Do you want to come into the house for some hot chocolate?" Rebekah leaned against the rail. Mark had done a great job.

"What time is it?" He gripped the pitchfork tightly.

"Five o'clock." Rebekah was still shocked that Patrick had called Mark and asked him to do the work. Relieved, but shocked.

"That late? I haven't worked with any of the horses." Mark maneuvered the wheelbarrow away from the stall door.

"Don't worry about it. You can ride tomorrow; it's too dark now. I know the stalls were really full. Did your mom come out earlier?"

Mark shook his head and pushed the wheelbarrow toward the back door. "She's going to come get me, though."

"I can take you home."

"I know. But she didn't want to trouble you." Mark shoved the door open with his foot.

Elise was as stubborn as her son. Sky bumped against Rebekah and licked her face. "Are you loving me, or do you have a salt deficiency?" She reached up and patted the horse's neck.

"Mom?" Pepper's voice rose over the squeak of the back door.

"Back here, sweetie."

"Elise is outside. She brought Reid home. She asked me to send Mark out."

"She's not coming in?"

Pepper shook her head. "Doesn't she like us anymore?"

Rebekah shrugged. "I don't think that's it. She's going through a rough time with Ted in Iraq." She turned her head to the back door. Mark was still outside. "That announcement about her blood type made her feel bad too, I think."

"Mom, do you think Elise would be a match since she has the same blood type, and she's blond and small like me?"

"I don't think the appearance of a possible donor has anything to with it. Besides, Pepper…" Rebekah paused. This was hard to explain. "I think waiting for a cadaver donor is best. I wouldn't want Elise to donate a kidney."

"Why?" Pepper climbed on the stall gate railing. Sky brushed against her.

"Because I would feel like we owed her. Like I could never pay her back." Rebekah squeezed through the gate, swinging Pepper out and then back in. She turned toward the back door again.

"Would you feel that way with my birth mom, if she were still alive?"

"Probably not."

"Why?"

"You would be connected to her."

Pepper shook her head. "No. I'm much more connected to Elise."

"We'll get the kidney off the list; it's the best way."

Mark came through the back door wheeling his bike. Rebekah hurried to open the barn door for him. "Wait. I forgot the wheelbarrow." He leaned the bike against Sky's stall.

Rebekah stepped out into the night. Elise sat with her head against the steering wheel. Was she crying? Or tired? Her head popped up. Rebekah waved. The winter sun had just set, and dusk hung over the farm for a final moment. Elise opened the window of the Volvo.

"Mark's getting his bike. Can you come in for a minute?"

"We should get home. I haven't started dinner."

Pepper stepped out from behind Rebekah. "Eat with us. Mom put a roast in the Crock-Pot this morning, and Dad has a dinner meeting."

Rebekah zipped her sweatshirt and turned her head toward Pepper. She didn't feel up to having company.

"Please, Elise?" Pepper stepped closer to the window.

Elise shook her head. "You have enough going on."

Rebekah paused. Elise's sadness flooded from the car. "Please come in," Rebekah said.

Mark rolled his bike around to the back of the car. "Where's Michael?"

"Checking out Reid's new computer." Pepper held the bike while Mark lifted the hatch. "You guys are staying for dinner."

"What's for dinner?" Mark wrestled the bike into the car.

"Pot roast." Pepper slammed the hatch.

"Cool."

"If you're sure." Elise gripped the steering wheel.

"We would be so disappointed if you didn't." Rebekah took a step backward. What did she have to go with the roast? She didn't have any potatoes or carrots. A can of corn? Probably a can of beets. Maybe even some frozen spinach.

"Do you want real hot chocolate?" Rebekah asked. "I'm out of the powdered kind."

"Sure." Elise loaded the last of the dishes.

Rebekah stood in front of her pantry. "I know I have some cookies in here somewhere." She pulled out a package.

"How about brownies?" Pepper twirled on the breakfast barstool.

"We don't have time to make brownies."

"Brownies would be perfect tonight. With vanilla bean ice cream."

"Pepper, would you like to take over the meal and dessert planning? Your comments about the vegetables at dinner were enough."

"Mom, I need a cell phone." Pepper opened the package of short-bread cookies.

"You don't need a cell phone."

"If I'd had one the other night, you wouldn't have been worried about me."

"If you and Ainsley hadn't walked across town in a downpour and then been flirting with high-school boys, I wouldn't have been worried about you."

"I think I need a phone."

"Pepper, I'm serious." Rebekah shook her head. "And don't ask Grandma for one for your birthday. I won't allow it."

"Okay, okay." Pepper bit into a cookie. "Can I ride in the corral? The moon is full, and the light from the back porch shines over that way."

"Did you finish your homework?"

"At the shop. Remember?"

"It's cold out, honey."

"I'll dress warm."

"Okay. For half an hour, and just in the corral."

"Mark, do you want to ride?" Pepper spun off her stool.

"I don't know." Mark clicked off the Internet. "Have you seen the cougar lately?"

Pepper's eyes got big. "No, but there was a raccoon in my tree again the other night."

Mark stood. "Is it all right, Rebekah, if we ride?"

"Sure. But, Pepper, you must be in the house by eight thirty." Pepper nodded, and Rebekah added a pinch of salt to the milk, sugar, and cocoa mixture and inhaled the sweet smell.

Funny that Elise hadn't asked Mark about homework. "Are we keeping you guys from getting home, from getting things done?" Rebekah stirred the hot chocolate.

"No." Elise sat down at the breakfast bar.

"How's your back?"

"Better."

"Good enough to ride?" Rebekah ladled cocoa into two mugs.

"Soon."

"I really need help keeping the horses exercised, especially the Appaloosas. Sky is doing great, by the way. You could ride him anytime." Rebekah put the mugs on the table. "I bet you're ready for things to get back to normal."

Elise nodded. "I bet you are too."

"I hope this doesn't sound wrong." Rebekah moved her mug clockwise. "But it helps to have someone else going through hard times."

Elise nodded.

"It feels like everyone else is living their perfectly normal lives while we're in survival mode, for who knows how long." Rebekah hesitated. "Patrick said, before the failed transplant, that he felt God had forgotten us."

Elise took a sip of cocoa.

"I'd never felt that way before, but I have since—like the other night when I couldn't find Pepper."

Elise nodded. "I felt that way about Ted volunteering to go to Iraq. Going to Germany was enough, but Iraq felt beyond God's plan."

"It's hard for me to leave this up to God. I wanted my plan to be his plan." Rebekah paused. The truth was that she no longer had a plan, no layout in mind, no outfits to match the specially chosen designer paper, no arrangements to create a perfect album.

No master plan to save Pepper.

She raised her mug. "Here's to happier times."

Elise clinked hers to Rebekah's. "Here's to getting through these times."

"Is the hot chocolate done?" Michael swung through the kitchen door, pushing it all the way open, followed by Reid.

"Here, let me help." Elise stood.

"Let them get it." Rebekah took a cookie as Elise sat back down.

"Where's Mark?" Michael picked up the ladle.

"Riding in the corral with Pepper."

"Rodeo Queen." Reid snickered.

"No more of that." Rebekah took another cookie and glared at Reid. "And I'm serious."

Reid ducked behind Michael. Michael ladled a second cup. "I don't get this. Isn't Pepper sick? Shouldn't she be in bed or something?"

"Are you worried about her?" Reid teased.

"I'm worried about anyone who would hang out with Mark."

"Michael." Elise stood.

"Just teasing."

"I'll go check on them." Rebekah grabbed her coat off the hook by the door, and Elise followed.

Mark stood in the middle of the corral and walked in a tight circle while Sky trotted in a wide circle around him. "Do it until he's tired." Pepper sat tall on the palomino, inside the gate. "Until he bows his head."

Rebekah leaned against the railing. Bear's warm body rubbed against her legs. Sky bowed his head.

"Now what?" Mark slowed.

"Move toward him."

Mark did. Sky turned and met him.

"That's so cool." Mark rubbed the horse's head.

Elise climbed on the rail beside Rebekah.

"It's called 'the joining.'" Pepper opened the gate. "It means that he accepts you as part of the herd and that he's submissive to you."

Part of the herd. Rebekah loved that.

Mark mounted Sky and began to ride. On the second time around he said, "Mom, you have an e-mail from Dad. I read it in the kitchen."

"Why were you checking my e-mail? You were supposed to stop that."

"Because Dad hasn't e-mailed me in a few days. I wondered if he had e-mailed you." Sky began to trot.

Rebekah grimaced. Poor Elise.

On the third time around, Mark slowed Sky. "Dad said if you don't get tested, you'll regret it."

Elise pulled her coat tight and turned away from Pepper, away from Rebekah. "Stop reading my e-mail," she hissed at Mark.

Rebekah caught her arm. "Elise, don't worry about it."

"How can I not?" Elise started toward the house. "It's all I think about."

lise parallel parked her car in front of the Scrap Shack. She had rid-
den Sky around the pasture that morning without any problems,
but as she rode, she decided she couldn't take advantage of Rebekah's hos-
pitality with her horses and ignore her the rest of the time. So here she was
at the store for Midnight Madness.

The six o'clock news came on the radio. "Three U.S. soldiers died in
separate bombings in Iraq today." Elise gripped the steering wheel and
tried to swallow. The panic stuck in her throat. She took a deep breath
and let it out slowly. She would check the BBC after Midnight Madness
to get an idea of where the bombings were. The chances that one of the
three was Ted were nearly nil. She knew that. Still, every time a report
came across the news, she fought her fear.

She had told Ted last night never to bring up her being tested again.
Not on the phone. Not by e-mail. Not to the boys. She knew that his
intentions were good, driven by his desire to see Pepper healed, but he
was making her life miserable. He had apologized. He seemed to finally
understand.

She turned off the ignition. The husband of their neighbor in Georgia
had been killed in the first days of the Iraq War. When the chaplain's car
had parked in the shared driveway between the two houses, Elise had called
Ted to the window. They'd waited. She half expected a scream or a wail,
the house to shake, the street to split in two, or at least the neighborhood

to tremble. Something. Tarry's life had just been blown to pieces. After the chaplain had left, Elise and Ted had knocked on the door. Tarry stood in her entryway, squeezing her two-year-old son. They played with the baby while she made phone calls. Ted went to the store and picked up milk and cereal. Elise washed the dishes and did a load of laundry. A month later Tarry moved to Sacramento, where her parents lived.

Where would Elise move? She wouldn't want to move anywhere without Ted. She wouldn't want to stay in Forest Falls. She wouldn't want to move to Seattle. She wouldn't want to be, without Ted.

She grabbed her box of Mark's photos and the scrapbook off the passenger seat. She had finally finished the sorting. Tonight she would begin grouping the photos.

Sandi slid her cutter through a piece of lavender paper. "John and I went into Salem last night. We saw *The Lion, the Witch, and the Wardrobe.*"

"Was it good?" Elise settled into her chair. It would be nice if John would take the boys to a movie, and that would have been the perfect movie.

"Loved it."

"So what's going on between you and John?" Elise opened the box of photos nonchalantly.

"We're just friends." Sandi shrugged. "I'll be honest, though. I like John—a lot."

Elise smiled.

"But he wants to give things time. It hasn't been that long since Maude died, and he wants to be sensitive to Ted's grief. You know, all of that." She sighed. "All the things I taught in my grief class." Sandi positioned the lavender paper on a page. "I'm fine with that. I can wait. I've learned not to put my hope in other people."

"What do you mean?" Elise sifted through the photos.

"They always let you down."

"So you have to put your hope in God, right?" Elise hoped she didn't sound cynical. It just sounded like such a cliché.

Sandi nodded.

"And then you can blame him if the kids don't turn out and your marriage fails." Elise laughed. Or your husband goes far away— No, wait, she could blame Ted for that. Unless he was dead. She pulled out a handful of photos.

"Elise." Sandi leaned back. "Are you okay?"

Elise pressed her fingertips against her temple. She'd said too much. Now Sandi would tell John, and John would tell Ted. "I'm just stressed."

Sandi took a deep breath. "My husband was a pharmacy rep; he traveled all the time. I pretty much ran the farm and worked part-time. We didn't have kids, and I was still stressed when he was gone."

Elise stared straight ahead.

"I know." Sandi sighed. "It's not the same as having a husband in Iraq."

Elise touched Sandi's arm. "And then your husband died."

Sandi nodded. "And then I realized what stress was." She pointed at Elise's scrapbook. "When are you going to get started on that?"

"Tonight. Well I was going to start grouping the photos tonight, but they're sort of out of order again. I think one of the boys was snooping— probably Michael." Elise pulled out the first three photos of newborn Mark.

Pepper and Ainsley clambered up the stairs. "Look, Mom!" Pepper held up a cell phone. "Ainsley has a camera phone, and we just took a picture of a raccoon."

Rebekah smiled. "Cool, sweet pea."

"It wasn't as scary close up as I thought."

Rebekah took the phone. "Well, don't make a habit of getting too close. They can be pretty mean."

Elise bent over her photos. She could just imagine the pictures Ainsley could take with a camera phone.

Rebekah handed the phone to Ainsley and then stopped at Elise's table. "Pepper said that Mark's birthday is next week," Rebekah said.

"I was going to talk with you about that. He wants to go to Seattle, but Michael doesn't want to go. Could Michael stay at your place?" Elise's other choice was to ask John. She knew Michael would rather stay with Reid, even though Elise hated to ask.

"Sure, anytime."

"Remember when we went to Seattle, Mom"—Pepper gave the phone back to Ainsley—"and Reid got sick outside the fish market?"

Rebekah nodded. "And he hasn't eaten fish since." She turned to Elise. "When are you leaving?"

"Thursday at noon, which means Mark will miss two days with the horses."

"No problem." Rebekah smiled. "Reid can take a turn."

"Make Michael help."

"Where are you going?" Sandi sat down with a brownie in her hand.

"Seattle. For Mark's birthday." Elise looked at her photos as she spoke.

"What are you going to do?" Sandi asked.

"Go to a couple of bookstores. Take Mark to the music museum. Maybe go by the aquarium and the market."

"And look at houses?" Sandi held her brownie in midair.

"Why would you look at houses?" Pepper pulled up a chair next to her mom's. Rebekah put her arm around Pepper and whispered something in her ear.

Elise shook her head. "I won't have time." She would pick up fliers, though. She glanced at her watch: 6:45. She wanted to go home and check the BBC.

Chapter 42

*R*ebekah scooted the scraps of paper into the recycling box. It was 11:50. Everyone had gone home but Sandi.

"John's afraid that Elise is going to move to Seattle." Sandi wedged her scrapbook into her tote.

"While Ted is in Iraq?" Rebekah dropped the box against the wall. "No, I think she wants to move next summer."

"He thinks she'll find a house while he's gone." Sandi zipped the side pocket over her cutter.

"That doesn't sound like Elise."

"She's not exactly happy here."

"What would make her happier?" Rebekah folded a chair.

"Who knows?" Sandi wheeled her tote to the top of the stairs.

Rebekah folded another chair and headed to the closet. "I don't think that she feels safe here."

"Why wouldn't she?"

"I think she feels judged."

Sandi folded a chair. "Rebekah, what are you talking about?"

"I think she felt like she never measured up to Maude's expectations. Now John keeps making negative comments about Mark."

"And tons of positive comments about Michael."

"The positive never outweighs the negative." Rebekah headed to the closet with two more chairs.

"Mark is a handful."

"Elise is doing her best."

"She babies him."

"So she's not a perfect mom. Let's indict her." Rebekah flipped the table on its side. "She moves here to make Ted happy, he gets orders to go to Germany, and then he volunteers to go to Iraq. It can't be easy for her."

"Military spouses deal with this every day."

"And now she feels pressured to get tested to see if she's a match for Pepper." Rebekah folded the table legs.

"Is she going to get tested?" Sandi plopped down on the couch.

"I don't want her to. She's not available to donate a kidney."

"John would help."

"Like he has so far?" Rebekah pulled the table to the wall.

"He's trying."

Rebekah collapsed on the couch beside Sandi. "Here you are helping me out, and I'm wagging my tongue—about a family that's none of my business."

"No. It is your business; you care about them."

Rebekah stood. Sandi was right. She did care about Elise, and it had nothing to do with her blood type. "I'll be honest. I didn't like Elise at first. She seemed pretentious and needy. But I've grown to appreciate her, to really like her."

Sandi sat forward, her hands on her knees. "I hope they don't move. I'd like to give her a chance, but you're right. I guess I wouldn't blame Elise if they did."

A bus parked in front of the shop. Rebekah hurried to the window. She had heard of busloads of quilters traveling from state to state to visit fabric stores. Wouldn't it be great if a busload of scrappers had found the Scrap Shack?

Women began to file off the bus. Retired women. Then a man, more women, and a couple more men. A group headed through the door. "Hi," the first one called out. "We're with a senior group from Portland. We're on a field trip."

"Welcome to Forest Falls." Rebekah smiled her cheeriest smile. "There's coffee upstairs. Let me know if I can help you with anything."

A white-haired man approached, looking for a forest-green album. He'd grown up in Idaho and wanted to start a heritage album. Rebekah showed him her Italian leather line that included a masculine-looking dark green book. The man thumbed through it as the shop phone rang.

It was the school secretary. Rebekah turned toward the wall, afraid that Pepper was not doing well.

"Hey, Reid isn't in fifth period. You didn't check him out, so I thought I'd call."

"He should be there."

"Michael is absent this period too."

The nice man with the green album stood at the counter.

"Thanks. I'll get right on it." She didn't want to close the shop. She rang up the elderly man's choice and told him that Mark Twain had scrapbooked. The man laughed. She called Sandi's cell as soon as the man turned away. No answer. A woman approached the counter with a handful of travel stickers and explained that the group went on a field trip once a month and this was the first time they had visited Forest Falls. Rebekah rang up her merchandise and then dialed John's number. Sandi wasn't there. Rebekah reminded John that Elise was in Seattle and then rattled off the story.

"I'll go check the park." John hung up quickly. Thank goodness he wasn't one to chat. Twenty-two customers and an hour later the last of the group left the shop. Rebekah wanted to high-five herself. If only a senior group stopped by the shop every day, even once a week. She had offered to teach a class to them if they came back.

She dialed John's home number again. No answer. He was the man without a cell; she would have to wait. As she hurried upstairs to retrieve the empty coffee carafe, the door buzzed. She hurried to the railing as John walked into the shop with the two boys slinking behind him.

"I found them at Ted's." John wore his leather jacket and black work boots.

Rebekah bounded down the stairs. "Reid."

"It was my fault." Michael stepped around his grandfather. "Lunch was really nasty. They had these vegetarian sticks that they try to pass as fish, which made us both sick—me because I like fish and Reid because he doesn't. Anyway, I suggested nachos at my house."

"You're not supposed to go home for lunch." Rebekah clutched the carafe with both hands. Elise made her boys lunches every morning; Reid told her that at least three times a week.

"I know we're not supposed to go home. That's why it's my fault. I suggested it."

"And then we got on the computer." Reid hung his head.

"And then they hid when they heard my key in the lock." John crossed his arms.

"How did you know they were there?"

"The two plates on the table. I knew Elise would never leave dirty dishes in her house."

Rebekah stifled a giggle; she'd left a kitchen full of dirty dishes just this morning. "John, could you take them back to school? Make them apologize to their teachers and see what punishment the principal has for them."

John nodded.

"Please don't call my mom." Michael put his arm on Rebekah's shoulder. "She's already stressed."

"We'll see." Rebekah put the carafe on the counter.

✂

Why had she been vague with Michael? Of course she was going to call Elise. She headed to the storeroom, dialing Elise's number.

"Is everything all right?" Elise asked.

"Just fine. Where are you?"

"Olympia."

"I just wanted to update you on a little expedition Michael and Reid came up with today." Rebekah sat down on a box of paper. "They decided to have lunch at your house and skipped fifth and sixth period."

"You're kidding!"

Rebekah could hear Mark laugh. Rebekah continued. "John found them and took them back to school and made them apologize to everyone. They got detention and missed practice, and they probably won't start in Tuesday's game."

Mark laughed louder.

"Hold on a second. I'm taking you off speaker." Elise paused. "I'm sorry—sorry about Michael."

"I think it was a good lesson for them."

"Was John furious?"

"He did surprisingly well. I think it was a good lesson for him too." Rebekah smiled. Michael wasn't perfect after all.

"Thanks, Rebekah."

Rebekah stood. "I miss you, girl."

"Thanks." Elise's voice relaxed just a little. She hesitated and then said, "I miss you too."

Chapter 43

*W*hat's going on?" Mark turned his sleepy head toward Elise. "Traffic."

"Where are we?" he yawned.

"Just north of Tacoma."

"What are you listening to?"

"Classical."

Mark scowled and closed his eyes for a moment. "I can't stand it. It's sucky music—old-lady music." He shifted his body away from her, hunkering toward the door.

Elise slammed on the brakes. The Toyota wagon ahead of her swerved onto the shoulder. She slammed harder, barely avoiding the corner of the car's bumper.

"Mom, are you trying to kill me?" He shifted in his seat.

She took out the CD. He turned his face toward her and smiled. She switched the radio on for the traffic report. "Northbound traffic is bumper to bumper from the Tacoma Dome into downtown Seattle due to an accident north of the Convention Center exit. Now for the news. Ten U.S. soldiers were killed in a roadside bombing in Iraq."

The cords in Elise's neck tightened as she switched off the radio. "What do you want to listen to, honey?"

"Nothing." He pulled his hood over his head and turned toward the door.

Two hours later they checked into the Alexis Hotel.

"This is a chick hotel." Mark walked ahead of Elise through the lobby, scanning the potted plants, overstuffed chairs, and ornate molding. They usually stayed in military lodging.

"Would you like to dine this evening at the Library Bistro?" the clerk asked.

"Mom." Mark rolled his eyes. "I'd rather get pizza."

"The Library Bistro sounds great." Elise took her Gold Card from the clerk and tucked it back into her wallet. "We'll get pizza tomorrow," she whispered to Mark.

"How did you find a chick hotel with a library restaurant?" Mark stomped toward the elevator. Thirty minutes later he sat in the faux reptile-skin booth with his arms crossed. "What are we doing tonight?"

"We'll go to the bookstore where I used to work, where your dad and I met, and then we'll walk along the waterfront."

"Not another bookstore." He tipped his head to the shelves that lined the walls of the restaurant, shelves filled with books.

"The fish and chips are supposed to be really good here." Elise put her menu down.

"I hate fish, remember?"

"You do?" She picked up the camera and took his photo.

Mark scowled. "Hello. Michael likes fish. I'm Mark. I hate it."

It began to rain as they walked into the bookstore. Elise breathed in the closed-up smell of the stacks of books mixed with the aroma of coffee from the café. The old wood floors creaked under their feet.

"Is there a chair where I can sit?" Mark asked.

"Come with me." Elise headed for the poetry section.

Mark slumped against a bookcase. "I'll wait here."

She stood where she and Ted first met, but it wasn't the poetry section anymore, it was the technical books section. She wandered to the fiction section and then found her way to poetry and to Yeats and pulled his collected works off the shelf. She read "When You Are Old" quietly and slowly: "Murmur, a little sadly, how love fled and paced upon the mountains overhead." She could move the boys to Seattle without Ted.

No.

That wasn't what she wanted for her family. What did she want? What did she want for herself? A house in an old Seattle neighborhood. She used to think she wanted to own a bookstore, but that was out of the question with big chains all over the city now. A Barnes & Noble or a Borders could be found in nearly every neighborhood. Maybe she could work at one. She winced. She put Yeats back on the shelf. She missed Ted. She wanted nothing more than to grow old with him.

She found Mark where she'd left him. "Aren't you going to buy anything?" he asked.

She shook her head. "Let's walk down to the wharf."

"Let's not. It's pouring. I want to see what's on TV."

"We'll take a taxi down." She pulled an umbrella out of her bag. "Then we'll go back to the hotel and see what's on TV." She wanted him to see the ferries on the Sound and the lights of the city, to smell the salt air and feel the biting wind surging in off the water.

Elise paid the taxi driver. She popped open the umbrella as Mark began to gag.

"What's wrong?" Had he been poisoned by the burger he had for dinner?

"It reeks down here." He gagged again. "What's that smell?"

Elise shook her head. Pepper must have told him the story about Reid getting sick in Seattle. Mark was copying Reid because he wanted to go back to the hotel.

"I'm not joking." He gagged again. A gull swooped down to the gutter. "It's right there." Mark pointed to the bird pecking at a rotting fish.

"Come on." Elise grabbed Mark's sleeve. "Let's walk."

"Happy Birthday." Elise clutched her camera as they walked out of the Experience Music Project and breathed deeply, trying to quell her anxiety from the loud music and flashing lights. "Ready to go up the Space Needle?" She tipped her head and looked upward. There it was, towering over them.

"Not really. We went up it two years ago." Mark tossed a gum wrapper into a garbage can. "How about if we go out for pizza and then back to the hotel?"

Elise frowned. He wanted to watch cable. "Then let's at least get a picture of you under the Space Needle."

Mark groaned as Elise clicked the camera. Her cell rang while she drove back to the hotel. Of course it was Ted. She handed the phone to Mark. He smiled and chatted away about Seattle, about the dead fish, and the music museum. "Seattle isn't as cool as I remember, though, Dad. Mom keeps driving around these funky neighborhoods, and the traffic is really bad."

She parked in the hotel garage. Mark handed her the phone. "How's the birthday boy's mom?" Ted asked.

"Fine. Missing the birthday boy's dad." Her tone sounded sharp.

"I haven't missed that many of Mark's birthdays." Ted sounded defensive.

"The first and the last." Had he missed any in between? Yes. He'd missed Mark's eleventh when he was in Afghanistan, but who was keeping track?

"How's Seattle?"

"Good. We're having a great time."

"See any houses?"

"A few." And they all cost at least three-quarters of a million dollars.

That night she dreamed about Cascade Pass. She followed her father up the stairs of their house. An old man with white hair stood in the kitchen with his back to her. He turned, slowly, surely. He smiled at her, a warm, knowing expression. Was it her father as an old man, the age he would be now if he had lived? No. This man was more than her father. She stepped forward, comforted, reassured.

She woke. The anxiety had eased.

Over breakfast Elise told Mark that they were driving to Cascade Pass.

Mark shoveled pancakes into his mouth. "Do you want to move *there*?"

She shook her head. The question was absurd. "No. I just want to see it."

"Why?"

She folded the *Seattle Times*. "That's where I grew up." She hardly ever talked about her family to the boys. It had been six years since Mark and Michael had seen her mother and sister. She had gone alone the last two times.

"I thought you grew up in Seattle."

"No. I spent a week every summer here with my grandmother. That was all. And then went to college here."

Mark slept as Elise drove north. The Saturday traffic out of town was much better than the weekday traffic had been. Mark fell back asleep as Elise turned east at Everett. An hour later, as her Volvo climbed the highway further up the mountain, the snow began to fall. "Mark, look." Elise slowed. Big, fluffy flakes floated through the evergreen trees. It was just as she remembered.

Mark grunted and fell back asleep.

The café where she had waitressed through high school was now an antique shop, the courthouse had winter pansies planted along the walkway, and the one-room library where as a child she'd spent hours after school had a Closed sign in the window.

Mark stirred. "Is this it?"

"Yes. Isn't it quaint?"

"It's smaller than Forest Falls."

The sawmill had been abandoned, the church freshly painted, and the big Victorian on the corner of Main and Baker Streets was a bed-and-breakfast. What would it be like to stay there for a weekend? Would anyone in town remember her? Surely a few would remember her father's tragic accident.

She turned onto Rainier Street. "That's my old house."

"Mom, that's pathetic."

The roof sagged, and the siding was nearly bare of paint. It had looked much better in her dream. "It's so small." Mark pressed his nose against the window.

"Only two bedrooms." No family room, no study, no formal dining room—no wonder her mother felt crazy half the time. No privacy, nowhere to escape.

"I didn't know you were dirt poor."

"We weren't." Or were they? "My father worked hard. We had what we needed."

What had she needed? Books and riding horses with her friends. They'd been so generous to include her. Just like Rebekah. She stopped the car across the street from the old house. She couldn't conjure up the image of the old man in her dream. Why had she come? The house looked abandoned. The house next door, where the Williams family had lived, looked in good repair. She wondered where the girls ended up. Should she knock on the door and ask? See if Mr. and Mrs. Williams still lived there? She read the name on the mailbox: the Andersens.

She drove to the far end of town and pulled into the cemetery. "This is where your grandpa is buried."

"Spooky." Mark pulled his hood onto his head.

Elise pointed to the field beyond the cemetery. "That's where I used to ride with my friends, when I wasn't holed up in the library. We would ride from here way up into the forest and then to the high meadows."

"Like the meadows above Pepper's?"

Elise nodded. She wanted to go back to Rebekah's, back to the falls.

"There's a horse." Mark craned his neck. "Two of them. Quarter horses." He opened the door to the Volvo and took off toward the fence. His hood fell against his back, and gigantic snowflakes disappeared on his blond head. Elise followed, pulling her parka snug.

The darker horse ambled over to the fence, and Mark reached out and stroked her neck. "I wish I had an apple."

Elise wiggled her camera from her pocket. It was the first settled moment Mark had had the whole trip. The other horse, a mare, approached them and then took a step backward. "It's okay." Mark reached out his hand to the bay. She sniffed his fingertips and then licked the wet snow from his hand. Mark turned toward Elise and smiled. She took another photo.

Elise wandered through the tombstones and found her father's simple block of granite. Who was the old man in the dream? *Was it you, God?*

She took a photo of the grave site and then shivered, slipped the camera back into her pocket, and pulled on her gloves. "Be careful who you make sacrifices for," her mother had told her. Her mother had gained nothing in life; she was a lonely old woman who watched television.

"Cascade Pass isn't so bad." Mark turned up the heat in the car as they drove back through the town.

"I was thinking about going home today." She missed Michael. She missed Forest Falls. She missed Rebekah and the Scrap Shack. Thinking about her father made her miss even John. And she missed Ted, always Ted. She swallowed hard.

The snow swirled as it fell. "We'd better hurry," Mark said, "or we're going to get stuck."

A settled silence filled the car as Elise concentrated on the curves in the mountain road. She tried not to focus on the snowflakes floating against the windshield in a mesmerizing pattern.

"Mom."

"Yes, Mark?"

"Why won't you get tested?"

"Tested?"

"To see if you're a match for Pepper?"

Elise pursed her lips together.

"Mom."

"I have many reasons." She spoke slowly as she maneuvered a hairpin curve. "Dad's gone, I have back problems, and what if you needed a kidney someday?"

"Those are the same bogus excuses."

Elise accelerated on a straight stretch. "What do you mean?"

"It doesn't matter that Dad's gone; everyone would help you. I'm never going to need a kidney, and you seem pretty healthy to me."

Elise gripped the steering wheel.

"I did some research." Mark slumped further in his seat. "An average of ten people in the United States die every day because they need a kidney transplant. An average of two American soldiers have died in Iraq each day since the war started, and, Mom, not one army medical person has died."

Elise steered with one hand and pressed her fingers against her left temple. "Rebekah said that kids take priority. Pepper should have a kidney soon."

Mark pulled his hood back onto his head. "Mom, Dad's chances are better than Pepper's. Why not get tested? Then you can decide."

lise called." Patrick stood at the sink rinsing dishes. "They're on their way home tonight but won't get in until really late. She asked if we could drop Michael off at her house after church."

Rebekah scooted the bag of groceries onto the breakfast bar. "Did Reid and Michael muck out the barn?"

"Mostly. Mark does a much better job."

"Patrick, that was a positive comment about Mark. What's going on?"

He shrugged. "The kid is a hard worker, and he's good with the horses."

She put the three loaves of bread into the drawer. Reid was into cinnamon toast these days, half a loaf at a time. The trick was to keep Pepper away from the white bread. "What else did Elise say?"

"That was about it."

"Anything about moving to Seattle?"

"No. Why? Did she say something to you?"

"No. Sandi thinks that's her plan." Rebekah dumped the apples from their bag into the fruit bowl. "Sandi said that Ted is seeing a lot of action."

"In the operating room? Or on the base?"

"Both. Mortars came in again night before last." Rebekah poked her head into the dining room. "Where's Michael?"

"Upstairs."

"Whew. I thought I'd done it with my big mouth again. Where's Pepper?"

"Out with the horses." Patrick wiped the counter around the sink. "Do you want to walk along the fence line before it's completely dark? I'll show you what I did today; I finally finished resetting that post."

Bear loped along beside them. "Hey, big guy." Rebekah patted his head as he rubbed up against her leg.

"He took off after a deer this morning. Chased him up the trail into the trees. Came back an hour later," Patrick said.

"He didn't get it, did he?"

"No. Well, if he did, he licked his chops clean."

"Bear, you wouldn't kill a deer, would you?" The dog wagged his tail and nuzzled her hand.

Patrick took a deep breath. "How was business at the shop this week?"

"Good, but I'm still not in the black. I had to pay utilities and the vendors. They say it usually takes a year."

"We don't have a year." Patrick picked up a stick. Bear ran ahead. "I think we should sell it. Would Sandi want to buy it?" He lobbed the stick into the air.

"Patrick, I don't want to sell the shop."

"It's that or the farm."

"Let's wait and see," Rebekah said. Good grief, they could start by selling a couple of the horses if they had to. She frowned.

Bear scooped up the stick and ran back. Patrick wrestled it from the dog's mouth. "I Googled 'kidney transplants' this afternoon and found some sites looking for donors. I was thinking we should do that and make up some fliers, send some press releases to the media."

Rebekah took a deep breath. She didn't want to do that. She didn't think it was wrong; she just didn't think it was right for them. Then again, if they found a kidney… But who would it be from? A townsperson she would bump into every day? Someone who came into the shop? Would she give them a discount? Or merchandise for free? The cadaver list was the best way to go. No emotional strings attached.

"I called the pastor today. I asked him to pray. I asked if we could share about Pepper's needs tomorrow during the service." Patrick knelt and rubbed Bear's head and neck.

Rebekah touched her hands to her cold face. At least Elise wouldn't be at church.

Bear ran after a rabbit.

"I don't want to beg people." Patrick stood. "But I think we need to be realistic. We need a kidney, and we need to be prepared to lose the shop and maybe even the farm."

The rabbit scurried through the fence and across the road. Patrick threw the stick again and ran after Bear toward the fence.

"Mom." Pepper's voice floated from the oak tree. She jumped down from the lower branch. How much had she heard?

"What's up with Dad?" Pepper wore her blue cowboy hat and Rebekah's riding coat. At least she was warm.

"He's worried."

"Are we going to lose the shop because of me? And the farm?"

"No, sweet pea." Rebekah pulled Pepper's head against her shoulder, bumping her hat.

Patrick turned into the church parking lot slowly. A light dusting of snow had transformed Forest Falls into a pristine village. Reid, Michael, and Pepper climbed out of the back of the truck, falling over each other. They ran up the shoveled steps of the church and through the carved doors.

Pastor Jim opened the service by congratulating everyone who had made it to church despite the snow. Then he asked for prayer requests. Patrick stood. Pepper, who sat next to Rebekah, ducked her head. "Most of you know that our daughter, Pepper, needs a kidney transplant. We're feeling desperate. Please pray that God will provide a donor kidney for her." He paused, opened his mouth to say more, and then sat down. Pepper's head popped back up, and she scanned the congregation.

John stood. Michael, who sat in front of Rebekah, bent his head. "As you all know, my son, Ted, is in Iraq. His army tent hospital has taken a few mortars in the last few days."

Michael raised his head. Had John forgotten about Michael being at church with them? Rebekah patted Michael's back. He shrugged.

"Please pray for Ted, and please pray for his wife, Elise, and their sons."

Pepper pressed her body against Rebekah's, hiding her head; Reid turned and rolled his eyes. Rebekah held her breath through most of the prayer.

The sermon was on John 6, the story of Jesus feeding the five thousand people. "If you love Jesus, he's going to test you just as he tested Philip." Pastor Jim sat on his stool and smiled. "Jesus knew Philip couldn't feed that many people; he wanted Philip to trust him."

The pastor read the passage and then continued. "Philip was overwhelmed, just as we're overwhelmed with what we face in our lives. Jesus felt compassion for the crowd, and he feels compassion for us. He knows you can't handle what overwhelms you on your own; he wants you to trust him."

Pepper slipped out of the row.

Pastor Jim stood. "You can choose to stay overwhelmed, or you can trust him."

Pepper leaned against the kitchen counter. "I hated having Dad announce that I need a kidney in front of the whole church, Mom. I feel like a freak."

"You are a freak." Reid spooned five mounds of ice cream into a bowl. "Reid."

"Actually, I'm tired of it too," Reid said. "It's all anyone talks about—teachers, coaches, parents. 'Has your little sister found a kidney yet? When is her surgery? Aren't you a match?'" He tossed the scoop into the sink with a clatter. "It's old."

The phone rang.

Reid slid through the dining room, balancing his bowl.

"Don't take that upstairs," Rebekah called out as she picked up the phone.

"He's going upstairs." Pepper spun around on the stool.

"Hello."

"Hi." It was Elise.

"Hey, I didn't think you were going to be at church. Then you snuck out before I could talk with you." She would have discouraged Patrick from sharing if she had known Elise was there. "Pepper said she saw you in the balcony before you grabbed Michael and dashed home."

"I decided to go at the last minute, but then I wanted to get home and check on Mark."

"Thanks for the smoked salmon and chocolate that you left in the truck."

"Thanks for watching Michael. How is Pepper doing?" Elise asked.

"Embarrassed. How are you?"

"Embarrassed."

"Why?"

"Because of John sharing in church."

"You have to admit it was sweet." Rebekah rinsed out the dishcloth.

"Yes." Elise's voice was soft. "But I had no idea Ted's unit had taken hits again. I wish he would tell me that stuff."

"Did Mark have a happy birthday?"

"Mark's birthday seemed really lonely with just the two of us..."

"Did you get what you wanted from the trip?"

"Seattle wasn't the way I remembered it. I realized I've been pining away for the past." Elise chuckled. "I'm whining."

"Elise—"

"Anyway, that's not why I called," Elise interrupted. "I have something I want to talk with you about."

"What?"

"May I come out?"

"Sure." Rebekah paced to the back door. What was up with Elise? "Come on out, and bring the boys. We're just hanging out, trying to stay warm. Mark can ride if he wants to—in the corral or field; the trail is too slick."

Chapter 45

*W*hat's going on with you, Mom?" Mark flipped the seat warmer on. Michael pressed his nose against the back window. Snow drifted from the treetops to the wet road.

"I just need to talk with Rebekah. You can ride. Michael can hang out with Reid."

"Except we're grounded from the computer." Michael breathed on the window.

Elise slowed for a corner. Rebekah had grounded Michael too. Good for her. Elise smiled.

"Mom, what's with you?" Mark slumped down in the seat. "You're acting happy—or something."

"Church was really good today." She took a deep breath. "The pastor spoke about Jesus's compassion and trust." Elise had been convicted about her lack of compassion—for Ted, for the wounded soldiers in Iraq, for John, oftentimes for Mark, and for Rebekah and Pepper. "What did you think of the sermon, Michael?"

He shrugged.

Elise continued, "Pastor Jim said that Christ will use us to show his compassion to others."

She paused. Ted had volunteered to go to Iraq because he felt it would be less disruptive for the family in the long run. His intentions were good, yet she had been curt with him since he had gone to Iraq. She had kept their conversations short, her e-mails to the point. She hadn't figured out how to IM him. How could she be so stingy with her love?

"This was the biggie." She turned into Rebekah's driveway. "He said if you love Jesus, he's going to ask you to do something you don't have the resources to do, something you can't possibly do on your own." She turned off the motor. "Because he wants us to trust him."

Mark opened his door. "Look at the horses. They're all huddled under the oak tree. The whole herd."

Did he have any idea what she was saying? Elise turned off the engine.

"Hi!" Pepper stood on the other side of the fence.

Rebekah climbed over it, toward Elise. "We had to break the ice in the trough."

Elise and Rebekah headed to the house. Michael ran past them.

"I can't wait to tell you this." Elise didn't notice the cold. She was too excited. She spoke softly. "I decided today, during church, that I want to be tested."

"Tested?"

Elise nodded.

Rebekah opened the door. "No, Elise, we already talked about this. You have back problems."

"I talked with Ted. He doesn't think it would keep me from donating."

"But he's gone."

Elise nodded. "I can get tested and all of that and then schedule it for when he gets back."

"And you don't plan to move to Seattle?"

Elise laughed. "Is that what you thought I was going to do?"

"I thought you might."

"I don't know what we're going to do in the long run. Right now, we're staying here. Tell me what I need to do to be tested."

Rebekah shook her head. "No."

Elise slipped off her shoes. "Rebekah, I'm serious."

"Why?" Rebekah pulled her boots from her feet.

"From the first moment I discovered Pepper's blood type, I knew I should do it. But I've been too afraid." She looked away. "Too selfish. But today's sermon…" Elise sat down at the breakfast bar.

"It was good, wasn't it?"

Elise nodded. "I really want to be tested, Rebekah. What do I need to do?"

Rebekah hung her coat by the back door. "Okay, this will scare you off. First they'll do a blood test to confirm that you're type B. Then there will be a tissue test. If you pass those, you need clearance from your dentist and ophthalmologist. You'll need a stress test and a CT scan and approval from a social worker."

"Slow down." Elise laughed. "Let's take it a step at a time. What's the first thing?"

"I'll call Jamie, our transplant coordinator, tomorrow to see when we can start the tests." Rebekah sat down on a stool. Tears sprang into her eyes. "Are you really serious?"

Elise nodded. "Don't tell Pepper yet. I don't want her to be disappointed if I'm not a match."

"Good plan." Rebekah pulled a tissue from her pocket.

Elise smiled. She felt happy—happier than she had felt in months, maybe years.

Patrick swung the back door open, scraping his boots on the mat. "Pepper and Mark are going to ride in the pasture. I told Mark he could ride Sky."

"Are you sure?" Elise asked, alarmed.

Rebekah nodded. "It's time. He's been doing great." Rebekah patted the chair beside her. "Patrick, sit down. We want to tell you something."

Elise stopped the Volvo in front of the school.

"Thanks, Mom!" Michael jumped from the backseat.

Mark opened the door slowly. Elise refrained from asking him about his homework. Mr. Jenkins had e-mailed her last night that Mark hadn't turned in his last three assignments. Elise hadn't answered.

"Are you coming out to Rebekah's to ride this afternoon?" Mark grasped the door handle.

"I'm going to Portland." She had passed the tissue test, and she would meet with the social worker today, but she hadn't told the boys what she was doing.

"Are you going alone?"

"No, Rebekah is going with me."

"What are you up to, Mom?"

"Errands. Maybe lunch." She smiled through her lie.

"You've been going to Portland a lot lately."

Elise drummed her fingers on the steering wheel.

"I think you're being tested to give Pepper a kidney."

Mark climbed out of the car and stood with the door open.

"I thought you wanted me to donate a kidney to Pepper," Elise said. "Both you and Michael said that."

"We do. Is that what you're doing?"

Was he worried about her? Elise nodded. She couldn't keep up her deception. "Dad will be home by the time of the surgery if I qualify."

"Mom, I'm proud of you."

"Thanks."

"Because I know it wasn't an easy decision."

She smiled. "Doing the right thing isn't always easy."

"It's kind of like taking care of horses." Mark yawned. "Some days I just don't want to do it, but it's the right thing to do. They need me." He paused. "I'm going to talk to Patrick about paying me less. Pepper said they don't have much money right now."

"Mark, please don't tell the other kids."

He nodded, closed his door, and wrestled his bike from the back. "Bye, Mom." He slammed the hatch.

✂

Rebekah dozed in the passenger seat as Elise turned on Terwilliger Boulevard and wound her way up the hill. Bare deciduous trees stood alongside fir and spruce trees, covering the steep slopes that lined the roadway. An ambulance blared, and Elise pulled off onto the narrow shoulder.

Rebekah stirred. Elise eased back onto the boulevard, heading to the parking garage. The Willamette River stretched below, bending toward downtown.

Her cell rang as they walked across the wide, long skybridge. "It's Ted," she said to Rebekah.

"I got your e-mail." He often jumped right into the middle of a conversation when he called. She knew that he was in a hurry. "I think that you should have the surgical procedure instead of the laparoscopic surgery. Anything that increases the chances of the kidney's success and longevity is worth it."

Elise agreed. Jamie had explained that more donors were opting for the laparoscopic procedure because the recovery was two weeks instead of six, but the transplants were more successful with the surgical procedure. It could mean years to Pepper in the future. "I'm really proud of you, Elise." He paused. "I just want to make sure you don't feel pressured. Especially by me. I was really out of line."

"You were." She chuckled. "I don't feel pressured, honestly. I feel this is what God wants."

"I'll be home to take care of you in less than a month." They chatted for another few minutes. Rebekah sat down at a table halfway across the skybridge. She seemed tired.

The weather had been cool in Iraq, in the eighties. "It's the rainy season." Ted chuckled. "And not a cloud in the sky."

"It's sunny here too. I can see Mount Hood and"—she turned toward the north—"Mount Saint Helens. I'm on the skybridge." It was the first sunny day in a month. Elise leaned closer to the window. Birds flew up from the river below and over the treetops. Miniature cars inched across the bridge.

"I totally support you in this, Elise. You're doing a wonderful—" Ted's voice became garbled.

"I'm losing you." She turned away from the window and pulled out the antenna on her phone. "Ted?" He was gone. She hurried to catch up with Rebekah, and they crossed over to the clinic.

"It will be a few minutes." The receptionist returned Elise's medical card, and she sat down next to Rebekah in the crowded waiting room.

"You need to see her alone," Rebekah said as the social worker called Elise's name. "I'll wait here. If they need me for anything, they'll ask."

Elise followed the social worker through the hall to a back office. "You're doing a wonderful thing to consider donating a kidney." The woman smiled. "We want you to know that being tested and passing the tests doesn't mean you're committed to donate. You can change your mind at any time."

Elise nodded.

"Your chart looks good. The blood and tissue samples match. You're healthy." The social worker leaned back in her chair.

Elise exhaled. "I had a back injury and took painkillers for quite a while." Elise uncrossed her arms. "I was worried about that."

"The kidney scan looks good." The social worker lowered her voice. "And so does your liver."

Elise tried to relax. If she hadn't damaged her kidneys or liver, maybe she hadn't damaged Mark, either.

"What does your family think about you donating? Let's start with your husband."

"He's an anesthesiologist, so from the start he thought I should be tested."

"I see he's in the army." She leaned closer to the paperwork. "Or retired army? Which is it?"

"He was retired, in the inactive reserve for a couple of months, and then he got called back in."

"Where is he now?"

"Iraq."

"Well, that complicates things." The social worker closed the file, marking the spot with her index finger.

"He'll be home by the time of the surgery."

"Are you sure?"

Elise wrinkled her nose and laughed. "Well, it is the army. I think he'll be home by then."

"Are you worried about him?"

"About his safety?"

The social worker nodded.

"Not really," she lied.

"I see you have two boys. Are they worried about you?"

Elise shook her head. "They're both very supportive of this; both encouraged me to do it. They would, if they could."

"Don't be surprised if they get clingy in the next little while. This is stressful for them too. Especially with their dad being overseas."

Elise nodded. They talked about Elise's availability, her support system, finances, and her recovery time. "You'll need to have someone else lined up to care for you after the surgery in case your husband isn't back in time." The social worker placed the file on her desk and clasped her hands together. "What concerns do you have?"

Elise shook her head. "I don't think I have any." She paused. "Well, maybe one. I don't want Rebekah and Pepper to feel indebted to me. I just want to do this, have it work, and then go on with our lives." Actually, she didn't think Pepper would feel indebted; it was Rebekah she was worried about.

"They *will* feel indebted to you."

"What can I do about that?"

"Accept it." The social worker paused. "There is one thing you can do. It won't help in the long run, but it might help right after surgery. Don't let Pepper see you for a few days. The donor is usually in more pain than the recipient; it will be a harder surgery for you. That often makes the recipient feel guilty. I doubt if you can keep Rebekah away after surgery, though." The social worker laughed. "But we can probably convince Rebekah to have Pepper wait."

Elise wrinkled her nose. "How soon do you think the surgery will be?"

"When do you think your husband will be back?"

"In a month. Pepper's been losing kidney function. Do you think she can last that long?"

"Hopefully. The coordinator, Jamie—"

Elise nodded.

"—will contact the surgery team and see what their schedule looks like. Pepper is definitely a priority around here."

"So, in just over a month?"

The social worker nodded.

"What's next?" Elise slung her purse over her shoulder.

"You'll meet with the coordinator again and go over the rest of the tests. You may meet with me anytime you want." The social worker pulled a document from a green file on the desk. "I have an agreement to go over with you, for you to sign. Go ahead and read it."

"Could Rebekah come in for this part? I think she'd like to be a part of this." Elise hesitated. "But first I want to call my husband."

Elise stood on the skybridge and called Ted. Hopefully he was still awake. "I'm a match. And approved. I sign the donor document in just a minute."

"That's wonderful."

"Ted, just one thing. I want you to be here. The thought of going through surgery without you here is as bad as Christmas without you, almost as bad as childbirth without you."

"I'll be there."

"Are you being overly optimistic? Because you know how much I hate hospitals."

"No, baby. I'm ninety-nine percent sure I'll be there."

"And if you're not here?"

She could sense him smiling from seven thousand miles away. "Things will work out."

Elise hurried back to the waiting room and then down the hall with Rebekah. They sat down in front of the social worker's desk. Elise read the document out loud. "Living Kidney Donor Agreement." She took a deep breath. "The donor will undergo an operation called living donor nephrectomy during which one kidney will be removed. The recipient will receive the kidney during the operation called renal transplant." She paused and then continued, "The kidney will be donated as a gift and will create no financial or material encumbrances on the recipient, either before or after the operations."

Tears filled Elise's eyes. A gift. Like compassion. A gift to be accepted by the recipient.

"Sign at the bottom if you agree." The social worker handed her a pen.

ears stung Rebekah's eyes. She pulled a tissue from the pocket of her coat as Elise signed the document. One tear escaped, then another. She put her arm around Elise. "Thank you," she whispered.

"Rebekah, don't make me cry." Elise laughed a little. The social worker handed her a tissue.

"Rebekah"—the social worker pointed to the recipient line—"as Pepper's mother, you sign here."

Rebekah signed, slowly and purposefully, and then hugged Elise again, a big mama-bear hug. "Thank you. That's all I can say. Thank you." Rebekah grabbed two more tissues from the social worker's desk and handed another one to Elise.

Rebekah drove on the way home while Elise slept. They would tell the kids. All four would be at the farm. Michael and Reid's practice had been canceled because of a wrestling match in the gym. Rebekah would drive straight home and then get her truck later.

Her plan had not been God's plan. God's plan, his design, was so much better. Pepper would be so relieved that Elise could give her a kidney, that it wouldn't come from someone she didn't know or a cadaver.

Rebekah stopped the Volvo in front of the fence. Mark walked in a circle on the inside of the corral; Sky trotted around him.

"Thanks for driving," Elise said.

"Did you have a good rest?"

Elise nodded.

The moms climbed out of the car and leaned on the railing. Mark kept his eyes on the horse.

"He's good," Rebekah whispered to Elise, "really good."

Sky dipped his head, snorted, and headed to Mark.

"Good boy." Mark's voice was gentle. He pulled the saddle off the fence and swung it onto the horse.

"Where's Pepper?"

"In the barn, getting the mare."

Rebekah swung the barn door open. "Pep?"

"Back here."

Elise followed Rebekah.

"We have good news, sweetie." Rebekah shoved her hands into her back pockets.

Pepper poked her head out of the mare's stall. She wore her blue cowboy hat over her braids. She smiled her pixie grin.

"We found a match." Rebekah smiled, stopping at the open stall gate.

"What?" Pepper slipped the bit into the horse's mouth.

Elise climbed on the rail. "I'm a match. An all-around kidney match for you. I signed the donor document."

Pepper shook her head in disbelief.

"Elise got tested. We didn't tell you; we didn't want you to get your hopes up." Rebekah opened the gate to the stall. "And I signed the recipient document. It's all settled."

Pepper kissed the mare on the nose, and then ran into her mother's arms, reaching out with one hand for Elise.

Patrick came home late. "They're working you too hard." Rebekah pushed a load of clean, unfolded clothes that were piled on her side of the bed onto the floor.

"I'm trying to do everything I can so that when Pepper has surgery, they'll owe me comp time." Patrick picked up the clothes and threw them in the chair.

Rebekah collapsed onto the bed. "I can't take this much longer."

"I'll help you fold them." He pushed the chair to the foot of the bed. He inspected each garment and draped the unwrinkled ones over the footboard.

"I tried to call earlier. We have good news." She pushed her pillow against the headboard. "Elise is a match."

Patrick dropped Reid's basketball jersey on the floor. "No."

"Yes."

"Is she going to do it?"

"She signed the donor form; she intends to. Nothing is for sure, right? We learned that the last time. But she looks like a very strong possibility."

"What a relief." He picked up the jersey. "I never dreamed that Elise would do this for us."

"That's not all. Jamie called late this afternoon and asked me to bring Pepper in tomorrow to check her function and symptoms."

"Why wait to do the surgery?"

"They have to schedule it with the surgery team, and Elise wants Ted to be home." Rebekah yanked a tissue out of the box. "I wasn't going to cry about this, because you know it's not a sure thing until the surgery actually happens, until the kidney starts to work." She dabbed at her eyes.

Patrick put out his hand for a tissue. Rebekah handed him hers and grabbed another one. He sat down beside her for a moment, then stood and headed to the door. "Come on. Let's go watch Pepper sleep."

They stood together, hand in hand, and stared at her as if she were a newborn. She slept on her back, her arms curled over her head. "Let's pray that Ted comes home sooner than expected." Rebekah leaned down and stroked a blond wisp from Pepper's eye.

"Let's pray that all of the Sheltons stay healthy and safe." Patrick squeezed Rebekah's hand.

She shivered. Elise had seemed to be the least generous person she had ever met. Now she was giving her a gift that no one else could. She shivered again.

"Cold?" Patrick asked, putting his arms around her.

Rebekah nodded.

"Let's go watch Reid sleep." Patrick headed to the door.

"Fair is fair." Rebekah turned away from Pepper. "If we don't, I'm sure we'll hear about it in the morning."

"Did you tell Reid about Elise?" Patrick asked.

Rebekah nodded. "And her boys too. They all seemed a little bit in awe."

✄

"Your kidney function is at twelve percent." Dr. Thomas felt the shunt in Pepper's arm. "They did a good job with this. You're ready to go."

"Elise is going to donate her kidney." Pepper zipped her backpack.

"Jamie told me." Dr. Thomas smiled and nodded. "In the meantime, you may have to start dialysis. We'll see where you are next week."

"Why?" Pepper asked. "If I'm getting a transplant?"

"We may need to do something sooner," Dr. Thomas said.

"Why can't we just do the surgery now?" Pepper asked.

The doctor closed Pepper's folder and stood up. "We have to coordinate everyone's schedule."

As they walked out of the office, Rebekah took Pepper's hand, knowing she was being overprotective.

Rebekah turned the pickup onto Terwilliger Boulevard, inching forward in the bumper-to-bumper traffic. A group of runners came through the trees in the park. She envied anyone who had the time to do more than survive.

"Mom, are you all right with Elise doing this?" Pepper unzipped her backpack and took out a skein of variegated blue and brown yarn.

Rebekah nodded.

"I thought you said it would be better if it came off the cadaver list."

"It's hard to explain, sweet pea. But if this is the kidney that God is going to give us, then I'll be forever grateful—both to God and to Elise."

Rebekah pulled on Pepper's arm when they reached the house. "Come on, Pep. We're home. You've got to wake up. You're too big to carry."

Pepper tucked her head under Rebekah's arm.

"Are you feeling okay, sweet pea?"

"I'm just tired." Pepper swung her legs out of the truck, one at a time.

"Let's get you in."

"I didn't do all my homework."

"Don't worry about it. I'll write a note." Rebekah pulled her daughter close, supporting her as they struggled toward the house.

lise dashed through the door of the Scrap Shack, trying to dodge the rain, with Mark's scrapbook tucked in her book bag. She hadn't even started the album, so she couldn't possibly finish it before the surgery. She hurried up the stairs, as Midnight Madness had already started. Elise pulled off her hood—and someone started to clap. Others joined in.

They were clapping for her.

Her face reddened, and she shook her head. "Don't. Please."

"No, do." Rebekah stepped forward.

"Any of you would do it." Elise put the books and pictures on the table. "In fact, all of you would have done it much sooner than I did if you could have. Pepper would be healthy by now."

"Stop." Rebekah took Elise's parka. "Just take a bow and say thank you."

"Thank you." Elise bowed.

They started to clap again.

"Stop. I'm embarrassed." Elise pulled her scarf from her neck.

"We're all praying that Ted will come sooner, that the surgery will happen ASAP. So"—Sandi grabbed her notebook—"we need a plan."

Elise said, "I need to finish Mark's book. Okay, I'll be honest. I need to start Mark's book." She laughed. "I'm feeling guilty about this—just as I knew I would." She definitely saw the value in creating the album for Mark; she just hadn't been able to make herself do it.

Sandi pulled the book across the table. "We'll do Mark's album. Just separate the photos. We'll even help you pick out the paper. Then you can do the journaling later."

Would they do that for her? "Are you serious?" She would enjoy working on the captions while she recovered.

"We'd love to, right?" Sandi grinned.

The other women nodded.

"I'll help too." Rebekah put her arm around Elise.

"No, you won't," Elise and Sandi said in unison.

"Rebekah, we're going to help you prioritize." Sandi opened the notebook. "You have to get the shop ready for me to take over. Where are you on inventory? Do any orders need to be placed?"

"I'll go over them tomorrow. Come in Monday, and I'll give you a list. We can negotiate your salary then."

"What salary?" Sandi held her pen in midair. "I am not taking any salary. Who said anything about salary?" Sandi's face reddened.

"I did. And Patrick."

"No. What are you talking about? I never intended to take a salary." Sandi pointed the pen at Rebekah. "I can volunteer at the hospital or the school or the animal shelter or here. I want to volunteer here." Sandi slammed her pen onto the table.

Rebekah jumped. "Sandi—"

"Rebekah, don't make me mad." Sandi picked up her pen and smiled.

Elise put her purse under her chair. Pastor Jim had opened a fund at church to help the Grahams, and she had written a check. She knew Sandi and John had contributed too. She could imagine families at school giving. Hopefully it would all add up—without Rebekah and Patrick ever knowing who gave.

"So," Sandi continued in an even voice, "your family will need extra help during the month Pepper has to stay in Portland."

Rebekah nodded.

"We can arrange meals. John can drive Reid around—Mark and Michael too." Sandi pointed her pen at Elise.

"Reid could use some extra attention. He's having a hard time. This will just make it harder. He feels...overlooked." Rebekah sat in a chair beside Sandi.

"Maybe John could just stay at your house for the whole month." Sandi tapped the pen on the table. "That way Reid will be home, and Patrick can go back and forth. Michael and Mark can stay there the first week—maybe longer so that Mark can take care of the horses. Do you think he would do that, Elise?"

Elise nodded.

"They'll want to be with Ted," Rebekah said.

"Maybe they could all get a hotel for a couple of days," Elise suggested.

"Mark loose in Portland while Ted is with you at the hospital? Doesn't sound like a good idea." Sandi tapped her pen again. "What will you need at your house, Elise?"

"What do you mean?"

"Meals, laundry, cleaning."

"If the boys are with John, we'll be fine."

"How about when you get home from the hospital?"

Elise shrugged. "Focus on Rebekah's family. Let's wait and see what we need. Ted will probably have everything under control."

"Elise, don't do this. Let *us* help you." Rebekah tore open a package of paper.

Sandi pointed the pen at Rebekah.

Rebekah laughed. "I mean let *them* help you. Just accept it. I'll help you later; I'll help you for the rest of your life."

Elise shivered. Pepper would need another kidney by the time she was middle aged. At least it was only once for Elise. "Help me with the scrapbook. You can't know how much that means to me."

✂

Coffee in hand, Elise sat down at the computer. Michael was up. Mark had five more minutes before his alarm went off. Maybe she had an e-mail from Ted.

Bingo. But first she opened an e-mail from Mr. Jenkins, determined to save the best for last.

> I wanted to let you know that Mark turned in seventy-five percent of his work last week.

Elise smiled but didn't reply.
She opened the message from Ted.

> Dad e-mailed me. He said that Sandi said that Pepper's kidney function is down more. How timely, considering what is going on over here. Long story, but Robert is better and will be back in Iraq by the end of this week, and I'll be on a plane two days after that. Talk with the coordinator at the hospital about scheduling the surgery in two weeks. Give the boys my love. Thanks for everything that you do for us.

Elise took a sip of coffee. Coffee! She hurried into the bathroom and spit it in the sink. She'd better stop now.

She yelled up the stairs to Mark. "Did your alarm go off? Up and at 'em."

An inarticulate moan drifted toward her.

Michael hurried out of the family room. "I need to be at school early. The chess team has playoffs for the tournament."

"Eat breakfast first."

"I'll take a granola bar."

"Take a banana too," Elise insisted.

"I got an e-mail from Dad. He might be home in nine days," Michael yelled from the kitchen.

"That's great. I got one too." Elise picked up a dirty sock from the dining room floor. "Hopefully we can do the surgery sooner." Elise headed to the garage and tossed the sock on top of the washing machine.

"Reid will be glad when it's over with." She heard Michael rummaging in the cupboard.

"Why?"

"It's all anyone in his family talks about."

Elise stood in the kitchen doorway. "How is Reid?"

"Neglected."

"Come on."

"No, he is. He feels acutely neglected."

"How are you, Michael?" She tousled his hair. At least she could still reach the top of his head.

He flung his backpack over his shoulder. "At least Pepper's really sick. Mark just fakes his problems to soak up all the attention."

After Mark headed out the door, Elise dialed John's number.

"Is everything okay?" he asked.

"Fine." She stood at the living room window. The trees across the street had grown green buds overnight. "Um, John, I want to thank you for your help, for spending time with the boys, helping me with the cars." She took a breath. "And I want you to know how much I like Sandi and that I wouldn't want you to make your decisions based on what you thought was best for us."

"Thanks, Elise." He paused. "I don't know what will happen with Sandi, but I appreciate your call."

Chapter 48

*M*om." Pepper stood at the window of the Scrap Shack. "Are we going to lose the shop and the farm?"

"I don't think so."

"What does Dad think?"

Rebekah put down her calculator. They were both overwhelmed with Sandi's generosity to manage the shop for free. That alone was a huge savings, and Pastor Jim had sent a gift from the church of four thousand dollars. So much for God forgetting them.

"Dad and I both see God at work." Rebekah had opened an account at the bank for Pepper's antirejection drugs. "I think things will come together. I think that God is working things out."

"I'll be good after the surgery, and I'll take all of the medicine that I need to. I won't complain; I won't be a whiner."

"It's okay if you complain." Rebekah winked. "Just a little."

"Jamie said the antirejection medicine might make me fat."

"Did she use the word *fat*?"

"No." Pepper sat down in a chair and took her knitting from her backpack.

"I think puffy is the word. It's from the prednisone." Rebekah put her arm around Pepper.

"Mom, not here." Pepper shrank away.

Rebekah looked around. They were alone.

"Mom."

"Oh, sweet pea, not you too."

"Not me too, what?"

"Not wanting hugs." Was that it? Rebekah paused and then whispered, "Not you growing up too."

"What else am I supposed to do?"

Elise flung open the door to the Scrap Shack.

"Hey, girl," Rebekah called out. "Two more days and you won't be single anymore."

"One more day until Valentine's Day. Other years it mattered that Ted was gone. This year I don't care." Elise glanced at her watch. "He should be boarding his plane in an hour."

"Hey, Elise." Pepper stuffed her knitting through the opening in her bag. "I was wondering something. Will it be your kidney or my kidney after the surgery?"

"It's a gift, sweet pea. It will be all yours."

"I'll take good care of it, I promise."

Elise gave Pepper a hug.

"Wait a minute." Rebekah stuffed her hands into her back pockets. "You'll let Elise hug you but not me?"

Pepper shrugged.

"I brought the rest of Mark's photos for Sandi. I grouped them in envelopes. She said she would pick out the paper today."

"Sandi will do way more embellishments than you like."

"I don't care. I'm just happy not to have to do this book."

"Is scrapbooking really that bad?" Rebekah asked.

Elise laughed. "Do you want to know why I really decided to donate my kidney? To get out of doing this book." Elise's cell rang. "It's Jamie," she mouthed to Rebekah as she listened. "That's right; he'll be here in two days." Elise paused. "Friday sounds great." Another pause. "She's right here. I'm at her shop." Elise handed Rebekah the phone.

"Looks like we're all set," Jamie said. "I just wanted to make sure that

Elise's husband was on schedule. She'll have her appointment with the anesthesiologist tomorrow, and then we'll do the final match Thursday and surgery on Friday."

"Excellent."

Elise pointed to the computer. Rebekah nodded.

Jamie asked about Pepper and then hung up. Rebekah handed Elise her phone.

"Look." Elise tilted her head toward Rebekah's computer screen. It was an e-mail from Ted.

> I tried to call, but the satellite must have tipped. I didn't make the flight today—our convoy was rerouted. I'm work-ing on a new flight, but I may not get home until Thursday, Friday morning at the very latest. Everyone here is pulling for Pepper. Everyone wants me home with you ASAP. I'm sorry.
>
> Hugs to the boys.
> Love,
> Ted

"Why was his convoy rerouted?" Elise covered her face with her hands. The final days were the hardest; she always had to fight her super-stitions that something horrible would happen at the last minute.

"He's fine." Rebekah read over Elise's shoulder. "He said everything is okay." She took Elise's hand. "You know how the army is—at least you keep telling me how it is. Missing paychecks, last-minute changes—all of that. Maybe they're doing road construction on the way to Baghdad." She was talking at lightning speed. "But I'll call Jamie, just in case we need to bump it out a few days. You know Pepper has stayed at twelve percent; she could probably go another week."

"Don't call. I'll do the surgery even if he's not here."

"Elise," Rebekah said, "I want to be fair to you."

"This is being fair to me. The sooner the better. Right?" Elise leaned against the counter.

Rebekah bit her lower lip. The sooner the better for Pepper, sure. She sighed. "Then I want you and the boys to come out the night before the surgery. John will come early that morning and get them to school. Patrick will drive you, Pepper, and me to the hospital. I can't stand the thought of you being alone."

Elise agreed.

"But we'll pray," Rebekah added, "that Ted will get here on time."

Rebekah slid the bag of groceries onto the counter. "How nice of your mom to make dinner."

Mark nodded from the breakfast bar as he slurped his tomato soup.

"Where are Reid and Michael?" she asked.

"Upstairs. They already ate."

Pepper reached for a grilled cheese sandwich.

"Sorry, sweet pea, no white bread." Rebekah wedged four frozen pizzas into the freezer. She had been late closing the shop, trying to get everything ready for Sandi, and then she'd remembered there was hardly any food in the house.

Pepper scowled and slumped down on the stool next to Mark.

"Soon." Rebekah slung the gallon of milk into the fridge. The doctors all said that Pepper would feel better right away.

Rebekah pulled out the whole-wheat bread. "I'll make you a sandwich while you go pack." Rebekah still needed to pack too. "Where is your mom?" she asked Mark, looking around.

"Outside."

"With the horses?"

He nodded, a little vaguely.

"I think I heard the cougar!" Pepper jumped up, knocking the stool over.

"I didn't hear anything." Rebekah bit her lip. *Please, no drama tonight.*

"Shh." Mark righted the stool.

The unmistakable scream of the cougar filled the air.

Rebekah dropped a slice of bread on the counter. "The horses are in? Right?"

"Yes. No. Sky isn't." Mark stood arrow straight.

"What?" Pepper asked.

"Mom is riding Sky—out in the field."

Bear began to bark. Rebekah flung open the back door. The cougar screamed again. "It's in the field." Rebekah snatched the flashlight off the shelf and grabbed her fleece. "Go, Bear!"

Pepper ran into the dining room. "Michael! Reid! The cougar!"

Mark followed Rebekah out the door and jumped over the fence.

"Don't go any farther. The cougar could be coming this way." The moonlight illuminated the pasture. Still Rebekah waved the beam across it. She could make out a figure running toward the forest. "There goes Bear." The cougar screamed again, this time farther away.

"Mark, check the barn. Your mom is probably in there." Pepper flew out the back door with Michael and Reid close behind.

"Where is it?" Michael yelled.

Pepper rushed to the fence. "Did you see it?"

Rebekah shook her head and pointed the flashlight near the trailhead. "I think Bear chased it into the woods. Our excitement is over."

"Rebekah!" Mark slammed the barn door. "Mom and Sky aren't in here. I bet she headed up the trail. She was upset. Dad had just called from Germany. He thought he could get home by tomorrow morning, but his flight was delayed again."

"How long ago—"

"It was dusk—over an hour."

Rebekah reached for her cell phone and started to call Patrick but stopped. What could he do? Chances were that Bear would protect Elise and Sky from the cougar. Still, what if something happened? She glanced from Michael to Mark and then to Pepper.

"I'll ride after her." Mark flipped the hair from his eyes.

"No." Rebekah started toward the barn. "I will."

"Mom." Reid followed.

"Let me go too." Pepper caught up with her mother and tugged on her sleeve.

"Pepper, don't be ridiculous. You have surgery in the morning." She turned. "All of you stay here. I'll be back with Elise in no time. Mark and Reid, you're in charge. Make sure everyone stays in the house."

"Let me go, Rebekah." Mark stepped forward. "Please."

"No, Mark. Your mom will be fine. She's probably riding into the pasture right now." She headed to the barn and then turned. "You obey me, all of you. Do you hear?"

They nodded in unison.

Rebekah swung bareback onto the mare, the flashlight tucked into the pocket of her corduroy jacket. She thought of her own night ride last summer. Elise had heard her talk about it. Had Rebekah's story encouraged Elise to ride tonight? Or had Sky spooked and taken off with her? Had she fallen? And now the cougar was headed her way.

The moon rode high above the treetops. Rebekah sucked in the brittle night air. The four kids stood by the back door. "Get in the house!"

Pepper and Michael ducked through the door. Mark and Reid stood like statues. The mare galloped into the field and headed up the trail. The bare branches of the trees and boughs of the evergreens stirred like an overhead web as Rebekah urged the mare forward. At least Elise was on the fastest horse, as long as she could handle him, as long as she was still on him.

The mare lunged forward, up the rocky incline to the plateau. Pine branches, knocked down by the wind, littered the trail. An owl hooted in the distance. "We'll find Elise and Sky before the lower meadow," she whispered to the Appaloosa. Why tonight? Why did the cougar come now? Why did Elise go riding alone? Why had Ted's flight been delayed again? Rebekah blew out her breath into the icy air. The temperature was dropping.

The mare shied at a crash below them.

"Easy, girl."

Bear leaped onto the trail. "Oh no, big guy. Did you chase the cougar straight to Elise and Sky? Or is he in a tree over my head?"

Bear barked and took off up the trail. Rebekah pressed forward, urging the horse through the tunnel of trees. The boughs of the red cedars hung low as if in mourning. Branches from the fir tees creaked and groaned as moonlit shadows fell across the path. A horse whinnied in the distance. Rebekah urged the mare forward; they were nearly to the meadow. The mare sidestepped, and her ears twitched. Bear barked as he raced back and forth. Ahead, Sky came into view, rearing as the cougar's piercing scream cut through the night. Elise bent over the gelding and held on tightly, her head against his neck.

Bear, a blur of black, brown, and white—his fur flying, his teeth bared—burst past Sky. The cougar landed behind them and ran up the hill with Bear close behind.

"Elise!" Rebekah shone the flashlight, waving it across the meadow. Sky snorted. "Are you okay?"

Elise tried to nod.

Rebekah raced to Elise, slowed, and jumped off the mare. Bear's barking grew fainter, stopped, and then grew louder. "I think he treed the cougar." Rebekah shone her flashlight up the hill.

"I'm sorry." Elise shook. "I was only going to ride up the hill and then go back, but when the moon rose, and it was so bright, and Sky was so sure…"

Rebekah laid her hand on Elise's arm. "You're not hurt. That's what matters." Sky jerked his head toward Rebekah.

"What do we do now?" Elise asked.

"Go home. Carefully." Rebekah swung back onto the mare. "I'll call the game department—and John."

Sky took a few steps forward. "Rebekah, I'm so sorry. It was a really stupid thing to do. I risked everything."

"Well, you're okay now. Right?" Rebekah tried to sound confident, but doubt crept into her heart. Elise was afraid. Would she go through with the surgery?

"Yes, I'm okay." Elise's voice sounded scratchy.

Rebekah pulled the mare to a stop. "Elise, are you going to be able to go through with this?" she whispered, scared to hear the answer. She wanted assurance so badly that the brief pause felt like a century. *Is Elise trying to back out of the transplant? Am I pressuring her into doing something she doesn't want to?*

"Don't worry, Rebekah," Elise finally said. "We're doing this tomorrow."

I'm more afraid than she is, Rebekah realized. *I'm afraid to let go of control.* If Elise didn't want to go through with donating her kidney, then Rebekah didn't want her to. She turned toward her friend. "Are you sure? I mean, whether Ted is here or not, maybe the surgery isn't the right thing for you to do."

"Rebekah, stop!"

"This is too much for you. It drove you into the forest in the dark—"

"I may be afraid, but that's not why I went riding." Elise looked Rebekah in the eye. "I took off on Sky because riding makes me feel strong. I want to do this."

Relief washed over Rebekah. "I guess the main thing is that we don't give way to fear, that we trust God," she said, aware she was talking mostly to herself.

Elise nodded and bent down against Sky's neck.

Rebekah took a deep breath. "Thank you," she whispered as Elise and Sky started into the night. Rebekah urged the mare forward until they rode side by side along the trail—the two horses and two friends in unison, pounding out a rhythm through the forest.

ey, baby." Ted's face floated above Elise. His brown eyes sparkled.

She was cold, freezing. "When did you get here?"

"Just now."

"Is Pepper okay?"

"Yes. She's already doing better. Your kidney went to work right away—while she was still on the operating table."

It wasn't Elise's kidney, not anymore. It was Pepper's. *Thank you, God.* Elise took a ragged breath. "You must be exhausted," she whispered.

"I'm fine. I'm just happy I'm here."

"I'm queasy." No wonder she hated hospitals; they were worse than she remembered.

"That will go away soon."

"Have you seen the boys?" She felt as if it had been weeks since last night, since she had reassured them that she was fine, that she really hadn't lost her mind.

"Yes. They're in the waiting room. Dad brought them up, and Reid too. He said all three boys were a mess this morning; he couldn't get any of them to go to school."

Elise shivered.

"Could we get another blanket, please?" Ted's voice was low and calm as he talked with the nurse. He spread a shiny space blanket over Elise.

She closed her eyes. "I did something really stupid last night."

"It wasn't stupid, baby."

"You heard?"

He nodded.

"Do you know what happened to Bear?" He was still gone when they had left for the hospital.

"He came back to the house this morning. Dad said the game department came out, but they couldn't find the cougar."

The beautiful, fierce cougar.

Elise reached out her hand to Ted. "Stay with me," she whispered.

"I will," he answered.

Elise opened her eyes to the morning light pouring through the hospital room. Where was Ted?

"Elise?" Rebekah pulled up a chair. "How are you feeling?"

"Like I've been hit by a truck." Elise turned her head.

"You had quite a night. Ted asked them to increase your pain meds three times."

"Really?" She remembered Ted sleeping on the chair with his head on the side of the bed. "Where is he now?"

"He went to see Pepper. Then he's going to get a hotel room and some sleep. He said he'll be back this afternoon." Rebekah held Mark's album in her hand. "Do you feel up to looking at this?"

Elise nodded. She leafed through the pages. Mark as a baby, Mark in Germany, Mark playing soccer and T-ball. The layouts were clean and simple with no embellishments, no stickers. Mark with Ted when he came home from Kosovo. Mark and Michael in Georgia while Ted was in Afghanistan. Mark in Colorado, snowboarding. Mark punching Michael. Mark and Pepper under the falls. Mark at the skating rink. Mark in Seattle and at Cascade Pass. Mark mounted on Sky.

Elise closed the book. "Tell Sandi thank you. It's wonderful. And more my style than I could have ever done."

Rebekah smiled. "Sandi didn't do it. I did."

"Rebekah, you've been so busy." Elise shook her head.

"I wanted to. I had to."

"Thanks." Elise wrapped her arms around the album. "How is Pepper?"

"Great. She's walking in the hall and asking for white bread." Rebekah laughed.

"You trusted God with her, with your baby." She reached for Rebekah's hand. "You risked letting go."

"I did."

"Rebekah, do you remember when we first met? When you said we were going to be good friends?"

Rebekah blushed.

"How did you know?"

Rebekah shook her head. "It makes me look bad."

"Tell me."

Rebekah grinned sheepishly. "God always hooks me up with people I don't li—with people I don't think I have anything in common with."

Elise started to laugh. "Ouch." She placed her hand against her side. "That's okay. At the time I couldn't imagine us being friends, either."

Rebekah smiled. "I'm so glad God has a bigger imagination than we do."

"Why can't I see Pepper? Do I look that bad?" Elise asked.

"What do you think?" Ted asked Rebekah.

"I think you look fine. Pale, sure. But as long as you stay in bed and don't limp around, Pepper won't know how much pain you're in." Rebekah fluffed Elise's pillow. "I'll go get her."

Elise raised the bed to a reclining position and closed her eyes.

"Baby, the boys are here." Ted touched her shoulder.

Mark and Michael stood at the end of the bed. Reid and John waited by the door.

"Come closer." Elise motioned to them. Her boys sat on either side of her.

"Hi, Mom." Mark touched her hand, and tears filled his eyes.

"Honey, it's fine."

"I didn't know it would be this hard for you."

"I'm fine, and I get to go home in two or three days. I'm sore, that's all."

Michael cleared his throat. "How's Pepper?"

"She's fine. She'll be here in just a—"

"Here I am." Pepper hurried through the door. She wore her own pajama bottoms and a blue hoodie.

The boys stood. Pepper poked Mark's arm as she walked by. "You've been crying."

"No, I haven't."

Pepper sat down beside Elise. "Thanks. I'm taking good care of our kidney, I promise."

Elise was getting tired, but she was glad to see Pepper. "I need to thank you, sweetie." A week ago she thought she was doing a wonderful thing for Pepper, but now she knew that God had done a wonderful thing for her. By giving up a little of herself, she had learned a measure of compassion, learned to follow Jesus a little more closely. She looked from Mark to Michael and then whispered to Pepper, "You taught me how to give."

*R*ebekah flung open the door to the Scrap Shack. "Sandi!"

Sandi leaned over the railing of the balcony. "What are you doing here?"

"Patrick is with Pepper." Rebekah ran up the stairs. "Elise is coming home today. I want to get her house spruced up—you know, have dinner in the oven and flowers on the table."

"How is she?'

"Better. Her pain is finally under control." Rebekah shook her head. "I don't know if I ever would have let her go through this if I had known how hard it would be."

Sandi ran her hand through her spiked hair. "According to John, you couldn't have stopped her. He's so proud of her."

Rebekah smiled. Ted had told her the evening before that Elise's goodness ran deep, that people just had to take the time to get to know her. Had it taken John twenty years? "I have a vase up here, from the last Midnight Madness. I stopped at the flower shop and bought a bunch of tulips." Rebekah rummaged through the closet. "Here it is."

"We've had a ton of business today." Sandi straightened the rack of sports stickers. "Teachers from school have come in, and more people from church."

"Great!" Rebekah headed down the stairs.

"I think it's their way of helping." Sandi followed.

"Wow, no matter what their motivation is, I'm grateful." Rebekah leafed through the mail. "I'll be back this evening to pay the bills." She put the mail back under the counter. "Sandi, thanks."

Sandi nodded.

"Patrick is taking next week off, so I'll be here. I need to see to the shop and to Reid." She started toward the door and then turned. "Not that John isn't doing a good job. What would we do without all of you?"

"What would we do without each other?" Sandi shooed her out the door. "Go get things ready for Elise. And tell her hello. Tell her we're all proud of her."

Elise opened her eyes as Ted pulled off I-5.

"We're almost home," he whispered.

She smiled.

They rode silently. The trees budded under the late winter sky. They passed a herd of horses huddled together under a grove of pine trees. Elise ached for her boys; she wanted more than anything for all of them to be in the same house together. It had been so long.

"Pepper looks good." Ted slowed for a hairpin curve.

Elise nodded and smiled.

"The boys are excited to see you. Dad's going to be with Mark at the house when we get home. I'll pick Reid and Michael up after practice."

She had no idea of all the logistics that had gone into caring for the boys. She had Sandi to thank for that, she was sure. Her back began to hurt, and she adjusted the seat.

"We'll get you more pain meds when we get home." Ted slowed as a farm truck turned in front of them, and then he quickly passed it.

"Careful." Elise sat a little straighter. "This is where the deer ran into the road in front of me."

Ted smiled. Did he think she was being superstitious?

"Look, there's some acreage for sale." Ted slowed for a curve and nodded to the right.

Elise took a deep breath. "Maybe we could come back in a few days and take a closer look." Something stood motionless across the field, a dusky gold against the dark pine. "Ted, look." She pointed toward the trees.

Ted whistled as he slowed the Volvo. "It's the cougar." He pulled to the side of the road.

The majestic cat, just fifty feet away, looked directly at the car. "He's not afraid." Elise opened her window. Ted leaned forward.

The solitary cougar turned, took a few steps, and then, with an elegant leap, raced toward the forest. He gracefully soared up the hillside, through the trees, away from her, away from Forest Falls, away from the horses and the children. She breathed in the earthy scent of pine and dirt, mixed with the promise of spring. She searched the hillside, the trees, and foliage for movement, but the cougar was gone.

"Let's go home." Elise closed the window. "Home to Forest Falls."

Acknowledgments

Many people helped bring *Scrap Everything* to life. First, I want to thank my husband, Lt. Col. Peter Gould, a member of the army reserve, for his all-around faith in me. My thanks also to our children, who, through our own deployment experiences, provided insights to this story. I'm grateful to Mary Varian and Kelly Raby for providing details about the lives of active-duty families; they shared from their hearts and encouraged me with their stories. My thanks to Danny and Kathryn Perez for connecting me with these dear women.

I'm grateful to Debbie Smouse and Faye and Keith Foster for sharing their kidney-transplant experiences, and to Cary Legros, RN; Tammy Seber, RN, BSN, CNN, Renal-Pancreas Transplant Coordinator; and Debbie Whitehurst, RN, BSN, Pediatric Renal Transplant Coordinator, for answering my many medical questions. (Any mistakes are entirely my own.)

I want to acknowledge scrapbooker Lorraine TenHaken and entrepreneur Bobbie Underhill for granting me interviews, Elizabeth Peters for sharing her scrapbooking stories, and Libby Salter for giving me actual scrapbooking experience. Also, thanks to Pastor Randy Shaw for inspiring me through his teaching and to Nancy Ellen Row for reading the manuscript in its early stages.

My lifelong thanks go to Wally, Marva, Teresa, Calla, and Sam Walker for their friendship and generosity and the opportunities they've given my family and me to hang out with them and their horses.

I cannot thank my mother, Leora Egger, enough for her endless love and support, in life and in writing. I'm also grateful to my brother Kelvin Egger for sharing his cougar story and for his care toward my family and me. A very special thank-you to Hana Gould for inspiring me to write this novel.

Most important, I want to honor God the Father, who provides the way to keep us from giving in to fear.

www.lesliegould.com
leslie@lesliegould.com

About the Author

LESLIE GOULD is the author of *Garden of Dreams*, a novel about friendship and faith, and *Beyond the Blue*, an award-winning novel about international adoption. She lives in Portland, Oregon, with her husband and four children. She likes spending time shopping for scrapbooking supplies with her two daughters and hopes that one day her girls will complete her unfinished albums for her. Leslie and her family enjoy soccer, camping, traveling, and appreciating the beauty of the nearby mountains and coast.